FACE OF A HERO

FACE OF A HERO

Louis Falstein

STEERFORTH PRESS
SOUTH ROYALTON, VERMONT

Library of Congress Cataloging-in-Publication Data

Falstein, Louis.
Face of a hero / Louis Falstein.
p. cm.
ISBN 1-883642-69-8 (alk. paper)
1. World War, 1939–1945 — Aerial operations, American — Fiction.
2. World War, 1939–1945 — Campaigns — Italy, Southern — Fiction.
I. Title.
PS3556.A485F34   1999
813'.54 — dc21   98-31407
                                                       CIP

Manufactured in the United States of America

SECOND PRINTING

1

MY MOTHER always said: "Ben was born in a caul. No ill ever comes to a man born in a caul." For thirty-four years I had not thought of it, letting this knowledge nestle comfortably in my subconscious against the time when I might need it. It came back to me several days after we landed in Italy and I saw all the battered planes and the young-old faces of my fellow Americans and I got the first strange sucking sensation underneath my diaphragm.

Mel Ginn, the nose gunner in our crew who might have got to look like Calvin Coolidge, if he'd lived long enough, scratched his sandy-colored hair and said, "I see they's killing lotsa gunners in this war, but they ain't gonna get me, I guarantee ya that." Mel usually added the "I guarantee ya that" to make sure his words were not taken lightly. "The way I look at it," the stringy young Texan continued, his rasping voice trailing off into a high falsetto, "they ain't gonna kill me 'cause I ain't lived yet. Just starting now, ya might say."

Mel didn't have a caul to sustain him, but he wore a locket of his wife's hair on his skinny, rib-silhouetted chest, next to a cross. But Jack Dooley came over on even less than that. Dooley's good-luck charm consisted of a WAC cap, olive drab, he'd got from one of the girls at Mitchel Field, USA. He had been clinging to her most of the evening, saying good-by to America through her, and after it was all over, she'd offered him her cap. "It'll bring you good luck," she told him.

"Well, as my name is Dooley," Jack related the story later, "I took the cap."

His name wasn't Dooley at all. It was Jack Dula. But he made it plain to us, his crew buddies, that he would be known as Dooley, and nothing else. Even the four officers in our crew were impressed by the husky flight engineer's ultimatum. And even Lieutenant Albert Pennington,

Jr., our pilot, called him Dooley. Jack was a powerful, self-confident youth of twenty-two, with bull shoulders thrust forward when he walked, his face framed in a scowl. He had high cheekbones and narrow eyes, wore his hair cut close to the scalp, and looked almost Mongolian. "The fickle finger of fate done me dirt on two accounts," Jack said, only partly in jest, "first by not making me a full-blooded Irishman, and second, by not making me look like one." His mother, who ran a saloon in Pittsburgh, was Irish. His father was of German descent. Jack ignored his father whenever possible, trying to comport himself the way he thought a real, full-blooded Irishman would. But on that evening of early May 1944, our last in America before hopping for overseas and combat, Jack suddenly realized that on the following day he would be off and there wasn't a thing he was taking with him that would summarize for him the meaning of the war. He was not going across to protect his mother; she was darn well capable of that herself. He had no girl, no beliefs one way or another about the war, no grudges. Somewhere in a book he had seen a sentence which summed up his philosophy about the war: "I don't want to make history, I want to make love." His mind, like the minds of the others on the crew, never leaped ahead to what might happen overseas. Like the rest of us, Jack was hoping that something would intervene and keep us from facing the enemy's guns. But it came suddenly, and he was saying good-by to America by hugging a strange, unattractive female, and when she offered her WAC cap for good luck, he seized it eagerly and stuffed it in his pocket and was ashamed to tell his crewmates about it for some time.

It was at Mitchel Field that we started thinking of good-luck charms and rabbits' feet and all the little symbols that we hoped would stand between us and disaster. For most of us there was little else to cling to; in many instances there was nothing else.

For most of us the war meant fifty missions, then back to the States. "After I get back to the USA," radio gunner Billy Poat said, "they won't get me inside a plane again even if they build one around me. I don't like any part of B-24s. They're flying coffins, take my word for it. Now if they put me in the infantry I'd be willing to fight their war from now till doomsday. But I got no use for this air war. I don't like to fight when you got no place to duck."

Nobody paid any attention to bean-pole Billy. He should have stated his objections when he had been put on the crew. That had been the time to talk. It had happened at Westover Field, Massachusetts, on a freezing January morning. Our crew had been constituted by the simple process of someone's picking our names out of a military hat. Picked a pilot, copilot, bombardier, navigator, flight engineer, radio gunner, two waist gunners, one ball gunner, one tail gunner, and called it a crew. "This is to be Lieutenant Pennington's crew," said the officer who had taken the names out of the hat. "Meet over at Row 4 and get acquainted."

We made a dash for the assigned spot, our eyes searching, probing, our handshakes trying to determine whether the man with whom you were shaking hands would be his brother's keeper. I surveyed the faces of these strangers and tried out their names: Pennington, Kowalski, Martin, Kyle, Dula, Poat, Trent, Ginn, Fidanza, and then I said somewhat haltingly, "My name is Isaacs, Ben Isaacs," and I watched their faces for reaction, and listened to the inflection in their voices when they said, "Glad to know you."

On that arctic day in the winter of '44, ten strangers were told they were brothers, stranger-brothers. The six enlisted men were moved into a barracks together, while the four officers went to live in a dormitory known as BOQ. They were given an airplane which they named *Flying Foxhole*, and were told to go to war. And now it was four months after their first meeting, but they were still strangers, although many of them already knew each other's weaknesses.

We knew, for instance, that our pilot, Second Lieutenant Albert Pennington had graduated from cadets with great distinction. He wasn't the type you'd cherish, though you might obey him. He was the lone-eagle kind, a tall Back Bay Boston aristocrat who had wanted to fly a fighter-plane. He was given a Liberator bomber instead, and with it a crew of nine to command. Big Wheel, as we nicknamed him at Chatham Field, Georgia, resented being saddled with nine men and the responsibility that went with it. The fact is, Big Wheel was an only child, raised as befitted a blue blood whose father, though not rich, had given him all of life's comforts and none of the responsibilities. He had gone to private schools from the age of five until he graduated from college. During the depression Albert Pennington, Sr., had lost his money. Young Albert was forced to find a way of earning a living. Fortunately Myrtle had come along. Beautiful Myrtle did not have the aristocratic pedigree of the Penningtons, but her father owned a prosperous photography business. Albert loved his wife, but making photographs palled on him after a while. When the war came he was drafted and assigned to the infantry. But Albert showed initiative and had himself transferred to the Air Force. "My heart was set on flying a Mustang," he told us later. "But I'm six feet three. Too tall to be a fighter pilot, they said. So they made a taxi driver out of me. But you wait and see. I'll get into fighters yet."

Big Wheel was openly patronizing, superior, disdainful of his men, particularly Chester Kowalski, the copilot. That did not prevent us from calling him "the best damn pilot in the business." Perhaps we said it to bolster our courage. Perhaps we said it because all air crews said that about their pilots. And having a good pilot was the most important thing. With a good pilot you could go places. And we went. . . .

2

Even christ was said to have ventured no further south than Eboli. Traveling under army orders we had no such choice and flew all the way to the heel of the Italian boot, to the barren, sun-parched plains near the little town of Mandia. From the air, the gray, closely clustered, tufa-rock houses looked white and clean, much cleaner than the dwellings in North Africa. From the air even the south of Italy looked good. The little towns below us had a lonely, unmartial look about them. They were built on top of hills, or pushing toward the top of a hill, as if seeking the sun. And we, gazing down upon the barren and strangely peaceful countryside, said over the interphone, "Wonder what the deal is here —"

"The way it looks to me," Dooley said, examining the land below from the waist window of *Flying Foxhole*, "I wouldn't give you a plugged nickel for this whole damned country."

"Don't cross the bridge till you get there, doc," Cosmo Fidanza said, hurt by the engineer's cynicism. "Wait till you *really* see Italy."

"I'm looking," Dooley said, "what's more, I ain't got no other place to go."

"Well, you just wait till we get down," Cosmo said. He said it haltingly, as if he himself were beginning to doubt the glowing stories he had told us about Italy. Standing dwarfed beside Dooley, like a small boy, our ball gunner peered at the sandy-colored land below as if he were searching for the glory that was Italy and the relatives his father had instructed him to see.

Below we saw the flying field of the Tigertail Group. It resembled all the other military airfields set out among the orchards of Italy; a Little America in an alien wilderness, a sprawling runway of steel and concrete and promise of asphalt, surrounded by army pyramidal tents, dusty olive trees, white casas, mess halls, and shot-up, torn-up bombers. The grounded planes were toy objects from three thousand feet up, but when we came down and our brakes brought us to a screeching stop, we saw for the first time how a Liberator looked after it had been in combat. Not sleek and shiny like our *Flying Foxhole*. Some of the fat-bellied ships sat on the ground like wounded birds with chewed-off wings and tails. Five-hundred-pound bombs were strewn over the ground as if left out in the sun for ripening.

We crawled out from underneath our ship and stood sheepishly waiting for someone to notice our arrival. But nobody paid any attention to us. The ground mechanics, who had seen combat replacements before, moved about the field slowly, lazily, as if they were in a trance. They blinked at us with bored eyes and asked with that same indifference which characterized all their movements whether we had any K rations aboard. We lied, saying we hadn't, and they lost interest in us.

Instinctively the ten of us moved closer together into a compact group, as if we were being threatened by this complete show of indifference. Only a PFC in greasy fatigues and freckles on his face remained to eye us curiously.

"Any you guys fum Tinnessee?" he asked.

"No," Leo Trent, our right waist gunner, replied, "I'm from Hollywood myself, but what I'd like to know at this point, since we have to stay in this damned hole, how is the chow here?"

"Stinks," the PFC said lazily.

"I see," Leo said gravely. His cap wasn't as cockily perched as usual. His whole manner was subdued, although he tried hard not to show it. In the crook of his arm he carried the puppy he had brought with him from Tunisia. "And tell me," he continued, "how are the women here?"

"Stinks."

"How about Italy?" Leo pursued, glancing at Cosmo Fidanza, who showed more distress than anyone else.

"Stinks."

"Young man," Leo said, "it's been enlightening talking to you. Thank you very much."

"I shore wished I'd find somebody fum Tinnessee," the PFC said wistfully.

"At this moment I think even Tennessee would be preferable," Leo said. He rubbed the little dog's ears, whispering, "Baby, it looks as if something has been put over on your old dad."

. . . . .

Several hours later, when the blazing Italian sun had disappeared behind the small olive trees, the enlisted men were shown their billet in a tumbledown wooden barracks, while the four officers were escorted to a tent about a block away. The separating of officers and men was a routine procedure which we had followed throughout our training in the States and on our trip across. But for the first time there was a hesitancy about separating, and even Pennington seemed reluctant for a moment.

On the door of our new home a crudely painted sign read: "WELCOME GONER" Mel Ginn shook his head in mock fear and muttered, "Welcome goner! It's the truth, I guarantee ya that."

"The average life of a gunner," Billy Poat said, "is supposed to be twenty-four minutes." He scratched his mop of red hair as if pondering the meaning of his words. Then he started mumbling about how he'd go to the commanding officer soon as he dumped his gear and ask for a transfer to the infantry.

We entered the cramped barracks and Leo shook his head despondently. "I swear I'll never be able to raise a self-respecting dog here. Look at all the spoilers! Must be at least forty of 'em. Let's get out of here."

Cosmo Fidanza's attention was riveted on a sign with a five-point star on it, the kind mothers and wives hung in the windows back in the States to signify that their dear ones served in the armed forces. This sign was inscribed: "To the four men who finished their missions and are serving with the armed forces in the States, the lucky dogs. Fitch, Regelman, Vlcek, Michaud."

"My aching back," Cosmo said. "Only four?"

I looked bewilderedly about the long barracks with the closely placed cots and mosquito netting. I had only one consoling thought: this is the end of a journey. . . . This is where they're fighting the war. . . . This is overseas, the last stop, I thought, the last time I would walk into a strange, stifling barracks to start life all over again, to make friends all over again, to grope slowly, painfully, toward some kind of an adjustment. Although nothing could be worse than this cluttered, butt-strewn, windowless barracks, this was the last of the lot. My thoughts were summed up by a sign above the door inside the barracks: "The best damned gunners pass through this door. Trouble is most of them don't come back!"

A gunner without a stitch of clothing on spoke to us from behind his mosquito netting. "Take a load off your feet, fellas. Grab them six empty cots." Then he turned over and went to sleep.

I approached my cot reluctantly. It was all made up, not in the fastidious GI manner of a stateside barracks, but hurriedly tucked in, as if more important business had come up. A gunner said to me, "The fella who had that cot was flying his last mission. Didn't come back from today's raid."

"Was he killed?" I asked.

"We never use the word *killed*," the man replied, "unless we got proof. When we got no proof we say a guy *went down*. This guy was in a ship that exploded over the target. But miracles can happen. That's why, sarge, unless you got the proof, people ain't killed. They go down. *Capito?*"

"Yes," I said, appreciating my first lesson in air-war language and Italian.

Although heavy with fatigue, I was afraid to stretch out on a bed which only recently held a man now dead.

3

FIVE DAYS after our arrival the pilot came to the barracks and said, "We're flying tomorrow." He towered over our cots, shifting his gangling six-foot-three-inch body. "I want you men to go to sleep early tonight." He had his say in a flat, dry voice, like a harassed adult who has grown weary of his young charges. "See you in the morning."

"Flying tomorrow," Trent said. "Know what that means?"

We were suddenly drawn together, all six of us, and even Billy Poat gave up his endless game of solitaire and joined our frightened little circle. Billy smiled a wan but friendly smile that reached toward his crewmates, as though he were trying hurriedly to bridge the gap between himself and the others. In the past he had labored hard to impress us with the toughness of his fiber. In fact he had tried too hard, and you suspected the lower he pitched his voice the more frightened he was. "Well, this is it," he said meekly. His words reached across to me and I felt as if I almost knew him although in the past he had always eluded me. His shell, which prompted people to say that you could be with Billy one day or one year and not know any more about him, was forced open for the moment. "I don't mind telling you," he said, "I'm pretty goddamned scared." He sat and looked into space and I wondered whether he was thinking of transferring to the infantry, or worrying about his mother's house in Rhode Island and the seventeen windows which she always made him wash. When Dooley put his arm around his shoulder, Billy didn't draw away. We sat there, hardly talking. Not one of us made a move to check his gear though it was nearly time to go to sleep.

The phrase revolved in my mind: *we fly tomorrow*. This was the end of the road. This was the culmination of more than two years of army life with its small indignities and small brutalities and sleepless nights and moronic drill sergeants and stupid second looeys. This was the end and the beginning. There had been years of talk about fighting back, striking back. There had been Ethiopia, a time to strike back. There had been Spain, a time to strike back. But it had been little more than talk by intellectuals with lacerated consciences and guilt feelings mouthing phrases about what must be done but doing nothing. Years of talk, lulling the senses. And I had talked no less than the others, perhaps more. And my friends had listened. "Ben knows fascism from first-hand experience," they had said. "Did you ever hear him tell about the massacres in the Ukraine when he was a kid?" I had told those stories of anti-Semitism and massacres often. I could not help remembering the taste of a mercenary's fist as it struck the mouth, or the blood-chilling cry: "Kill the Jews!"

It had been no effort to talk, to curse Hitler and Mussolini, to hate fascism. The difficulty had been in bridging the distance between belief and action. Now the decision had been made for me. . . .

Across the narrow aisle Mouse Fidanza's five-foot-two-inch frame wriggled inside the winter flying suit which he was trying on for the first time. Cosmo's tiny face, his pointed little chin and nose, peered out of the heavy clothing, beaming like a child's. I was struck by his child's face. Although he was nineteen years old, Cosmo hadn't put a razor to his face.

"How do I look?" he inquired.

"Rugged," I said. "You look like Steinbeck's conception of an aerial gunner: the executioner of the air."

"Don't tell me, doc. Keep it a secret." He cocked his index fingers and thumbs as a kid does for guns. "Brrrrr."

I couldn't reconcile Cosmo with war. Everything about Cosmo was too tiny for war. He was too small, his fingers too thin, his voice too squeaky, his physique too delicate. His was the strangest case of all: he had wanted to be a monk, seeking the peace and tranquillity of a cloister which would keep out the thrust of the world. At the age of eighteen, when he had almost achieved that removal, the Army made a belly gunner of him.

I thought of Cosmo and how unfit he was for the task before us. And I thought of tomorrow, wondering whether I should take along my eyeglasses. Until now I'd managed up in the air without the glasses.

What would my crewmates say when they saw me put on the glasses in the air? Would they laugh and say, "Pop ought to get himself a desk job"? I might hide the glasses and put them on in my turret when nobody saw. I didn't mind them calling me "pop" and "old man," but what would Steinbeck say about an air executioner with glasses on?

.   .   .   .

I couldn't sleep. Mel Ginn, on my right, couldn't sleep either. Earlier he had puttered with his flying equipment, testing his oxygen mask, tracing the many cords extending from the winter flying suit, and strapping his dagger just above the left knee. While testing his equipment Mel sang the only song he knew:

"Warshing out my stockin's,
Warshing out an' shaving —"

Then he sat down to write a letter to his wife, Sharon. But he didn't get far in his writing. He started perspiring, the way he usually did when trying to compose a letter, and gave up. Writing for him was almost as great a chore as speaking. When he spoke Mel's words sounded stiff and inflexible as if he had learned to use them only recently. His voice was almost inarticulate; it had a painful, rasping quality. As a consequence, Ginn was the butt of most jokes in the crew, and Dick Martin, our bombardier, rode him mercilessly. He was a good mechanic and knew his guns. But he couldn't write a letter. "I sure wisht I was one day older," he said, before the candles were blown out, "I guarantee ya that."

Mouse Fidanza, before retiring behind his mosquito netting for the night, went down on his knees and, burying his little head in his hands, prayed fervently to his God. When he got up from his prayer, he saw the approving glances of his crewmates. There was a gleam of triumph in his smiling brown eyes; this was one thing he could do that was of service to his buddies. But though he prayed passionately, Mouse couldn't sleep either.

I thought it incredible that the world was asleep while I lay awake thinking of tomorrow. I couldn't believe that I was really overseas, in Italy, and that tomorrow I would be hurled through alien skies in a bomber, to be shot at by enemy cannon. I wondered how it was that air force had never discovered my inefficiency, my lack as a gunner. It all seemed so unbelievable. I had said good-by to my wife only ten days ago. Ruth came to Mitchel Field all the way from Chicago for a last farewell. She had not fully recovered from her latest heart attack, and she tried to hide the shortness of breath that always showed when she got excited. But the flushed cheeks gave her away. We were at the post theater on our last evening together, postponing the time when we must say good-by. We were afraid of being alone and of saying the things we knew would sound clumsy. We sat in the crowded theater with Myrtle Pennington, Big Wheel's wife, who had come in from Boston. Beside Mrs. Pennington, whose sweeping gestures and daz-zling smile took in the whole of our crew, my wife looked like a little girl. All of us, all but Dooley who had run off with an unattractive WAC, sat stiffly in the overlighted theater, watching comedians who were not funny, laughing dutifully, but thinking of moments that were slipping away.

Ruth looked like a child that evening. But there was a gravity and introspection about her that comes to those who live constantly with pain and are reconciled to it. She certainly didn't look anywhere near twenty-seven, and my crewmates dug me in the ribs and whispered "cradle snatcher." Ruth smiled at them. I could tell by her smile that she was tired. She smiled and looked at them a long time as if probing quickly, trying to determine the caliber of these men to whom she was entrusting her husband. And I whispered to her, "How do you like them? A good bunch. I'm very lucky." But Ruth continued probing as if she were determined to make absolutely sure these men would take care of her husband and bring him back to her. She had to be sure, for she was twenty-seven and her rheumatic heart would not carry her be-yond her middle thirties. There was little time left and she had to be sure. And finally she said, "I'm satisfied you have a good crew. I'm pleased." After that we said little that had any meaning. I was glad she had met my crewmates and spoke to them and approved of them. Now it would be easier for her. A little bit easier. Now she was ready to let me go. She could not go herself on account of her damaged heart. She was giving herself through me. For Ruth my participation in the war was an expression of outraged humanity. She was motivated in her ha-tred of fascism by emotions that were probably more universal than mine. As a third-generation American born in a small town in Indiana

of well-to-do Jewish parents, Ruth hated Hitler for what he had done to
the people of Europe. She knew he must be fought for what he threatened to do to America.

From the theater we went to the post cafeteria and drank beer.
Again we sat in a stiff, unmoving group, but around us, at the other tables, the flyers who did not have their wives or sweethearts with them
began to cut up. They sang and shouted and embraced the WACs.
One pilot, tears streaming from his eyes, sang grimly:

> *"I'll be seeing you,*
> *In all the old familiar places —"*

One of his gunners broke in with:

> *"Don't sit under the apple tree,*
> *With anyone else but me —"*

There was a desperation in the boisterousness, as though they were
crying: Look what a good time we're having before going across! But not
one of them got drunk. The reality of tomorrow could not be effaced
any longer. The men whose wives and sweethearts were with them were
lucky. My crewmates, lonely and bewildered, clung to Myrtle and Ruth,
basking in the warmth and the gentleness of their femininity. And the
girls, realizing what was happening, embraced the men with their
glances and conversation. Then Ruth and I finally escaped into the cool
mid-May evening. We walked slowly and held hands and attempted to
speak several times, but again the words were clumsy. At one time Ruth
whispered to me, "I know you will come back — safe." She tried hard to
restrain her tears until she got inside the bus. Then the tears burst forth
and the bus moved away and Ruth was gone, passing out of my life,
drifting into the black Long Island night, and I stood there clinging to a
fire hydrant as if that were the only solid object left in the world.

That had been ten days ago. Since then, I'd seen half the globe
from the waist section of *Flying Foxhole*; I had made my last will and
testament; I had reconciled myself to the fact that there were to be no
more delays, no more reprieves.

I sat up and parted the mosquito netting and reached for a cigarette. I lit it and lay back on the cot. My thoughts resumed their

morbid vigil. Who among us would stand up tomorrow? I had no doubts about the pilot and none about Dooley. But I wondered about Lieutenant Chet Kowalski. Nice fellow though he was, our copilot had no confidence in his own flying. Working in the co-seat with Pennington he had lost the little confidence he ever possessed. It was a mystery to all of us how Chet had got his pilot's wings. No doubt he was the handsomest flyer I'd ever seen. The women went insane over his big, dark eyes, his wavy, black hair, aquiline nose, and black mustache. He had a great talent for dressing, and everything about him sparkled, even in the Italian mud. But he couldn't fly a plane. He knew we were aware of his deficiencies and that we did not trust him with the stick. He resented Pennington to the point of hatred because the pilot was patronizingly sorry for him. But evidently Chet was prepared to pay the price. Back in Hamtramck, Michigan, where Chet had sold plastics, his wife was already proud of him; she and their growing son, and all those who had seen his splendid photograph in the *Free Press*. It was quite possible Chet had chosen Pennington deliberately. Perhaps he felt there wasn't anyone he'd rather fly with in combat than Big Wheel.

I felt confident Dick Martin would stand up. Our bombardier was the most unmilitary-looking officer I'd ever seen. At twenty-six he was plump and had fat buttocks and waddled like a duck. Everything about him was effeminate, especially his voice which turned into a hysterical shriek when he yelled, "Bombs Away!" Dick, who had been in civil service in New York, clerking in the Sanitation Department, ran around flexing his biceps and demanding that people feel his muscle. While training in the States it had never occurred to him to put on a parachute harness in the air. But there had been no flak in the States. We would see tomorrow.

I wondered about Andy Kyle. Our navigator was only twenty-three, but he seemed to possess the wisdom of the ages. He was kind and gentle and had a smile for everyone at all times. He didn't smoke, drink, or swear. As soon as we'd arrived in Italy, Andy painted a legend on his flying cap: "MO MULES THE SHOW-ME STATE." He went around slapping us all on the shoulders as if he were fanning the team spirit before a college football game. "We got a dream crew, men," he said, "let's keep it that way." And then he explained what he meant by dream crew. "It's a perfect crew, like ours, with a perfect record, a very heroic combat

record, with Distinguished Flying Crosses for all the men and Air
Medals galore. But no Purple Hearts! After we finish our fifty missions,
we'll go back to the States in our own ship and tour and sell war bonds.
Just like the guys who flew *Memphis Belle*. How's that for a shot?"

I heard Dooley snoring. The others were awake. And they must be
thinking thoughts similar to mine. I wondered if they resented me for
being their tail gunner? I wondered if they tolerated me because in
war one cannot choose one's companions? I wondered if they suspected how really frightened I was of planes and how completely in-
efficient I was with the guns? Perhaps I should have told them back in
the States. My ineffectualness might jeopardize nine lives. But with
luck, and with their help, I hoped, I would cover up. . . .

4

I HEARD THE screech of brakes, and
Sergeant Delmonico of Squadron Operations burst in, shouting:
"Time to get up, you hot rocks! Time to fly the big-assed birds!" His
cheerful tone made it seem we were awakened to go on a picnic.

We sat up bleary-eyed, staring at each other by the candlelight. It
was two in the morning, and a gentle May breeze drifted in through
holes that had once been windows. The moon peered in over the
open barracks door. It was such an incredibly peaceful moon one's
mind could not project itself to the business ahead. We dressed hurriedly, almost eagerly, and ran to the mess hall. I tried eating the powdered eggs but something inside me constricted and I gave them up
and sipped the acid black coffee instead. Then, stabbing the dark
with our flashlights, we ran to the briefing shed which was already
filled with gunners whose eyes were searching worriedly for the red
ribbon on the huge map. The ribbon pointed to the Target for the
Day: Wiener Neustadt, a double-credit mission.

It was still dark when all ten of us assembled near our ship in the dispersal area. *Flying Foxhole* was all shiny and silvery with a taut, unblemished, aluminum skin. Nevertheless I was struck by a change in her appearance. It was not a tangible change. The plane suddenly seemed angry, like a predatory bird. Her great bomb bays were weighted down with ten five-hundred-pound bombs. Her ten guns were stripped of their covering, and the munitions boxes were heavy with chains of copper-shiny, dull-pointed, fifty-caliber bullets. The transformation was complete. The soaring eagle that once shared with us the poetry of peaceful flight over the green-carpeted jungles of Brazil, the sunrise on the equator, the black majesty of the Atlas Mountains in the Sahara Desert, that eagle had overnight actually become a bird of prey.

All around us fat-bellied Liberators sat heavily on the ground, hiding their death-bombs from the Italian moon. And nearby, amid the pygmy olive trees, and even underneath the wheels of the planes, crickets maintained their feeble chatter, asserting the night was theirs and we were intruders. Suddenly the whispering night was violated as the propellers started churning, and soon the world was a roaring, thundering inferno. The ground crews were warming up the engines, revving them up and idling them. We moved away from the plane for the last quick smokes and last few words on the ground. Chet Kowalski passed out the Escape and Money Kits. His face had a one-day growth of beard: it was the first time I had seen him unshaven. We tried some words, but nobody sounded convincing, not even Lieutenant Andy Kyle who attempted to inject some cheer.

Like the others, I was listening to myself. I tried to sort out my fears: fear of the unknown, fear of combat, fear of being wounded and made helpless, fear of not doing the right thing in an emergency and imperiling the lives of my comrades; fear of death. I was pitifully conscious of my inadequacy. I was too old. My fingers were too thin and delicate, my eyesight was faulty. Even my anger against the enemy, the object that guided me toward this moment, even that left me. "If I was a Jew, like Ben," Dooley often said, "maybe I'd feel like fighting in this thing." But it was four-thirty on a cold Italian morning, and I was many thousands of miles away from Ruth and security, and instead of anger there was a terrible, numbing fear. I was appalled by the realization that though we were huddled together momentarily against the unknown, we were in fact strangers, bound ever so precariously only by mutual fears.

Lieutenant Andy Kyle, staring at his black navigator's watch, called, "Time."

All ten of us slid in underneath the bomb bays up to the flight deck. After *Flying Foxhole* was airborne, we dispersed to our various stations. I made my way up the incline to the tail turret, and there I suddenly stopped. I could not bring myself to climb inside the turret. In the past I had avoided this exposed part of the bomber, fearing — of all things — that it might fall off or be blown away while I was in it. The turret was narrow and confining and offered no avenue of escape. Back in the States, while in gunnery school, I had invented countless excuses to be allowed to fire from the waist section. In fact, I had qualified for air combat by firing the waist guns. By some miracle no one had ever called attention to the discrepancy of a tail gunner avoiding the turret assigned to him. During training in the States I had overcome to some extent the feeling of insecurity in the air, by keeping my eyes shut when taking off, by not looking down, by holding on to something solid when the plane lurched.

I started climbing inside the turret and felt an icy sweat on my forehead. I closed my eyes to avoid looking at the vast emptiness floating beneath me. My several layers of clothing, topped by a bulky electrically wired suit, Mae West, and constricting chute harness, made the slightest movement difficult. Cords extended from my suit, throat mike, and helmet, and I realized if the need ever came to flee the turret, I would be held by all these threads like a fly caught in a spider's web. I started to preflight my twin-fifty guns by giving them a dry run, and set about charging them nervously. I fed the ammunition belts on the gun feedways by touch, cursing the infernal mechanisms. Unable to see the gun feedways which were shielded by steel jackets I leaned forward with difficulty and put my ear close to the jackets, hoping to hear the click when the shell was lodged in the slot underneath the extractor. My anxiety increased with failure and the awareness that even if I succeeded in charging the guns I would still remain at the mercy of any minor malfunction. I felt hopelessly miscast in the role of warrior. The situation was both alarming and absurd, and were it not so tragic one might laugh, laugh at the fact that a clumsy, old fool got inside a tail turret of a bomber under false pretenses. I tore frenziedly at the munitions boxes. Blood was trickling from several cuts on both hands. I thought desperately of calling for help from Mel, our crew armorer. But Mel was in the nose section of the ship and I did not want to be heard on the interphone pleading for help on such an elementary matter as charging one's guns. I could hear Dooley's voice taunting me: "Some career gunner you are, Ben! Looks to me like a short career!"

We were half across the Adriatic Sea, pointing toward Yugoslavia, when I finally succeeded in charging my guns. I remembered the advice of one of the more experienced gunners in the barracks who had warned me to keep my turret door open. "It will be cold and you'll freeze your ass off," he had said, "but in case you want to bail out, all you hafta do is roll back toward the camera hatch — if your door is open. If it's closed, you might never get out."

"Navigator to crew," Andy said over the phone. "Navigator to crew —" Andy's voice sounded colder than I'd ever heard it — "we're over Yugoslavia. Enemy territory. Take your places. Gunners in your turrets. Open waist windows."

I switched on the gun buttons and rode the turret in azimuth until my back was completely exposed to the biting winds. I tried the guns in elevation, and for an instant I felt the master of an intricate and deadly laboratory.

Billy Poat and Leo Trent pried open the windows in the ship's midsection, and the icy wind struck me in the back. The waist gunners stuck out their single guns. Mouse Fidanza pumped down the spherical turret until it was completely exposed under the ship's belly. Then he crawled inside it and latched the door.

The wind came in burning blasts and I heard Billy and Leo on the mike swearing. "Colder than a witch's tit," Leo said, "my aching back." I could almost hear his teeth chatter.

"Colder than a grave digger's ass on the Klondike," Billy said. They moved away from the open windows and toward the center of the ship to avoid the searing gusts.

Silence followed on the interphone. It was an alive, ominous, sinister silence. It was the silence of fear. The silence of premonition. The silence of doom. I was grateful when Dooley broke that silence. "I'm gonna transfer some gas from the Tokio tanks, fellas, so put out your cigarettes." There was a grateful response on the interphone, a feverish, brief chatter, as if the engineer's words had resurrected the dying.

Again we were plunged into silence until Chet Kowalski called, "We're at thirteen thousand feet. Time to put on your oxygen masks." Chet's voice didn't have its usually apologetic and humbled quality. His voice was part of the war, calm but heavy with a fear that nobody could deny him. Neither he nor his voice could be rejected now, over enemy territory, cut off from the most secure aspect of life itself: the earth.

The echelons were strung out for hundreds of unseen miles, and in the distance the ships appeared like specks hanging against the backdrop of clear sky. Occasionally the rays of the sun set aglow the silver skin of a bomber, and I raised my head, peering suspiciously in that direction.

Below us the great expanse of mountain land was green. It was warm and inviting. It was peaceful below. I saw rivers and small, wooden bridges. Fields were combed with furrows, and some of the dwellings had new paint. But no smoke issued from the chimneys, no living objects moved underneath. I was suddenly aware that the lands beneath us were drained of life; the beautiful, warm earth was abandoned by its former dwellers and consigned to the gods of war. And yet I had the strange feeling that out of the forests and valleys and ravines and trenches, eyes were probing the skies anxiously, looking for our passage.

A speck darted across my vision and I cried into the mike, "Unidentified aircraft at eight o'clock." I had said exactly the right thing, as I had read it in manuals and seen in training films. The aircraft rose high, as if climbing straight up, then it turned over on its side and started dropping slowly. We raised our guns and framed the intruder in our sights.

"It's one of ours!" Dooley cried, elated. "It's a P-38!"

"Yes, 'tis," Mel confirmed Dooley's findings. It was the first thing he had said all morning.

The pursuit ship slid in closer to our formation and turned over on its side again to reveal its identity conclusively to the many suspicious and trigger-happy gunners whose fingers were nervous on their weapons. In the next few minutes several more twin-boomed Lightnings appeared as if by some magician's stroke. They flew in packs of four, high above the bomber formations, like shepherds guiding packs of clumsy, vulnerable charges. Mel Ginn, forgetting his fear of the mike, shrieked exultantly, "That's our escort awright! Purtiest sight I ever seen, I guarantee ya that."

The formations continued climbing slowly, laboriously, as if seeking a safe altitude from the impending clash with the enemy's antiaircraft batteries. We crossed the muddy Danube into Hungary. From twenty-one thousand feet the land below us lost its color and assumed the outline of a war map. A slight mist hung over the enemy country. Behind our box of seven bombers I watched the other Liberators close in tightly as if seeking safety in compactness and unity. The four-engine planes seemed to respond to the same fear that gripped us inside, and flew in tight formation.

The mist below, the wing-tip formations, the terrible silence, built up the dread until I was aware of a physical pain underneath my heart. I longed to hear the voices of my comrades, but there was only the tortured silence that enveloped us with a heavy, stifling blanket. The whole universe was joined in the conspiracy of silence. The universe was holding its breath, I was sure of that. We were at the vortex of the universe. Nothing existed beyond this nucleus of fear.

Pennington's voice announcing the Initial Point tore me back to the present. "We're coming on the IP," the pilot said. "Everybody stay off the interphone. I'll be listening in on Command for instructions." Immediately following his announcement, Kowalski said, "Time to put on your flak suits."

I pulled on the unwieldy flak vest with its forty pounds of steel bits. I donned the flak helmet. I could neither see nor move.

Andy Kyle's voice came over, unrecognizable, distant, almost frozen. "Start throwing out the 'window,'" the navigator said. Leo and Billy reached into the boxes on the floor and started throwing out long strips of silver foil which were supposed to interfere with the enemy's radar antiaircraft devices. The "window" slapped against the sides of the bomber and streamed away with the prop wash like confetti.

"Bomb-bay doors open." Dick's voice. Calm, distant, like the others. Saying the right things as we had rehearsed them many times in the States. Only the tone was different, the voice floating in space, frozen with fear.

The bomb-bay doors swung up and the fierce wind struck the ship's exposed belly and penetrated its vitals. The bomber shuddered from the thrust of the wind and I felt as if I were riding stormy seas. I watched the other bombers' bellies swing open, and the great black bombs were poised on their racks, waiting to be dropped.

The world was all engine roar. Beyond the silver foil glistening in the sun as it streamed away, everything stood still. The black death-bombs hung down from the racks like ugly tits. "I don't believe it . . . I don't believe . . ." I whispered to myself. "What am *I* doing here?"

"FLAK!" Mel screamed "Flaaakkkk!"

I raised my helmet and looked at the Plexiglas, past it. I saw black puffs appear in the sky. They were like the pictures I had seen on hot, drowsy afternoons while training in Georgia. The black puffs were abreast of our formation and seemed to hang there. There was something fat and ugly about their jet blackness. They were completely soundless, hanging like black roses planted by unseen hands. For a brief moment I seized upon the crazy hope that these black puffs were also harmless. For I saw them blossom out on both sides of *Flying Foxhole* and all along the path of our formations, and yet the ships plowed through them.

A violent thrust, and our ship was lifted up in the air. A hissing sound. Somebody's voice, disembodied, hysterical: "One of the engines was hit —"

"Stay off the goddamn interphone!" It was the pilot. Voice grim, businesslike. He was in full command. Four years of training. Nothing can stop the army air force! Pennington's voice was reassuring. He was listening in on Command as the flight leader, Colonel Haasert, guided the formations over Wiener Neustadt.

For miles the sky was all black puffs, lightless, explosive lanterns pointing the path to destruction. I had thrown off my flak helmet and my eyes were glued on them. My teeth chattered and the lower part of my jaw rattled like a jeep bumping over tufa rock. A strange hissing sound penetrated to my ears, and the pungent smell of high-octane gas attacked my nostrils when my oxygen mask slipped off by accident. Below us there was smoke. The smoke hid the target and obliterated all living matter. There could be no life below, I thought, only antiaircraft batteries firing their salvos from gun emplacements in hell itself.

"They got our range!" It could have been the voice of any of my comrades.

I was lifted by a violent jolt, and without thinking I seized the turret hinges and held on as if that would afford protection. But the turret rose and fell with me. "Solid. Grab hold of something solid," I thought. I felt suddenly that my actions were being stripped of all semblance of logic. Only noises were distinct: shrapnel hitting the ship were like pebbles striking against the side of a speeding automobile; flak bursting nearby sounded like one railroad train passing another at high speed. Swish . . . ssswishshshsh. Hissing sound of escaping gas.

I heard the agonizing sound of Duraluminum torn as a shell struck our hydraulic system and the fluid burst from its containers and sprayed the gunners in the waist section. It penetrated to the tail and covered the Plexiglas of my turret. I hid my face in my gloved hands and doubled up, and my whole body contracted. The gas smell became more pungent. The shell fragments tore at *Flying Foxhole*'s skin with glancing taps and hammer blows. The ship reeled and groaned like a stricken bird.

"We're losing too much gas!" Dooley cried. His plea lingered momentarily on the interphone and died without response, as if all the rest of us had lost the ability to comment or articulate any opinions. In the next instant Dick Martin's voice came like a warning scream: "BOMMBS AWAAAY!" I had never heard it so shrill, feminine, anguished, hysterical.

Flying Foxhole moaned as Dick relieved its belly of the bombs. It rose perceptibly, freed from its terrible burden.

We made a sharp turn off the target and the ship lurched on a forty-five-degree angle. I glanced back into the waist section fully expecting to see the ship out of control, with only brief seconds left before bailing out. But through my tear-filled eyes I saw Billy and Leo both kneeling, their faces hidden in their arms. A thought flashed through my mind: were they praying? Neither one of them put much stock in prayer. No, they were hiding. Hiding. In full view of the Jerry flak guns. I slapped the oxygen mask back on my face and straightened up and started climbing out of the turret with the intention of joining the kneeling waist gunners. But a bursting shell sent shrapnel through the Plexiglas dome, spraying my helmet, severing electric-suit cords and tearing the solenoid off the left gun. I hid my face in my hands and it occurred to me this must be the end. There seemed no way out of the enemy's fire. This must be the end, for human intercourse had ceased on the ship which was caught in a maelstrom of destruction. This was the end because none of us functioned any longer; each one of us was rolled up in his own envelope of fear, awaiting the final blackout. I was praying . . . I heard my lips in prayer . . . a Hebrew phrase I learned as a child in the synagogue. *Shma Israel* — I had not used that phrase since childhood. I had never believed it. I did not believe it now. *Shma Israel.* Hear, O Israel. . . . My befogged mind registered the irony of it: an unbeliever praying, knowing it would not help, grasping at a tenuous thread that held no promise of delivery.

I sought desperately for an image that would make death seem meaningful and worthwhile. I recalled a picture of the massacred Jewish children of Kiev, lying eyeless and charred on a heap. . . . I recalled the Uprising of the Warsaw Ghetto. . . . The hated image of Hitler. . . . Could any of these images be summarized into a song of defiance when death leered at you? I could not grasp at any of these images for courage. My brain was a hopeless jumble, a frozen mass.

My eyes were glazed with tears but I looked up and stared at the sky filled with black puffs and smoke. The struggling planes were like helpless clay ducks in a shooting gallery. The last semblance of formation flying was gone, and the Liberators were all over the sky in panicky flight. In the distance I caught a glimpse of a bomber exploding; the front half of the ship nosed down and spiraled slowly earthward, turning crazily, like a long piece of paper dropped from a tall building. The other half of the fuselage appeared nailed to space momentarily, then it too floated down in a slow spiral. No chutes came out of that ship. No men. All ten men were trapped inside. Ten men (was this Gilbert's crew? Whitey's in that ship) hurtling toward destruction, riveted to the steel, entombed by the law of gravity, clinging to their parachutes but unable to use them. For those of the ten whose hearts had not stopped beating, two minutes, one hundred and twenty seconds of living death was in store before the last moment when their bodies shattered against the alien soil.

I vomited into my oxygen mask and closed my eyes and dropped my face on the gun-handles. A lump squeezed upward from my diaphragm like a swelling hard fist that made breathing difficult. I sucked on the oxygen, sucked on it greedily, but the lump continued squeezing upward as if attempting to choke the remaining gasps of breath out of my body. I was alone in the vast death-sky, without comrades, without mother, alone and swaying briefly with only a turret hinge to grab for support. It no longer mattered what happened to me. . . .

•   •   •   •

"We're out of the flak now, we're out of the flak now. Can't you hear me, tail? What's the matter with the tail gunner? Hey, Ben! . . . Go see if he's alive." I recognized the pilot's voice. I bolted into consciousness and sat up.

"I'm okay —" I articulated slowly. I looked at my hands and then I guided them along my body, probing in the dark for any damages.

"You hurt, tail?"

"N-no —"

"What about the others?"

A wave of hysteria broke loose on the interphone in response to the pilot's query. The voices of my crewmates mingled and fused.

"One at a time!" Pennington shouted. "Goddammit, speak one at a time!"

"If we don't stop this gas from escaping we'll blow to hell!" Leo Trent screamed.

"The hydraulic —" Billy Poat cut in.

Pennington pressed the mike button and held his finger on it, and when he finally let go, the interphone was silent. "This is an order!" he cried with rage. "I said one at a time, and this is a direct order!" He articulated the words slowly, as if remembering in this desperate moment the magic power with which the army had endowed him when he was made pilot and thus commander of the bomber. "Any bastard talking out of turn, I'll have him court-martialed."

The pilot's outburst had a sobering effect on the crew, not so much because he threatened court-martial (most of us doubted that we would come out alive) but because he entertained the hope of reaching ground safely to appear before a court-martial.

We checked our panic and reported, each from his station, listing the damage to himself and the ship.

"Number Two engine knocked out," Dooley informed the pilot, "and we got gas escaping. The whole ship's drenched. We'll never make it to Italy —"

"Hydraulic system knocked out," Billy Poat cut in on the engineer, "which means we won't have any brakes for landing, even if we *do* get back to our base. Our left rudder is shot to hell, and —"

"The formations are gone," Mel Ginn interrupted, "and so is the escort. We're alone up heah in the sky. What we gonna do?"

Pennington waited until all the questions and cries had subsided, then he said in a voice he tried hard to control: "We'll try to patch her up the best we can and limp home. The other alternative is to bail out here, over Austria. It's up to you fellows. Want to bail out over enemy territory? I'll leave it up to the crew. If anybody wants to bail out, speak up." He paused, and when there was no response, he continued, "Now, let's start patching her up. Dooley, you come down off your turret, let Dick take your place while you go to work feathering the Number Two engine and transferring her gas to the three good engines. Fidanza, bring up your ball turret, that'll save some drag. You men in the waist, try to stop the hydraulic leak the best you can. Isaacs, you stay in the tail turret. If you see enemy aircraft, don't shoot. Report. If enemy fighters make a pass at us, we'll lower our wheels and surrender. One bullet would set up enough of a spark to blow us to hell. Poat, you stay away from the radio; don't send. We don't want any sparks. Andy, start navigating; let me know when we get to Yugo over Partisan territory because we might have to bail out there. Now everybody strap your chutes on — in case you have to go out in a hurry — and get to work."

We were alone in the hostile skies. All the air force formations had passed over us a long time ago, ignoring us, streaking home at forced speed after the bloody encounter, some carrying wounded on board who were patched up temporarily; some carrying dead comrades to whom it did not matter how soon the homing field was reached. With the formations of the tired, oil-spattered, flak-torn bombers roamed the swift packs of P-38 Lightnings and P-51 Mustangs like solicitous shepherds keeping a sharp lookout for their clumsy charges. And behind them, unshepherded and undefended, mangled B-24 Liberators were strung out helplessly across enemy skies. These were the stragglers for whom the Nazi Focke-Wolfe-190s and Messerschmitt-109s lay in wait, the clay ducks and the dead pigeons, many of whom would be listed in squadron operations bulletins later in the day: Missing in Action.

We were alone, patching, plugging up our ship, realizing how little we knew about a plane and how ill-prepared we were for fighting. All the days we'd goofed off at school, and all the times instructors in the States had ignored our questions by saying, "You'll get that in the next phase of training," all that came back to us now with a terrible impact. But despite our ignorance we tried to bind the wounds of our stricken ship. Dooley worked like a man possessed, rushing back and forth along the catwalk from the flight deck to the waist section where Billy Poat was helping him with the hydraulic system. Billy was drenched in the reddish hydraulic fluid. He had stripped off his chute harness and tossed it away. He was too occupied to be afraid.

There were only three of us at the guns: Dick, Mel, and I. The rest of the crew were struggling with the plane. Pennington and Kowalski both gripped their sticks to keep the rudderless ship from going into a spin. Above the camera hatch Cosmo Fidanza sat hunched up as if he were still in the ball turret. Mouse was praying.

The sky over Yugoslavia was like the Austrian sky: clear, blue, hostile, treacherous. My eyes were bloodshot from staring at the emptiness, searching for enemy planes. My teeth had stopped chattering. I was no longer afraid, I was simply stiff and numb as if all emotion had been drained and I was no longer capable of feeling. I did not dare hope we would come out unscathed. But if by some miracle, we came out of it, I did not see how I could face going on another mission. If we came out of this I would go to the flight surgeon and have myself grounded. I would tell him the truth that I'd tried but I was unable to go through with it. I was too old, too slow, my reflexes were all mixed up. I was a novice with the guns. He could take my sergeant's stripes, my silver wings, and put me on KP for the duration. I would say all these things to him, but the real truth I would keep from him, namely, that I didn't have the courage to go on. A washed-out gunner in the States had called it "a yellow streak of common sense." At that time I'd considered him a worthless coward and broke our friendship. Now I envied him, though I disliked him no less for what he had done. And I was beginning to dislike myself for the thoughts that were licking at my mind. In the rush of self-pity accompanying these thoughts I resented the people who were safe in America. Whatever bond I had with human beings was not with my wife or mother or friends; it was with the nine men in *Flying Foxhole*. But even my oneness with them was transient because my mind was scheming how to abandon them if and when we returned to our base.

If, at any time along the route, the pilot had suggested we bail out, I would have gone out without any hesitation. By bailing out I would avoid carrying through my decision of getting myself grounded and afterward facing my comrades. If I bailed out I would be a hero. . . .

"We'll keep flying," Pennington said, dismissing all warnings about the ship being soaked through and through with the 100-octane gas. "We'll fly a little bit longer," the pilot said in a voice that carried no decision but a plea. It seemed less complicated to say, "We'll fly a little while longer," than to order: Abandon Ship.

The sun was no longer overhead. We came over the rugged range of peaks that separated Dalmatia from the Adriatic Sea. I left my turret and went to the waist section. From ten thousand feet up the sea was steel gray and cold. Two small craft appeared on it like water bugs zigzagging and leaving little penciled marks on the surface. Ahead of us we glimpsed the shore of Italy. And the barren land that had been strange to us only yesterday was suddenly Home. How quickly and subtly the transformation had taken place. "If I ever get my feet on that solid ground there," Billy Poat whispered to me as we both stood at the waist window watching the land below, "they'll never get me up again."

"Doesn't that look lush!" Leo exclaimed. "Never thought this place could look so good. *Viva l'Italia!*"

"Keep your shirts on," Pennington burst in on the conversation. "Ground Operations is calling us but we're up s— — creek. Don't respond, Poat. Lay off that radio. I'm afraid of sparks."

"It's six of one, half dozen of the other," the bombardier said. "Why don't we abandon ship?"

"We'll fly a little while longer," the pilot said.

"It's a kind of a shame," Leo whispered in the waist section, "to be home and yet not to be home. Don't those bastards down below know we're Americans?"

"Jerries have been known to fly captured B-24s," Billy said.

Then we heard the tower at the field call for our Identification Friend or Foe.

"Use your IFF," the tower warned, "or we'll shoot."

"F— — you," Pennington said. He steered *Flying Foxhole* away from the field and started losing altitude slowly and cautiously. "Maybe the stupid bastards will spot our markings if we come down a bit. A fine mess!" he suddenly cried, showing emotion for the first time. "You go through hell, come out of it, limp all the way home and when you get here they're zeroing in their guns to plug you. Plug their own men!"

"Dick said before we ought to bail out," Kowalski said.

"Bail out if you want to," Pennington said. "Anybody who wants to, go out, it's okay with me. I'm going to try and land this ship."

"Don't be a hero, Albert," the bombardier said. "Heroes usually end up in the graveyard."

"You have my permission to hit the silk," Pennington repeated, "I'm going in."

"Who wants to bail out with me?" Dick Martin asked. When there was no response, he reconsidered, saying, "Okay, I'm staying 'cause it's my crew. But I'm doing it against my better judgment."

We circled above the field in a wide pattern, dropping altitude slowly. Through the field glasses which Andy Kyle passed around we saw from the waist windows how the antiaircraft guns were tracking us, riding with us, waiting for the command to start firing. Then the guns were suddenly lowered and we saw an ambulance streak down the field. Ground was sending: "Okay, Pennington. Got your markings. You're identified. Note change of wind. Come in north runway. Over."

"You fukken well told I'm coming in!" Pennington cried in triumphant anger. "Take ditching positions, you men in the waist, we're going in."

We remained at the open waist windows, ignoring the pilot's order. We crowded near the windows in order to be in a position to jump in the event the ship started sliding or giving off sparks. "After all I gone th'ough," Mel Ginn said, "I ain't gonna get myself blowed to hell on the home field, I guarantee ya that."

We came in on our final lap, and the ship's three landing wheels poised below the fuselage like huge talons. The flaps came down from the wings and the ship settled slowly. We struck the runway and bounced back in the air and hit the ground again. We felt the pilot slam on the brakes but they didn't hold. It was at this moment, as we were streaking down the steel mats at 100 miles an hour, heading for the huge rock wall at the end of the field, that Dooley seized two parachutes, threw one to Billy Poat, pushed Mel and me away from the waist windows and screamed at the radio operator: "Open the chute out the window!" The two men held their chutes out the windows, pulled the handles and spilled the nylon against the prop-wash. They secured the chute lines around the waist-gun mounts and held on. We were down three-quarters of the runway when suddenly the chutes billowed out, and the ship sat down on its tail like a fatally stricken bird. Its nose wheel reared up in the air. The ship skidded fifty feet and dragged to a stop near where several jeeps and the ambulance were awaiting us.

All ten of us piled from the ship. We scrambled down and without looking back we ran in our heavy clothing away from the ship, away in all directions. Then, when we felt safely distanced from our plane, several of us fell down and kissed the barren, parched soil, then got up and ran again.

5

I LAY ON MY cot and listened to the happy chatter of my crewmates. Our flirtation with death had given us a oneness. Already I felt a part of this war life, as if I'd been part of it for a long time. I no longer felt self-conscious about stretching my limbs on the cot that so recently belonged to a man who hadn't come back.

I was completely spent, and were this the end of the experience, I might have collapsed on my cot and relegated to some future time the minute dissecting of the morning's events. But already I was conscious of tomorrow, of the many tomorrows and the additional forty-eight missions I must fly. And this awareness of tomorrow mingled with the joy of having cheated death today.

The idea of going to see the flight surgeon was absurd. Up in the air the mind played one dirty tricks. But down here the terror of the mission was beginning to recede. It had been a nightmare, but now I was awake. I was on my cot listening to my buddies and I was intoxicated with being alive and whole. I stretched my limbs underneath the mosquito netting and reached for a cigarette and a great joy swept over me. Despite the needling pain in my bloodshot eyes, I kept them open. I wanted to see everything that went on in this wondrous world.

The voices of my comrades drifted to me lazily, Dooley crying while he hugged little Cosmo Fidanza, whose cheeks were red with the thawing out: "Oh, that fukken Wiener Douche-bag sonofabitch! I never thought we'd make it."

"I know what you mean, doc," Cosmo chirped happily. He wasn't the cussing type, being an undergraduate man of God on detached service with the army, but he couldn't help saying, "I prayed like hell."

"We wasn't far away from that final salvation you always talk about," Dooley said, putting a headlock on Mouse.

"You'd be surprised, doc," Cosmo said. "The Almighty wants you to hang around this world as long as possible. That's why I prayed so hard."

"Maybe that's what brung us out, your prayer," Mel said, sitting on his cot, a cross dangling from his throat. "Don't know what else brung us out, I guarantee ya that."

"I know now I was right about wanting the infantry," Billy Poat said. "Up in the air what can you hold on to? How can a guy fight when there's nothing solid to grab?"

"I never looked at it that way," Mel said reflectively, "but I see what you mean."

"Ever since I was a kid," Billy said, "I remember when my old man and old lady had a fight, I'd run for a big oak tree we had in the yard, and put my arms around it and hold on. I'm telling you, that was solid, take my word. Never fear it'll move on you, like people, or planes. You can always rely on trees. But what have you got up in the sky?"

Leo Trent was listening in on the conversation and playing with his little dog. He kissed the pup and ran his cheek over its soft brown fur, making clucking sounds with his tongue and stabbing the dog with his large Roman nose. "They almost got your old dad today," Leo said to the dog. "You almost lost your daddy, baby." Leo poured out the endearing words effortlessly and unselfconsciously. He was completely absorbed by the puppy. "For a while there I thought I'd never see my baby again. Come give daddy a kiss."

We were very close that afternoon, having learned together, and having accomplished something, though we said little about the damage our bombs had inflicted. Mostly our thoughts were about being alive. Flirtation with death had caused all of us to fall in love with life. The stretching of a limb, a sigh, a drag on a cigarette, all motions and movements flowed with a sensuousness I'd never known before. All these pleasures had a new meaning. It was like being reborn.

It occurred to me I must write to Ruth, but I didn't know what to tell her. A subtle wall was being erected between my wife and me because we had not shared this experience. I realized with a shock that my wife was a civilian, *safe* back in the States. And I suddenly resented those who were safe. I was appalled at the ease with which I abandoned myself to self-pity even in my hour of triumph. But aside from the corrupting but very comfortable stabs of self-pity there was no denying that my most profound experience had been shared with me not by Ruth but by nine comparative strangers. They were now a part of my life, part of my joys and sorrows. We had not chosen one another as brothers; it had been ordained for us. Mel Ginn, a rancher from western Texas, was my brother. I didn't know much about him and he was suspicious of me because I came from a large city. He was amused by my clumsiness with the guns. He was puzzled that an "old man" had got himself mixed up in the fighting. Mel had never met a Jew before and this confused him also. Before our first mission we had little to say to each other. But today we had been through life together. Before our first mission Leo Trent and I had little in common. Leo used to sell perfume in Hollywood before the war. His heart had been set on becoming a pilot, but he had been washed out of cadet training "three hours before graduation." That was his story. It rankled that his younger brother, who was twenty-one, two years Leo's junior, was an ace Marine fighter pilot in the Pacific while Leo became a "venereal gunner." He was not a good gunner (this we had in common), and up in the air I saw him paralyzed with fear (this too we had in common). Leo and I had never become close, perhaps because we each knew the other to be a coward who resented being found out. That's why he was wary of me. He credited me with an insight that always sat in judgment on his weaknesses. Also, he mistook my aloofness for snobbery. He did not like riddles. But I wanted him to like me. He was, after all, my brother.

It was wonderful to be alive, to contemplate the distant future which we had helped to shape this morning. Dropping our bombs, destroying Hitler's factories, we had gone to the heart of the matter.

To be *doing* finally, no longer to be *talking*, was what made it all so rewarding. And this particular feeling only Ruth could understand: I was afraid my crewmates would laugh at me if I told them about it.

* * * *

After the evening meal at the squadron mess hall we went to the officers' tent as if we were trying to perpetuate our crew honeymoon. We sat on the four cots and bomb racks and talked about the mission and tossed the little pebbles which made up the tent floor.

"We did okay," Andy Kyle said. "We worked like a real bunch of old-timers." Our navigator thought for a while and continued: "There was only one thing wrong and that concerns me alone. I don't like the idea of not having a gun to fire. When somebody shoots at you, you like to shoot back. Now, you guys understand that's not a complaint."

"I got no gun either," Dick Martin said, "but I don't give a continental."

"At least you drop the bombs," Andy said softly, as if he feared to offend his buddies. "At least you press the button that releases the bombs. But what's a navigator like me do? He sits and doodles on the flight deck — just like a passenger. The only time a navigator feels useful is when he's in a lead ship navigating or when a crew gets separated from its formation. At least if I had a gun —"

Big Wheel, who had been writing a letter to Myrtle on an up-ended K-ration box which served as a table, looked up as if he'd noticed us for the first time. There was a suggestion of a smile on his tight-lipped mouth. "I don't know what you're complaining about," he said half-jokingly to Andy. "Didn't you take charge of the mission log and note all pertinent facts?"

"Yeah," Andy retorted bitterly. "I noted the fact that 'At 1900 the pilot turned over the stick to the copilot and proceeded to the waist section of the ship where he relieved himself — in the relief tube. He returned at 1905.'"

"Well, that's what you get paid for," Pennington said, laughing. We all joined in the laughter because it was a rare sight to see our pilot laugh and because we believed that this was the beginning of a binding relationship in our crew, the kind one reads about in storybooks and sees in movies.

Our laughter encouraged Pennington. He abandoned his letter-writing and joined in the conversation. "If I'd only had a fighter plane this morning," he said wistfully, "instead of that fat B-24."

"You didn't do so bad," Andy said.

"I hate these clumsy crates," the pilot said. "They're perfect targets. The Jerry antiaircraft gunners must be saying to themselves: 'What a bunch of fools they are up there, sitting in those coffins.' A Liberator doesn't fly. The fukken thing crawls." There was laughter again when Pennington concluded, because we shared his passionate denunciation of the fat-bellied Liberator. I suspected, however, that there was a note of condescension in his cursing, as if he were coming down to the level of the crew.

Sitting on a bomb rack, listening to the talk, I closed my eyes and felt secure and enveloped by a thousand silver threads of sleep. Suddenly I heard Kowalski's voice. "I been to Squadron Operations," the copilot said, his tone heavy with grievance. "We're alerted again for tomorrow's mission!"

Outside the tent I looked at the sky. It was no longer the beautiful, serene sky. It was an object filled with treachery and an unknown tomorrow.

●   ●   ●   ●

Sleep was gone from my eyes. I reached for a v-mail form to write to my wife. I felt it imperative to inform her — and through her, the whole world — that I had a double-mission credit. If anything happened to me on tomorrow's mission, she would know her husband died a hero. But was that the only reason for writing her? What manner of hero was I, seeking this reassurance from Ruth? Didn't she consider me a hero already? Ruth knew perfectly my reasons for being here. I was here because I hated Hitler, hated fascism, and feared they would come to America. I was here because Hitler made me conscious, again, that as a Jew I must assume the role of scapegoat. I had almost forgotten that being Jewish carried any stigma with it, though I had known anti-Semitism and pogroms as a child. From the age of fifteen when I arrived in America, being Jewish had not stood in the way of my becoming a teacher, of being happily married, of leading the kind of existence that would let me attain my limited aspirations. Only in 1933, with Hitler riding into power, was the old wound reopened.

Where was my anger? Intellectually there was no question in my mind about what was the right thing to do. Fighting was the right thing. Then why the vacillation? Why the need to be reassured that I was a hero? Why the doubts? The word *escape* etched itself in my mind. War was a perfect *escape!* I tortured myself with the thought: perhaps you wanted to die a martyr, and thus, instead of being accused of running away from life, you would be hailed as having died a hero. How many were privileged to be martyrs? The whole world would approve of you — even Ruth from whom you *escaped* on account of her illness. You escaped into war and now you resent all those who do not face death as you must. Eat your cake and have it too. What a goddamn mess!

But why place so much emphasis on *escape?* Why put things in a negative light and torture oneself when sleep was so precious and necessary? I wondered how strong the element of escape was in Pennington's case. The mundane work in the photo shop could not compare with flying a Mustang. They had refused him a Mustang, but he was a flyer nevertheless and he lived in the hope of getting a fighter plane someday. He was a hero for the whole world to see and approve, and this without the aid of Myrtle or his father who had never given him any responsibility. Behind Big Wheel's cold aloofness was a reckless, romantic streak. Dooley had made the observation, "I sometimes wonder how a levelheaded guy like him can be so crazy. The sonofabitch looks like he's always either chasing somebody or running away."

The war was also Chet Kowalski's great experience. Compare the dreams of a shiny officer's uniform and piloting a ship in the wild blue yonder with the realities of selling plastics on Joseph Campau Street in Hamtramck and spending bored evenings at home with an unattractive wife five years his senior. He had let himself be carried along by the swollen tide of the army, going along in a semi-somnambulist state, content with having reached the exalted rank of second looey. Unlike the ambitious Pennington, our copilot had never made any effort either to influence or resist the course. He had found himself in cadet school by chance. He was graduated a pilot though he showed no aptitude in that direction and despite the fact he'd put out little effort. And suddenly he was faced with the realities of war. And while this held true for most of us, I felt that if this was all we were going to fight the war on,

34 ♦ LOUIS FALSTEIN

with no more fundamental beliefs, we would wind up in a hell of a mess, "I guarantee ya that." True, the mercenaries of the Foreign Legion were able to carry on limited campaigns without any other credo than escape into anonymity and a bare sort of security. But we had to fight on something more positive. He is thrice armed who knows his cause is just. But the army had kept our cause a deep, dark secret. My crewmates fought on nothing. They fought without anger. I would never fight, face injury and death if I did not have some feeling about this war. My comrades were going into battle tomorrow simply because they felt it was their duty, because others had been doing it, but without any conviction that their deaths would have any meaning for the world. Theirs was the kind of a courage I did not possess. I thought I understood what Leo felt when he whispered to his pup, "I sure wish I was a little dog like you and didn't have to worry about flying tomorrow." And Mel Ginn wrote a farewell note to his wife. He sat perspiring over the letter more than usual because he put in his feelings for Sharon and his fears. It was the kind of letter most gunners wrote and put away and if they failed to come back somebody would discover it while scavenging among their belongings and dispatch the note to a wife, mother, or close relative. After he had finished writing, Mel wiped his narrow forehead and dug into his field bag and pulled out a pair of woolen socks. He fondled them lovingly and said: "See them socks? Them's my good luck pair. They brung us out today and they'll bring us out tomorrow." He did not add the usual "I guarantee ya that." Instead, he turned to Dooley who was getting ready to go to sleep and said: "Don't forget that WAC cap. Might come in handy tomorrow."

"You fukken a . . . ," the engineer replied. "I wouldn't get off the ground without that cap."

Cosmo prayed on his knees and put the little steel-jacketed Bible in his flying suit.

I thought of my caul, which was nothing but an old wives' tale, but comforting nevertheless. I put my glasses on the table so I would not forget to take them along in the morning. I crawled into my narrow cot and tucked in the mosquito netting. I waited for merciful sleep. But I was wide awake. I was awake and oppressed by thought: never mind the caul, what you must really do is line up your emotions with your beliefs, you must win the small, private war inside of you before going on to fight the big one, otherwise you'll quit or go raving mad.

6

$\mathbf{W}$E WERE torn from our sleep by Delmonico's stomping feet. We went to the mess hall still groggy with the fatigue from the previous day's raid. But already we walked in unhurried, tired silence, like veterans.

After briefing we went to Squadron Operations to pick up our chutes. I glanced at the Alert List on the bulletin board, hoping our names weren't there after all. The eagerness with which I reached out for this reprieve made me feel ashamed of myself and for a moment I stood before the board, staring at it blankly, trying to reconcile my ambivalent feelings. I saw it for myself:

> Lt. Albert Pennington, Jr. *(They didn't leave out the "Jr.")* and crew.
> Flying in #7 position *(Purple Heart Corner is what the gunners call that position.)*
> Name of ship: *Dinah Might.* *(And then, she might not!)*

There was something reassuring in the irrevocableness of the sentence.

The trucks hauled us to the dispersal area and we passed among the ships that appeared like black, monstrous shadows in the night. Near the hangar we saw *Flying Foxhole,* waiting to be repaired. The ship looked ghastly in the dark, sitting on its tail like an embalmed creature. Her skin was torn, the shine and sleekness gone. She was almost sadly human, squatting in the dark, damp night. She was the first chip to break away from what Andy had fondly called our dream crew. She had never been a beauty, no B-24s are, except from a certain few angles up in the air, but *Flying Foxhole* had been a "fast" ship and had flown like a proud bird. She was our first casualty.

We clambered down off the truck with our flying gear and Andy said, "Well, here we are again." His words had a familiar ring, as if they'd been said many times before. He grinned his big, buck-toothed, friendly grin and continued, "Well, men, what's the shot today?" His presence cast a brief, flickering warmth and I was grateful for his effort. His words, meaningless though they were, snapped the aloneness in which each one of us was wrapped and conversation came easier after that.

I looked suspiciously at the battered ship which had been assigned to us for the day's mission. *Dinah Might's* paint was peeling and even the naked pinup of a blonde woman on the forward end of the ship was full of cracks and patches. The crew chief, a sleepy lad who was waiting impatiently for our takeoff so he could go back to his warm sack, pointed to a flak hole in *Dinah's* breast and said: "Got it yesterday over Wiener Neustadt. A Jerry twenty millimeter went right through it. Killed the bombardier."

I prowled around the ship, poking critically and morbidly inside the ancient turrets. Dooley was arguing with the crew chief. "This god-damn coffin ain't had an engine change in three months," our engineer complained. He was taller than the oil-spattered chief and stood over him, his eyes even narrower than usual, his face frozen in a bitter scowl. "The goddamn putt-putt is no good," Dooley continued, "and the generators act like they're gonna fall off. How the hell do they expect us to fight their fukken war if they don't give us a ship?"

The crew chief shrugged his shoulders and said: "I'm sorry, sarge. I ain't the one assigning the ships. That's all we got now. Maybe one a these days we'll get some ships from the States. Could be. Maybe they figger they need 'em more in the Zone of Interior than here. But this is all we got right now. Squadron's got seven, and that's what's going up. Sorry, sarge."

Pennington came over and settled the argument. "We'll handle her," he said. "Let's get in." Dooley glared at the pilot but then he loosened his scowl and declared, "If you'll fly her I will too!"

The moon was still up when we took off. As soon as we joined the formation, each one of us inside the bomber set about checking our stations and preflighting our guns as if this routine were an old habit with us. I tried keeping occupied so as not to think of what was in store for us. I charged my twin-fifties with effort, preflighted my turret — it was so old I doubted whether they would even use it in training back home — checked the mike, oxygen meter, oxygen tube, and the electric juice for my flying suit. I transferred my lemon drops from the inverted flak helmet to the breast pocket of my coat, next to the glasses. Finding nothing else to do, I crawled out of the turret, lay down on the incline between the camera hatch and the tail, and closed my eyes.

We were hours away from the target, which was Turno-Severin, in Romania, six hundred miles away. We were scheduled to hit the target at 1105. Everything had been precisely calculated by those who did the calculating at air force headquarters in Bari. We were expected to carry out those calculations. 1105 became the focal point in my life. My life became dependent on that precise hour and minute set by the brass in Bari. Nothing else mattered. Nothing but 1105! What happened to the rest of the world had no import. I felt justified in concentrating all my being on 1105 and if at this precise moment Ruth suffered deep pangs of loneliness as a result of having gone back to the confining small town to stay with her parents, if at this moment she cried out in loneliness and anguish and guilt because she could do little to help, I could not be expected to help her with her burden. I had no greater ambition in life than to look at my watch and find it was 1130.

I listened to the uneven engine-throb of battered old *Dinah Might*; the rhythm was broken like a nervous heart's, and every time it missed a beat I cocked my ears suspiciously. My mind was feverishly engaged in charting what my actions would be at 1130 that morning. How would I react to being alive and whole? How would I express my joy at having cheated death again? But the image of flak and burning planes, the image of fear, constricting, paralyzing fear, crept over me. I was suddenly taut and full of foreboding. I got up and smoked a cigarette and watched Billy and Leo, whose eyes met mine. We regarded one another with the resignation of old people at funerals. In our naked glances there was no affection or shame or feeling of oneness. Fear of dying is an individual thing. Each man, no matter how close a buddy he has, dies alone. He takes little consolation that he might die in the presence of a comrade. A man dying wants his mother. Billy was leaning hard against the right waist-gun mount as if that solid object would sustain him when everything else in the world failed. Cosmo sat round-shouldered, holding his little steel-jacketed Bible in his gloved hands, his eyes prowling hungrily over the small print, his lips moving imperceptibly. He looked like a little ball, and the way his shoulders hunched you saw how he would look sitting in his spherical, confining turret under the belly of the ship.

We were all wrapped up in our own thoughts. The interphone was silent except for routine conversation dealing with the transferring of gas or sighting of aircraft. The morning had a fine, sunny, June quality. The morning cast splendor upon the beautiful lands below. The sun appeared miscast on this war morning. June appeared miscast. The sun and June were engaged in battle with war to decide who would have hegemony over the hearts of men.

Lying in the tail section of the bomber with the sun streaming through the Plexiglas of my turret and even softening the angry contours of my guns, I thought of an Italian cart and burro I had seen earlier that morning. The burro was pulling the two-wheeled cart very leisurely along a winding road lined with small olive trees. The driver of the cart was lying on his back, relaxed, sleeping. This picture ate into my mind indelibly. I wanted to be that Italian, sleeping peacefully in a cart, being pulled along leisurely by a burro, going nowhere, on a warm, caressing June morning. The sleeping, bedraggled Italian became for me the essence of living. It did not matter that his life was one of misery and hunger and defeat. For me, a man not facing 1105 lived a life of fullness and promise.

I speculated about Turno-Severin, a name which puzzled Mel Ginn no end. The people of Turno whose marshaling yards we were going to hit, were they expecting us this morning? Did they know the meaning of 1105? Or were they going about their June morning business unsuspectingly? Did they realize that two hundred American bombers laden with incendiary, high demolition, and antipersonnel bombs were converging from the Italian mainland over the Yugoslav skies, thrusting toward that spot so well charted on the shiny maps? The people of Turno probably hated the Jerries as much as we did, and yet, because Jerry was there, we would destroy them this fine June morning. By the same token, they might destroy us this June morning.

I was fighting time, urging it on, rubbing my watch underneath the glove in order that it might tick faster. Flak could not be as frightening as the thought of it. Brooding over what might happen was worse than death itself. Play games, I said to myself. Think. Take an image, an exciting image completely removed from the business at hand and sink your teeth into it and forget. Think of images that arouse anger. Think of the future — a life without wars; fix an image of that future in your mind and hold on tight. Because that is why you are here . . . but will I be alive to see that future?

I sat in my turret and I heard that frightful sound of the bomb-bay doors rumbling open and the wind biting into the vitals of the ship, and I saw the "window" streaking away like confetti, and suddenly my lips were articulating phrases from the *Marseillaise* into the rubbery oxygen mask. I was shouting crazily into my mask as if trying to drown out the roar of a world coming to an end. Then I heard Dick's high-pitched voice: "Bommmmmbs Awwway!" The song died in my throat and I squeezed my knees tightly together as if this action would safeguard my genitals from the enemy's 88s. I sat hunched over, holding my breath, waiting for hell to break loose from its moorings. But the ship was silent except for the gusts of wind lashing at its belly. The universe was silent. It was as if Turno-Severin down below was lying in wait, holding its fire for a more propitious moment. Unable to contain myself any longer, I threw off the flak helmet, sat up and opened my eyes. I saw one solitary burst of flak about one thousand feet below us. I thought this must be the forerunner, the sky would soon be black with them. But the sky was ominously silent. We turned off the target in a sharp evasive action and the long wings of *Dinah Might* flapped with the bank as if they were in pain. Pennington cried out to Chet, "Let's get the hell out of here! It's too quiet to suit me!"

We rode in choking silence for five minutes and then somebody's voice seeped in through the earphone: "What are they waiting for?"

Then it dawned on all of us that we were outside the reach of Turno's antiaircraft guns. I threw off my heavy flak suit and a great feeling of exhilaration seized me. I had never experienced such joy! Death had been cheated again and the resulting effects were overpowering. We began to shout into the interphone like a group of happily hysterical boys who had won the war and to whom life was assured forever more. I pulled off my rubbery oxygen mask and tried lighting a cigarette. At eighteen thousand feet the match flickered yellow and the flame was small. I took a quick, famished drag on the cigarette and slapped the mask over my nose again to keep from getting dizzy. Then I dragged on the cigarette again. I had been up for more than eight hours, had eaten nothing, and the cigarette smoke coursed through the emptiness of me like a rich, intoxicating drug. I dragged on it deeply as if it were life-giving and life-sustaining. Below, behind our formations which were coming away intact, I saw the target. Huge, black pyres were blossoming upward like bouquets. From my safe distance, sitting warm and protected in my turret, I regarded the rising smoke over Turno like a creator examining his handiwork. My triumph was too complete to consider that we had probably killed many innocents. Once out of the enemy's gun range, it required no effort to approve of yourself. You were getting even with Hitler.

I looked at my watch and it was 1135.

We came down to about ten thousand feet. I stowed my oxygen equipment and sat back in the turret and glanced sleepily at the silver bombers stretching behind me. Above our box I saw the fighter-escort of P-38s in the sparkling sun, and I started mumbling to myself: "My sweetheart of late is a P-38. . . ."

I felt safe and secure sitting in the turret of the old wreck *Dinah Might* whose engines sounded as if they were on the verge of falling off. I felt safe, hemmed in as we were by two hundred bombers and protected by fighters. I felt secure listening to the chatter of my buddies who were turning this trip home into a picnic.

"One thing about a toggleer like me," Dick Martin said, "I don't like my bombs to hit cultural institutions like whorehouses, for instance."

Dick waited for the laughter to subside, then he said: "See that spot below, that little white house near the Danube? That's my Uncle Snuffy's Bar and Grill. Let's all pitch in and send Mel down to get us some food. Snuffy's menu today features sirloin steak, French-fried potatoes, applesauce, blueberry pie à la mode, coffee with real cream, all for fifty cents. How would you like that?"

"How would you like to go into a power dive, solo, and forget to come out of it?" Dooley said. "I'm hungrier than a she-wolf with seven pups, and this guy talks about steak!" He did not hide his resentment and envy of Dick, who was an Irishman without any effort or fanfare.

"Well, if you don't want to try Snuffy's," the bombardier retorted, "you can go to Ptomaine Tavern or Heartburn House when we get back."

"F— — you," Dooley said. Then, changing his tone, he inquired: "Hey, Cosmo, how you doing down there in the ball, you little peckerhead?"

"Fighting the good war, doc," Mouse chirped back in a high alto voice.

"Giving 'em hell, eh?"

"With both barrels, kiddo."

"How would you like to go to town with me when we get back and help me find an Eyetie signorina?"

"I'll go to town with you, you big lug, but you'll have to find your own." And then in a more serious vein: "I was thinking I ought to look up my grandparents and aunt and uncle. They're in Gallipoli. It's not far from the base . . ."

We were soaring above a sun-drenched valley in Yugo and Andy Kyle said wistfully, "See that pretty farm down below? It looks like Missouri. I could settle and live there the rest of my life."

Beyond the valley lay the last peaked range of the Dalmatian mountains. The mountains smiled up at us in their silent, majestic dignity, and it seemed as if they too approved of us. I was completely at peace with the world and with myself. I felt that my life was full of meaning. I looked at my reflection in the thick armored glass and saw my own face, which was thawing out slowly, and I shook my head in approval, in immodest approval, forgetting that not so very long ago my mind had been a frenzied, incoherent mass. It was only after noon and we were flying over the Adriatic Sea and the rest of the day loomed before me like life itself. I did not think of tomorrow. I thought with what pleasure and pride I would walk the earth again, how I would sip the Red Cross coffee when we came down. Then I thought of lying on my cot behind the mosquito netting, clad only in my shorts. And later in the day, when the fierce Italian sun set, we would all go to chow together. And in the evening I would sit on the stone step outside our barracks and watch the men in their aimless wanderings and watch the lizards scamper about the ground and up the small, dust-bitten olive trees. And then, by the candlelight I would write to Ruth and to my parents, and perhaps to some friends. Life, I thought luxuriously, was full of limitless possibilities.

7

WE GOT OUR first pass to town after bombing Genoa. We rode to town eagerly, hungrily, consumed by curiosity and the need to get away from the war and loneliness and thoughts about the next day's mission. We had not seen Italy except from the air. From the air Italy appeared unsullied. But we had yet to see it from the ground. Mouse Fidanza, standing up in the truck and assuming the role of guide and interpreter, said proudly, "Now you'll really see Italy!"

"Are you sure the babes around here are pretty?" Leo Trent asked dubiously. We were passing little gray tufa-rock dwellings with black holes where windows should be. Everywhere was the smell of dough and sour wine and rancid oil. Our truck roared through Mandia while the black-clad Italians hugged the houses in the narrow streets. I had the impulse to wave to them but soon I realized with a terrible shock that I would be waving to people whose backs were turned toward us. And those who faced us stared hard at us as if we were not their allies and our trucks belonged to conquerors instead. I saw Cosmo's face turn pale, almost green, and the words die in him.

Walking along the streets we were mobbed by children in rags, crying:

"*Caramelle,* Jo?"

"*Sigarette,* Jo?"

"Wanna shack up, Jo?"

"Wanna lay, Jo?"

"*Fikken, fikken, molto buono,* Jo . . ." (A combination of German, Italian, and American, as though there hadn't been time for reconversion.)

In a courtyard, not far from Mandia's arch of triumph which had withstood the assault of two thousand years, a whole family was soliciting for a girl who was upstairs. Only the father, a man with heavy whiskers and red suspenders, stood off to one side, letting his wife and brood of young ones sing the girl's praises.

"She's younga, Jo."

"Six-a-teen year old, Jo."

"Five hundred lire, Jo."

At the amphitheater, in the center of town, not far from the American Red Cross, a ragged eight-year-old was soliciting for her sister. She pointed toward a tunnel where the desirable one was waiting. With her was a little girl with a swollen belly and running sores on her spindly legs. "Piecea ass," the little one chirped, "piecea ass . . ." They were probably the first words she'd learned.

"I'm ashamed! I'm ashamed —" Cosmo Fidanza cried. He ran from us, scattering the little Italians. "Get out of my way," he shouted, swinging his fists to make way. He was too disgraced to speak Italian. He was humiliated for the Italians and for his comrades who were making sport of the Italians and heaping scorn upon them. And he was humiliated for himself. Italy had been a dream, now crumbled and shattered like the little bombed-out *casas*. He escaped inside the Red Cross building, seeking refuge in this piece of America which was enjoying extraterritorial rights in the midst of shame and sorrow.

We walked in silence for a while, in full possession of the narrow sidewalks, while the black-clad Italians took to the road. In the middle of the main piazza, Dooley made an angry pass at a stray dog that got in his way. "What are you trying to do?" Leo cried, shocked.

"That little Eyetie dog!" Dooley retorted. "I didn't like the way he looked at me."

"Why, you darn fool!" Leo protested. "Dogs are the same all over." A moment later, Leo was poking fun at the people.

"Let's find a whorehouse," Dooley said.

I had a strong desire to hide from the hostile stares of the people, as if I were guilty for their humiliation. I went to the Red Cross where Cosmo was sitting in a corner, a torn copy of *Stars and Stripes* in his hands. I saw he had been crying. Later on Trent, Dooley, Ginn, and Poat came in. All of them were tipsy, except Billy.

"The one I had didn't smell so good," Leo Trent said, sniffing up his large nose, "although she did screw like a rabbit."

"You can't beat this college life!" Dooley exclaimed. "But I still think we ought to go to a pro station."

Ginn didn't say a word. He was not completely at peace with himself for having been unfaithful to his Sharon. But after a while he found his speech. "What the hell!" he said. "Eyetie women are gooks anyway." There was no comparing them with American women. Therefore making love to an Italian whore was nothing to be ashamed of. He'd never think of doing it to an American whore. "A fella's got to have some fun, ain't he?"

We were speeding through the blacked-out Italian night toward our base. The truck roared through the slumbering town and the driver opened his exhaust as if trying to awaken the people to the fact that we were there, and we were Americans.

"I'll never go to town again," Cosmo whispered to me. I was tempted to say the same.

Back at our barracks, Cosmo sat on his cot and prayed fervently. The others chattered loudly, comparing their adventures in Mandia. They did not sound or look like conquerors. Mel, who had a greenish bath towel wrapped around his thin loins, looked rather comical, and so did Leo in his striped pajamas that were so unwarlike. And yet the Italians who had seen them in Mandia in the afternoon turned from them and got out of their way. And the hungry children looked upon them, and me among them, the way we had looked upon the conquering armies that swept through the Ukraine when I was a child. For us there had been the German armies, followed by the Austrians, then the Poles in 1920. They had come like waves of black locusts to denude the land. They had corrupted our sisters and violated the beds of our mothers. I hated them with the clean passion of a child, but like the children of Mandia, I had cloaked my hatred with smiles and words of praise for the conquerors.

I had hoped that we, who were Americans, would be different. We had not come to enslave, but to liberate Italy. I had been wrong. I had been fooled. When the army had briefed Mel and Dooley and me on Italy, the most pertinent fact quoted was the high rate of venereal disease in that country. "Stay away from the gooks!" we had been told. It wasn't Mel's fault he strutted like a conqueror.

And yet, I consoled myself, Mandia had seen conquerors before. Hannibal had been there, on his road to Rome, and the Germans had been there. Mandia was older, much older than any of its conquerors. The town, which had structures older than Christ, was tired with age and hunger and defeat and shame. The people of Mandia lived in crumbling gray houses and on their cracked walls were still remnants of Mussolini's granite chin and the credo: "CREDERE — OBBEDIRE — COMBATTERE." It was ironical to read the warning on the air-raid shelters "*Défense de Fumer*" (Smoking Forbidden), because they had no to-bacco unless we gave them our American cigarettes for which they scampered about madly. The people of Mandia were dressed in black, always in black, as if they were forever mourning. They walked among us without laughter, often without acknowledging our presence. They no longer called us allies, and their young men, seeing the liberties we took with their sisters, regarded us with naked hostility. The well-to-do, and there were a few of those, hid their daughters from us behind drawn shades, and the poor gave us their daughters so that they could eat. They deferred to us and sold us their wine which we nicknamed Purple Death because it blinded our men. They scraped and bowed before us in their innumerable *sale da barba*. Some of them begged and stole from us and they told us to our faces that the only *Americani* they liked were the colored *Americani* who were gentle with them and did not flaunt their superiority and did not try to strip them of their dignity. Even their streets were not their own, except for funerals. I saw a black procession behind a band of musicians and it moved unhur-riedly down the ancient streets as if there weren't any need to worry about the American military trucks. The trucks pulled up as the pro-cession moved along, and some of the drivers inside the vehicles even removed their fatigue caps.

"I won't go to town again," Cosmo repeated. He sat rigid on his cot for a while, whispering, "It's a sin, it's a sin. We will have to do penance for this sin." His black, mournful eyes were directed at the rotten floor planks as he spoke, as if he were trying to ignore the presence of his comrades whose actions played such a large part in his humiliation. "I won't go off the base so long as we're here," he whispered. "But what will I write my parents? They expected me to visit our relatives in Gal-lipoli and write them glowing letters about the way things are here. If there was a way I could change into civvies, some torn black clothes, maybe I'd sneak over to Gallipoli and see my grandparents and explain things to them. But I won't go in a uniform."

"I think you ought to go anyway," I said.

"My father thinks Italy is like it was thirty-five years ago when he left it," Cosmo said, ignoring my words. "He thinks it's still a land of song, music, and wine. He doesn't know what the war's done. He tells his friends he'd like to go back to Italy to die. He wants to be buried under an olive tree. Well, what am I going to tell him?" the ball gunner said, looking up at me questioningly, as if I had the answer. "The truth would kill him, but it's sinful to tell a lie." His words and his thoughts seemed to have reached an impasse. He picked up the Bible and resumed his reading. His little shoulders were bent more than usual, as if upon them rested the burden of martyrdom for Italy's prostration and shame and his comrades' arrogance.

8

NEXT DAY we bombed Ploesti. Over the target we heard the enemy interceptor command order all the Jerry fighters to proceed to France immediately. When we got back to our base we found out from jubilant groundmen that our troops had invaded Normandy. We embraced and said this was a good day to celebrate because with the Second Front open the war could not last much longer. But when we got back to our barracks our plans for a brief holiday were altered. One of the crews from our barracks had failed to return.

Six empty cots stared at us. We stayed away from the cots all afternoon, fearing to touch them. Even our little pup, Stowaway, sensed the tragedy and did not go near them.

Nobody had seen the crew go down. They had been erased from the sky. And by the same token they would be erased from the Squadron

Operations bulletin board when Sergeant Delmonico wiped out the name of Lieutenant C. Maxwell and crew. They would be entered as MIA — Missing in Action. Tomorrow, or a day after, a new crew fresh from the States would take their place.

Our barracks was a dismal place. The cussing was subdued. Nobody shouted or talked out loud. The barracks chief startled us by his suggestion that we all gather around the six cots of the MIAs and help ourselves to their razor blades, Brazil boots, pistols, sunglasses, leather jackets, K rations, cigarettes, socks, underwear, writing paper, and other items. "It's better for the gunners to have them things than to let Supply get hold of 'em. And they'll sure enough come after it tomorrow morning, like a flock of vultures." I saw the logic in the barracks chief's reasoning and so did my crewmates, and those of us who had been squeamish scavenged through the items, saving only the wallets, letters, and photographs to be turned over to the chaplains of the various faiths for return to the Zone of Interior.

"Them orderly-room commandos!" Mel said derisively, hiding his hoard of razor blades in a little box under his cot, "a buncha vultures, I guarantee ya that."

"Come on, take something!" Dooley said. "I wouldn't give those ground-gripping bastards the sweat off my *cojones*." And in order to assuage the guilt feelings for our own greed, we poured bitter scorn on the men who stayed on the ground and were safe.

"If one of them ramp-rat, USO fighters walked in now, I'd let him have it!" Dooley said fiercely.

At that moment, the enemy was not Hitler, but the men, Americans, who worked in the mess halls, Supply, orderly rooms, medics, transportation; all those who did not fly bombers, with the exception of mechanics.

It was strange, this Little America, complex, divided, stratified. Though we all ate in the same mess halls and stood in the same endless lines and dove into the same foxholes when the Jerry planes came over to bomb us at night, we lived in two distinct worlds. A clear, starry sky had a different meaning for a flyer than it had for a ground man. For us a clear sky meant a mission on the following day while for the ground man it often meant hours at the beach. When a flyer received his weekly ration of four cans of beer, he drank them all in one evening, fearing he might not be around to drink tomorrow. We envied the ground man because he could contemplate tomorrow and the day after. He could think of the future. He was safe — like the civilians back home. We lived like an exclusive blood fraternity which no ground man was allowed to invade. They seldom ventured into our barracks. Behind our backs they called us "hot rocks," "hot pilots," "wild-blue-yonder boys." They argued that the flyers were crazy; how could a man in his sane mind go up there day after day and be shot at? But many of them tried to emulate the flyers in the way they crushed their garrison caps. And some of them put on gunner's wings when they got far enough away from the base. A few of them volunteered for combat.

· · · ·

Master Sergeant Arthur Sawyer was a small, rotund man in his middle thirties, with a round, hard belly and a perennially red face. Sawyer was in charge of our squadron orderly room. When dealing with combat men, Sawyer always had a wide grin on his face. He always greeted you with: "How ya, sarge." His smile disappeared when he dealt with his own men, the orderly-room commandos. The Italian KPs ran for cover every time they saw the top kick come into the mess hall. He came like an ill wind, striking out at his charges with loud roars and streams of invective. But there was more to Sawyer than that. Major Paterno, the ground officer in charge of our squadron, considered Sawyer "the best top kick in the business," though the major knew that Sawyer misappropriated funds and worked hand in glove with the squadron mess-sergeant, diverting food to the black market in Mandia. Every month Sawyer sent a thousand dollars to his wife in Clearwater, Florida. "My poker winnin's," he said. Even the colonel must have heard about Sawyer's share of profits for food sold to Italians, for blankets stolen and issue clothing diverted from Supply. But nobody did a thing about it. And nobody expected that anything would be done about it.

Major Paterno, who was sweating out his rotation after eighteen months overseas, sat in front of the orderly room every day, dozing in the sun or reading *Stars and Stripes*. A friendly, ineffectual, tired man in his late fifties, the major owned a small supermarket in Philadelphia — as a result of which he had been given a commission on the basis of being an "efficiency expert." His knowledge of Italian prompted the army to send him to Italy, but once they got him there, they forgot about him. Whereupon Colonel Hill, Group CO, appointed Major Paterno squadron executive officer. As part of his program of bringing efficiency to the squadron, the major's first act was to appoint a detail to build a rock garden. Little pebbles in front of the mess-hall were painted red, white, and blue, and a corporal in charge of the detail was ordered to plant some grass seed. But the hard, rocky, south Italian soil rejected most of the seed and only a few blades of grass appeared among the pebbles. This became known as "Paterno's Victory Garden."

Whenever I saw the major, he just sat, sat and dozed in the sun. When he saw us pass on the way to the mess hall or to the medics' *casa*, he bestirred himself and asked in a friendly, tired tone, "Did you fly today, did you?" If the answer was yes, he queried, "Did you hit the target, did you? All the ships come back, did they?" Then he went back to sleep. The war was beyond him. His mind was already dwelling on home, Philadelphia, and retirement from the army. He closed his eyes to the war and to what Sawyer was doing. Perhaps he considered it the natural course of events for Sawyer to line his pockets. Perhaps he considered the army a place where a good man who knew his stuff was entitled to make himself a little nest egg. Perhaps that's what it was: a man must look out for Number One in the army, too. Private enterprise overseas! Arthur Sawyer was salting away the dollars. He brown-nosed, glad-handed, and yessired the officers and laid himself out every time the colonel appeared with his jeep to haul away several cases of beer or a side of beef.

For Sawyer the army was not only a career, it was also a good business. He sold pornographic pictures of Italian women in the nude or in the act of having sexual intercourse with one of the mess corporals of our squadron. Sawyer paid the girls lire or C rations for posing, then he made regular calls in the barracks, including ours, selling the photographs. He charged fabulous prices, and since the men did not consider lire money, they paid. Sawyer's models were sometimes old women with dry breasts hanging down like withered udders, looking at you with bewildered, often tear-filled eyes. And some of them were young girls, children of thirteen or fourteen, smiling audaciously at you with those knowing corrupt smiles of children who have been thrust prematurely into a cruel adult world.

Always when Sawyer came to our barracks, a feeling of revulsion rose in me and I had a strong desire to chase him out. But he was impervious to rebukes. "How ya, sarge," he grinned. "How about some nice pitchers?"

On Sundays Sawyer went to Protestant church services at the mess hall. In his *casa*, which was fitted out with an inside toilet, he had an oil painting of his wife hanging on the wall. The oil was done by a Mandia artist from a snapshot. The pretty, vacuous face was Sawyer's pride. "Ain't my wife purty?" he demanded of all who entered his *casa*. "Purtiest woman you ever did see, and best. I wouldn't touch no other woman with a ten-foot pole. I hold if a fella wants his wife back home to do right by him, why, he oughta do the same by her." Even though Sawyer was known to take most of the pornographic pictures himself, sometimes even posing the shots, he had the reputation of being faithful to his wife. In Clearwater, Florida, he was known as a "hero fighting the enemy of civilization, Hitler," according to a newspaper clipping he proudly displayed at the mess hall. The gunners loathed him and many of them could not fathom the logic of risking their lives while Sawyer was growing rich. They shrugged their shoulders and said, like Dooley, "What do you expect? That's the army for you! That's war for you! The suckers get shot at, the smart guys get rich!" Everywhere there was this acceptance and acquiescence and cynicism. The cynicism was like a drug, easy to take until you become submerged in selfpity. You could become so completely immersed in it that you lost sight of the big thing, the war itself. You had to be on guard always not to be swept along by cynicism and fatalism. Like a chant you had to go on repeating to yourself constantly: this war is bigger than Sawyer; this war is a good war despite Sawyer. A strong man knew these things, but you had to make up these little chants for yourself constantly. . . .

9

Dooley wired our barracks for electricity. He stole a hundred-watt bulb from Group Operations, from right under the colonel's nose, you might say, and hung it over his cot. He burned it even during the day as an act of defiance. Mel Ginn, having placed his wife's photograph on the table he and I shared, built a box for his underwear, and a radio made out of razor blades. He was completely absorbed by copper wires, earphones, and blades; he sat on his cot, his face grave, his ears alive to any noises that might come over his contraption. No music issued from his radio, but the fact that static came over sporadically was considered by all of us such a great achievement that each time there was a gurgling noise in the earphones Mel called us excitedly, and each one of us listened in turn.

Big Wheel bought a motorcycle from a British antiaircraft gunner in Bari and all the officers except Andy, who was busy studying merchandizing and writing letters to his wife, were forever repairing the cycle. Pennington went to work on plans for erecting a *casa* with a built-in toilet. "It will be the good old USA type," the pilot said, "the kind a man can sit down on and take a load off his feet." Practical man that he was, Big Wheel wrote to Myrtle and told her he saw no reason why he should hang up a pinup of some strange movie actress, who wasn't as pretty as his wife, anyway. Myrtle obliged with a photo of herself in scant clothing. All the officers in our squadron flocked to the tent to admire our pilot's all-around taste. Dooley saw the pinup and came back raving: "That wife of Pennington's would look naked in a flak suit. She's stacked like a brick s — house with plenty to spare."

Leo Trent fixed up a box for Stowaway underneath his cot and he said he was thinking very seriously of extending his perfume business to Mandia. "If these women around here only used some perfume,"

Leo said, "the war would smell a lot different." Billy Poat painted ten bombs on the back of his leather jacket to indicate the number of missions our crew had flown. Every time we came down from a mission, Billy painted another bomb before doing anything else. Over at the end of the barracks, Billy lived like a hermit, driving a nail here and there in the wall, hanging his forty-five pistol at this angle or that, puttering in preoccupied silence, as if he were constantly thinking of the seventeen windows in his mother's house in Rhode Island that needed washing, or ways and means of transferring to the infantry where a man had the earth to hold on to when hell broke loose. Evenings he sat and stared at the cracks in the wooden floor or played a tense game of solitaire.

Even Cosmo Fidanza fixed up a little nook for himself by hoisting some pictures of Jesus and Mary on the wall, instead of the usual pinups. He went to Catholic services each evening except Tuesdays when there were GI shorts at the open-air movie theater. These short subjects were of a more recent vintage than the full-length features which often dated back to Cosmo's childhood. Mouse spent all of his time on the base. He had vowed never again to set foot on Italian soil in the uniform of the US Army. Often he ventured as far as the gate and stared past the fields, stared critically, mournfully at the passing Italian *vino* carts on the road, then came back to the barracks and crawled into his sack. Even the Catholic chaplain was unable to persuade Cosmo to give up his self-imposed exile.

And there was the comical aspect of Chet Kowalski having to cut off his magnificent beard because he looked too much like Italo Balbo.

But our most important bridge with life was the writing of letters. It was like a bodily function. Writing a letter was like clasping a solid hand. We wrote them furiously, constantly; we all wrote them with frenzy and devotion and this function was accepted like breathing itself or religion or fear. Mel Ginn sweated over his letters and mopped his brow and complained, "Ain't nothing I can think about to write to Sharon. I sure wisht I could think of something to say."

Leo Trent had a great deal to say. To him writing came without any effort. He carried on a furious correspondence with Helen and several less important females in Hollywood, one of them having had a "walk-on in pictures." Leo sat over his makeshift table chuckling over the stories he invented about aerial exploits and hair-raising escapes. His imagination took him on low-level raids over Berlin, solo. He compiled record bags of enemy fighters under the most impossible conditions. He described the suffering of his buddies who were succumbing to malarial mosquitoes by the hundreds. Leo worked over his inventions assiduously. One suspected the image of his kid brother, the marine flyer in the Pacific who was shooting down Jap planes, was constantly before Leo's eyes when he wrote to his friends. Leo never forgave Phil for becoming an officer, while he had been washed out of cadet training and made a gunner. In his letters home, Leo was always a hero. What he did not know was that most of the figments of his imagination never reached the States because our crew officers — to whom his letters were referred — wielded their scissors on the lurid passages, but said nothing to Leo about it.

Despite the constant engine roar and casualty lists we tried to establish a pattern of life in little habits formed and observed like checkpoints on a navigator's map. You looked forward to such things as smoking a cigarette on your cot after coming down from a mission, of playing all kinds of games with yourself to keep from falling asleep when you wanted so to stay awake and be aware of living. Then there was the flavor of the afternoon shower which Dooley improvised in the stony latrine and which had to be coaxed along because the hot water and the cold did not often flow simultaneously. There was the ceremony of going to evening chow together and reading in the hammock suspended from two olive trees. We sat on the barracks steps in our shorts and gossiped until dark, when poker and pinochle games started in earnest. There was little else and hardly any variation, but coming down from a mission all this seemed like such a great deal to look forward to.

And beyond the determination to introduce some normalcy into a barbaric existence, and the striving for continuity, there was the constant battle to adjust oneself and not to stick out in too many places as an old fogey, a creaking old gunner with bad eyes and hot temper and strange ways. I was yet to learn the art of falling asleep with a half-dozen men playing poker at my table and two or three of them sitting on my cot and smoking constantly. I knew they expected me to go blissfully to sleep. But often I lay there, chastising myself: why can others sleep and you cannot? I told myself I had to endure it because after all this was a just war, and one must discard the luxuries of privacy and the intellectual snobbery of civilian life. And even though I was raging mad and wanted to turn over both cot and table — as I would have back in the States — I contained my rage, lay still, and turned all the blame on myself. Often while in the process of doing something I suddenly stopped and said to myself, "You are acting too old, must act younger. . . ." There was the great need to be accepted and approved. And this lightened the burden of the unicolored existence where the only object that did not fall into the drab color scheme of khaki or fatigue green was Trent's red-striped pajamas.

·　·　·　·

Dooley came in and said our crew was alerted to fly tomorrow. "They're loading eight five-hundred pounders," he said significantly, meaning we were going on a long, hazardous trip.

It was ten o'clock, and we knew this without looking at a time-piece because precisely at ten each evening a gunner from the adjacent barracks stepped outside and cried out in a voice of angry impotence: "Jeez, how I hate this fukken place!"

10

THE JEWISH crew chief, whose ship *Violent Virgin* we were flying on the mission to Munich, whispered to me as I was taking the last nervous puffs on a cigarette before takeoff, "If I was you, Isaacs," he said, "I wouldn't take along your dog tags to Germany. If the Nazis bring you down and see that H for Hebrew on them tags, it'll be tough on you."

"That's nonsense," I said, taking offense quickly, although momentarily I was grateful for his solicitude. "There's the Geneva Convention setting down behavior toward prisoners of war." Then I proceeded to explain to him that according to this convention, signed in Geneva by the present belligerents, a prisoner of war was required to give only his name, rank, and serial number. And no more. The Germans, we understood, had ways of coaxing information by intimidation, ruse, threats, and physical violence. They threatened to inject recalcitrants with syphilis and other diseases; they put men in solitary confinement, and on occasion they killed "while the prisoner was trying to escape." I never dwelled on these matters or I could not go on flying. Like a young person who rejects thoughts of death, I tried not to speculate on what would happen to me if I were shot down over Germany.

"But you're a Jew," the crew chief said significantly.

"That hasn't a thing to do with it," I said, resenting his reminder. "I'm an American." I suddenly disliked this chubby, inoffensive man for adding fuel to my already considerable fears, for spreading rumors for which he had no proof, and for displaying a persecution complex which always surprised me when I found it among American-born Jews.

I dismissed his warning and thought no more about it until we started crossing the Alps into Germany proper. Suddenly I took off my identification tags, without any thought or reason, and dropped them in one of the dark crevices on the turret floor where nobody would find them. My action was completely irrational, influenced no little by the terrifying mountain peaks that rose to a height of sixteen thousand feet. The Alps looked like a monstrous forest of jagged rocks jabbing up at us, as if they were the first harbinger of what was to follow once we entered the enemy land.

Aside from the dog tags I had no other identification with me, and according to the same Geneva Convention which I had quoted to the ground man earlier that morning, my captors were entitled to execute me as a spy. But for some reason which I could not explain to myself, being executed as a spy did not hold as much terror for me as being put to death as a Jew. I hadn't the slightest idea what they did to captured American soldiers of Jewish extraction. I started cursing the crew chief who was safe, back in Italy. I ground the metal dog tags with my fleece-lined boot, mumbling crazily to myself: So the Nazis will inject syphilis in my veins. They'll kill me. They've killed six million Jews already; this will make it six million and one. The point is: one must act with dignity. Remember: in the face of threats or intimidations you tell them only name, rank, serial number; name, rank, serial number; name, rank, serial number. . . .

"We've just entered Germany," Andy Kyle said over the inter-phone as if he were conducting a tour. "Right underneath you, men. This is it!"

I looked down past the armor-plated glass at the land twenty thousand feet below us. And though the land was clean and furrowed and neat, it seemed to me as if it were in the throes of some terrible plague. The land appeared diseased. I tried to spit down but the slashing wind only pasted my sputum against the Plexiglas. Angry at this failure, I unplugged my heated suit cord and made my way to the relief tube in the waist section, where I urinated defiantly on Hitler's Reich.

Some flak batteries picked us up before we got to Munich. Over the target the sky was full of black puffs. By some strange impulse I pointed my twin-fifties downward and opened fire. I fired the guns with my eyes shut, my face buried in my knees. I did not see where I was firing. I surmised my fire was directed in the general direction of Hitler's beer cellar below, in whose damp confines were hatched the first foul eggs of National Socialism. My eyes were shut. I heard the flak bursts around the ship like claps of thunder, like trains passing each other at high speeds, like pebbles striking a moving automobile. I heard a scream over the interphone, it sounded like Cosmo Fidanza who was hanging below the ship's belly, his child's eyes probably wide with terror at the black puffs bursting all about him. I heard his scream, and suddenly I was sitting up, my eyes wide open, shouting: "Bastards! You dirty bastards!" I pumped bullets at the smoke-quilted city below. The recoil of my guns shook the turret. My oxygen mask came loose, my flak helmet fell off my head, and my heated suit caught fire. But I continued firing in a mad frenzy as if in this one act I was getting even with Hitler and his fat burghers for all the lives they'd snuffed out, for the tears they'd caused, for the dreams they'd shattered, for the lives postponed, for Ruth who was at this very moment exiled to the choking atmosphere of a small town to sit and watch the waste of precious days. And I was getting even for myself, because they threatened to brand upon my flesh the yellow Star of David after I'd discarded it with all the rest of the nightmarish memories of a ghetto childhood.

"Bommmmbs Awwwway!" Dick's words snapped me out of the reverie. I made a motion as if to wipe the perspiration off the exposed, upper part of my face. My breath felt hot and moist inside the oxygen mask. I stood up in my turret and bent forward and watched the bombs go away and a feeling of exultation gripped and held me. I was completely oblivious of the flak bursts as if they no longer had the power of harming me. I watched the clusters streak earthward like savage bouquets. "Hit!" I screamed. "Hit —" I was anxious for the many clusters of bombs to explode in crowded areas of the city among the men and women who had grown fat on the loot of Europe and on the bones of the world. I wanted to see Munich blown up, Munich the infamous, Munich of Chamberlain's umbrella and peace for our time and appeasement. . . . I was eager for our bombs to blanket the city, erase it, kill its inhabitants and let the tongues of flame from its slow pyre reach toward the heavens to ask for forgiveness. There were no innocents below, as there were in Yugoslavia or Romania or even in Austria, where you felt sorry when bombs went astray and often killed civilians. Below me was the battlefield, all of it was the enemy. . . .

I didn't realize we were out of the flak until I heard the waist gunners shouting to each other while they were pumping up Cosmo's turret to examine his wound. I stowed my guns, and ignoring the pilot's query as to why I had fired my guns when there had been no enemy fighter interception, I started rubbing out the fire which was eating away at my suit. The electric wires had shorted along the shoulder blades and a fire had chewed away at the cloth, singeing my flesh.

Billy and Leo pumped up Cosmo's turret and opened the tiny door. They pulled him out slowly and stretched him out in the waist section. Cosmo was bleeding in the right thigh, where a piece of flak the size of a fifty-caliber bullet was lodged. They reported to the pilot.

"We'll peel off and go home by ourselves," Pennington said without any hesitation. The pilot's bold suggestion caught the rest of us unaware. In view of Cosmo's wound, not one of us raised the obvious objection against leaving the well-protected formation to go home alone. What disturbed me, and the others, no doubt, was the alacrity with which Big Wheel seized upon this challenge of returning alone by a route where one hundred and fifty enemy fighters were known to roam among the crevices and gorges of the Alps, preying on stray American bombers and decimated formations.

We banked sharply and peeled off, after Big Wheel had called the flight leader and told him he had a wounded man on board. We left the security of the formations behind us. We were alone in the sky over

Germany, flying at sixteen thousand feet. Pennington flew the ship just above the peaks, maneuvering it as if the clumsy 110-foot wing-spread of the Liberator was suddenly shrunk to the diminutive size of a swift Mustang. And *Violent Virgin*, though old and battle-scarred, responded to the pilot's masterful touch, as if she were eager for him to forget that she was not a graceful Mustang at all, but a lumbering B-24 that has no business flying so low among the peaks of the Alps.

Cosmo lay in the waist section on a blanket, staring moist-eyed at the webbed bulkheads of the ship and puffing self-consciously on his first cigarette. His lips moved slowly: "I'm not going to let them take me to the hospital."

"Now you just take it easy," Leo said tenderly, touching Cosmo's arm and keeping a worried eye out the waist window for enemy fighters.

"I won't go to the hospital," Cosmo repeated. "They'll keep me there and you men will be flying your missions and I'll fall way behind." A note of alarm crept into his voice. "You men will finish your missions ahead of me and you'll go back to the States and I'll remain in Italy alone."

"Whoever told you a thing like that?" Leo said.

"I won't stay in Italy by myself!" Cosmo cried. There was the suggestion of hysteria in his voice and Dooley came back to the waist section from his top turret. The engineer bent over Cosmo and put his arm around him and said affectionately, "Why, you little peckerhead! You know goddamn well we wouldn't fly with no other ball gunner but you. Would we now, men?" he said, turning to Leo and Billy who alternately peered out the open waist windows and at Cosmo. Leo and Billy shook their heads vehemently, but Cosmo was not assured. "You'll fly without me," he whispered. "If my crew is going to fly without me, why —"

"All right, all right," Dooley said clumsily, determined to stop any flow of tears.

"You men are going to leave me," Mouse cried. "You don't think I'm a good gunner. You never *did* think I was good. You had me around because I prayed. You figured it was good insurance to have somebody around that had an in with the Lord. I know, I know. . . ." He began to weep. The ship was momentarily silent, as if each one of us was thinking what weapons there were to stop a man's weeping;

thinking back to remember whether provisions were ever made in the Table of Operations to give solace to a man who was suddenly turned child as a result of the war.

"I don't understand you," Dooley said in a perplexed tone of voice. "You know damn well we're all your buddies."

"You won't be for long. You'll leave me!" Cosmo cried.

Dooley reached into a medical kit and gave Cosmo a morphine needle. Cosmo lay back, his breathing leveled off to an even rhythm. He smiled at his buddies like an underfed angel and mumbled sleepily: "You're the best bunch of guys in the whole world. Never was a crew like this . . . wonderful crew like you men . . . I'll sure pray for you . . . all . . . God bless you . . ." Cosmo closed his eyes and slept.

When we came over home base, Pennington shot red flares over the field to indicate wounded aboard ship. Instead of circling the field in the customary landing pattern, Big Wheel banked sharply as if he were trying to convince the control tower and the rest of the world that rules which applied to others did not hold for Lieutenant Pennington. While other flyers needed several miles for a landing approach, Big Wheel set the ship down on the ground from an almost vertical position, and we hardly felt it when the three wheels made contact with the earth. A meat wagon waited for us at the end of the runway, but Cosmo refused to be separated from the crew. "I'm not going to the hospital," he cried. "Why can't I stay in the barracks, near my buddies?" He grabbed hold of Dooley and held on like a panicked child. He was not ashamed of being a child at that moment, and we envied him for it.

"At least you come with me, Dooley," Cosmo begged.

Dooley shrugged his shoulders. His cheeks were still crimson from the cold of the flight and he was strapped in his chute harness above the bulky flying clothes, but he got inside the ambulance with Cosmo, smiling wearily. "All right, you little bastard, I'm going with you. Now shut up and drink your beer!"

11

NONE OF THE four squadrons was able to put up more than one or two airworthy ships. About thirty crews in Group were idle; three hundred men with time on their hands. But not too much time . . .

. . . .

We visited Cosmo at the fifty-third Field Hospital. In the evening we went exploring in Mandia. On Via Cavour we wandered into a laundry that had once been a smithy. A shingle over the door read: "LAUNDRY FOR AMERICAN SOLDER. IZONING FREE." We found four laundresses inside and an American Negro corporal. Dooley ignored the corporal and started introducing Mel, Leo, and me. Mel interrupted him. "I ain't gonna stay here!" he snorted, looking at the colored American. "I'm getting outa here right now, I guarantee ya that."

"Me, too!" Leo declared. "Let's wham it out of here. Let's go where Americans congregate."

Gina, the youngest of the girls, who was about seventeen but had the stunted body of a child, flushed, as if she understood what was happening. She ran around from behind the partition and put a restraining hand on the Negro corporal who had got up to leave. "Please stay," she said to him in Italian. "I beg all of you to be our guests. Would you kindly sit down?" She turned her face to us in supplication as if our decision affected the course of her future and that of her coworkers, Angelina, Maria, and Lenora.

Leo and Mel left in a huff and Dooley, shrugging his shoulders, ran after them. "I'll see you guys later," I said, completely unsure of what I was doing, torn as I was between two loyalties. I had intended staying only long enough to apologize to the laundresses and to the corporal. But then I sat down and suddenly I felt at home. For a long stretch of time we said nothing. I was trying to put my thoughts into Italian which I wrestled out of a pocket dictionary. But the effort proved too much. I gave up and sat back and smoked. Soon I felt there was no need to talk, I was accepted on my terms of silence. It occurred to me that perhaps the girls realized their female presence and warm chatter — which I hardly understood — was enough in itself and little else was required to make me happy.

I sat and smoked and once in a while Gina would lift her little face from the iron and the corporal rose and took the iron from her and fanned the coals inside the iron to flaming heat and returned it to her across the wooden counter. He gave her the iron without speaking. She said, "*Grazie.*" He replied, "*Prego,*" and sat down again.

One bulb hanging down from the ceiling cast a sickly light over the four girls who were busy with their irons, needles, and washing. The counter was piled high with American military shirts, blouses, shorts, socks. There wasn't any other color in the damp-smelling room except khaki and the black the girls wore. Occasionally the laundresses looked up from their work and smiled. And I smiled back at these underfed, misshapen girls with bad teeth and sallow faces and I remembered their husbands or brothers or sweethearts I had seen in North Africa where they were our prisoners of war. They smiled at me with a warmth and a forgiveness which almost brought tears to my eyes. I was ashamed, but at the same time I felt that they understood the Americans' belligerence, ignorance, prejudice, stupidity, provincialism, and feeling of superiority; understood and forgave our adolescence; understood that underneath we were lonely, insecure, war-frightened, and often ignorant why we were in Italy at all.

The Negro corporal smoked in silence. He did not look at me once. He sat wrapped up in his own little fortress, in a world which, strangely enough, was closed to his fellow Americans who were white but which he could reveal to Italian whites. I could not help feeling that he resented my intrusion. It occurred to me I should leave him to this little world in which he felt comfortable, was accepted as an equal, having traveled thousands of miles away from his own ghetto home to find it in an alley in a small town in southern Italy on a street known as Via Cavour. I was ashamed of the irony of it, because I knew it had not escaped our hostesses that the black *Americano,* who was a part of an army that had come professing democracy, found a welcome only among Italians. The rest of the world was the familiar sign: OFF LIMITS.

Gina said: "Both of you belonging to the same army, perhaps you should learn each other's names." I saw the twinkle in her eye and I thought she was chuckling inside. But in the next instant her face was serious and she said, "What is your name?"

"Ben."

"And this is Carlo," she said, playing the hostess.

"I'm glad to know you," I said self-consciously.

"Nice knowing *you*," the corporal said. "Smoke?" He held out his pack of Luckies which had a tear at the end. (Only Americans tore the ends of cigarette packages like that; if ever you were shot down and met up with a person who posed as an American in a PW camp, watch the way his pack looks; a sure way of telling an American. . . .)

I took a cigarette from him and after that talk came easier. The girls started asking questions. The corporal, who spoke Italian well, acted as the interpreter.

"Ask him, Carlo," said Gina, "whether he is married?"

"Yes," I replied, "and my wife's name is Ruth."

The girls weighed the name Ruth on their tongues and giggled.

"She must be very beautiful, your wife," Gina said through the corporal.

"To me she is," I said, looking at the Negro. "Every day she is getting more beautiful," I added, thinking it was only a month since we parted, and already there was this removal and the inevitable romanticizing, and though I had never considered Ruth pretty, the metamorphosis was now taking place and she appeared to me not the shy little girl who was not much bigger than Gina, with nearsighted eyes and funny ears that stuck out, but a ravishing beauty, a pinup girl, the American Dream. Already I was reshaping the image of my wife in my own mind to fit a lonely soldier's dream. "Yes, to me she's beautiful," I repeated. "And also very nice," I added.

The corporal translated my words to the girls and they all nodded enthusiastically as if that is what they would expect of American men: to have beautiful American women because everything about Americans must be as the moving pictures portrayed them. And in the next moment the words came tumbling out of me and I told them eagerly about Ruth: how I had met her in Chicago five years ago. "The first thing I noticed about her were her wrists," I said. "They were the most delicate wrists I have ever seen. Everything about her was delicate and fragile, like rare porcelain, including her voice."

The corporal translated my words, but my thoughts ran swiftly ahead of the words. I wondered how I could best sum up for them what Ruth was like and what she meant to me. And it occurred to me that more than anything else, Ruth brought to my mind the loveliness of a Keats poem: delicate and fragile, but possessed of a fierce flame. In her body, wracked with pain, there was a spirit which was indomitable. And I heard myself saying impatiently to the girls, "*Capito?* Do you understand what I mean?"

The laundresses nodded and so did the corporal, and I was grateful to all of them for letting me talk, for listening to me with kindness.

"And where is Ruth now?" one of the girls asked, as if we were now one closely knit family and there wasn't any need to stand on formalities.

"In a small town near Chicago," I said. "The name of the town is Michigan City. She will remain there with her parents," I said, "until after the war."

"And how does she occupy her time?"

"By waiting — for the war to come to an end. She is not very well."

"Oh, I'm sorry to hear that," the corporal said.

We were silent for a while, then Gina resumed: "It is quite a coincidence that both you and Carlo are from Chicago. In fact, I think it is wonderful. Two Americans thousands of miles away from home, introduced to each other by a strange Italian *signorine*, only to realize they come from the same place. For all we know you may have been neighbors." I searched for mockery in her voice because I caught the twinkle in her eye when she said "you may have been neighbors." And I thought how flimsy was our armor, and how little we had to offer to these people whom we were determined to "teach democracy." She knew, of course she knew, with the wisdom of the swiftly ripened children of Europe, that the corporal lived in the Negro ghetto on the south side of Chicago and I somewhere in the north and that we were strangers and that we passed each other along the thousands of streets and our worlds never met. I wanted to assure her — and this she could not know — that after we had won the war, Carlo and I would be strangers no longer. I believed it sincerely and yet I did not say it because it was difficult to talk of a bright future to people who were undernourished and living in misery. In addition, I feared their mocking laughter, and Carlo's also.

"Ask him, Carlo," Gina said, "does he go to church?"

I said: "No, I don't go to the synagogue."

The corporal told the girls matter-of-factly that their new friend was a *Giudeo*. They gaped at me wide mouthed and shook their heads and Gina said kindly: "This cannot be. The sergento looks like such a fine person. He must be joking."

The corporal laughed. "We have many *Giudei* in the American army," he informed the girls.

"But *Giudeos* worship a false god," Lenora, the only buxom one among them, said. She looked at me apologetically as if saying: this is not personal.

"And who is to say who worships real or false gods?" Carlo said calmly. He was coming out of his shell. His words carried a quiet strength and dignity.

"But you are a Protestant, Carlo," Gina said heatedly and with a note of grievance in her voice. "According to the *padre*, Protestants also worship a false god. Why don't you become a Catholic, Carlo?" Gina pleaded. Judging by the Negro's soft laughter it was evident that this request had been made on previous occasions. "Your Protestant God," Gina continued earnestly, "has he been so good to you?" She turned from him abruptly as if he were a hopeless case and said to me, "We shall make a believer out of you."

"But I have beliefs," I said.

"What kind of beliefs?" she asked dubiously.

"I believe we will win this war and have a brighter future."

The girls all giggled and Carlo regarded me searchingly.

"God," Gina said. "We will make you believe in the real God. We will teach you how to pray."

"And if I learn to pray *your* way," I said, remembering how my father had tried teaching me prayer when I was a child and never succeeded because I doubted that God could hear the hurried, muffled whispers, "would some of the things I desire come through?"

"Why, of course!" Gina said without hesitation. "What do you desire?"

"I desire that the children outside this door get rid of their rickets and swollen bellies. I desire that the war come to a victorious end; that the guilty be punished and the innocent learn to laugh again."

"Certainly," Gina said, shaking her head reflectively as if she were enumerating my points; then, turning to the girls: "Don't you think so? If he prays earnestly enough?"

"But he must pray a great deal," Lenora said, "because he is asking for a great many things at one time."

"They will all be granted," the stunted seventeen-year-old Gina said. "And for our part we will light a candle for him each time he flies a mission." She looked at me and asked: "Are you flying tomorrow?"

12

IN THE morning I wondered whether the laundresses had lit a candle for me. We had been briefed to strike the Romania-Americana oil wells in Ploesti. I had taken along a few additional flak vests and draped them around my genitals, thighs, and feet. But a man flying over Big P needed more than that. And I thought of the candle, absurd though it was. The image of a burning candle clung to my brain as we came off the target. Suddenly I heard Pennington's congealed voice: "Enemy fighters at twelve o'clock high!"

As if in response to the pilot's scream, Mel's nose guns started chattering wildly and Dooley swore briefly and opened fire.

"Watch them, Leo!" Pennington cried, "they're sliding over to three o'clock. Coming in on a pursuit curve." Leo's gun started palpitating and the battered plane shook from the recoil.

"Ben, watch them!" This was Leo's voice.

Suddenly they came on. It's happened, the thought flashed in my mind. No drunken leer, no hobnailed boots, no swastika on a sleeve.

No storm trooper pointing a bayonet at you and screaming *Sieg Heil;* instead, swift planes that looked like our own P-51s, like toy-machines suspended from heaven by some puppeteer. What harm could come from them? I wondered. Then a swastika streaked across my vision, and though my mind was in the slow process of registering incredulity and disbelief that I was not seeing the coiled serpent in a motion picture newsreel but facing it, my fingers were pressing the triggers. Forgetting the sight, I rose in my seat and, throwing off the flak helmet which kept sliding down on my nose, I started tracking the enemy pursuit planes. It dawned on me that the battle had been joined and I was not afraid. In fact, I was calm.

The plane shook from the recoil and I shook inside the turret as if electric shocks were passing through me. Pennington was screaming with the helpless cries of a man who does not have a gun but points out the dangers to those who are armed: "Watch him coming toward three o'clock, Leo!"

"I see him! Oh, you sonofabitch — watch him, Ben!"

"See him!"

They came singly, sliding down with deadly grace in their pursuit curve. Then they came like a pack of wolves, starting their fire at the front end of the ship and raking us in a complete semicircle with the fixed machine guns mounted in their wings. Then they came from the top, and some came from underneath to probe our belly gunner's effectiveness. The world was a churning dogfight. The firing and the short, crisp oaths mingled in my ears, and the directions: watch him at three; Roger, he's sliding down to six, watch him, tail; okay. . . .

I felt no emotion. My calmness surprised me. I felt no cold or heat. I did not hear the enemy's fire. I saw only the wings of their ships, the wings lighting up with bullet-bursts like fireflies at night. The whole thing appeared so improbable and fantastic that even while I was firing, there was this insane thought: pinch yourself and see whether you are awake; this must be a dream, this cannot be you . . . Briefly I toyed with the dreadful idea that the enemy might recognize it was I, Ben Isaacs, whose eyeglasses were tucked away in the upper breast pocket, firing at them, and they would lose what little respect they had for my guns and slide in closer to our formation. I began to pucker my face, to grimace savagely, trying to impress Goering's yellow spinners with the grimness of my purpose. I pressed hard on the triggers.

I watched an enemy fighter saw one of our ships in half with his bullets. The Liberator fell apart in two pieces like a watermelon sliced through the middle. Perhaps as a reflex action I pressed the triggers too eagerly and both my guns jammed and I sat helplessly for a moment. Somebody screamed: "What's the matter, tail?"

"My guns are jammed!" I cried. With one hand I rode the turret in azimuth and elevation, pointing my guns at the enemy fighters, while with the other hand I tried fixing my guns, one at a time. The MEs were firing at us, and I sat there pointing my guns at them. But my guns were dead. I tore off one glove and felt the burning cold extractor. I charged the gun, and luckily it started its song again. The other gun remained dead.

"What's the matter, tail?" one of the waist gunners asked, worried.

"I'm okay," I said.

"Keep it up, men!" Pennington cried with a choked voice. He was at the stick, both he and Chet, and neither of them had any guns to fire. All four officers were crouching, feeling helpless, superfluous, and afraid. Only the gunners were busy. In the upper turret Dooley's oxygen mask slipped off and fell down to the flight deck. Dooley forgot all about the mask. He flew without oxygen for twenty minutes. He shot down one enemy plane. When our escort finally showed up, late, and the enemy broke off the engagement and fled, Dooley collapsed in a dead faint.

The enemy suddenly vanished from the skies as suddenly as they had come. And my mind was slowly adjusting itself to emotions and thoughts I had never before experienced. The meaning of triumph. I had never known the meaning of triumph. I had feared I might lose my head, become paralyzed by terror, but none of these things had happened. There wasn't the hysteria I had experienced over Munich, firing at remote objects on the earth. Here we had matched guns with professional soldiers. We had adopted their language, their tactics, their weapons.

In the one act of firing, I felt as if an end had come to all the years of temporizing. By pulling two triggers, just squeezing them gently, I had felt a completeness.

It was amazing, I thought, how again the simple proved to be the most direct. The most eloquent rebuttal to brutality was brutality in return. Such was the logic of our life, of our civilization, and of the moment. A man could express himself most fully only through killing. Any other way was compromising. The world was not for passive people. They perished. Only they who fought back would remain alive, even if only in the consciousness of those who came after them. The dogfight had lasted twenty minutes, Andy Kyle later told us. To me it had seemed like a second. But into this second a lifetime of grievances had been crowded. My guns had spoken for the pogroms I had lived through, for the pregnant mothers whose bellies I had seen torn open, for the cellar days of my childhood, for the yellow Star of David, for the anguished screams of people, my people, who were at this very moment burning in Hitler's extermination ovens, for Guernica, Coventry, and Pearl Harbor.

Pennington came back to the waist section and slapped the gunners on the back and said: "You men were wonderful. You really gave them hell and I'm proud of you."

We were embracing and feeling the nearness and pride that comes from fighting back and emerging triumphant. We had not been passive as we had on other occasions when going through flak. Fighting it out with a pack of enemy fighters made us feel like masters of our own destiny. Our triumph was a crew triumph, although Andy protested, saying, "I didn't do a thing. I just sat on the flight deck biting my nails. If I'd only had a gun!"

Oh, we were in a frolicking mood on our return trip. We romped over Bulgaria, Albania, and Yugoslavia. Sofia threw up some flak at us as if to dampen our spirits, but we were not to be denied our fun. Dick Martin said, "You're a bunch of heroes, that's what you are! Now you take Dooley, for instance. He does his best fighting when he faints."

Mel Ginn thought that was very funny. "It's the goddamn truth, I guarantee ya that." He roared with laughter. "That old Dooley is the craziest sonofabitch I ever did see."

Dick said: "This reminds me. I got an uncle living in Bulgaria and he runs a bar and grill called Snuffy's. We ought to send Mel down to pick us up some sirloin steaks. With French-fries — and ketchup. For dessert I want apple pie à la mode."

"Food!" Trent said wistfully. "What do you eat it with?"

"I once knew the color of milk," Dooley said, "though I never touched the stuff."

"I'll ask you a riddle," Dick said over the interphone. "What keeps a B-24 in the air? Give up? A miracle!"

"In my log you're sucking hind tit," Dooley said to the bombardier.

"Well, fifty cents more and you could have been born a white man," Dick retorted. He waddled into the waist section, small, round, pudgy, a can of insect powder strapped to his chute harness. The insect powder was a precaution against bugs, if he got shot down.

"*Grazie*, Nazi," Dooley said.

"*Prego*, dago."

Over Yugoslavia one of our ships fell out of formation and dropped back. The pilot of *Wolf Pack* called Command and informed us they were all abandoning ship. "See you in church," Lieutenant Wensley, pilot of the ship, quipped. "And tell those sons of bitches at Squadron Operations if they had decent ships to fly and didn't send men up in coffins, we wouldn't be doing this."

The bomber dropped back in the hostile skies and was hidden behind a cloud bank.

"Count the chutes going out of that plane," the pilot said to me.

I peered at the cloud as if trying to dissolve it. I strained my eyes for chutes in the sky. But there was nothing. Earlier that morning I had seen Wensley's gunners in the briefing shed where we exchanged silent greetings and the inevitable thought must have run through their minds also: wonder who among us will come back from this one?

Our happy mood had evaporated. Dick Martin took one more stab at it. "Why worry about what's going to happen to you? The way I see it the sun has enough hydrogen left for only two billion years."

It *did* seem kind of pointless to worry. We were near home, where cots awaited us. There might be a letter from Ruth. Later there would be a sunset. What more could one ask of life?

I stowed my guns and took a last quick look at the turret as I had looked at my classroom in previous years before leaving it for the day, seeing that everything was in order. "Killer Isaacs," I thought to myself, putting away the lemon drops with the thin black silk gloves which I wore underneath the electrically heated gloves. "A silk glove killer!" I was eager for Ruth to see me, dressed like a man from Mars, looking very tough and warlike. I wondered what my friends and my students would say if they saw me now. They would not recognize me. I remembered a gunner in Savannah who, looking at my hands, exclaimed, "Jeez, you got thin fingers. How do you ever expect to fire guns?" I chortled to myself, thinking, "You sold old Ben short, all of you." Suddenly the heartburn came on, searing my empty insides and reminding me that my excursion into self-adulation was at an end and I better lie down.

When Billy awakened me we were roaring over the home field We came in at fifty feet and the whole world seemed to shake and vibrate and thunder joyously in token of our return. We got out of the ship and when the trucks dropped us at Squadron Operations, I put away my chute and started toward our barracks. The earth felt cushiony under my feet and the sun caressed me and I felt strong.

•   •   •   •

Billy painted the fourteenth bomb on the back of his leather jacket to denote the number of missions our crew had flown. And we found Cosmo, who had returned from the hospital all mended and ready to fly, but looking much thinner. "Now you men are four missions ahead of me," he said gloomily. "How will I ever catch up?"

13

THE JULY sky was naked.

Wing hit at Brod, Belgrade, Sofia, Salonika, Budapest, Miskolz, Constanza, Pitesti, Giurgiu, Osijek, Zagreb, and Ploesti. Group sent up everything that stayed in the air for any period of time, determined to destroy the enemy oil output and his accumulated stocks, cripple his lines of communication, choke his marshaling yards, and generally mess up the Balkans.

Our crew was on the Alert List all the time. In three weeks we hardly had any rest.

14

$\mathbf{W}$E FLEW SO much the days lost
their meaning. The days were fused into a nightmare of flying. I
longed for sleep. I dragged myself out of the cot each dawn, bleary-
eyed, like a sleepwalker, and plodded to the squadron mess hall and
drank the acid, ill-tasting, warmed-over coffee. I regarded the mess
personnel with hostility because they seemed to be living in a normal
world of sleep and peace.

I no longer bothered going to the briefing shed. It made no difference to me where we flew. I wanted only sleep.

Some nights the Jerry planes came over to bomb us, but I was too
tired to climb out of my cot and seek a slit trench in the fields. I lay in
the barracks and pulled a blanket over my head as a protection against
the enemy bombs. In fact, I didn't care about the bombs.

I was too weary to care whether our target for the day was Big P or
a little marshaling yard in Yugo with only one flak gun. I pulled my
bag of flying gear along the ground to the truck that drove us to the
dispersal area and to the ship assigned to us. I climbed inside the ship,
hoisting myself through the camera hatch with great effort. I went
through the motions of preflighting my guns. Then I spread out my
gear, stowed my oxygen mask, and stuffed the indispensable lemon
drops inside the upper pocket of my winter flying suit. I lived almost
exclusively on lemon drops. Lemon drops and cigarettes. Every time
I tried to eat the powdered eggs — they usually turned rubbery and
yellow by the time we got to the mess hall — I vomited.

After the ship was airborne, I closed my eyes and dozed. There
had been a time when my fear of planes kept me from closing my
eyes. But now it hardly mattered. I listened to the engine throb in my
half-sleep. My ears had become attuned to the engines and propeller

pitch and I could hear them in my semiconscious state. It was like a heartbeat. When an engine missed a beat, I opened my eyes suspiciously as if I could hear better with my eyes open.

I lived on the rubber-smelling oxygen like a person addicted to a drug. I often thought how pleasant it might be to get shot down over a nice, peaceful, green field in Yugo where one could stretch out and sleep for a year.

I was tired to death. I did not care what happened to me, to the war, to the world. I did not have the energy to write Ruth or my parents. I scribbled innocuous v-mails, telling the folks back home I was resting, getting sun, doing fine.

Dooley began harping on the old theme: "Why don't you quit, you old bastard? Let us young ones fight the war."

"Not today. Maybe tomorrow." My stock reply.

"It's a shame making an old guy like you fight a war," Dooley said, relishing the bit of sarcasm. "Want me to help you with your flying gear? Or maybe we oughta get a stretcher to carry you to the ship? What do you say, pop?"

We were all wound up and taut. We snarled at one another and cursed savagely and this gave us moments of relief. But there was too much tenseness inside of us, too much pent-up aggression to be relieved by mere oaths and constant sarcasm. We could hardly tolerate one another, and yet, after eight hours up in the air, we were inseparable on the ground. After a mission we went to chow together, wordlessly, and we sat on the steps in front of the barracks together, and sat at the open-air movies together. It was as if the crew would fall apart if one of us wandered off by himself any distance. Not one of us seemed strong enough to be alone.

Pennington was so exhausted he looked like a long, drooping stalk that might break at any moment. He dragged his thin legs along the ground and his fleece-lined boots scraped on the pebbles. He lost what little desire he ever had to communicate with his fellow men, except to reprimand someone for an imaginary infraction of air discipline. Sometimes he bellowed for no reason at all: "And what's more, from now on there will be no more smoking in my ship!" But his flying was faultless. It was worth all the abuse, to fly with him.

Chet Kowalski, who always flew with several days of beard growth, looked more decrepit than anyone else. Our copilot took to religion.

He went to Catholic services three times a week.

Andy Kyle kept smiling wearily through his buckteeth. "Well, here we are again," he said. "Wonder what the shot is today?" It seemed to me I'd been hearing these words all my life.

Dick Martin no longer waddled. Our bombardier's plump buttocks shrank. And yet he had amazing founts of hidden energy; he never complained, nor did he seek his cot as eagerly as the rest of us after a mission. At night he sat in the war room at Group Op and listened to the British Broadcasting Company classical music hour.

The faces of my comrades were with me all the time. They were even in my dreams. I was certain these nine faces had been with me since the day of my birth and would be there until the hour of my death. The faces, and the voices that came thinned out over the interphone and from Command as if they'd been processed through a wringer. I heard the voices in my half-sleep:

"Clear the props —"

"Starting Number Three engine —"

Then there were the voices on Command, a group leader talking to the planes in formation: "A-Able, calling B-Baker, come in B-Baker. Get your ass in that formation, where the hell you think you are — out on a Sunday jaunt?" The voice disembodied, belonging to the sky, the war, fatigue. The voices had been with me all my life. There had been no other life. There had never been peace.

I did not even remember what my wife looked like. I saw her thin wrists and delicate, transparent skin, but for some reason I couldn't put her lovely features together. She lived on a tree-lined street in Michigan City and there was a knocker on the door, a gold-plated knocker. When the little colored girl came to clean she was always put to polishing the knocker first. That's fine bourgeois stability. That's planned living! It's orderly living. I didn't even bother buttoning my fly any more. It was too much trouble and nobody cared. I too had had an orderly existence once, way, way back. Got up at seven-thirty, took the Division Street car to Wells Street, started teaching at nine, ate lunch two minutes after twelve, resumed classes at one, quit at three-fifteen, corrected papers at home, ate supper at six, read the paper, listened to the radio, went to sleep. A good, orderly, stable life, and my fly always buttoned, or zipped up. . . .

There were only the faces, the sweaty, weary faces of my comrades; the voices over the interphone, the engine throb, and the vast sky. The earth was an appendage of the sky and sometimes the earth was beneath us and sometimes it was sucked away from us and the only thing in the world left to cling to was the jamb where the turret door once hung.

We lived in a twilight world where feelings, perceptions, and emotions were dulled and numbed. There were no longer any primary sensations. Even Benzedrine tablets no longer kept us awake. The fatigue was like several layers of blankets smothering you with its weight.

My brain was forever conjuring up little tricks. It played games with me, testing and torturing me all the time, promising me there was a way out after all. All I had to do when things became unbearable was go see the flight surgeon and appeal to him to have me grounded. I envied the men upon this earth who were not consumed by vacillations. I knew why I was in the war, yet I pounced on all the minute details to prove to me I was expendable. I seized upon the universal cynicism in the army and the inefficiency. Why were ships sent up that were not airworthy? Dead flyers were strung out all along the Balkans and Germany because engines had not been changed, radios not checked, guns not tested. This did not make the cause less just, but for one given to vacillations and doubts, and seeking an escape, it made it more difficult. To escape, one needed a rationale. I seriously questioned my value to the army. Soon I would be thirty-five; almost twice as old as Cosmo. In the tail turret, where I sat dozing, I was a lifeless passenger, taking up space, endangering the lives of nine other men. Who could dispute Dooley when he called me "old man"? I wondered whether behind the sarcasm there was resentment against me. Did he, and the others, think I was competing with them? Perhaps they suspected my participation in the war was an attempt to run with the young ones? Could it be that I had a compulsion to be martyred? I was going crazy, torn by my doubts.

It struck me funny, to think all the strings I had to pull to get into combat. There was the time in basic training in Miami Beach, after I'd been qualified for combat, they sent for me, and some Jo, maybe he was a looey or a corporal, I didn't remember which, started throwing questions at me. There I was in the office with men who had come to the US from enemy countries like Hungary, Romania, and Austria. I had come from the Ukraine, an allied country. They wanted to make absolutely sure I was loyal, the Jo said; make sure I wouldn't sabotage a bomber which cost about a quarter of a million dollars, he said; wanted to make sure I wouldn't loosen a screw in a B-Two-Dozen, or tell secrets to some Jerry pilot while he was giving me short bursts. "I see you were born in the Ukraine, soldier. When did you leave?" I said we migrated about 1920. And he wanted to know why, and I said because there were bands of mercenaries roaming through the countryside, robbing and killing Jews and my father decided America would be a safer and better place to live, and since my father decided, we all went. It took us almost six years to get to the States, so we must have had a strong yen for it, I said. . . . Then there was the time in gunnery school over at Tyndall Field, when I failed in the blindfold test for taking apart and putting together a machine gun. The result was I walked around blindfolded for two weeks, until I mastered the technique. And what for? It's the goddamnedest thing you ever heard of in your life, taking apart and putting together a machine-gun. Who ever takes a machine gun apart in the air? If a gun goes haywire you're out of luck. If you tried fixing it with your bare hands, your fingers would drop off from the cold. . . . And then there was the time with ground firing where I couldn't hit the side of a barn and I had to bribe the firing officer to give me a passing mark. Big deal! . . .

Only one sensation came effortlessly. Lying in the tail section of a bomber, dozing, I felt the heat of my electric suit bathe my body caressingly. The warmth penetrated to my belly and thighs. My mind conjured up pictures of voluptuous women, like those painted by the Italian masters, deep fleshed and graceful, clean, naked, in white beds in a room with white curtains ruffled by gentle breezes, far, far away from engine throb. . . . To think of women and love making on the way to a target was one way of escaping thoughts about the target. I counted on Ruth's forgiveness; after all, wasn't I at war? I was aware how incongruous and unreal these preoccupations were. But nothing seemed real anymore. Seeing a woman through the haze of your fatigue at twenty-five thousand feet in the air on the way to bomb some city and be shot at seemed just as unreal as being up in that bomber. Conjuring up little pleasant fantasies, one was less prone to think of death, although death seemed the only peace.

But none of us talked of death except Cosmo Fidanza.

15

BILLY PAINTED the twenty-seventh bomb on the back of his jacket. Our crew was granted a three-day pass but we were so tired, we all went to sleep. The first day we slept around the clock; the second day boredom set in among some of the men, and on the third day most of us escaped into Mandia.

Dooley piloted us to one of the innumerable cobblestone alleys in the ancient town, saying, "The girl working behind the bar in this joint sure is stacked! And she's only fifteen."

"Did you slip her the eel?" Trent inquired.

"Not yet. But I will," Dooley replied, leading us into a small, high-ceilinged, almost formless room. There was no electricity in the room, which was run in conjunction with a laundry. It seemed as if the dampness had been imprisoned behind the thick walls for centuries. Behind a high wooden partition, which served as a bar, there were a few hastily built, small shelves, and on the lonely shelves there were a few lonely bottles of liquor. Inferior war liquor: cognac, vermouth, champagne, wine, whiskey. Everything inferior but not cheap, even the past glory of Italy: *vino.* Everything inferior and hastily improvised to catch the American's stray lire.

Luisa, a buxom, dark-haired girl with a sensuous face and jet black eyes, sat behind the partition, holding a sheet of paper and a stumpy little chewed-off pencil. Every time we ordered a round of drinks, Luisa wrote down the amounts on the piece of paper. Then she turned her obstinately impassive stare at us. The room was too small for her to look elsewhere. She sat on a high chair, safe behind her partition, safe from Dooley's itching palms.

"This is her," Dooley said, proud of his discovery. "How would you guys like to guide that thing over a target?"

"I'd love it," Trent said. "Lush thing, isn't she?" He plucked at his wispy mustache, looking her over like a connoisseur. "Your old dad wouldn't mind it at all," he concluded, rubbing his palms as if he were about to join a feast. "Of course," he said, whiffing the air with his big nose expertly, "perfume makes all the difference on a woman. With me it's the first whiff that counts. Honey," he turned to the girl, leering, "don't you ever take a bath?"

"No undershtanda," the girl replied calmly, almost coldly, from behind the partition.

"You don't understand, huh?" Leo said. "Ben, why don't you tell this lush thing in Italian that I'm from Hollywood, California, where they make pictures? You know all these foreign languages."

"I don't know this one," I said.

Leo took a sip of *vino*. He said to the barmaid, "Me Hollywood. Cinema. *Capito?* Cinema . . ." He started cranking the air with one hand, holding the other over his eye in front of Luisa as if he were filming her. "Me Hollywood."

"Me Mandia," she said.

"Oh, nuts," Leo said, sitting down in disgust, "how are you going to educate these foreigners?"

"Luisa," Dooley coaxed, "come on out and I'll pinch your ass."

"No undershtanda."

"Come on, honey," Dooley pleaded. "Just let me get a good hold of you. I ain't had my hand on one in such long time! I'll pay you for it. Got *molto lire.*"

"No undershtanda."

"You understand all right!" Dooley cried. "Just putting on an act, that's what she is! I'll bet when the Jerries were here she spread for 'em. Bet she understands when the officers come around."

"No undershtanda," the fifteen-year-old girl said calmly.

"Oh, f— — you!" Dooley shouted.

Tony, the proprietor of the bar and owner of the laundry, came rushing in to see how the bustling establishment was doing. There were four of us in the small room, Dooley, Trent, Ginn, and myself, beside Luisa, and there wasn't any room for anybody else. Tony stopped on the threshold, bowed quickly, and said, "*Buon' giorno.*" His pants were crowded with patches but Tony looked very enterprising, a young man taking advantage of a situation. The Americans had many lire and Tony was enlarging his establishment. He pointed to a long, dark foyer where an emaciated artist was painting what he thought was an Esquiresque female. The artist, who had long stringy hair and wore a dirty white smock, held his paintbrush in one hand, a lit match in the other. He stabbed at the black wall with desperate strokes, trying to complete a detail of the painting before the precious match burned out. He was almost part of the wall, peering at it, straining his eyes while guiding the brush.

"How you like?" Tony inquired.

The question was purely rhetorical. Nobody replied. I felt a little resentful, realizing Tony was preparing for a long war.

"Why don't you wire this place for electricity?" Trent said.

"Shure, shure," Tony said, plunging into the darkness of the foyer.

We sat and drank the ill-tasting *vino* in the formless, damp-smelling room. We sat shifting in our chairs, looking at one another with boredom. How many times had we seen one another in exactly such pose? How many bars had we sat in, sipping from glasses and looking at our buddies with naked boredom? Where had all this started: this boredom and consuming loneliness? It seemed to me that it had been going on forever, with little change. Miami Beach had been pretty much like Panama City or Mount Holyoke or Springfield or Savannah, or even Natal in Brazil, or Dakar or Tunis in Africa. They had all been the same. Sitting and staring after everything had been said and there was nothing more to say.

"I'll sing you an Irish song," Dooley said, "and those that don't like it can go blow." He started his favorite, "When Irish Eyes Are Smiling," attempting to sing it in tenor voice the way he thought an Irishman should sing, but his voice dropped to a cracking baritone. The small, thick-walled room hurled Dooley's voice back at us, and we could not escape it. Dooley was high, and it was not safe to interrupt him, especially when he sang, and an Irish song at that. (For Dooley only one thing was sacred, and that was an Irish song.) But this time he sounded as if he were croaking. He drank and sang and embraced each one of us in turn and proclaimed: "You're the best bunch of buddies any sonofabitch could ever wanta have. I say it as an Irishman and a gentleman. I say it as a lover and as the biggest whoremaster you ever seen." He was half-solemn, half-joking, and his narrow, Mongolian eyes twinkled drunkenly as he talked. Dooley was going through his act, which was only half an act. "One thing about me," he continued, grabbing the pocketknife with which Leo had a habit of carving whenever he was bored, "one thing about me, even though I'm only twenty-two, which is almost half the age of this old fossil, Ben, the sonofabitch, I'll bet you I've lived more, loved more, whored more, brawled more, drank more, and sang more than anybody in this room, bar none."

"That's the truth, I guarantee ya that," Mel chimed in, playing his usual courtier role with Dooley and beaming with his junior Cal Coolidge face.

"And so," Dooley continued, ignoring Mel, "if they get me tomorrow or the next day, if the law of averages catches up with me, I'll go like an Irishman should. F— — 'em!" He wiped his lips with a big fist and turned to look at Luisa, who sat like a frigid statue behind the partition. "Before I die, honey, I'd like to get inside of you."

"No undershtanda," the girl said.

The emaciated artist came in from the dark foyer and asked quietly: "Match, per favore?"

We gave him a box of matches and he thanked us profusely and went back into the darkness of the foyer and resumed lighting the matches and stabbing at the wall with his brush.

"Oh, I'll get you all right," Dooley sang, leaning back in his chair, leering at the girl.

And she replied, "No undershtanda."

We sat, all of us, four drunken, dazed, lonely hot rocks, our feet stuck out, our Natal boots gleaming, our overseas caps over our eyes, sat and stared at the girl behind the partition, each imprisoned with his own thoughts, each ready to explode.

"I could go to bed with this thing and stay there the rest of my life," Dooley said, his eyes consuming the girl.

"So could your old dad," Leo said from underneath his overseas cap, "perfume or no perfume."

Mel started giggling and Dooley lashed out at him: "And so could you, you bastard, and that hypocrite, Ben, who acts like he never seen the inside of a whorehouse. Don't give me that crap, pop. Tell me," he asked angrily, "wouldn't you like to ride this thing here? Did you ever seen such bomb bays! And that fuselage!" He halted his angry diatribe and addressed the girl: "Come on out of there, you!"

"No undershtanda."

"I don't know why we liberated these people," the engineer cried in disgust. "No undershtanda," he mocked the barmaid. "Well, I'll make you understand."

Mel started giggling but changed his mind. The room was entombed in silence again. I heard the artist's brush scratch blindly at the wall as if he were in a race with the war, determined to complete his nude before the Americans left Italy. He put down his brush and came out to beg for more matches. "*Per favore*," he said, "*ancora* matches."

"No more goddamn matches!" Dooley cried, jumping to his feet and menacing the slight Italian in the dirty white frock. "*Via*, you goddamn dago! Always chiseling! That's all these wops do, chisel. Get the hell outa here!"

The frightened artist retreated, mumbling: "*Scusa —*"

Luisa sat behind her bar unperturbed, impassive, as if what was happening on this hot Italian afternoon in July 1944 was a routine occurrence.

Leo said, "Last night I had a wet dream in Technicolor."

"What do you know about that!" Dooley snickered. "Everybody else gets 'em plain, but just 'cause he's from Hollywood — tell me, was it in *glorious* Technicolor?"

"*Si*," Leo replied, carving his name on the table with savage strokes.

We ordered more *vino*. Our senses were clouded over, but not sufficiently. The devouring loneliness fed upon us like lice on the bodies of the little *bambini* outside. We stared at one another. Dooley held his little *vino* glass in his fist as if he were choking it. He glared at us with his drunken twinkling eyes, trying to make up his mind against whom he might take out his spite. His eyes lit on me. "Hey, Ben," he said, his voice heavy with sarcasm, "when is this war of yours gonna be over?"

"When you finish it," I said.

"I didn't start it," the engineer retorted.

"Neither did I."

"But it's *your* war."

"It's yours as much as mine," I said, going over ground covered many times before. "And if you don't like it, why did you study to be an engineer, why didn't you wash out? Nobody forced you to fly."

Instead of his usual — what somebody else can do I can too — Dooley rebutted, "I don't want no part of this war. I wanna get the hell outa this God-forsaken hole. The guy that invented Europe oughta have his tail kicked from here till Wednesday. Stick this war up Aunt Mabel's whoozis and it won't be no skin off my ass."

"Mine neither," Mel said.

"You shut up, Texas!" Dooley pounced on the nose gunner. "Nobody axed you. Go screw a sheep."

"I come from *cattle* country and you know it!" Mel protested indignantly. "I wouldn't look at no sheep."

"My ass bleeds for you."

"And my heart pumps pure piss for *you*."

"You're full of the well-known article."

"Close your mouth 'cause your tail is sucking wind."

"Blow it out!" Dooley shouted. "Blow it out!"

Luisa sat behind her partition, part of our tense world, yet apart from it. She wrote with her stump pencil while we poured the rotten, muscle-paralyzing *vino* down our throats as you would pour fire-extinguishing chemical on a burning Liberator. But the *vino* only covered our tenseness, it could not extinguish it.

"There are two thousand, seven hundred whorehouses in Havana, Cuba," Trent observed drunkenly without raising his eyes from his carving.

Dooley held up his glass and cried, "Let's drink to all of 'em!"

"Every fukken one of them," Trent said, taking up his *vino* glass.

"Cuba is a civilized country," Dooley said wistfully, remembering our three-day stay there. "Very *molto buono* women. Here in Italy if you want a good piece, you gotta go all the way to Rome. And when you get there you gotta shack up with a babe for three days and give her a hundred bucks for it, and in order to get screwed you gotta go to the Sistine Chapel with her first and look at those goddamn pictures on the ceiling of big guys with little peckers by this fellow Da Vinci or Angelo or some dago like that. And then this whore she makes you go see the Vatican and the catacombs and the Coliseum and the art galleries and opera. And all the time this goes on, you provide the rations! Didja ever hear anything like it just for a lay?"

"It was much simpler in Havana," Trent said, sighing with nostalgia. "The girls were prettier. They smelled better on account they used perfume. Even the dose of clap you got there was of a higher caliber than in Italy."

"You said a mouthful," Mel agreed, feeling secure that his comrades were all agreeing again. "What I say is you cain't expec' much fum a country where they ain't even got no screens or no toilet seats. Why, you know somepin," he cried, his voice rising indignantly, "we been in It'ly purty near two months and I ain't seen one head o' cattle."

"You don't say," Trent said mockingly, putting the last touches on his carving with vicious strokes of his knife.

"Oh, shut up, you guys!" Dooley cried. "Point is I gotta pitch a bitch tonight."

"Not me," Mel Ginn said. "I ain't touching them ugly syphed-up gals in Mandia. What's more, we better be getting back to the base 'cause we're liable to fly tomorra."

"Oh, s— —," Dooley sighed. "Radar can pick up everything, why can't I?" He sat in his chair, unsteady, leering at the girl behind the partition. He saw Luisa come from behind her perch and made a leap for her, grabbing the girl from the rear. She began to scream and Tony came rushing in, disturbed and pale, and behind him stood the frightened artist. Tony begged Dooley to let the girl alone; she was, after all, a stupid little girl, a child. Dooley shooed him away, but between the four of us we freed the terrified girl from his embrace. He sat down panting, defeated, sweating. "Where the hell is the *vino?*" he demanded.

"*Si, si.*" Tony sprang behind the bar, grabbed the bottle and poured the dark red liquid and bowed.

Dooley drank until his eyes no longer focused and his tongue no longer obeyed his mind which was paralyzed with alcohol. "I had my first drink when I was five," he mumbled slowly, glaring at the table where Leo had carved beside his name the letters: HOLLYWOOD, CALIF. "I been drinking since. My grandfather, Go' bless him, is ninety-three. Still drinks a pint a day. And don' let anybody kid you about me being only half Irishman. I'm fu' blooded, see. . . ." He chattered on, leaning his face on his arms, opening and closing his eyes: "After this fukken war is over I'm going back to Pittsbur' and marry me a fine girl, see? The prettiest, cleanest, nicest American girl you ever did see. S' nothing like an American sweetheart, not in the whole fukken world, I don't give a damn what any of you hot rocks say."

"Nothing like it," Trent agreed. "Now you take this girl Helen, back in Hollywood —"

"Goddamn right," the engineer continued, interrupting Leo. "And I'm going to marry this girl and I'm going to build us a *casa*, a *molto buono casa*, and I'm going to have a bunch of Irish kids running around the fukken yard. See?"

"Roger-dodger," Mel prompted.

"And any sonofabitch that's going to open his yap," Dooley continued, "and mention this coffin they call an airplane, this Liberator, or talk Jew-war to —" He stopped suddenly and looked toward me and said, "Oh, excuse me, Ben. It slipped out. I didn't mean nothing by it. It's just an expression —"

I caught Mel and Leo looking at me as if they were trying to gauge my reaction to Dooley's words. And I sat there confused, taken aback by the suddenness of the remark, wondering whether I should take umbrage or let it pass as I had done on many previous occasions. This was not the first time it had slipped out like that; I had heard the sniping, snide remarks against Jews in the past. Back in the States it had been quite prevalent, men asking you point blank: "How come you don't have a desk job like most Jews? How come you're a gunner?" And you said: "Look around you and you'll see many Jews who are gunners. This other thing is a lie." And there had been the hope back of your mind and the certainty that when you finally got to combat, men would judge you strictly on the basis of your deeds. My hopes were realized to a large extent. I found no Jew-baiting among flyers, although there was some among the orderly-room commandos. The men who were close to death each day did not seek scapegoats among their own. Only once in a while it slipped out, and you were shocked and hurled back to your childhood days when being a Jew had been a stigma, a daily, tormenting, conscious thing, and at such moments there was the feeling that you were being set aside to be judged not only as a person, but also as a Jew.

"I apologize," Dooley said, putting his arm around my shoulder. "Let's have a drink on all being good buddies."

All four of us got up and embraced and thumped one another on the shoulders and cried "my good buddy" and sat down again and each one of us resumed his own thoughts, jumbled and incoherent though they were. I had an overwhelming desire to rise and run back to the base and write to Ruth. It was a desire, a need driving me mad, a need to communicate with her, to speak to her, to share with her, perhaps to cry with her for the waste and the hollowness of days. I started getting up. "Let's get going," I said.

"Just one more drink," Dooley said. "Just a *poco* drink." We ordered one more, and Trent had his arm around my shoulder, talking with difficulty: "Know what I'm going to do when I get back home, I mean, if God grant I finish my missions? I'm going to have dog kennels. Raise 'em like they should be raised." He grimaced as he hugged me, puckering his lips and shaking his head. "I just love those little fukkers. Gimme a pup and I'm the happiest *guaglio* you ever saw . . ."

"Me," Mel joined in on the conversation, "when I get done with my fifty, I'm going inta cattle raising. Get me a GI loan and set up for m'self. Me and Sharon."

"I just love dogs," Leo pursued. "They'll never screw you like —"

"Me, I'll take cattle," Mel insisted.

"I'm going to build," Dooley said out of the depth of his drunkenness. "Build houses, that's what I'll do. And Ben, over there, he's going to teach. And Billy is going to wash his mother's windows and Big Wheel is going back to photography." Suddenly he was laughing loudly, pounding his fist on the table violently.

16

The BUDAPEST raid had been a milk run. After the mission the men showered and escaped from the hot barracks. Only Cosmo and I remained. Cosmo had not gotten over his panicky outburst over the target. He sat on the cot, trembling. "I'd go to sleep," he said, "but I get the awfullest nightmares soon as I fall asleep."

The heat hung thickly over the barracks. Flying gear was heaped on the bunks; socks and shoes were strewn all over the place. Oxygen masks hung down from the mosquito-net poles; cigarette butts covered the floor. And everywhere was the oppressive khaki world.

I dressed quickly and ran out of the barracks. I had a need to find color, any color but khaki. I hopped on a truck going to the beach. The Tyrrhenian Sea was a lovely blue. I stared at the water, determined to shut out this other world. And yet, it was maddening to sit on the sand and to watch only men. Everywhere there were men, just like on the base. If I could only see one skirt billowing in the wind; the softness of a thigh; the swelling of a breast. The universe seemed empty, cockeyed, lopsided. The sea murmured restlessly, as if it too lamented the absence of woman. I got up and started running. I thought if I ran far enough along the beach I would come upon the Sand Dunes, Indiana, and there Ruth would be waiting for me. Around the next bend, I thought, the cottage must be there! And the sea, it was transformed for me into Lake Michigan. Suddenly a Liberator wheeled overhead and I stopped, exhausted, the spell broken.

I left the beach in disgust and escaped to the Red Cross in Mandia.

Let me tell you something about this Little America. The Stars and Stripes flew proudly over the ugly, gray, two-story building which had once been a monastery. Inside, old murals on the walls had been covered by pinups of Lana Turner, Betty Grable, and other leggy females. Long yellow sheets were tacked to the woodwork with the latest bulletins from Normandy, Bessarabia and the CBI.

In the enlisted men's section of the building there were two Ping-Pong tables, but seldom were there Ping-Pong balls, unless you knew the faded, peroxide Miss Nellie Bullwinkle, Red Cross director in Mandia and *chargé d'affaires* of the doughnuts and coffee offered to flyers, Free of Charge, after a mission. Miss Bullwinkle's hands were full, so she had two assistants, both American girls. They were tall, one blonde, one brunette. They were both slim and unattractive, but the demand upon them was great. They were seldom seen in the EM part of the Red Cross. They slept with officers only — above the rank of first looey, while Miss Bullwinkle, who would not rate a second look on any street in the States, slept with a colonel from Wing who was an ex-stunt flyer, crowding fifty.

Nellie Bullwinkle's skin was flabby and sallow and it looked as if she had never exposed it to the hot Italian sun. She was dumpy and plump. But that did not prevent her from wiggling her substantial hips in response to the men's devouring stares. She knew the men came to the Red Cross for more than doughnuts and coffee. They came to stare at her. She was the exotic bird in their midst, she and her two assistants, brought to Italy for our edification.

Aware of what a rare article she was in this wilderness, Miss Bullwinkle played her little role in history right up to the hilt. Her march down the main piazza on a late afternoon was something to behold — the way she held her head up, and the twinkling of her thighs. Then you saw her smile and you knew she forgave the Italians for being Italian. And she probably forgave them for being so uncivilized as to have urinal walls built so that you could see the men's knees from outside. When she came abreast of the urinal, Nellie Bullwinkle simply looked in the other direction, ignoring it out of existence. The American military urinal down the street, near the air-raid shelter, presented no problem at all to the Red Cross director. These units were built from the ground up; they had a roof over them, and two entrances. A shingle over one entrance read: "Officers Enter Here"; and the other: "Enlisted Men Enter Here."

Having passed these obstacles, Miss Bullwinkle smiled again, a sort of detached, tolerant, forgiving smile which she bestowed upon the town. It was as if she forgave the Italians their pesky flies, the stench, the breast-feeding of babies in the middle of the piazza or on a doorstep of a *casa*; forgave them the dirt and disease and the promiscuity of their daughters and the drabness of their lives and the shabbiness of their clothes. I had the feeling, watching her smile, that she forgave them everything — so long as they realized they were natives, and kept their place. Being an American must have been a renewing experience for Nellie Bullwinkle each morning; and being an American among an inferior people must have been a challenge. But serving one's country had always been the highest aspiration. And Miss Bullwinkle served. Day and night.

Her job was to keep the boys happy, keep them smiling, keep them from thinking too much about home. She ran dances for officers in their part of the Red Cross building. At these dances, when she was able to coax some of the well-to-do families in town to allow their daughters to come, papa and mama usually came along and sat dourly in full glare of the lights, watching daughter's every move as she cavorted with an American officer. Miss Bullwinkle also ran concerts with Italian operatic talent. But these were not popular with her "boys," except Dick Martin and a few others. They preferred a good rendition of "I Wanna Buy a Paper Doll That I Can Call My Own" or "I'll Be Seeing You in All the Old Familiar Places," to a foreign song like "Sorrento" or "Vicino al Mare."

Inadequate though Nellie Bullwinkle was, she was part of our life in the war. She was part of the mosaic, one of its brighter, though no less tragic, aspects. She was the image of Mother, though she tried hard not to be. The young ones, all of us, in fact, sought the image of Mother to temper the violence of our lives, but Miss Bullwinkle gave it to us only when she was tired and off guard and didn't pretend.

It was distressing to watch her trying to recapture her youth, trying so desperately, although there weren't any women around to compete with her except the two unattractive assistants.

My curiosity regarding Miss Bullwinkle had another aspect. Besides sleeping with the colonel from Wing, she had a clandestine affair with our copilot. The colonel didn't know it, but everybody else at Wing and Group knew that every afternoon, when not flying, Second Lieutenant Chester Kowalski spent the siesta period at Miss Bullwinkle's *casa* with her. True, the Red Cross director was almost twice Chet's age, but nobody underestimated his achievement. To say that the men were envious is to put it mildly. Few officers could boast of such a deal. Imagine! Shacking up with an American woman! Even our commanding officer had to fly all the way to Naples or Rome to get his. Think of all the 100-octane gas he used up, taxpayers' money, if you please. What added magnificence to Kowalski's triumph was his being only a second lieutenant, a copilot, no more.

If we were envious of Chet, we were also grateful to Miss Bullwinkle. The affair with her worked a profound change in our copilot. Some of his old sparkle returned, and he even acquired a little audacity and talked back to Big Wheel. He still didn't trust himself with the stick, but the conquest bolstered his morale considerably. He became less withdrawn, less apologetic, and on occasion he joined in the banter up in the air. He knew we all regarded him with wonder and respect for having captured Nellie Bullwinkle.

Chet felt rehabilitated, accepted. It had been the same in civilian life. Each time he failed in business — the stationery store in Hamtramck, or the plastics shop his father opened for him — Chet got involved in a love affair that redeemed him. All his being was directed toward pleasing women: his looks, his mannerisms, his actions. He was able to express himself fully only with women. After his marriage and the birth of his son, Chet gave up chasing after women. He resumed it only after entering the army. All through our training in the States, he had girls. Even in Savannah, where servicemen roamed the streets by the thousands and the ugliest among the women acted as if they were luscious movie actresses, even there Chet had himself a pretty Southern girl, "a real sex machine," he called her. He would pick up the girls at the Savannah Hotel Bar or the De Soto Bar and turn them over to Dooley or Trent and walk away triumphantly, leaving the girls gaping.

After our arrival overseas, Chet wilted more quickly and perceptibly than anyone else on the crew. He quit shaving each morning and took along more flak-pieces than anyone else, devising ways of protecting his genitals. He was completely unreliable up in the air. The other pilots in Squadron wondered why Big Wheel flew with him. But Pennington had his own reasons. He accepted Chet and retained him as a way of proving to the world that while most mortals needed copilots, he could fly a ship single-handed. There was no doubt he was also sorry for Chet.

Chet's relationship with our pilot was similar to the one he had had with an exacting, domineering father who drove him, early in life, to seek the gentle female world. He hated the pilot no less than he had hated his father, although he was afraid to show it. After our first mission Chet took to religion. Then Nellie Bullwinkle entered his life.

•   •   •   •

It was late afternoon when Chet entered the Red Cross building. He came in gleaming, his Natal boots shining bright, like a song. He looked like a god striding among men. He winked at me and touched Miss Bullwinkle's shoulder possessively. She turned around and saw him and blushed like a little girl. "I must go to the hospital with the lieutenant," she lied to the admiring men. They both left in her jeep.

•   •   •   •

I got back to the base at ten o'clock. I knew it was ten o'clock because the gunner from the adjacent barracks had just roared out his nightly defiance: "Jeez, how I hate this fukken place!"

Cosmo, who was talking to Dooley, sat in the same position as I had left him in the afternoon. "We're flying too much," he complained to the engineer.

"It'll let up after awhile," Dooley said, smoking his last cigarette before turning in for the night.

"But why do they fly us so much?" Cosmo insisted. "Don't they know about the law of averages? Every day I look around me and there's less of the old guys around. It's like now you see them and now you don't. At services, you get used to the way a man prays, you get to like his voice and his face, then, all of a sudden, he isn't there any more. You can't depend on anything. I don't like it." He looked at Dooley with his frightened and confused child's eyes.

"Next time we ain't flying you come to town with me," Dooley said. "Relax a little. It'll do you —"

"I'm not going to town!" Cosmo cried. "I hate the town. I hate Italy!"

"Fine thing coming from a wop," Trent said, looking up from his toes.

"You better go to sleep," Dooley said to Cosmo gently, wearily.

17

AT NIGHT Cosmo tossed on his cot. He screamed in his sleep and woke up most of the men in the barracks. "Six o'clock! Look out at six o'clock! Flak at six o'clock! Ball gunner to crew, ball gunner to crew, my turret is coming off the hinges! MAMAAAA!" His piercing cry knifed through the night stillness.

He woke up with a start and his face was white and beady with sweat. I saw his terrified eyes in the half-moon coming through a hole where there had once been a window. "Oh my God!" he muttered.

All of us, except Billy Poat who buried his head in the blanket in order to shut out Cosmo's cry, crept to the ball gunner's cot and lit cigarettes and sat bleary-eyed and tried to pacify him.

"I had a terrible nightmare," Cosmo whispered, eyeing Dooley imploringly.

"What you need is a few days off," Dooley said, putting his large hand on Mouse's knee. "We'll talk to the flight surgeon."

"What do you mean?" Cosmo asked, alarmed. "Want me to fall behind on more missions? Rest of you are four ahead already."

"You ought to get grounded for a while," Trent said bluntly. "Your buddies won't mind. We know you're not trying to — to —"

"You mean *quit* flying," Cosmo said. "Why don't you guys say what you mean?" He was reflective awhile, as if he had thought about it before. "I won't quit," he said firmly. "Not me!"

"There's plenty extra ball gunners around," Mel assured him.

"I'm sticking with my crew," Cosmo said, "unless you guys don't want me."

"Oh, sure we want you!" Dooley proclaimed loudly. "We wouldn't change you for nobody. Why, the way you drove off them MEs over Ploesti, and that good-luck Bible of yours, we got the best ball gunner in the business." He put his arm around Cosmo and Leo sat on the other side of him, and we all whispered consolingly, assuring him we approved of him and wanted him and needed him. Dooley tried to joke once, saying: "Why, you're the only ball gunner I ever seen that can get inside that fishbowl with his parachute on." We laughed, though it wasn't funny, and our laughter seemed macabre in the stillness of the tense night and its loud snores and the brutish roar of a bomber warming up mysteriously on the ramp.

"I'm a drag on you," Cosmo said slowly. "I wish I was dead —"

"You cut out that damn fool talk!" Mel said.

Cosmo paid no attention to Mel. He seemed oblivious of our presence. "In my dream the turret came off the hinges and I got caught in it and fell into the sea. . . . I have a feeling I'm going to die."

"Now that's a fukken way to talk," Dooley said. "Why, you little peckerhead, the way we been going lately, we'll *finito* our missions before you know it. And after the crew's done, we'll sit on our asses right here in Italy and wait for you to get done with them four missions. We ain't going back to the States without you. And that's a goddamn fact, as my name is Dooley."

"I guarantee ya that myself," Ginn said.

"I'll never see the States again," Mouse whispered.

Dooley scowled and his eyes narrowed into penciled slits. "I oughta smack you for saying things like that," he said.

"Your old dad is surprised at you," Trent said. "I don't understand that kind of talk, do you, Ben?"

I shook my head in negation and said, "No," and tried desperately to summon words that would bridge the distance between us and Cosmo. Already there was a distance between us, and Cosmo was accomplishing what he had set out to do since that first visit to town when he had fled in shame and in panic: he was retiring into a martyrdom, as he had once attempted to retire to a monastery. I sat there, touching him, holding him, thinking desperately that I must pull him back, not let him go — but how could hollow words compete with a savage determination on his part to expiate the sins we were committing against the Italians?

"Every day they're dying," Cosmo said. His face suddenly looked old. "Only they're dying up in the air, so you don't see 'em. But go down to the GI cemetery near Bari. Last time we were there, for Janski's funeral and that crew that overshot the runway, I asked the captain in charge how business was. And he said, 'They're bringing 'em in like hot cakes.'" He thought awhile. "That's what wars are for, so people would die. But why do innocent people suffer? Why do kids suffer? But I suppose," he added reflectively, answering his own queries, "I suppose the Lord deems it best. He decides these matters. And I have a funny feeling — like a pressure under my heart — that the Lord is calling me. I think He wants me to —"

"You're gonna get that nonsense outa your head," Dooley said with anger. "You know what Andy Kyle always says: we're a dream crew, and we're gonna make it!"

"With all the good-luck charms, we can't miss," Trent said with mock optimism as if he were trying to exorcise evil spirits that had taken possession of our comrade. "There's your own good-luck Bible. And there's the little pup and he hasn't failed to greet us once when we come down."

"And my good-luck socks," Mel chimed in. "I ain't gonna warsh them till we *finito* our fifty — and then you kin have 'em to finish them four missions —"

"And there's my WAC cap," Dooley said, "and Big Wheel's red flannel drawers, and Andy's Mo Mules cap, and Dick's can of insect powder and Ben's caul —"

"And all of us praying," Mel said. "You praying to the Catholic God, us praying to the Protestant God, and Ben, over here, praying to the Jewish God. And the officers praying too. By God, we got 'em all on our side," Ginn exclaimed. "We cain't miss."

"I didn't mention it even once in my letters," Cosmo said. He appeared to be listening to himself. "How could I tell Pa what I saw here? It would of killed him. He thinks Italy is still the way it used to be: a land of song and happiness. Wants to come back and die in Italy, in Gallipoli. He should see what Mussolini's done to it . . . and what the Americans've done to it . . . my own buddies. Oh, Lord God!" he sighed, "I don't like it here!"

18

COSMO WAS killed over Zagreb. The mission had been a milk run. The flak had been erratic and inaccurate. The Croatian Ustachi antiaircraft gunners were way off the mark. But it doesn't take much flak to kill a man. One piece of shrapnel the size of a cigarette killed Cosmo. It came through the waist window, ricocheted off Billy's gun, plunged into the ball turret and lodged in Cosmo's throat. By the time we discovered it and pumped up the ball turret, he was dead. His jugular vein had been severed.

19

WE TOOK A day off from the war and traveled to Cosmo's funeral. Besides the nine of us, there were a dozen others from our squadron. Some came along to pay respects, others came for the seventy-mile ride and the chance of sneaking into Bari later and raise a little hell. Some came to mourn the dead and reaffirm their own aliveness, like old people, dueling with death, keeping one step ahead of it, going to their friends' funerals.

The day was beautiful with that rich midsummer Italian beauty. The impoverished countryside yielded to the richness of the sun and the violent blue of the Adriatic. The rocky countryside was dotted with rundown, peeling, pink villas, now abandoned; rock dwellings of peasants that looked like inverted ice-cream cones from the distance; and dust-eaten, undersized palm trees. The vineyards were covered with a white, powdery dust. The olive trees were small and undernourished like the people themselves, fighting to keep erect in the barren soil. We saw no animals along the route to the cemetery. There weren't any cows or chickens or even stray dogs. They had all been eaten. Thin, emaciated horses and burros plodded along the well-paved highway, pulling *vino* trains. The bony animals did not bother to look up when our two trucks roared by them, the exhausts sounding full-throated and menacing. Nor did the drivers of the *vino* carts look up. They were accustomed to the roaring exhausts of the *Americani*.

We stood around the rims of the open trucks, each one of us wrapped up in his own silence, our eyes roaming over the morning landscape. Despite the various army camps along the road, the countryside appeared as if the war were a remote thing. Around the army camps, the British, Hindu, Polish, Kiwi, or Australian soldiers moved about slowly, lazily, as if they were conscious that the war was many hundreds of miles up to the north and they were not directly involved in it. We were the only ones at war, taking a day off from war. I was suddenly struck by this ambivalence of the airman's existence who lived half his war life in surroundings completely removed from combat. Unlike the infantry where one was up in the line for a certain period, the airman shuttled between combat and safety, between flak and his own ground men who hadn't the remotest conception of war and didn't give a damn about it.

At Taranto our trucks were held up by a British military policeman who gave the right-of-way to a small convoy of His Majesty's troops. Dooley bellowed at the pink-faced MP: "Let us through, you Limey bastard, we're going to a funeral!"

"F — — you, Yank!" the Briton roared back. Then he turned his back on us and all the vituperation and cussing and name-calling did not move him. It was as if he were getting even with the Yanks for calling him Limey, for keeping him out of their Red Cross clubs, for making fun of his planes, of his small British Isles, and for making his trucks drive on the right side of the road.

"We'll be late for a funeral!" I cried, shocked at his adamant stand. I suddenly loathed this man who stood in the midst of Taranto's snarled traffic, his broad back turned on us because it did not matter to him that we were on our way to bury a man who had died at war. One half hour later, after we'd finally crossed the bottleneck bridge and left Taranto, I was ashamed and humiliated at the ease with which I had abandoned myself to hating a harassed traffic cop who happened to be British and who by chance worked as an MP instead of toting a rifle up north.

We came upon the United States Military Cemetery abruptly, camouflaged as it was, off the main road. We found it, hacked out of an olive orchard, surrounded protectively by olive trees. We jumped off the trucks in silence and there it was, a slice of America that would remain in Italy long after all the other Americans had removed themselves. I had seen the graves before, but I was startled anew at the way they were lined up precisely, six feet deep, twelve inches apart, the crosses and six-point Stars of David all exactly the same size. GI! I walked among the graves which were being dug by Italian laborers, and I looked at some of the names: Allan, Constable, Kaplan, Zinner, Johnson, Mankiewitz, Velasquez, Pappas. Some of the men I had known in the States; Kaplan and Zinner had been in my barracks. Kaplan had been a Brooklyn boy who had talked very little despite Brooklyn's reputation for producing garrulous people. Zinner had been a motorman on Philadelphia's subway.

We found Cosmo's casket in a pyramidal tent. It was draped with an American flag. Other pine boxes were stacked almost to the ceiling. A shirtless corporal sat in the tent, reading microfilm comics. The color of his skin was almost as coppery as his identification tags. He did not look up as we came in. "Which one you wanna see?" he asked, bored.

He opened the casket and we looked at Mouse. He appeared small inside the six-foot regulation-size casket. He had a foot to spare. He had always complained there wasn't enough room for him in the ball turret. There was something completely incongruous about that boyish face and child's body clothed in a military uniform with staff sergeant's chevrons and the silver wings of a gunner. By what quirk of fate had this child usurped the prerogatives of man? I had never realized how small he was until I saw him in the casket.

We looked at Cosmo and looked at each other without saying a word and then we drifted to a shady place near a *casa* to wait for the Catholic chaplain who was to come from Bari. We squatted and smoked and field-stripped our cigarettes out of respect for the dead, and smoked some more. And out of respect for the dead we talked in low tones.

"The way I look at it," Mel whispered to Billy Poat, "the guys that's dead don't need to worry about sweating out no more missions."

"You got something there," the radio operator agreed. His overseas cap sat on the back of his head, and the sun caught the sparkle of his red hair.

"What I always say is," Mel continued in a humble tone, yet encouraged by Billy's acquiescence, "we all gotta go some time."

"True enough," Billy said harshly, as if he were suppressing anger because of the occasion.

"Ain't none of us live more'n once."

"Some don't even live once," Billy said bitterly.

Mel regarded Billy. Billy's words confused him. "Wha' ya mean by that?" he asked, disturbed.

"The kid was hardly twenty," Billy said. "He didn't have a chance to know life. Bet he never even got close to a woman."

"Still'n all —"

"Wars should be outlawed," Billy said heatedly, directing his angry gaze toward the precise wooden crosses on the graves. "We oughta make the politicians fight wars. And the priests too. Why don't the Pope in Rome speak out against war? They're all the same! I got no use for any of 'em." He picked up a pebble and threw it at the *casa*.

"Oh, I don't know about that," Mel said, perplexed. "I wouldn't say that," he said.

One of the Italian grave diggers, a squat man with a torn vest and the inevitable cap, came over to our group and took off the cap and begged: "Cigarette, Jo?"

He got his cigarette. You couldn't refuse an Eyetie who was in the process of digging your comrade's grave. Besides, he undoubtedly knew that even *Americani* grew humbler in the face of death. Dooley held up a match for the grave digger to light his cigarette. The man said "*Grazie*," and went back to dig Cosmo's grave.

"If you want to look at it properly," Leo said, entering the indolent discussion, "there have always been wars and there always will be. It's human nature to fight." He leaned his elongated head against the white *casa* and took a deep drag on his cigarette. "Man's a beast," he concluded.

"Cosmo was no beast," Dooley disagreed. "All he wanted to do was pray. They shoulda let him be a monk."

"I mean generally speaking," Trent said. "Wars have been going on since history began."

"Then why don't the politicians fight it?" Billy insisted. "They always start a war. Let them fight it. I wouldn't object."

"Me neither," Mel said. "I'd go home tomorra, I guarantee ya that."

A gentle breeze came off the Adriatic and rustled the leaves of the palm trees. Birds kept up a respectful chirping. They buzzed the plot of ground lined with crosses and disappeared among the foliage, plunging in and out, flapping their tiny wings playfully, singing about the day and the sun and the strangers who sat in sorrow and contemplated death.

Pennington came by and regarded us critically and said, "Where the hell is the chaplain?" and walked away.

"It's the damned Europeans," Trent resumed, fumbling with his knife, searching for an object on which he might carve his name. "Europeans always start wars and then we have to come over and finish what they start. I'm for letting them finish their own wars."

"Me too," Mel agreed. "If they's so goddamn dumb as to start wars alla time, let 'em fight their own."

"Europe ain't worth saving," Dooley said. "If it was up to me I'd let 'em all kill each other off and there'd be no skin off my ass."

"Europe shore is a mess," Mel said. "I'm s'prised President Roosevelt don't know that."

"Roosevelt's a politician too," Billy said. "He's like the rest of 'em. Take my word for it."

Another grave digger, a tall fellow, gaunt and skinny, came over, cap in hand, and whispered: "Cigarette, Jo?"

"Which grave's he on?" Dooley asked, scowling at the Italian.

"Cosmo's."

"Here," Dooley said, handing the man a cigarette. "Hurry up and *finito* the grave."

"*Si, Si, finito,*" the grave digger said, smiling gratefully. "*Presto.*"

"Yeah, *presto,*" the engineer mocked the man as he resumed his work on the grave. "It'll take 'em all night to dig that grave. I never seen a lazier bunch of people than Eyeties."

"Niggers is lazier," Mel said.

"You're fulla s— —," Dooley said. "Niggers are Americans. The Ninety-ninth Fighter Squadron is an all-nigger outfit. And if it wasn't for them chasing off the MEs that day we got hit over Graz, maybe you wouldn't be here."

"That don't cut no ice," Mel rebutted. "I come from Texas and I oughta know."

"Even Pennington thinks those black boys from the Ninety-ninth are the best flyers around."

"They're the craziest," Mel corrected the engineer. "A nigger is liable to do anything in the air. By God, man, don't ya know that? They ain't got no sense. They just gets in a plane and flies. You guys fum up No'th —"

"Hold it down to a roar," Pennington said. "Don't you fellows know where you are? This is a cemetery."

"f— — you," Dooley muttered under his breath. He hissed the words out of deference for the dead and some fear the pilot might hear him.

"There is one advantage to being dead," Trent observed, "they bury you next to officers."

Our attention was called to four Italians who came to the entrance of the cemetery. All four of them, the old couple and the middle-aged one, were dressed in shabby black clothes which were neat and pressed as if they had been saved and readied for a funeral. My attention was riveted to the old man, whose nose was shaped like Cosmo's. He was small, with a long, pointed face and gray mustaches that were much too large for his face.

"Fidanza," the younger of the two men muttered to the guard at the gate. The guard exchanged a few words with them in Italian and told them to wait at the gate and came over to the officer in charge. "That bunch of wops say one of the KIAs is their relative. Old man says he's the grandfather. They'd like to see the stiff."

The captain in charge, a pudgy man with a bald spot, turned to Pennington and said: "How about that?"

"Ask them if they're from Gallipoli," Pennington said.

"Gallipoli, *si*," the Italians nodded almost in unison, smiling humbly, deferentially. The older woman began to weep.

"It's all right," Pennington said. "I notified them to come. You see, the kid talked about wanting to go and see them, and then —" He broke off abruptly and turned away from our grateful glances and said brusquely, "Some of you fellows go to the tent with them."

The four small, black-clad visitors followed us to the tent. The corporal looked up in surprise and undid Cosmo's casket and went back to his funnies. They moved up front and stood over the casket. The older of the two women cried softly as if fearing that a loud outburst might displease the *Americani*. The old man ran his gnarled hand over his eyes and shook his head. He continued shaking his head all the time while we stood in back of them, filling up the tent. The corporal put away his funnies. He looked up at the old woman who was weeping as if he had never heard a woman cry over a dead man before. He rose and walked out of the tent.

We remained standing in the tent. We seemed to be standing there for ages, watching the four small, work-bent figures. No words passed between us. There was something heartrending about hearing a woman sob in these surroundings. It was heartrending and yet heart-filling to hear the sobs of a woman in this world of men. It was just the thing: a woman's sob at a burial. And all of us listening to those sobs were weeping ourselves, weeping through her. I saw Dooley biting his lower lip and there was a tear on Andy's cheek. Trent started to sob but checked himself and ran out of the tent. We escaped after him and assembled near the *casa* and reached for our cigarettes. I pitied Andy, who didn't smoke.

Cosmo's relatives remained inside the tent a long time. They came out and stood in front of the tent, uncertain what the *Americani* expected them to do or how they were to behave until the funeral was over. I started toward them, not knowing what I would say to them. I did not know enough Italian to convey to them how I felt about Cosmo, and about them. There was a gulf between us and I wanted to impress upon them that it was an artificial barrier which was our fault and not theirs. I wanted to tell them about Cosmo and his devoutness, his gentleness, and the fact that he had often talked about them with affection. What else was there to say about Cosmo? They had seen him in the casket. He had been a child whose voice was too squeaky, his hands too small, his disposition too gentle to make his way successfully through this dog-eat-dog world. That is why he had sought removal to the peace and tranquillity of a cloister. And now he was finally achieving that peace in the soil of his ancestors. A native's return, with his relatives on hand to greet him. And to weep for him. In this one way Cosmo was fortunate; no other man buried here had a woman weep over his grave.

The old woman continued sobbing. But she was an Italian, and sobbing did not seem out of place for Italian women whose children were dying of hunger, whose sons were dead or prisoners of war and whose daughters were selling themselves for κ rations or cigarettes. Weeping and black garments went well together.

The grave was all ready. The sun was setting beyond the olive trees but the chaplain hadn't arrived. The Italian laborers were clamoring to go home because their day's work was done, but the captain in charge ordered them to stay until after the burial.

We tried at conversation with Cosmo's relatives. We offered them our cigarettes. There was even a suggestion from Dooley that we give them some money. But they refused our offerings with polite firmness and many *mille grazie*.

"They don't act like Eyeties," Trent whispered.

"If you take that little old lady and put some good clothes on her," Dooley observed, "she'd look like an American grandma."

"How *about* that!" Mel put in. "And that lil ol' man, damn if he ain't the nicest-looking fella I seen in a coon's age. Don't look like no Eyetie to me."

"When you come right down to it," Andy Kyle said, "he looks like a farmer from Missouri."

For a while the barrier was down and despite the language difficulties we got along, telling them as much about Cosmo as our Italian allowed us. And they nodded to all we said with encouraging *si, si, è capito.*

The Catholic chaplain finally arrived in a jeep. He was a thin, stringy captain with a nervous tick in his left eye.

Everything was done in an indecent hurry after that. The chaplain donned his vestments, the corporal put on a shirt and came out dragging his bugle lazily. We carried the casket to the grave. The chaplain went through his prayer as if he were in a hurry to get back to Bari, and the Italian laborers stood by impatiently with their shovels, waiting for the order to start shoveling the soil onto the grave. The corporal, his funnies sticking out of his back pocket, blew taps. There was the silhouette of a Liberator about ten thousand feet overhead. The bomber was either coming home from a raid late or going on a lone mission; perhaps it was on the way to Naples with men who had finished their tour of missions and were returning to the States.

It looked like perfect flying weather. As Cosmo's casket was being lowered into the hard tufa-rock soil you had the feeling that he didn't have to worry any longer how the sky looked and what it held for tomorrow.

The captain in charge of the cemetery said to us as we were leaving, "Drop in any time."

"If I don't see you again it will be too soon," Pennington replied.

A laugh. We were on the way to Bari. In Bari there was a large Red Cross. There were shops and wine. In Bari there were whores who were not nearly as ugly and seedy as those of Mandia.

On the way to Bari our truck roared by Cosmo's relatives who were riding in a horse cart.

"Go easy past that cart," Lieutenant Pennington shouted to the PFC in the cab, "I don't want that horse frightened."

The driver smiled and said: "Okay, lieutenant." But he paid no attention. He stepped on the gas and opened the exhaust. We waved as we tore by the cart and the old people waved back sadly. Allied soldiers who were passing by and saw us wave to the four Italians in an old cart drawn by a bony horse probably thought we were drunk already. The British no doubt swore and said: "The Yanks are fukkin up again, making it worse for us the way they're spoiling the bloody natives."

In Bari all nine of us got drunk.

20

THE SQUADRON assigned another ball gunner to our crew. We all resented him when he moved in to take Cosmo's cot, but after one mission we accepted him. His name was Charley Couch and he was 29 but he looked older than I. He had about 25 missions to his credit and was the only survivor of his crew. In the first brief hours of our acquaintance we found out that he was from Arizona, where he prospected for gold; that he played no-limit poker in the day room, despised his wife and had false teeth. When not flying or playing cards, his main preoccupation was reading *Studs Lonigan*. "I been reading it for years," he said, chuckling, "ever since I got in the army. I hope to finish it by the time I get out."

It soon felt as if Charley had been around a long time.

•   •   •   •

Dooley ran off after the supper meal threatening to "beat the s— — out of some orderly-room commando. I just gotta beat up on one of them guys," he said, "or I won't be able to sleep." Trent, after a tearful session with his little dog, tagged along with Dooley to restrain him from doing anything rash, he said. Billy Poat stayed in the barracks and shuffled his cards furiously. The wine he had drunk in Bari made him retch all night long. But fearing he might awaken the men, Billy sat out on the cement stoop all night long, holding his head and moaning.

"One of these days I'm gonna blow my top," Billy threatened in the afternoon. "I applied for a transfer to the infantry months ago. It better come through soon, take my word."

I went out for a walk. No place in particular. I prowled among the tents that were emptied out suddenly, their occupants going to the base theater. The gear was strewn about as if the inhabitants had been called away in a hurry. Passing by the barracks I saw small groups of men huddled over card games. But for the most part the barracks were as empty as the tents. Most of the men in the field had gravitated toward the open clearing near the ramp to watch a moving picture. I heard the sound track of the film, disjointed words and exclamations, a feminine voice that startled me momentarily, all emanating from the never-never land several wing-tip lengths down the road. On the road men were still hurrying toward the movie, punctuating the darkness with their flashlights. I passed the mess hall and there the night cooks were working, preparing the food that few of us would eat in the morning. On the ramp a bomber was warming up. In Group Operations I saw several men poring over maps, and the light was on at Squadron Public Relations where a corporal sat over a typewriter, perhaps writing to the Cleveland papers all about Cosmo Fidanza, the hometown boy who died in action. The corporal, who wore glasses, pecked away at the typewriter with two fingers. It seemed strange to hear the click of typewriter keys; strange, unreal, yet reassuring. Above me the wine-colored sky was pinned with twinkling, sparkling stars. Like a war map. I had never seen the galaxies so resplendent and so clear. But there was treachery in that magnificence. The sky would never beguile me again.

I started for our barracks but the feeling of loneliness drove me from the door. I went back down the road to the officers' tent. Andy alone was in the tent and when he saw me come in he was startled for a moment and folded up a sheet of paper on which he'd been writing.

"Hello, Ben," he said distantly. "What's the shot?"

I sat down on one of the four cots and stared at the footlocker on the pebbled floor. The locker spelled out Dick Martin's full name, rank, serial number with a reassuring permanence.

Andy fidgeted. I had never seen his face so somber.

"I wrote to Opal," he said haltingly, as if he were still pondering whether to share his secret with me. "Told her if anything happens to me, she isn't to mourn. She's a — too young and too pretty to sit around and mourn me. I'm going to seal this letter and put it in my footlocker. If —" he hesitated, "if anything happens to me, I'd like you to have the letter sent —"

"Nothing's going to happen to you," I said.

"I'm not so sure any more," he said quietly, almost in a whisper as if afraid to voice his fears too loudly. "Once upon a time I had an idea about a dream crew. But now — you know all this afternoon I've been sitting here feeling sorry for myself. And this sentence kept bobbing up in my mind: 'Married only one week when you left . . . married only one week when you left.' That's absolutely crazy because I came here on my own and nobody forced me. But I can't help thinking about that wedding of mine and that I was with Opal only one short week before we left. You remember the wedding, Ben?"

"Sure." It seemed so long ago. Several lifetimes ago. When we were innocent and naive and thought the sky was for lovers to whisper about and death was a distant threat only old people worried about.

"In fact it was only three months ago, the first week in May," Andy said. "Remember how you guys arranged that party at the De Soto Bar and —" His face was suddenly animated.

It had not been a wedding, properly speaking. The crew had gathered in the barroom of the De Soto, one of Savannah's swankier hotels, and we drank while Andy and the pink-cheeked girl who had come in from Kansas City on the previous day, sat primly and smiled. Both of them looked like a couple of kids fresh out of high school. I remember watching them through a pleasant film of liquor, saying to myself: This is the Ideal All-American Couple: pink-cheeked, sandy-haired, open-faced, well-nourished, smiling. The All-America Smile and the Nothing Can Stop the Army Air Force Smile. The smile covering the bewilderment, shyness, apprehension about the near future, the need to love in a hurry, passionately, because the days were numbered and the nights even fewer and their life together would be encompassed in one week. They smiled when they wanted to weep, sat and drank when they should have run off by themselves for that brief period of passion and probing and discovery and fulfillment. "I hope theirs will be right," I said to myself and I was reassured, remembering theirs was a childhood romance. But still, how could one tell? The world was in a frenzy. Boys and girls plunged into marriage in order to assert life before death intervened. They clung together briefly, for a day, a week, a month. Then they were torn apart. The young wives followed their husbands from one base to another. Like gypsies. The great migration. The way Ruth followed me from camp to camp. They lived out of suitcases. They learned a new language:

"My husband was just made PFC —"

"Harry got himself a good deal —"

"Al's CO is pretty chicken, if you me —"

"Phil and I are sweating out Special Orders —"

"My aching, busted back —"

"What do you expect of the Army?"

Like the others, Andy and Opal had meant to wait until he graduated from Missouri State and got set up in merchandising. Become an efficiency expert. Have a baby. Build a home. The American Blueprint. But then the war.

So instead they had a quick wedding a week before Andy was sent across. At the wedding, Dooley, Corporal Jack Dula, the ex-steel puddler from Pittsburgh, got up and sang "I Love You Truly" with a grim, perspiring determination. The officers and men around the circular bar stopped clinking their glasses and regarded their girls with moist eyes.

Leo Trent addressed Pennington all evening long: "Lieutenant, let's get the troops out of the rain and pour us some drinks."

"Roger-dodger!"

Every one of us was deliciously high, feeling deliciously sorry for ourselves, sensing what heroes we were already, although back of our minds was the blind hope something might happen that would keep us from going across.

"To the best navigator in the business!" Chet Kowalski was decked out in his officer's uniform with the golden second-lieutenant bars. He looked like an ad, he was so beautiful in his pinks and those shiny pilot's wings. Beside Chet sat a pretty, dewey-eyed southern gal who regarded him lovingly, caressingly all evening long. "Ah'm just having oodles of fun," she sang. "Ah just am!"

"Drink up," he said to her. "Drink up. You know the old Army saying: here today, gone tomorrow. In a week —"

"Don't say that, honey, 'cause Ah'm having so much fun —"

And then there was Lieutenant Dick Martin who after three drinks shrieked at Mel Ginn: "Go on! Who ever heard of Ozone,

Texas? You can hide most of your Ozone in Macy's bargain basement. Now I'm a cultured man and broad-minded and all that, but when you try to palm off your Ozone on these innocent people —"

"But I ain't said a word," Mel cried. "Feller is setting here quiet and minding his own business and 'fore you know it —"

"You said enough!"

Everything was good for a laugh that evening.

Chet was playing with the southern gal's knee underneath the table, Leo Trent was whispering to Dooley how he would like to change places with Andy for just this first night and "grease the skids" for him, and I was watching the smiling couple and thinking of Ruth who was sick and resting in her room several blocks from the De Soto Hotel. Around me everything was moving at a feverish tempo as if the world was aware that time was short and one must live quickly.

The wedding party broke up at twelve. Andy and Opal, still smiling, escaped to their room in the hotel amid congratulations, winks, good-humored warnings of "Don't do what I wouldn't do," and admonitions on the part of the pilot to be in good shape for tomorrow's practice mission. We were too charged to return to the base. Several of us wandered down Bull Street, Savannah's main thoroughfare. Despite my intoxication I felt the cold hostility of this city which had been our home for three months. Neither the caressing, warm inflection of their speech nor the overpowering scent of the magnolias could erase from my mind the scorn which I felt the natives of the city had for the men in uniform. At times I thought they regarded us more like an army of occupation than Americans in their final stage of training before going overseas. Were we unwelcome because many of us "from up Nawth" walked stubbornly to the rear of the buses that were marked "Colored Only"? Or were we too noisy for those who turned toward the past when Savannah had been the Pearl of the South? Perhaps we were too feverishly seeking all the things that meant life before going across. Savannah was our last stop.

"This here town," proclaimed Dooley as if he were issuing an edict, "is the asshole of the USA, including territories and possessions!"

Mel Ginn, a southerner himself, said: "You ain't just a bird-turding."

We paraded down empty Bull Street. My comrades were chattering noisily. The liquor had chased our timidity, and there weren't any officers to impose their restraint. I had a strange desire to find the little old woman who worked at the Servicemen's Club.

"What do you want her for?" Billy asked.

"I want to thank her," I said. "What's more, I want to tell her she's my choice for Miss Savannah of 1944."

"But why, pop, why?"

"It's a secret," I said. My own secret. The little wrinkled old woman never smiled at me. She did not even know my name, but every time I entered the Club she invariably said to me, "Good evening, son." It was the friendliest thing I heard in Savannah. And now I had to seek her out and thank her, before —

"Shshsh," Cosmo said, putting a finger to his pursed lips. "Let's not make so much noise, men. The civilians are sleeping." And he roared with laughter.

"f— — the civilians," Dooley said, acting the fierce warrior already. "What they ever do for the war?"

"Civilians don't do a thing 'xepting make money!" Mel proclaimed. "I heard the fellas working down at the shipyard make four dollars an hour."

"Still I wish I was a civilian," Billy Poat said. He towered above the rest of us. His bow legs and little feet made him look like a cowboy.

"Come to think of it," Leo screamed, "you're all a bunch of civilians on detached service with the air force."

"Well, doc, they can detach me altogether," Cosmo giggled.

Dooley roared with delight at Mouse's wit and bear-hugged him. "That Mouse! He's quick as a marble and twice as sharp."

Cosmo put up his hands and made like a machine gun. "Rat-tat-tat. I'm giving it short bursts, guys. Look at those Nazi planes go down in the drink."

"Roger-dodger. Keep your sights on him!"

"Got him!" Cosmo yelled.

"He's a killer!" Dooley exclaimed. "Look at that little peckerhead mowing down them enemy planes. He's a regular killer."

"That's me, doc. Killer Cosmo they call me in Cleveland."

"With a ball gunner like that we can't lose. Look out, Adolf, here we come!"

"Ain't this the craziest bunch o' bastards you ever did see!" Mel cried wonderingly at the empty street.

"Wait till we get to Italy!" Cosmo said.

"How you know we going to Italy?" Mel inquired. "I hear we's going to India, China, Burma, North Africa, England, and Alaska. Every day I hear rumors we's going some other place."

"We're going to Italy," Mouse said. The few drinks gave him assurance. A cherubic smile played on his lips. He looked like a little scarecrow dressed in a soldier's uniform with a PFC stripe and the silver wings of a gunner. He looked like a child dressed to play the part of a warrior in a school drama. "I know we're going to Italy," he said mysteriously. "Wait till we get there, doc! We'll have some fun! I know. My folks come from Italy. That's where you get real wine and everybody sings."

"What about nookie?" Trent asked. "Your old dad isn't going across to fight no wars unless there are babes around."

"I guess there'll be plenty of that for you hounds," Cosmo said with the generosity of a host who cannot refuse even the most outlandish requests of his guests. "Prettiest women in the world are in Italy," he said proudly.

"Good deal!" Mel cried, forgetting about his wife in Texas whom he had recently visited on a three-day pass.

"Whoopee!" Dooley exclaimed. "Italy, here I come!"

"Off we go into the wild blue yonder, flying high . . ."

"Three cheers for Mouse!"

"From now on he's Super-Mouse!" Dooley said with finality.

All this happened so very, very long ago.

"It almost seems like it never happened," Andy said. He listened to the sound track of the film, a feminine voice sounding canned and distant. "What scares me to death is that I'll never see her again." He looked up, smiling feebly, ashamed of having spilled his innermost thoughts.

"Men finish missions every day," I said.

"But many don't," Andy said quickly. "What about those that don't? Like Cosmo, for instance. For a long time I really believed nothing would happen to us. I was the most hurt guy in the world when *Flying Foxhole* got shot up so badly on our first mission. When men got killed on other crews or when crews went down, I said tough luck, wasn't in the cards for them, but we'll make it. But when Cosmo got it, well . . . I guess when you're twenty-three and just married, you feel nothing's ever going to happen to you. It'll happen to the other fellow, but not you. But often the other fellow *is* you. Do you understand what I mean?"

"You feel that way even when you're almost thirty-five," I said. "The only way to keep going is to think always: it won't happen to me. It'll only happen to the other fellow. But if it does happen, let it happen suddenly. Don't want to be a hero on crutches or an eyeless hero."

"If I had only had a little fun, I'd say okay, give it the works. But I haven't lived at all. And I'm not reconciled with dying. Tell me, Ben, are you?" He seized my arm and pressed it.

"I don't know," I said, confused. "There's a war going on inside me all the time. You tear yourself to shreds because you're a coward and always scared; because you hate war and violence. I've never had a fistfight in my whole life. Each morning before going up I say to myself: it's not important what'll happen to you. You're a grain of sand, life is short anyway, you'll have to die sooner or later, might as well die a hero. I don't think it's quite as difficult to die when almost the entire world approves of you —"

"Maybe if I were your age," Andy interrupted, "and had had a little bit of fun, I wouldn't mind facing this other thing."

I wanted to laugh, then checked myself and said, "People don't want to die at any age." I was amused, then suddenly I felt very old. "I've been mulling this over in my mind," I said, thinking out loud, trying to straighten out in my own mind the contradictory thoughts. "I've been thinking: it isn't fair for a kid like Cosmo to be killed and an old guy like me spared. After all, I've been around almost thirty-five years, had the good with the bad. But then, but then this other thing comes up. The more you learn of living, the more you like it. It took me so many years to get set in a country, in a home, to sink roots. Went through a hell of a lot of bother —"

"But you got something to believe in," Andy cut in. "If only I had something to believe in. Oh, I know we have to fight the war. Hitler attacked us and nobody can take a swing at the US and get away with it. We're a fighting nation. Never lost a war yet, and by God, we aren't going to lose this one. You know I'm for a fight to the finish, Ben," he said pleadingly, moving his bomb-rack seat nearer the cot until we were almost touching knees. "But my heart isn't in it. What the hell is this war all about, anyway?" He grinned sheepishly, guiltily as if he were ashamed of the blasphemous thoughts that were being revealed for the first time. "Is it worth it for what happened to Cosmo? Look at it! Look at it!" he shouted heatedly, forgetting his shame, "only a handful of us fighting while the rest of them are looking out for Number One. Why should I get shot at with the rest of the world goofing off? I didn't even spend a full week with Opal." Andy picked up a pebble and tossed it at Dick's locker. "Let me put it to you this way," he said. "Hitler never bothered me in Kansas City. I know it's not patriotic to say it and I'm a coward and all that, but if I'd played my cards right I could have stayed in defense work instead of volunteering for cadets. I know you feel different," he added quickly. "Hitler killed a lot of — your people."

I shook my head vehemently and heard myself cry, "That's not fair, that's not fair, Andy." I resented the insinuation, unintentional though it was, which put the burden of the war upon me. "That was not the primary factor," I said, trying to articulate the thoughts for myself as well as for Andy. There were many things that needed saying because you were on the verge of exploding by keeping them to yourself. But how do you tell a man that you hate fascism? How do you personalize such things as crematoria, concentration camps, book burnings, thought control? How do you tell a man that knowing all this, your guilt would have been enormous if you had not gone to war? I was a round-shouldered kid when I came to America. I was afraid to raise my eyes from the ground. When I heard that in America Jews could become policemen, and even judges, I could not get over it.

Would Andy laugh at me if I told him I was in this war because I wanted to keep America free? I wanted to tell him I was in it not only because I was *against* Hitler; I was also *for* something. I was convinced that after we had won it, life would be better for all. People would get along better; not only Missourians and Illinoisans, but Italians and Americans too. . . .

But how do you tell these things to a frightened man, a man facing death? I was afraid Andy would laugh at me. Americans had an ingrained suspicion of words, any words smacking of patriotism.

Andy sat silent for a while, contemplating the pebbles on the tent floor. "Oh, I'll fly my missions," he said. "I'm no better or no worse than anybody else. I certainly wouldn't pull a stunt like Bowles pulled yesterday, shooting off his toe and claiming it was an accident. I wouldn't

do a thing like that, nobody in our crew would." He regarded me searchingly to see whether I believed him. He got up and went to sit on his cot.
"Oh, I don't know," the navigator sighed. "It's all mixed up in my mind.
In one way I feel I'm a sucker for being in this. In another way I feel useless. I'm supposed to be a navigator. The army spent a fortune to train
me. But do I navigate? I'm just a passenger in the ship, while the lead
navigator does all the work. You men could fly without me. It wouldn't
be so bad if I had a gun to fire. You don't know what it means to be shot
at and not shoot back. You're helpless, useless. You go crazy. If I could
only keep busy up in the air — maybe I wouldn't have the time to worry
so much about death. . . ." He slapped his thighs savagely and stood up
and walked to the cone-shaped entrance of the tent. "I don't know what
to think. I've never been so mixed up and so scared in my life. . . ."

21

AT BREAKFAST, Dooley started a
row with one of the cooks. Corporal Kingston was snoozing in the
corner of the mess hall when we came in. In front of him were the
large metal pots with greenish powdered eggs, thick, greasy bacon,
cold, toasted Italian bread, and muddy coffee. Dooley looked at the
mildew-colored eggs and shouted, "What the hell kind of chow they
giving you? They expect you to eat this s— — and fight a war!"

The cook opened his sleepy, red-rimmed eyes and regarded
Dooley quizzically. "I'm surprised at you, Sarge," he said mildly. "You
talk like you wuz new here."

"I'm fed up with this crap!" our engineer cried. "My buddy got
killed fighting this goddamn war, while you, you bastards —" He
broke off, choked with emotion, and seized the table and held on as if
trying to arrest the fury that overwhelmed him. "What's happening to
all the food they're supposed to send here? Who's getting it?"

"Search me," Kingston replied.

The corporal's calm tone only infuriated Dooley more. "Why, you sonofabitch. If I'm gonna fight this fukken war for you, you're gonna feed me and my buddies right."

"I'm giving you what I got, Sarge."

"The hell you are! After we leave here, you and the rest of 'em in the kitchen are gonna have fried eggs. You'll eat fit to bust while we're up there getting our balls shot off."

"That's right," the cook said slowly. "And there ain't nothing you or I kin do about it."

"I can punch you right in the nose," Dooley said, pushing us out of the way. He made a lunge toward Kingston who stood up to meet him. "You can punch me awright, but that won't get you no fried eggs or butter —"

"Why, you fukken bastard!" Dooley knocked over one of the egg pots and grabbed the cook by the throat and shook him. "Where are them eggs?"

"Lemme go, lemme go —" Suddenly there were tears in Kingston's eyes. "Look in the kitchen . . . break up the joint for all I care! Set the fukken place on fire!" He freed himself from Dooley's grip and retreated several steps. "Go ahead, set it on fire," he chattered, "I'll thank ya the rest of my life. You — you think I like it the way you guys is fed?" He was suddenly looking past Dooley, looking at us. "My heart breaks every time I see you eating the stuff. I go crazy watching you. I been to Operations every day for a year begging 'em to take me outa here. Put me in a plane, I tell 'em, I'll fly. But they want me in the mess hall. What am I supposed to do?" He eyed us pleadingly. His lips were trembling. "I'll change places with any of ya any time. Most of you gunners'll go home after your fifty. But I'll stay here. Be here, rot here so long as this fukken war lasts. Go stir-crazy here, plum' loco —" He reached into his pocket and took out a cigarette and tried lighting it, but he couldn't. He threw it away and ground it up with his heavy, grease-spattered shoe.

Dooley ran into the kitchen and came back empty-handed. "Them steel cabinets is locked. Who's got the keys?"

"Top kick Sawyer," Kingston said, "and the mess sergeant, and the colonel too. They never go hungry. And neither do their *signorine* in town. If you wanna know what happens to your eggs and butter and flour and meat, the whores got 'em in Mandia, the private ones, I mean. And the black market."

Dooley ignored the cook and turned to the gunners. "What do you say we break the locks?" But the dozen or more men remained seated at the long tables. The gunners just stared at Dooley, understanding his rage. But they knew it was an impotent rage

Kingston shrugged his shoulders and got out of the way. "Look here," he said wearily. "You'll break the locks and tomorra you'll be court-martialed and busted down to a private and put in the stockade. The sun's too fukken hot to be in that open stockade. Drive you mad, like it did old Ingersoll last week. You can't fight the army. Only one thing to do: fly your missions and get 'em *finitoed* and go home. I wisht I could do that."

We dragged Dooley out of the mess hall. Outside, the hordes of dogs that seemed to increase daily, pounced eagerly on our un-touched breakfasts. Near the steaming water kettles where men washed their gear, First Sergeant Sawyer grinned and said: "How ya, men? How's things going?"

"I hear tell they's a war on," Mel said with sarcasm, "would you know?"

"Now, I wouldn't," Sawyer said, going along with the joke, "it's all news to me." His shrewd little eyes were on Dooley who stood there glaring at him with naked loathing. "What's on your mind, Sarge?" he said, somewhat uneasy.

"You're a dirty sonofabitch!" Dooley said. "I could kill a son-ofabitch like you!" Before we had a chance to seize Dooley, his fist caught the rotund Sawyer on the jaw and he lay sprawled on the peb-bled ground.

"Oh, I'll get you for this," the enraged top kick shouted after Dooley. "I'll get you."

•   •   •   •

We were in the barracks getting ready for bed when several gunners from the adjacent barracks dragged in Dooley by his arms and legs and asked where to dump him. "We found him in a ditch," one of the gunners said.

We laid him out on his cot. His face was all raw and puffed and discolored. His eyes were completely shut, with blood caked around them. His cheekbones were mounds of torn flesh. He appeared dead momentarily but suddenly he came to life with a violent burst of energy. His arms flailed out and his legs struck out and he tried to sit up. He began to roar like a madman, his mouth frothing.

"He's got the DT's," Billy said. "Let's grab him."

We jumped on him and pinned him down to the cot. I held Dooley's right arm while Billy grabbed the left one. Mel sat on one of his legs, Trent on the other. Dooley heaved and bellowed and spittle came out of his mouth. The other gunners got off their bunks and stood around the cot and watched.

I held on to the engineer's arm, not wanting to hurt him yet afraid to let go. But beyond this action of ours which curbed his violence, we didn't know what to do. We were helpless. We held him in silence, hoping he would be calmed eventually. I looked away from Dooley's face because it was smashed to the point of being repulsive. Curiously, I was not sorry for him — I had always resented his aggressiveness and streaks of violence. The heartbreaking thing was that a boy of twenty-two was shrieking madly, piercingly, threshing about helplessly while his comrades stood about looking resigned to suffering, like old people.

"He musta got drunk and tangled with some orderly-room commandos," one gunner said.

"It was Sawyer," Trent said, "with a bunch of his goons. Dooley let him have it this morning."

A torrent of oaths descended on Sawyer, the orderly room, and all men who did not fly planes. The oaths brought us all closer together and gave momentary relief and satisfaction, like breaking the window of an enemy; they made the youngest among us feel grown up and strong; they belied our impotence and gave us a heady feeling that we were fighting back, whereas there was little we could do or would do. But Billy tried it, simulating a husky voice, "I'll take my pistol and go down there and shoot those chicken-livered bastards full of holes. Who'll go with me? When I finish with 'em they won't tangle with no gunners again. Take my word."

Billy didn't go. Dooley threshed about until he was exhausted and his roars were replaced by abject pleas. "I want my buddies," he whispered through his blood-caked lips. "Where's my buddies?"

Mel said: "Here I am, Dooley. It's me, your old buddy, Ginn. And here's Billy and Trent and Ben. All your buddies is here."

"I want Cosmo —"

"Cosmo's gone," Mel said.

"Cosmo —" Dooley moaned.

"You wanna sleep," Mel said, bending over and speaking into Dooley's ear. "Your buddies is all here and we're gonna stay right here till you go to sleep. Go to sleep, Dooley," he whispered like a mother rocking a child to sleep. "Your buddies want you to go to sleep."

"My buddies." Dooley wept, tears coming through the bloody slits of his eyes. "I got the best buddies in the world. They'll never leave me." His voice came from a distance. "Never leave me —"

"That's right," Trent said, bending over the engineer. "We'll never leave you."

We stood over him until he fell asleep.

22

Betty lou, one of the ships that had come over with us from the States, ditched in the sea coming back from the Regensburg raid. When the ten bodies were recovered they all looked like a lot of shattered bone. Fortunately the dog tags were found, so the bone was taken to Bari to be put away. We all traveled to the cemetery. I felt I'd been there so many times. Cosmo's grave was still unmarked.

· · · ·

Ten men who had flown their missions without a scratch and *finitoed* them, hopped a plane for Naples where they were to catch a ship for the Zone of the Interior. The B-24 crashed on takeoff, exploded, and the medics who searched the runway after the smoke had cleared away couldn't even find dog tags. So there was no funeral.

·   ·   ·   ·

Vern Matchek and his crew didn't return from the Brux raid. Somebody said nine chutes were seen over the flak-covered target. In his barracks, 227th Squadron, the men were helping themselves to boots, shirts, etc. Vern's girl was staring at me through the portrait. I wanted to take the picture with me because it would be thrown away after it gathered dust on the shelf. The worst part was the new man taking Vern's cot wouldn't even know who Dorothy was. Vern had a rubbery face, imitated Red Skelton, played the guitar, and sang: "I got a gal, she lives on a hill, she won't do it, but her sister will. . . ." He used to say his ambition upon returning to the States was to walk into a Croatian bakery in Scranton and order a loaf of fresh rye bread.

Danny Smith didn't come back from the same raid. He was nineteen, with apple cheeks. He had roomed with me at Tyndall Field in gunnery school. One week before graduation from school, Danny tried to form a No Swearing Club because how would it look if he sat around the dinner table on his furlough and forgetting himself, said: "Ma, pass me the fukken butter, please"?

·   ·   ·   ·

The British intelligence officer revealed in his talk in the War Room that ten per cent of American flyers shot down by the enemy gave information voluntarily, even before they were interrogated. This, he said, was an indication of terribly low morale among Americans. (No wonder Axis Sally knew so much about our plans!) Morale? There was no such thing. The men were fighting this thing on sheer guts.

·   ·   ·   ·

A poem entitled *Italy* which someone posted in the latrine:

> *Everyone's heard of Italy,*
> *A land across the sea,*
> *Famous for its sunshine,*
> *And here and there a flea.*
>
> *That is what they told us,*
> *Before we landed here,*

But what we found waiting,
We'll never forget, I fear.

Poor and dirty people,
Goats and sheep and pigs,
Mud up to your ankles,
Mules and two-wheeled gigs.

It rains the whole damned winter,
It's hot as hell in June,
The only thing that's like the States,
Is the same old golden moon.

The flies breed by the billions,
And ruin all your grub,
The whole damned place is lousy,
My kingdom for a tub.

Let's get this damn war over,
For that we'll fight like hell,
The Huns can have this country,
And all the wops as well.

Then someone write a hist'ry,
And this time let's be frank,
Not cover it with glory,
It stinks, it stunk, it stank.

On the squadron bulletin board I saw the following orders: Staff Sergeant Elmer Fritch "has been reduced to the rank of private for being apprehended in a House of Prostitution in Lecce without his identification tags."

.   .   .   .

Russ came in drunk late at night when everybody was asleep. "I'll pay six and a half dollars for a can of beer," he said, "and throw in my flying glasses too. Who'll sell me a can of beer?" He flew in the morning.

Nagoobian came in late, also drunk, shouting loudly: "Who wants a shalmon shandwich?"

Sandy came in drunk, made a hell of a racket, woke up Dooley and started pouring water on him. Dooley flew off his cot, grabbed Sandy's cot, broke it, tore the mosquito netting, and peace, unquiet peace, reigned.

•   •   •   •

There was a rumor that Axis Sally gave birth to an illegitimate child in Florence.

•   •   •   •

I read in a stateside paper that American GIs were so terribly spoiled by good army chow, their mothers and wives would have to look to their laurels when the boys came home. Whereupon I went to the mess hall and had the following: beef hash, potatoes, spaghetti, beans, bread and pudding (starched).

23

Our box, led by Pennington, came off Ploesti all shot up and reeling, fleeing like a bunch of frightened geese. In the distance, sitting off the target, ME-109s were lobbing twenty millimeter shells at us, and several JU-88s fired rockets. Then our escort came over, P-38s and P-51s, driving away the Jerry fighters, and I was beginning to hope the worst for the day was over. But we weren't twenty minutes off the target when Big Wheel noticed a lone Liberator flying about five thousand feet below us. The bomber was obviously straggling on its way back from the target, abandoned by its formation. The straggler had one feathered prop and with our field glasses Andy identified it as belonging to one of the groups flying out of Foggia in the north. "I'll go down and fly formation with that fellow below," our pilot said casually. He called the deputy lead, instructed him to take over squadron lead, and our ship peeled off and started losing altitude.

It dawned on us slowly what Pennington had done. The first one to react was the copilot. "Albert, what the hell are you doing?" Chet screamed into the interphone.

"I'm going to escort him back home," Big Wheel said in an even tone of voice, as if his action were of the most ordinary kind.

"Have you gone crazy?" the copilot demanded. "Whoever heard of one bomber leaving formation to escort another? There are fighters in the area for this kind of work."

"But the fighters haven't come down," Pennington said calmly, "and I can't let this fellow go home alone. He needs help."

"But what help can a clumsy old bomber give that fellow?" Chet insisted. "If the Jerries hit us, two bombers will be lost instead of one."

"Shut up," Pennington said impatiently as if he were through explaining and now it mattered no longer what anybody thought.

"I won't shut up," Kowalski retorted.

"And neither will I," Dick Martin said from the nose section of the ship, where he was covering up the bomb sight before returning to the flight deck. "You have no goddamn right to do this," the bombardier said. "You're not flying a single seater yet. This is no goddamn P-51!"

"Shut up."

"You make me shut up!" Dick cried. "Who the hell do you think you are? Get the hell back in formation."

"The next bastard that opens his mouth —" The pilot did not finish. The voices poured in on the interphone like a torrent. We all shouted our protest at the quixotic act which put our lives in jeopardy beyond any need. Pennington tried to reason with us: "This fellow is in trouble," he said. "That's why I'm going down to help him."

"*You're* going down!" Dooley shouted. "If you went down yourself, I wouldn't give a damn. Nor would anybody else. But there are nine other men in this ship with you."

"You're a bunch of frightened namby-pambies," the pilot said, bringing our ship down to the straggler's altitude and moving into position off his right wing as if he were flying in the Number Two spot.

"I'm going to fly right here in this position till we get home," he said with finality.

"Be a goddamn hero!" Dick Martin cried in disgust. "Fight the war yourself. Tomorrow you can find yourself a new bombardier."

"Bombardiers are a dime a dozen," the pilot retorted. "Besides, all *you've* been hitting lately is hospitals, old people's homes, houses of prostitution, and children's schools. And while we're at it," he went on, "if anybody else doesn't like the way I fly my ship, they too can quit!"

"You can get yourself a new engineer right *now*," Dooley declared. "I'm coming right down from my turret. If the enemy fighters come over, I'm sure you'll take care of 'em all by yourself."

Dooley came down from the upper turret. Trent quit his gun and so did Billy. Charley Couch, our ball gunner, came up from his belly turret shaking his head, mumbling, "I don't like this. I don't like it a-tall!"

"I'll fly this thing myself," Pennington said without acrimony or threats of court-martial. His calmness infuriated me and I finally quit my guns and lay down in the waist section with the others and smoked. But I was too enraged to lie still. Rage took the place of fear and I was prepared to die rather than be a party to Big Wheel's insane scheme. And yet, his scheme was not so insane. He was helping a straggling ship abandoned by its own group. But he was acting out a hero role, ignoring the rest of his men, even denying the rest of us a share in what he was doing. We had not even been consulted. He was attempting to make an escort plane out of a clumsy bomber whose sole work it was to drop bombs and hurry back. It was as if he decided to do escort work in whatever was available to him — since the air force refused to give him a P-51. And so he made a Mustang out of a B-24. The fact that we were along was a secondary matter. It always had been a secondary matter with him. He had never taken us into his confidence. He had made all the decisions in flight. But up until today our resentment had been tempered by the knowledge that he was "the best pilot in the business." We had overlooked the insults he leveled at Kowalski, his shortness of temper with members of the crew, his scorn for the opinions of others and his unbearable sullenness since Cosmo's death. He was fighting a good war, and that mattered. And he was flying us toward the fifty mission mark, and that too mattered.

Although my heated-suit plug was connected, I suddenly realized I was freezing. I was cold and trembling. My fear was transferred to another plane of thought. The realization that Pennington no longer held our trust, that this was the end of our association, made me grow numb with insecurity. This feeling was like the one I had had when I left my father's house, after years of arguments, and made the final break. And now, too, I felt the alarm and the insecurity because I knew this was the blow that shattered the family, removing its head. None of us wanted to lose Big Wheel, for all his harshness and recalcitrance and illusions of grandeur. Over and above the fact that he was already reputed to be one of the best pilots in the squadron and made first lieutenant, he was, after all, part of us if only for all we'd experienced together. We took a personal pride in his love for flying and boasted about his prowess in the air like children praising their father. We all had implicit faith in his flying — but not in him. He wanted to fight the war on his own terms. He did not attempt to escape his responsibility in the war, but he made no secret of his displeasure at having to fly with us. But Big Wheel had built up a legend of indestructibility and we had seized upon that legend and nurtured it as Mel nurtured his good-luck socks.

When we returned to home base, all of us, with the exception of Kowalski, went to Squadron Operations and raised a fuss. I expected disciplinary action for Big Wheel, hoping Captain Hall would give him a dressing down. Instead, he promptly told us we would have a new pilot. Pennington was removed from our crew.

24

SECOND Lieutenant George "Casey Jones" Petersen, our new pilot, had fifteen missions to his credit. He had been checked out as First Pilot only recently, a fact which sent goose pimples down our flesh. We had an innate fear of ex-copilots. A copilot was considered as superfluous in a plane as an appendix in the body. He was an object that took up room needlessly, used up precious oxygen, got liquor rations, and generally got in the way. A copilot, it was said, was one who had not washed out of pilot training school. He was the stepchild of the air force, according to the men flying heavy bombers. Lieutenant Petersen was a copilot. Now he was our pilot, replacing Pennington.

. . . .

On the run to La Spezia, we all watched the new pilot's actions like a bunch of wary hawks. Dooley hung around the flight deck ready to pounce on the stick if Petersen made any errors. Andy and Dick were also close by to be on hand in the event of an emergency, although their knowledge of the instrument panel was no greater than Dooley's. Although Kowalski flew in the copilot's seat, he was too frightened to be of any assistance.

Each one of us, having reluctantly taken our stations, remained on the alert, noting the new pilot's flying habits. His sloppy takeoff so upset Billy, our radio operator, that he strapped on his chute and threatened to go out the waist window. When he turned in to join the formation we looked at one another terror-stricken. In our minds we were making comparisons between Petersen and Big Wheel. Pennington never flew a plane full throttle unless it was an emergency. We noted right away that the new pilot *used* a plane, while for Big Wheel flying was an expression of freedom from the chains that confine most humans to earth.

"Look at the sonofabitch burning sky!" Trent said to the rest of us assembled in the waist section. He did not use the mike button and our conversation did not go over the wires.

"Drives this thing just like he used to drive a truck back in Minnesota. That's what he did for a living —"

"My aching, busted GI back," Poat moaned, crowding near the open waist window as if he planned to go out if something went wrong.

"And did ya see that railroad fireman's uniform he had on?" Charley Couch asked. "His old man's a fireman on the Chicago-Northwestern, sent it to him."

"And *this* hot pilot plans to go into commercial flying after the war!" Leo said sarcastically. "My poor mother has never had a better opportunity to collect that ten thousand insurance than she has right now."

"If we get back from this one," Billy said in his threatening tone of voice, "I'm going to the flight surgeon and ask him to get that transfer for me. Either they put me in the infantry or I'm through."

"We shouldn't of went to Squadron Operations about Big Wheel," Dooley said regretfully. "For all his faults, Big Wheel —"

Each one of us was being eaten up by the qualms caused by our break with Pennington. Because the break had been the result of a decision we ourselves had made, the qualms were even worse. In the army a man could seldom put the blame on himself for whatever went wrong because he was never asked to make his own decisions. But that morning, coming off La Spezia, we blamed ourselves. The choice had been given us and we lost out.

We kept the windows open and strapped on our chutes although there had been no flak over the target and the formations were coming back intact. Hardly anyone spoke over the interphone so gloomy were we and so sorry for ourselves. Then, suddenly, we heard a friendly voice, the pilot's voice, husky and matching his big body: "'What's the matter with this here outfit?" he said laughingly, "doesn't anybody ever talk? Wake up, you guys. Let's have some chatter. Talk!"

Charley Couch, who had had no ties with Pennington and was not subject to our nostalgia, was the first to take up Casey Jones. "I'll tell ya a story," he said with a sing-song drawl, "tell ya about myself. I'm just sitting in this here plane trying to figger out what I'm doing here. And I come to the conclusion it's all my wife's fault."

"And what's the matter with your wife?" Casey Jones said, laughing.

"It's what's wrong with me," Charley said. "I was in an automobile accident when I asked her to marry me. I guess I thought I was dying and that's why I asked her. She grabbed — pronto. So she married me and my life's been so miserable, I welcomed the chance of becoming a gunner. That's how come I'm twenty thousand feet over nothing in particular freezing my *cojones* off —" Suddenly he began to cackle like an old man. "I'm a sinful ole bastard, ain't I? But I come from a good fam'ly."

"Me," Casey Jones said, "I like it up here. I never had it so good. Look at me! An officer with shiny bars. Rugged, ain't it? I'm getting

paid while I'm learning a trade too! The gov'ment is practically subsi-
dizing me —"

"Well, now, Lieutenant," Charley started.

"Cut out the 'lieutenant' stuff," the pilot said, "we're all buddies
up here. Call me George or Casey Jones or Petersen or Big Swede if
you like."

"Okay, Lieutenant," Charley said cautiously.

The talk flowed freely between those two and momentarily I felt that
two strangers were usurping the right of *our* crew, taking over our ship.

"After the war's over," the pilot said, "I'm going into commercial
aviation."

"Let me tell you something about Snuffy's Bar and Grill that's
right down below us," Dick Martin said.

The ice was broken. The constraint was gone. Dooley came back
to the waist section and said to us off the interphone: "He don't fly so
bad. I kinda like him."

"Looks like a good Jo to me," Trent said.

Maybe, I thought to myself, maybe the change was for the better.

•   •   •   •

In the evening Casey Jones came to our barracks and brought us his
liquor rations. Then he sat down to play pinochle with Dooley, Trent
and Ginn. "How come you don't hang around BOQ?" Trent asked.

"I don't like officers," the pilot said, dealing out the cards. "They
put on too many airs. What a difference a pair of gold bars make with
these Ninety-Day Wonders! They think they're something extra-
special. I'm a guy that worked for a living."

The gunners all roared with delight.

"This caste system pisses me off no end anyway," Petersen continued. "But wait! Wait till these officers get back home to their old
jobs as office boys and elevator boys. They'll know what rugged is. I
never had it so good, and I admit it."

"Boy, you got *some* pilot!" one of the gunners said to me with envy
in his voice as we were both taking a shower before going to bed.

"Best goddamn pilot in the business," I said.

25

THE TRANSPLANTING of a crew
was like a surgical operation. Ours seemed like a successful operation, although the changes wrought by it were painful, of course. We
now had a new copilot also. Casey Jones insisted on a new copilot
after that mission to La Spezia. "Kowalski was too scared," the pilot
told us afterwards. "He shouldn't be in no combat plane." And as if to
allay our suspicions that he was thinking of breaking up our crew, or
might be personally ill-disposed toward Chet, Petersen added, "If I
didn't have a crew to worry about I'd fly with Kowalski. But I have to
consider the rest of you guys."

We agreed with him.

Kowalski was removed from our crew. He did not protest. With
Pennington gone from his side there seemed little fight left in him.
He had been so completely dependent on Big Wheel, he would trust
no other pilot. He accepted his removal from the crew without a
whimper. He might have requested this removal himself, but Casey
Jones saved him the embarrassing task.

Chet was cut adrift.

He remained with the rest of the officers in the tent. But he had
no crew, and I heard at Squadron Operations that no pilot would fly
with him.

There must have been a cold loneliness, being cut adrift like that
in the army.

Kowalski's removal from our crew left no void, as there had been
in the case of Cosmo. If there was any grief among us it was the
feeling of self-pity that comes with any violent change in one's
mode of living. Of the ten in our original crew, only seven were still
together.

The romantic thoughts of a dream crew — which most of us had and only Andy had voiced — were gone, as was the compact we swore to back in Georgia that we would die one for all and all for one. One day after Pennington had been separated from our crew, he became a stranger. He ceased being of interest to us, and though we exchanged greetings at Operations, there was little between us, except the past. Lieutenant Chester Kowalski ceased being part of our life as soon as he was removed from our crew. Ours was a little universe revolving in its narrow orbit, the crew. Those who were outside the crew and its experiences were outside our world and concerned us little. From now on what happened to the man who wore a crazy railroad-fireman's uniform on missions and drove a plane as if it were a truck was of interest to us. And that held for Oscar Schiller, our new copilot who was almost bald at twenty-six and had a grandmother living in Vienna. Every time the air force bombed Vienna, Oscar suffered un-told agonies. And we, though we hated Vienna, suffered with him.

26

WHEN THE annals of World War II are written, and all the songs have been sung about the terrors of Bougainville and Omaha Beach, about Leyte and Cassino, about Stalingrad and Aachen, I plead for one song about Vienna. The Vienna that Americans knew from the sky, not the Vienna of the Strauss waltz memories and *Gemütlichkeit*. For those who flew heavies out of Italy, Vienna was synonymous with Death. The name Vienna was so hated, flyers changed the name of the C ration Vienna sausages to "Vy-ennas."

The briefing officer who looked like a misplaced geography teacher, said in part: ". . . and if you get shot down over the city of Vienna proper, take the Number 132 trolley and go to the Ukrainian Displaced Persons Camp where they will hide you."

"Well, now, sir," a gunner said, "usually a trolley line goes in two directions. This camp, is it north, south, east, or maybe west?"

"You'll inquire when you get down there," the lieutenant said without batting an eyelash.

There were snickers in the crowd. Imagine: an American flyer, dressed in his bulky winter flying clothes, carrying his dagger and pistol, standing in the middle of Vienna, unmolested by the civilians whom he has just got through bombing, asking directions to a Displaced Persons Camp!

"Sir," the gunner continued, and you couldn't tell whether he was new, being funny, or just indifferent to his approaching doom, "supposing you get on the right trolley, what'll a fella use for carfare? You can't yank out a ten-dollar bill from your Money Kit and ask the conductor to change it, can you?"

The briefing officer scratched the round bald spot on his head and said: "It *does* sound complicated, doesn't it? Best thing I can advise you is *not* to get shot down over Vienna."

But Vienna had four hundred heavy guns firing at you.

"Not all at once," the briefing officer, who had never seen flak fired except on a screen, said. "The guns will not come to bear on you all at once. As you come off the IP onto the target, 200 guns will pick you up —"

And set you down.

Vienna fired the versatile German 88 millimeter guns at you. The versatility of the 88s consisted in their ability to kill you in a horizontal or vertical position. In Vienna the black death muzzles were turned toward the sky. They were controlled by radar. Radar shot impulses at your formation, calculated the distance when the impulse bounced back, communicated the findings to the control tower, then hell broke loose. Scientifically.

You clutched at your Bible, your good-luck socks, your memory of a caul, or a WAC cap that a girl gave you at Mitchel field. You cried, Mama, O God, save me, save me, but hell was loose from its moorings. Calculated. Allowances made for wind drift, muzzle velocity, and shell deflection. Your brain was a frozen, jellied mass with only one message coming through feebly: the end, the end, this is the end.

Over Vienna a man sat next to death for twenty minutes. He was riding along Death Boulevard and there was no sidestepping or turning aside or turning back. For the route had been carefully plotted for him over at air force headquarters in Bari by the men on Air Staff who got paid for doing that kind of work. They, the strategists, had calculated the latitude and longitude and all the sundry factors leading to the target and chose, after weighty deliberation, the unswerving path. There could be no deviations! The lead navigator (a captain, at least) was there to make sure there were no deviations. And if, by some accident, the formation drifted off Destruction Path, or Flak Alley, or Death Boulevard, the lead navigator called the colonel (a West Pointer who never liked deviations) and said: "Sir, give me a correction of three degrees to the right, please." The colonel replied, "Roger," and made the correction. Scientific. A man had been sent through navigator school, had been commissioned, had cost the United States ten thousand dollars in training, and all for the purpose of leading a formation of American bombers (ten men in each bomber) down a path where the enemy shot the hell out of them. And if the lead navigator snafued, there were the box leaders, and after them, the navigator in each ship.

The enemy knew our course hours before we arrived. Our course would be over their factories or railroads or installations. This was not a matter of guesswork. This was not a matter of sidestepping or bobbing and weaving, of hitting the dirt, of stopping short, of retreating. A B-24 does not fly backward. There was something inevitable, irrevocable about a plotted course. The course led over the object to be bombed. The antiaircraft guns were lined up accordingly. There wasn't any guesswork for either side. No element of surprise.

"Oh, my aching — Look at that black stuff coming up."

Vienna.

The British scoffed and said it couldn't be done. Daylight bombing, they said, would be a failure. Couldn't sustain the losses as a result of enemy antiaircraft action. Too severe.

They were telling us!

Vienna was never Diversionary, nor was it ever Secondary. It was not a Target of Opportunity. Vienna was always Primary, A for Able, Maximum Effort Target. Strategic. The city was one of Hitler's main arsenals. There were aircraft plants around Vienna, ball-bearing factories, oil refineries, underground installations. The railroads serviced the East Front and the Balkan Front. Vienna had a very important industrial suburb: Wiener Neustadt. Remember?

Vienna was very strategic. And ours was a Strategic Air Force.
You could get killed over Vienna.

•   •   •   •

Casey Jones brought the ship off the target with a sharp turn to the
right. The Number Four engine was smoking from a direct hit. We
were losing gas.

"We'll catch up with the formation," the pilot said to Dooley who
was on his guns in the top turret, "then you'll come down and feather
Number Four and transfer the gas to the good engines."

We did not count the holes in the ship. There were a hundred of
those, but that didn't matter because a checkup revealed that nobody
had been hurt. We were worried about the dead engine, which
would slow us down. But we anticipated no undue difficulties because our escort of Lightnings and Mustangs picked us up off the
target to fly us home.

"You know something," Martin said, "I think we missed the target."

"Who gives a s— — ?" Petersen said.

Over Lake Baloton, in Hungary, Dooley started transferring the
gas. When he'd drained Number Four, the engineer went to work
transferring the remaining gas from the auxiliary tanks, the Tokios.
His pumps indicated that the auxiliaries were all drained. But Dooley
didn't know, at the time, that you could not trust the pumps on a B-24.
He computed his gas at six hundred gallons, all that was left of the
twenty-seven thousand gallons we'd started out with on the mission.

"Are you sure?" Casey Jones asked, a note of concern in his voice.

"That's what the pumps say."

"We couldn't of lost that much gas," Casey Jones said. "Take another check, will you, mate?"

The panic crept over us in slow, subtle stages, like water inun-
dating an area.

The formation was streaking for home, there were wounded
aboard on many of the ships. And in order to keep up with the pace
set by the formations, the pilot was feeding the three remaining engines a rich mixture of gas and oil.

"I don't know," Casey Jones said. "Be frank with you, I don't understand what happened to our gas. There should be more of it in
those Tokios."

"Not according to my pumps," Dooley said. He wasn't sure of himself.

"In that case, fellas, it's going to be a tight squeeze," the pilot said. "We might even have to bail out over Yugo."

"Maybe we ought to fly her on auto-lean," the copilot suggested, "even if we have to leave the formation. Save gas that way."

We dropped out of formation. Chatter died in the ship. We moved as little as possible, as if hoping that inaction would nurse along our gasoline a little longer. "If Pennington were at the stick," I thought. The ship held no mystery for him. But Pennington was probably on the ground, in Italy, smiling sardonically at our dilemma. Or so it seemed to me.

Over Yugoslavia, Casey Jones called to say: "My indicator is mighty low, fellas, but I'll try the Adriatic. Take a chance. Might have to crash-land after we cross it. Unless you want to abandon ship here. What do you say? Rugged either way."

There was no response to the pilot's words. The silence indicated that the decision was being left up to him. Only one of us had been in a crash landing before — Charley Couch. He was in the waist section smoking a cigarette when the pilot's words came over the interphone. Suddenly he seized his head with his hands and started shaking it vigorously.

"Oh, God, no," he whispered. I saw his face drain of the blood and it was almost chalk white. "Not again," he whispered, rolling his head from side to side. "This time I'm afraid Mama Couch's boy ain't gonna make it. Oh, my God, my aching scrotum. I shore musta sinned awful bad." He sprang to his feet and looked about him in terror as if he'd just awakened from a frightful nightmare. Pressing on his interphone button, he screamed into the mike: "Lieutenant, I'd do anything but crash-land if I wuz you. I done it once, walked away from a ship that hit the dirt, but wasn't many that walked away with me. We gotta set her down, Lieutenant. why doncha try an' set her down?"

"We're over water now, Charley," Casey Jones replied. "But we'll fly as long as we can. Might even try and make it for home base."

The mention of home base kindled a brief hope. Momentarily I believed we would make it. We had made it before. Always there was something, but we had made it. Perhaps my caul had something to do with it after all. There were these uncomputed, incalculable, unforeseen factors in war that made the difference between life and death. How else explain the incident of the tail gunner who had been shot away from the ship and went hurtling down in his turret and yet lived to tell the story? And yet, the realization that I was placing my hope on miracles increased my anxiety. I knew that a B-24 was not built for crash landings. (The ship was built to stay on the ground.) But never having been in a crash I did not know what to fear or what to expect. The fact of the matter is, there are all kinds of crash landings. It depends on the space, the terrain, the control of the ship.

We crash-landed suddenly. Six miles from home base. The crash came with such suddenness, our flaps were down only twenty percent. There had been just enough warning from the pilot, who screamed: "DITCHING POSITIONS! HURRY! WE'RE GOING IN FOR A CRASH!"

I was sitting on the floor, leaning my back against the ditching belt, facing to the rear of the ship. Against me, Charley Couch was propped, my legs wrapped around his body, Trent sat between his legs. We were all propping our necks with our hands when the twenty-eight-ton ship telescoped into the ground on its belly. There was a deafening thud accompanied by the anguished cry of crumbling aluminum. I felt as if my insides had been pulled out of me; my eyes were sucked into the back of my head, the delicate fibers dangling, stretched, on fire with pain.

When I was able to open my eyes, I saw dust outside the open waist windows, dust rising on both sides. I listened for explosion or the sound of fire. But I saw only dust. Then I noticed Billy Poat's lean, bent figure. He rose with difficulty, gripping his middle as if he were holding on to his guts. He moved toward the waist window, leaned over it, and fell out. I heard him shout, call for help. Inside the ship, Trent was bleeding from the head, Charley Couch was moaning softly, trying to get to his feet. He finally succeeded and moved toward the waist window. He was shaking his head like he did when the pilot had made the suggestion about crash landing earlier. His store teeth were dangling, protruding out of his mouth. I saw one of his hands go up, fix his teeth by lodging them in proper place as if he were fixing his toilette before going out to meet a girl. Then he too leaned over the waist window and fell out.

I tried to move, but could not. My hands were feeling about my body for blood; there wasn't any. I could move my right foot, but not the left one. When I tried to sit up, my body would not give. It seemed nailed to the ship's belly which was dug into the hard rock.

In the front end of the ship were Casey Jones, Oscar Schiller, Andy Kyle, Dick Martin, Mel Ginn, and Dooley. I heard Dooley's voice. It was very weak. "We can't get out up front, you guys. Pilot's arms, legs broken . . . in his seat. Mel's hurt awful bad, unconscious. We're locked in, you guys. Do something. . . ."

Then I heard the chattering: Italian. And Billy Poat's voice. "In here," he said, "*mi amicos.*" I saw the heads of two Italian laborers.

"*Aspetta, aspetta,*" one of them said. I pointed toward the front of the ship where the rest of the men were entombed, but the Italians continued saying "*Aspetta, aspetta,*" and carried Trent and me out and laid us on the ground about fifty feet away from the ship. Then they ran to the front of the plane, led by Billy and Charley who were both bleeding from slight wounds about their faces. They examined the ship carefully, speaking mostly in sign language. One of the Italians took off across the road and came back with an acetylene torch.

"If there's gas in that plane," I heard Billy say, "they'll be blown to hellengone. And so will we," he added as an afterthought. But he did not move away from the plane.

"I'm for trying it!" Charley counseled. "Ain't no other way to get 'em out. By the time the field sends down the meat wagon, fellas are liable to be dead."

"Okay, *paisan,*" Billy nudged the Italian. "Drill!"

Did the two Italians realize that they were endangering their own lives by applying the torch to an *Americano* plane which was full of 100 octane, volatile, highly explosive fumes? If they did, they gave absolutely no indication of it. They seemed completely concentrated on the gun bit which was chewing away at the aluminum body of the plane. Billy and Charley were shouting to Dooley whose face appeared in the glass over the copilot's seat. The glass had not shattered. "Hold on . . . Just hold on," Billy yelled.

The two Italians changed off on the torch. Both of them were dripping sweat from the heat of the hot July sun. Both of them smiled as they worked. Their smiles reached across to us like warm handshakes. Without these two Italians, two men working on a *casa* six miles away from the airfield, without them my comrades would have perished. By the time the ambulance arrived with Doc Brown and three medics, the two strange Italians, or gooks, as we Americans called them, sawed off enough of the ship to reach the entombed men. Schiller and Andy almost made it on their own power, but Casey Jones was carried out like a sack of broken limbs, and Mel Ginn was an unconscious, bloody mess.

27

ACROSS FROM my cot lay Casey Jones Petersen in a white cast. He looked entombed in the cast, like an Egyptian mummy. His arms were broken, and where his legs had been, there were cotton-swathed stumps. Only his face showed out of the cast, and there were openings at the bottom for bodily functions. He couldn't move, nothing of him moved except his eyes. An orderly, or nurse, held the cigarette for him when he smoked. "The Doc said I'll be like a new man after one year in the cast," the pilot said to Billy, who was on the next cot. "A year won't take long." He didn't know his legs had been amputated. "Looks like you fellows might start shopping around for a new pilot. What do you think, Poatska?"

"Oh, you'll make it, Lieutenant," Billy said.

"I sure busted you guys up real bad," Petersen said. "I'm awful sorry."

"Did the best you could," Andy said. He and Schiller had walked away from the crash, suffering from shock. An MP had found them wandering on the road and returned them to the base. Every day Andy came to visit us at the hospital.

"How's Mel?" Dooley asked continually. He could hardly sit up on account of his bruised back, and his eyes were still half shut from the lacerations and cuts. He kept repeating the question in his sleep: "How's Mel?" When awake he couldn't keep his eyes off the stumps which had been Casey Jones's legs. When Dooley discovered Mel was on the Critical List with an internal hemorrhage and busted kidney, he said, "If that kid dies, it'll be on account of me. The whole thing's on account of me." He was sure now the crash had been his fault, but somehow he couldn't put his finger on it. "I f—— up some place," he muttered. He was constantly striving to get up from the cot to be nearer Mel, but the nurse forbade it. "You aren't ready for it yet," she said.

"Please, nurse, can I talk to him one minute?"

"Somebody ask for me?" Mel inquired. His eyes didn't focus any longer and he wasn't able to see, but his voice was still clear, though weak. "I don't look my best today," he would say by way of a joke, "but I'll be okay by tomorra when you come to see me, I guarantee ya that."

"Sure you will," said Mel's neighbor. He was a Negro from Engineers, with a busted arm that was in a white cast. He was able to walk around, and when the orderlies were not in the ward he offered his help cheerfully. "Anything you want?"

"Wanna write a letter to my wife, Sharon," Mel said. "I ain't wrote to her in a coon's age. Trouble is, fella —" He hesitated, looked at the colored boy without seeing him and said: "What's your name, fella?"

"Phil."

"You're my buddy, Phil, my good buddy. Trouble is, Phil, I don't know what to write half the time. Feel queer as a three-dollar bill ever' time I sit down to write. Why don't you just write and tell her I'm doing fine. Just doing dandy. I'll be much obliged to ya. . . ." He slumped in his bed as if the effort of speaking and the attempt at humor was too much for him. He looked so thin, emaciated, and his skin had the pallor of death.

The heat was unbearable. Though the rooms of this former high school turned hospital were without doors, the air stood still and heavy. Everywhere there were army cots placed so close together there was hardly any room for a patient to put his feet down on the cement floor. The severe cases, like Mel and Petersen, lay in real hospital beds. Above some of the beds were pulleys and weights and limbs dangling from them in the real stateside manner. There were about thirty men in our large room. Nurses flitted in and out, looking very busy, always looking busy and solemn and just a bit surly as if they disapproved of the goings-on. And always there was a captain from Public Relations walking forlornly among the cots with a stack of Purple Hearts and a list of names. When Dooley saw the captain for the first time he said, "When they write me up for one of them things, I don't want it. I want no part of it." The captain was about to say something, but he turned away and left the ward.

The only comic aspect in this unbearable place was Leo's shaven head. His golden hair had been cut right on top of the head where his wound was. A bandage covered the spot. Charley, in the cot next to Leo's, slept most of the time. Dick Martin hobbled about on a crutch. I, too, was promised a crutch.

⋅   ⋅   ⋅   ⋅

Pennington came to visit us in the evening. I was sorry he came and was relieved when he left. I knew it wasn't fair to blame him for our disaster. But I couldn't help feeling it was on account of his heroics that this thing had happened. I watched his face while he talked to us, but he was genuinely sorry and wanted to be helpful. Nevertheless, I hoped he would not come again.

⋅   ⋅   ⋅   ⋅

The nurse brought me the only book she found on the premises: *Salsette Discovers America*, by Jules Romains. One passage in the book fascinated me to such an extent I couldn't get over it: "Your cooks don't like to prepare sauces [said the protagonist, about America]. Now, sauce is cooking, sauce, I mean, in the broadest sense." Sauce in the broadest sense!

⋅   ⋅   ⋅   ⋅

There was no question about it: our crew was *finito*. They would send Casey Jones back to the States to be placed in a hospital somewhere near Duluth where his wife might come to see him, and hold his cigarette for him. Mel was bleeding internally and there was no way to stop that bleeding. The doctors, majors and lieutenant-colonels stood over him, consulting. But nobody could help him. Mel was bleeding to death. "Phil, where's Phil?" he chattered feverishly. "Have you wrote that letter to my wife, Phil?"

"I'm working on it —"

"That's my good buddy." The words came with difficulty now. "You're my buddy for life. After I get up —"

Billy Poat lay on his back, stiff, unmoving, staring at the dirty ceiling that had once been pink-colored. Billy stared at the ceiling with a feverish concentration as if he were entranced by the dirt and the flies scampering over it. When he looked at you, his eyes were far away, as if he were contemplating some terrible decision. Dooley hardly spoke at all. The guilt for the crash seeped slowly into him, like a poison. He was sure the crash had been his fault, although he didn't know what he had done wrong. But at the field, the crew chiefs were not long in determining the cause. They said if Dooley had advised the pilot to raise the bomber's wings alternately and drain the gas from the wing tanks, instead of relying on the faulty pumps, there would have been no crash. An investigation of the ship disclosed 200 gallons of gas in the auxiliary tanks — after the crash. But Dooley was not told about it while in the hospital. Nothing existed for him except Mel's thin moans. His own injuries did not concern him. He couldn't lie still. He couldn't sleep at night. He was forever watching Mel's bed. It was like a deathwatch. When he thought Mel needed attention he shouted for a nurse, doctor, or orderly.

·   ·   ·   ·

I had always associated hospitals with the color *white*. Hospitals were quiet, cool, drowsy places, with long, clean corridors and muted bells and effortless efficiency. Nurses and doctors and even orderlies all worked with purposeful concentration. Ruth had been in such hospitals in Chicago. I'd always loathed them because my wife spent so much time in them, but now I reflected on how restful it would be to lie in one of those quiet, cool, white rooms. And sleep. I had an insatiable need for sleep. Sleep to shut out thoughts of tomorrow and of the chaos here. I would sleep around the clock if they let me. But even in a hospital one was still in the army.

The color was khaki: the cots, the blankets. There were no sheets. The food was served on plates instead of mess kits, but it was still C ration food. Vy-ennas. The orderlies wandered about indolently in the manner of overworked PFCs and corporals who have learned in the Army that the best way to avoid doing anything was to pay no attention to the world about you. And there was the noise, constant noise. Noise and unbearable heat and somber-faced nurses, and naked, peeling walls and hard cement floors. The only note of boisterousness was supplied by the venereals who were billeted in tents out in the courtyard. There was no order in the place. There

was only chaos and confusion. It was amazing that anybody at all
ever got well there.

.   .   .   .

Through my constant half sleep I heard planes overhead. I knew they
were coming back from a raid because it was late afternoon and the
heat was suffocating and my cot was wet with perspiration. I wondered
what target they'd struck today. I wondered what day it was. It didn't really matter what day it was. I was lost in the vastness of time. Time and
events were a swift whirlpool and I was spinning on the rim of it and
there was never an end. I had been in this whirlpool all the conscious
years of my remembrance. There had been no other existence. Perhaps there had been a time once, when the hour, the day, the year was
of import, when one moved of one's own volition. But that must have
been long ago. Before the army was invented. Before merciful sleep
was invented. It was T. S. Eliot who wrote in that poem: "Good night,
ladies . . . good night, sweet ladies . . . goonight . . ." A very profound
line! When I got out of the army I would sleep forever.

.   .   .   .

I had a most alarming dream. I dreamed I shot off my big toe on the
right foot quite by accident while cleaning my pistol. My comrades took
me to the medics' *casa* where Doc Brown examined the wound and
said: "I'll give you a letter to the Adjudication Board in Bari, recom-
mending that you be grounded. You can't fight any more. It'll take that
wound some time to heal, and after it heals that stump will bother you
in altitude. Besides, you've had enough, Ben." He put his hand on my
shoulder, kindly and warmly. "You're too old to fly anyway. It was all a
fluke, letting you fly in the first place. How many missions have you
now? Thirty? That's good enough. You're a hero. Fought a good war."
My comrades nodded agreement and said: "Doc, he tried his best. Acci-
dents happen, though. He didn't mean to shoot off that toe. He's an okay
guy, Doc. Nothing phoney about pop." We all got in a jeep, and suddenly I was alone on the road to Bari. I was abreast of the big sign: AMER-
ICAN MILITARY CEMETERY. Suddenly Cosmo came out on the road and stared
at me. "Where you going, doc?" he asked. "No place," I said. I woke up.

What alarmed me was that my subconscious had gone berserk with
neat schemes of escape. So the vacillations had been there all the
time, lurking where one could not reach for them and tear them out

by the roots. The dream frightened me; in fact, it terrified me; in it I grasped too eagerly for safety, abandoning my comrades. I was ashamed, and yet it was no lie: I wished it were reality, not a dream. I was tired of endlessly fighting, trying to reconcile my fears with my beliefs, and fighting against the army. The struggle had sapped all my energies. The crash had capped it all. I was too old, too tired, too sick. . . . I wanted to go to sleep and never wake up again. I was tired of this life of conflict and violence. I almost envied Casey Jones. For him there was no more violence. He would be cared for the rest of his life.

But Petersen was a cripple! What would Casey Jones say if he were in my position? "God, you're a coward!" I lashed out at myself, "You're like putty. You must repeat this over and over to yourself: *This is the only positive thing you've ever done!* If you quit you'll never be able to live with yourself. Nor will Ruth live with you when she finds out the truth. Look, take stock, think instead of whimpering like a fool. At thirty-five a man should act grown up. Others think you're grown up. In Chicago they think you're a hero. Most of your friends are either on Limited Service in the army or overage and out of the war. You're probably the oldest gunner in Group. It's not an honor, but nothing to be ashamed of. You've flown thirty missions. Not an honor, but some people give up much earlier. And the war. Think! We're winning. The Allies are deep in France and the Russians are in Romania. You're part of it. This is your war, remember? Rekindle your anger. You must rekindle your anger. Remember, your life is like a tracer bullet; let it glow once — just once — briefly. Let it light up the sky for others to see. Don't snafu the deal, oh, brother, don't snafu the deal. Tomorrow you must get off the cot, crawl if you have to, but get out of here!"

•   •   •   •

At night Mel cried feverishly. The nurse kept coming back armed with a hypodermic needle. She had ceased counting three-hour intervals. The doctor had instructed her to give him the needle. "Might as well keep him as comfortable as possible," he had said. "The poor fellow won't last much longer."

"And when you write that letter to Sharon," Mel whispered hoarsely, his mind already wandering on the periphery of death, "I wancha to say I'm a faithful husban' to her. And if she stick by me I'm gonna make it up to her. 'Cause I don't care any for them Eyetie gals.

I guarantee ya that . . . Just put down ever'thing I say, Phil, 'cause I'm busy right now fixing to shoot down that there ME-109 —"

Dooley crept off his cot and started toward Mel's bed. The engineer's face was frozen with terror. "Mel —"

"What is it, Phil? You writing down things like I said?"

"It's your buddy, Dooley —"

"Well, you just tell her I meant to write alla time, but somehow — didn't ever get 'round to it. She'll unnerstan'. She knows I'll make it up to her. When I git back home —"

The nurse came in the ward and saw Dooley standing over Mel's bed and said: "You had no business getting off your cot, soldier. You're not well enough to —"

Dooley paid no attention to her, concentrating his stare, his whole being, on the dying man.

"Soldier, go back to your cot!"

"I gotta help him," Dooley muttered, talking to himself.

"You can't do a thing for him," said the middle-aged, sallow-faced woman who walked with a slow and tired gait and looked so out of place among the young, sturdy, swift-moving nurses. "You can't do a thing for him, boy. And you're liable to injure yourself —"

"Somebody's got to help him, you can't let him —" He seemed afraid to mention the word "die."

"We're trying to make him as comfortable as possible," the nurse said. "As for you —"

"Comfortable!" Dooley cried. "You're letting my buddy die! If my buddy dies it'll be all your fault. It'll be the army's fault! I'll hold you all responsible!" He was suddenly hysterical, hurling his own feeling of guilt at the army, transferring the guilt that had been on him like a terrible weight since the crash. "I'm warning you!" he cried, waving his arms. "I'm —"

"All right, son," she said gently.

Her words struck him like an unexpected blow. He had not looked for gentleness or even conciliation. "All right, son," spoken softly by this woman who looked like a mother, caught him off guard and he was suddenly defenseless. She had her arm around his waist, leading him back to his cot. At first he tried to shake her off but soon he gave up the struggle, and when she helped him onto his cot and raised his legs after he lay down, Dooley could stand it no longer and wept like

a little child. Only a man does not weep like a child. A man's sobs are
the sounds of anguish and despair. They come to the surface with the
difficulty of dry heaves.

The ward was silent a moment, then Mel resumed his chatter. "Tell
her when I get back home, Sharon and me is going in for ourselves.
Ain't gonna have to live with my old folks no more. Gonna get us some
cattle and start in for ourselves, like we said. I do declare, if'n there's
one thing I miss in this Eyetieland, that's seeing cattle. Sure is funny, a
land without no cattle. Now you take western Texas —" He sniggered,
amused at the thought. He coughed. He lay still for a while. I heard the
roar of engines, away in the distant sky. Dooley's cot creaked. He sat up.
We were all sitting up, our eyes glued on Mel's bed, listening to the last
thin fibers of his voice. "I can't breathe so good . . . must be my oxygen
hose working loose . . . Damn . . . Nose gunner to bombardier, nose to
bombardier, over; open my turret door and check my hose, I can't
breathe. . . ." He coughed. "Oh, God . . . oh, God, oh, God —"

He died before morning.

28

A WEEK AFTER Mel's funeral we
were given three days at the Santa Casada Rest Camp, seventy-five
miles from roaring engines and war. The sunlit majesty of this place,
the peace and serenity frightened me at first. It was as if we were given
a respite in heaven only to be returned to hell eventually. The change
had been too sudden, both in scenery and in mind. From the flatlands of Mandia we were catapulted into a mountainous region that
looked down upon the pure blue Adriatic, with Albania visible across
the sea, though it was forty miles away.

Santa Casada was a white village hugging the coast tenderly like
a lover. A summer resort which had been a playground for wealthy

fascists, it was built on rock tiers, all of them turned toward the sea and toward the sun. The sun set the white dwellings afire during the afternoon hours, and the village rested, sleeping in intoxicating indolence. And the war was so far away! In the evening Santa Casada came alive with a different kind of splendor. The people poured out into the street facing the sea, Yugoslav refugees, American military personnel, Italian generals in their seedy gray uniforms that always needed pressing and were always bedecked with many rows of faded ribbons. The generals walked gloomily, their eyes hugging the ground. The two American Red Cross girls, pert, swift, proud, usually took their constitutional along the promenade, and so did the Italian *signorine* who started circulating among the men in the hotels soon after nightfall. And topping Santa Casada were the two great hotels that stood on the highest hill and looked down on this world of peace. In the larger of the two castles the officers resided. We were in the less sumptuous one.

At first, upon our arrival, after Trent, Dooley, Couch, and I were shown our room, we scattered in all directions to see the wonders of the place. I felt like someone who had been chained to a bed for a long time, and now, though still weak, was reaffirming life, tasting it anew and finding it strong, like wine. I felt my legs grow stronger as I ran about the great palace, touching the wonderful flush toilets, tile sinks, fingering the white tablecloths in the dining hall and listening to the two musicians, fiddler and accordionist, who played while we ate noisily. The first evening at dinner when a Red Cross girl sat down at our table, I hardly knew what to say and we all grinned at her sheepishly like a group of embarrassed youngsters.

The change from barracks and hospital to this place was incredible, swift, and shocking. There should have been an intermediate step somewhere. But the flight surgeon had given us only three days for our rest. I was grateful for the rest, but I worried about the stresses set up in one's mind when he had to leave this paradise and return to combat. I wished they had not billeted us in a palace. I felt self-conscious, living on the mountain top like a conqueror, while below the people starved.

The hungry Yugoslav refugees at Santa Casada and their children were housed in wooden shacks and cavernous old *casas*. They were fed bean soup. Meat was a rarity among them. Their children were all thin and spindly legged and hunger stared out of their eyes. And most of them were dressed in discards of British uniforms which were largely patches by now. They, and the natives of Santa Casada, the Italians, marched below our windows. Sometimes I saw an envious glance and I moved away from the window ashamed. I wondered what the Yugo fighters and the Yugo girls, among whom an ascetic morality prevailed, thought of us and the fact that at night whores circulated among us. I felt ashamed for our American ostentation and bad taste and inequality of effort. And the incredible thing was that I felt guilty of being there altogether. Perhaps Billy, Dick, and Andy were smarter when they chose to go to Rome. Because Rome was somehow part of the war. Perhaps I felt guilty because I liked Santa Casada so much and longed to remain there. Dooley, Trent, and Couch ran around furiously, sailing, swimming, drinking in the village. Everything was done grimly, desperately. We could not relax.

When the rest camp idea had been suggested to us by Doc Brown, Dooley protested, saying he'd rather fly. "I don't need no rest," he had argued. "Is Petersen resting? I can just see him looking at them stumps of his, thinking of me! It'll be like that all his life: Dooley the sonofabitch, Dooley the sonofabitch. . . ."

"They'll make him a pair of artificial legs," Trent consoled the engineer, "and he'll be like a new man. You watch and see."

"He wanted to be a commercial pilot after the war," Dooley said. "That was his dream. Remember he used to say: this is one time where a guy joined the army and really learned a trade . . . Now I can see him in another kind of a trade. Like the crippled vets after the first war, navigating on one of them small platforms close to the ground, begging for pennies."

"You're crazy as a loon," Trent said. "You know damn well they're gonna take care of the vets after this war. Listen to your old dad: we won't stand for no nonsense!"

"I can just see it: me walking down a busy street, maybe even in Pittsburgh, and there's Petersen, the half-man, pushing himself on one of them platforms with pencils in hand, a little tin can tied around his neck for pennies —"

"Cut it out," Trent said, annoyed. "You're crepe-hanging all over the place."

"Sonofabitching war!" Dooley cried. "Kills you before you live. That's what happened to Cosmo. If only he'd of shaved once. . . . And them it don't kill, it burns out. I feel like I'm all burned out inside. Just a lot of fukken ashes. How's that air force song go?

> We live in fame,
> Go down in flame —

"That's only a song," Trent said.

"But it's true. It's got you either way, this war has. If you don't go down in flame, like the song says, you get burned out inside."

"You talk like the original man with the paper asshole."

"I gotta keep flying," Dooley said. "That's the only kind of a rest I need."

The guilt ate at Dooley, and we all had it to a lesser degree. I had it because I felt I was cheating on the war, trying to escape from it. I felt guilty because I did not give enough to the war; there were too many reservations in my mind. I seized too eagerly upon the universal cynicism among the troops, the fatalism, and the undeniable fact that war was an amoral act and that it did not exalt or purify or uplift; it killed, crippled, dulled, paralyzed, and wrecked beyond repair. War, contrary to the notions of some doddering old fools, was not a normal pursuit of man. It was the most degrading, unnatural, and abnormal pursuit ever foisted upon man. And yet, there was Hitler, and you had to fight. I felt guilty because I too became a victim of the survival cult so prevalent among men who flew missions. Survival, fifty missions, was the goal — not the winning of the war. But survival for its own sake was a corrupt thing, like living only for the sake of living.

∙ ∙ ∙ ∙

The air was cool with the sea breeze and the dryness of the mountains. Albania, across the Adriatic, disappeared in the purplish mist of the approaching evening. The song of the Yugo kids ceased, their mentors having bedded them down for the night on the stone floors of the refugee camps. The street was alive with talk: Slovene, Italian, and American. Yugo soldiers saluted us as we walked up the terraced street, and Charley muttered: "I'm a sinful ole bastard, pop, but I don't look like no officer, do I?" A huge Yugo MP saluted us and said: "American *aviaticheri* very good. Sure."

"Peculiar people, these Yugos," Charley said. "I was out in the street this morning and didn't one of them Yugo kids ask me for candy or cigarettes, like the Eyeties do. And their gals don't proposition you either. Wonder what makes 'em different?" He scratched his mop of reddish hair. "These people act more like Americans than any I seen. Don't you think?"

We walked in silence for a while, and the thought occurred to us simultaneously: we both had money in our wallets and we wanted to buy food and wine for the Yugos.

"I wish we could pitch a bang with a bunch of 'em," Charley said. "After all, them Partisans been saving plenty of our boys that bail out over Yugo. I feel lower than a snake's bottom walking around with *molte liras* in my wallet while these people don't have the price of a drink."

I was grateful to Charley for expressing the thought. I, too, wanted to repay the Yugos, and to make amends for the castle on top of the mountain and the prosperity which Americans exuded while they were in rags. Perhaps being with these people, I thought, would provide that anger and reaffirmation which I needed more now than at any time since coming overseas. "You'll make us happy," I said to the Yugos in my very halting Ukrainian-Russian-Polish, "if you drink with us."

Several Yugos accepted our invitation and descended into a cool Italian wine cellar. As soon as we came in, the worried proprietor sent his young daughter into the house which was in back of the bar, in order that the *Americani* might not be tempted by a young *signorina*.

"It's all on me," Charley cried, adding in Italian, "*per favore*, eat and drink. I got *molte liras*, and you're welcome to as many of 'em as you like." Charley ordered food and wine. The proprietor brought the wine. As for food, there wasn't an ounce of meat in all of Santa Casada. "Only the *Americani* have meat," he said. Charley spied an old Yugo who was blind and had the granite face of Timoshenko. The blind man did not drink. An accordion rested on his lap and on top of the instrument were poised his two powerful hands. "Why don't this man drink?" Charley asked, aggrieved. "Ain't he a Yugo?"

I translated Charley's words and the blind man beamed and said in Slovenian: "I shall share your wine only on one condition — if I may reciprocate by playing."

"That's good enough!" Charley said.

The granite-faced man played. His fellow countrymen sang. Charley beamed upon them, prompting: "Drink, men, drink." And to the Italian proprietor he said: "*Ancora vino. Ancora!*" In the corner of the bar sat an Italian general, beak nosed and sad eyed, muttering to himself and to his wineglass: "*La nazione è disgraziata, la nazione è disgraziata.*"

"Hey, Jack," Charley cried angrily, pointing a finger at the general, "hold down that moaning. Don't you see we're singing here?"

The Italian general raised his sad eyes and said: "*Non capisco.*"

"*Non capisco,* s— — !" Charley retorted, red with drink. "Ben, tell that wop general to shut up or I'll ream him out good. It ain't every day you can chew out a general and get away with it."

The Yugo accordionist sang a plaintive Dalmatian song and his countrymen joined in. I sat in their midst but I felt a reserve about them, as if they didn't trust us. Was it that my khakis were whole while they wore patches? Was it our castle atop the hill while they lived in shacks? Was it our plentiful food, though C ration, compared to their thin soup? Was it our magnificent armor as compared to their too few rifles? What was there about Americans that made all Europeans suspicious, reserved, and at times incommunicative? These people were our allies, but with our usual ostentation and patronage we made them feel like poor cousins to whom we offered alms on occasion.

"We got to get more Yugos to drink with us," Charley cried. "I'm a pore, sinful bastard, but ain't no Yugo gonna be thirsty so long as Mama Couch's boy's got lire in his wallet."

"No, no, Charley," I tried to stop him. He stumbled over to the bar, flourished some money before the diminutive proprietor, loaded his arms with bottles of red wine and ran out into the street. He roamed the streets searching for Yugos and every time he recognized one he'd stuff a bottle of wine into the hands of the bewildered man and say "Chvala (thank you)." He ran around in a frenzy, dispensing the wine, buying melons and forcing them upon the refugees. He emptied his pockets of cigarettes and when the Yugoslavs refused to accept his offerings, Charley was almost in tears. He cried that they were doing him a favor accepting his gifts, but beyond that he couldn't say what was on his mind. He came back to the wine cellar exhausted but triumphant, as if he'd repaid his debts and his soul was at peace. "I never had so much trouble giving things away," he said, flopping in a chair.

Before we parted, the accordionist who looked like Timoshenko said to me, "It would give me great pleasure if you consented to come to my house and meet my wife. And please bring your friend. You will find us down the road, near the cloister. The name is Professor Blaj Bralle."

. . . .

Professor Blaj Bralle and his wife lived in one barren, cavernous room. Some cloth was stuffed in the hole which was the window. The furniture consisted of two broken chairs and a mattress on the floor. Nothing else. Mrs. Bralle was in her forties, thin, like most Yugoslavs, who were undernourished, and about fifteen years younger than the professor, who called her "mama." When she spied the bags of food we'd pilfered from our own mess hall — plus the fruit we bought in the village — and several bottles of wine, Mrs. Bralle flushed and said in Slovene: "You shouldn't have done it. I must protest. How do you expect people to eat when they've just had supper?"

The blind man laughed and said: "Mama, open a bottle of wine, instead of making profuse apologies. Our friends have come to enjoy themselves —"

"Now, what a way to talk!" She was ill at ease fussing with the bags and I wondered whether we had done right bringing them food and thrusting our riches upon them with our usual bad taste.

Mrs. Bralle looked up embarrassed and cried in despair: "We have only one glass for the wine. Oh, how can that be!"

"Our honored guests will forgive us," Blaj said. "They know all our things were left behind in Belgrade and by this time the Germans have likely destroyed them."

"But the least they can do," the hostess complained, thoroughly distressed at the state of affairs, "is for one of our guests to sit on the other chair. Please do," she begged, addressing both of us.

"*Molto grazie*," Charley said and sat down beside me on the cement floor. The chair remained vacant. She threw up her hands and looked about helplessly at the barren room and said, "In Belgrade it was different! But what can we do?"

"Nothing, Mama, nothing," the professor said, sitting up straight in his chair, his accordion poised. "You need not apologize, our friends understand. And they forgive us. And now," he cleared his throat as if he were going to sing, "I shall oblige you with some accordion playing."

He directed his sightless eyes toward me and added: "Would you kindly translate that to your comrade?"

Charley nodded his head and said: "*Bene, bene.*" He was nursing a wine bottle in his hand. He squatted on the floor, his feet spread out. "Ask him what he's gonna play."

"I thought I might oblige you with some Bach," the blind Yugo said, "but first I have a little surprise for you." He smiled shrewdly, gripped his instrument and tore into the old marine song: "From the halls of Montezuma, to the shores of Tripoli. . . ." He beamed as he played it and I was sure he thought he was rendering a song dear to our hearts, probably a song which we sang with our last dying breath. He finished it triumphantly and Charley cried: "Hot dog! Ask him if he knows 'The Wabash Cannonball.'"

"And what is this Cannonball?" Blaj inquired, wiping the perspiration off his brow. I said it was a song popular among some American soldiers. "Then I must learn it," the professor said soberly, as if he were already beginning to concentrate on the task. "If it is a favorite song among our allies, I must learn it. I know all the Russian songs." He moved his chair closer to us.

I remembered I had a cigar in my pocket. I offered the cigar to our host but he refused at first. Finally he took it, fondled the cellophane wrapper for a long time and undid it ceremoniously. "Ah, my dear friend," he exclaimed, "what a treat! It's been so many years since I've smoked one of these. In Belgrade when I was director of a conservatory . . . But of what interest is that to you? Are you sure you're not depriving yourself —"

"Smoke it, please," I said.

"Now?" he asked, somewhat taken aback by my bold suggestion. "Oh, well, why not?" he reconsidered, his face beaming. "Mama," he exclaimed like a little boy, "we'll proceed to smoke this wonderful thing! Mama, smell it." We lit the cigar (they did not even possess a match). "Mama, come here. The sheer fragrance of it." He took several puffs. "Now I'm happy. I shall smoke it slowly and I shall proceed to learn this favorite song of our allies, 'The Wabash Cannonball.'"

While Charley and I were teaching our blind host "The Wabash Cannonball," a young Italian priest came in. He wore glasses on his smooth, plump face, and his roundish body was robed in a black cassock. Behind him trailed a boy assistant. "I heard the music," he said in sonorous Italian, "and I cannot resist music, particularly the way the professor renders it."

"Thank you very much, Father Fortugno," the host said in Italian. "Won't you meet my very dear American friends?"

The priest's face looked familiar. I remembered seeing him earlier in the day on the beach. He had been in a pair of bathing trunks and I had taken him for an American mess sergeant. I suddenly forgot about Father Fortugno and his black priestly robes and let my mind dwell on the fine leveling process that might be accomplished by the mere removal of clothes. In their bathing suits enlisted men looked like officers, and Americans might be taken for Italians or Yugoslavs. Without their clothes, even God would have difficulty telling his children apart. The trained eye could discern the American from the others by his bulk, size, or girth. But even God would have trouble distinguishing between an American officer and an American enlisted man — in a bathing suit. The only solution would be to have separate bathing facilities for officers, enlisted personnel, Yugoslavs, Italians. Subdivide the beach. And then how about subdividing the field officers from the lower brass? But the best solution was to take their clothes away and they'd have a grand time. Mix them up a little and tell them they all looked alike, all made in God's image.

Father Fortugno took the chair which the hostess relinquished and folded his hands over his belly. His boy assistant remained standing near the damp, dark wall. The priest leaned back and listened to the music, seemingly at peace with the world.

I was curious about the relationship of these people. I had seen the priest in Santa Casada, acting more or less like the self-appointed host and unofficial mayor. I had seen him on the beach and at our officers' affair where he had been the only Italian present. His cloth gave him entry where even Italian generals were excluded. This man, who was probably younger than I, was already growing fat with a nice round belly and a pinkish double chin. Compared to the scrawny fishermen and storekeepers of the town he looked like a man from another world. His magnificent church which had served rich provincial fascists at one time was now being used as living quarters by the Yugo refugees. He had no flock to speak of, but he didn't seem distressed. He walked the streets of Santa Casada with easy, measured step, his arms folded behind his back. He had that priestly gait so familiar in

Italy: a gait that seemed so patient and reposed. You saw them all over Italy, priests and Jesuits, walking singly or in pairs, arms clasped behind their backs. They gave the impression of being completely oblivious of the cataclysm about them.

"I will oblige you with some Puccini," the host said to Father Fortugno, who was leaning back in the none too secure chair, puffing blissfully on an American cigarette. "Are you in voice tonight?"

"Hardly," the young priest replied. The question brought him to an upright position and he flushed. "Oh, my voice," he said, "that is my tragedy." He recited the words in his lyric native tongue, looking about the room with supplication.

"Yours is a rare voice," the blind man said, smiling in the direction of the priest. "But I think a little wine will not be amiss."

"But what about glasses?" the poor woman said. "We cannot have the Father drink out of a bottle."

"That's just TS," Charley said, picking his way through the Italian with difficulty. "Priests gimme a pain," he whispered to me in English, "maybe that's 'cause I once studied for the ministry. Nuts!" he said, "let him drink out of the bottle." And with that he lost interest and returned to his own bottle of wine.

Father Fortugno pondered for a moment and reached — what appeared like — a difficult decision. "I will provide the glasses," he said somewhat agitated, summoning his assistant. He whispered something in the boy's ear and detaching a key from a bunch that hung under his cassock, he ordered the boy to be off quickly and return without delay.

We sat in the semidarkness of the flickering candle which mercifully obliterated the peeling walls and naked mattress in the far corner of the room. The boy returned several minutes later, carrying five golden beakers. "Father!" the hostess cried when she saw the exquisite golden vessels. "You mean to use them here?" And her arms swept about the barren room.

"And why not?" the priest said magnanimously. "I have kept them under lock and key since the *Tedeschi* came. This is an excellent opportunity to put them to use again. After all," he said, grinning broadly, "how often do we have the honor of drinking with our American friends? I can see no task more sacred than to bring about understanding among us all."

The blind accordionist fondled a golden beaker in his powerful hands and said laughingly, "The church is always such a comfort!"

The priest, having taken a drink, said eagerly, "Shall we sing now?"

Blaj began to play and Father Fortugno launched into an aria. The priest's face grew red and the veins stood out on his neck. I feared his voice which changed from tenor to alto would crack. The boy assistant who clung uneasily to the wall, trembled, watching the padre's efforts. Only the hostess didn't appear concerned with the singer's labors. There was a flush to her cheeks which suddenly made her look young. I wondered if the beakers, the golden shining beakers, had accomplished that miracle. She seemed to be moving on air, with ease, grace, and elegance, as if she were entertaining distinguished guests at the Professor's Conservatory of Music in Belgrade. She was oblivious of the cavernous room and the rag stuffed into the wound where a window had been. "May I pour you more wine?" She sang the words unselfconsciously. "Oh, just a bit more wine! And how about something to eat?" And her own beaker she held delicately, basking in its sparkling reflection. She shone over the little world of men and cast a warm glow over us, and we reached out toward her like lonely men reaching out toward the image of Woman and Mother. I was happy enough to want to cry.

The two men concluded the aria, and the host, wiping his granite-like forehead, said: "You are in fine voice today."

"No, *signore*, I'm in very poor voice. And for bel canto singing one must always be in good form. These uncertain times," he added, looking at us, "they affect one's voice too. And what is an Italian whose voice fails him?"

"An Italian who does not have a voice to sing with is not an Italian," Bralle observed soberly, resting his hands on the accordion. "Beyond any doubt you are the most melodious of nations. I am partial toward our own Dalmatians and the Russians, but I think you are more melodious."

"Coming from the maestro it is a compliment!" the priest exclaimed, lighting an American cigarette. "We Italians are born with song on our lips. Even our speech is song. We express our sorrow in song. My favorite theory, *signore*, is that if statesmen conducted their deliberations to the accompaniment of a Verdi libretto, there would be more accord in the world. I venture to say we might even abolish wars."

"I'll drink to that," Charley said readily.

"This war we cannot abolish," the blind Yugo refugee said. "This one we must finish."

"And why must you finish it?" the priest inquired. "Do you believe there will be victors?"

"Yes, *we* will be the victors," the blind man said quickly. "We most certainly will! Not the church, *padre*, no. This time the *people* will win."

The priest smiled, flicked the ashes off his cigarette and moved closer to his host. Their exchange which was growing heated was obviously not the first. "I make no distinction between people and church," Father Fortugno said. "To me they are synonymous."

"No, no, no," the professor cried impatiently. "The church has compromised itself too much. The people will never forget the photographs of Franco tanks being blessed by your Roman Catholic priests."

"Those were acts of individuals," the young priest retorted. "The church cannot assume the blame for that. Your Marxian concept that religion is the opium of the people will not hold. Human beings must believe, particularly during times of stress, like now. They must have something spiritual to hold on to. The church gives them *that* something."

"Your flock has run away," Blaj said, "and they are probably cavorting with the Fascists in northern Italy or with the Nazis in Germany."

"I shall get a new flock. My church is ready to receive anyone who seeks its aid. We are patient, *signore*. Time is on the side of patience. I believe people will turn toward us more after this war than they had after the last one. Observe," he said, turning toward Charley and me squatting on the floor, "how religious American soldiers become."

"Maybe for the duration of the war," Charley started saying. He was interrupted by the blind man. "When people do not know why they fight," Blaj said, "it is possible they might turn toward religion." He faced in our direction and smiled. "I must apologize, my friends, for this observation. But after talking with many Americans at Santa Casada, I have come to the conclusion that few of them know why they are fighting. Most of them do not have their heart in this war. They are armed magnificently — with guns, but spiritually they are naked. If we had their arms we would conquer! Oh, how quickly we would conquer, *signore!* You realize our Partisans fight with their bare hands, and yet look what we have accomplished. Our men and women are like the proverbial giants, because they believe in their cause. That is why they do not need your religion."

"Religion might strengthen you in your cause," the priest said.

"It has not in the past," Blaj retorted. "Religion has always kept our people in chains."

"Not religion," Father Fortugno took exception, "some interpreters of religion."

"However you put it," the blind man said, "the church is finished in the Balkans and the whole of Eastern Europe."

"My dear Signor Bralle, you underestimate our capacities and talents. Perhaps we shall retreat in your Balkans, but we shall advance in America. After the war the United States of America will need us, and we will respond."

The two antagonists ignored us completely. Though their argument centered on America, they did not find it necessary to canvass Charley's or my opinions on the subject. It appeared as if their minds were made up that Americans were a mass of adolescents who had lire, liked whores, and drank Cokes. If they were wrong in this assumption, neither Charley nor I proved it.

By midnight when most of Santa Casada slept, the Yugoslav refugee and Italian priest finally came to an understanding. "I shall certainly drink with you, Father Fortugno," said Bralle, "to a future where nations will speak to each other through song. When that time comes, Italy will have the most eloquent of ambassadors!"

"And will not Yugoslavia?" the priest returned the compliment. "Let us drink a toast to that future."

I awakened Charley and we held up the five golden beakers and drank a toast. "To a singing future," the hostess said.

"Down the hatch," Charley said.

·   ·   ·   ·

In the morning I decided to visit the Displaced Persons Camp for Jews which was about twenty miles from Santa Casada. I can't explain my eagerness; I know it was not based on the suggestion of the Jewish chaplain at our field who had urged me to see these refugees and "cheer them up."

On the way to the camp along the rocky coast of the Adriatic while the jeep was churning our breakfasts inside of us, I almost told the driver to turn back and forget about this mission. But something drew me irresistably to these people.

We came upon the camp suddenly. There weren't any wires or compound. The camp headquarters, workshops, and synagogue were all located in a large villa overlooking the sea. Almost two hundred Jewish refugees, escapees from Germany, Austria, Yugoslavia, concentration camps, and the Warsaw ghetto, worked in or about the crumbling old villa. The general manager of the camp, a Mr. Weiss, introduced himself to me in a soft Yiddish. He had been a shoe manufacturer in Belgrade. For some inexplicable reason he wore a mustache which had a painful resemblance to Hitler's. He marched me into the hall holding my arm and telling me proudly how their workshops were all busy and producing. "Would you believe it," he exclaimed, "our co-operative here is self-sufficient? Yes, absolutely self-sufficient! We take your American and British discarded articles, like clothing, shoes, wires — but only discarded — and create new clothes and shoes and bedsprings and toys. We depend on no one." He kept squeezing my arm, emphasizing the self-sufficiency of the camp as if that was of paramount importance. "All those who can work are busy. But we have many old people who cannot work any longer. Most of our young people have been slaughtered by *him*. Oh, what great woes *he* has caused us!" The word Hitler was not mentioned; Hitler was referred to as *he* or *him*.

Mr. Weiss let go of my arm and summoned the few old people who were wandering about aimlessly in the hall and corridors of the villa. "Follow me," he said eagerly. "We are honored today. An American Jew has come to see how his brothers live." The old people stirred. They followed Mr. Weiss into the hall reluctantly. Curiosity had been wrung out of them, as was the zest for living, I thought, watching them move slowly in response to the manager's summons. At that moment I was sorry I had come; I felt like an intruder; I felt looked upon as an intruder from another world that did not know the smell of crematoria and the yellow Star of David. And if they resented me I did not blame them. *They* were the survivors of the six million slaughtered Jews, not we American Jews.

Mr. Weiss said something about "the guest," referring to me, and a few of the old people began to show some curiosity. They formed a circle, touching me, fingering my gunner's silver wings and my chevrons; all this performed in grim silence. Finally an old man with a little goatee murmured, "A Jew . . . A *free* Jew, yes?" He whispered the words, weighing them on his tongue as if the sound of them was the proof of his surmise.

"He's a flyer," said Mr. Weiss proudly, "and he's been bombing *him!*"

"A bombardier!" a little old lady exclaimed. "A bombardier, God bless him!" She suddenly began to weep, grabbed her skirts and ran out summoning the younger folks in the shops down the corridor. "A Jewish bombardier who has been bombing *him* has come to visit us!" She screamed and pointed toward us. "There he is! May he live to one hundred and twenty, Riboinoy shel Oilom. Come, Jews, behold him!"

I stood in the center of the hall surrounded by people who were hurling questions at me; people, particularly the old ones, touching me as if I were a curio or a statue, a man from another world, a world from which they had been torn. They kept hurling the word *bombardier* at me and I nodded, realizing how silly it would be to tell them I was a gunner who fired bullets and not the man who dropped bombs. They wanted a bombardier for that was the symbol of striking back at *him*. The bomb! I remembered how while we were in Tunis some black Jews had stopped us on the street and inquired: "And which one of you is the bombardier?" And when Dick Martin had responded, rather sheepishly, they had blessed him and promised to say a prayer for him.

"Do you know, son," said an old man tugging at my sleeve, "six million of your brothers and sisters are slain? Remember that, my son, when you drop those bombs on *him*." He pulled at my sleeve as if he had a secret to tell me which could not be shared with the crowd. "I see your bombers going over the Adriatic each morning," he whispered. "I make it my business to get up early to see them. Everybody asks me: 'Chaim, why do you rise so early, almost in the middle of the night?' But that's my job. I guide you across the Adriatic by saying a prayer to the Lord. And when you're safely across, I go back to bed. It's the least I can do."

"I'm from Vienna," a middle-aged man with thick-lensed glasses said to me. "I make bedsprings out of telephone wire. In Vienna I had one of the largest furniture stores. Have you ever bombed Vienna?" I nodded. His face lit up. "Ah, *gut! Gut!* I have a great house there, but I do not care. Bomb it. *He* is there! I do not care if you destroy the house so long as you wipe out the evil genius. I don't care about the house at all." Suddenly he grasped my hand and cried: "Thank you! Thank you very much!"

"Young man," a little wizened woman piped, "would you do me the honor and visit our *casa*? My husband can no longer walk. I would like for him to see a Jewish bombardier." At the *casa*, in the one room occupied by two army cots, they offered me an orange. It was the only food they had. "Take it, take it," the old woman insisted. "You need the strength."

Then she sat on the cot and rocked slowly, and the wrinkled face and the shawl on her head suddenly made me think of my grandmother. The similarity was striking and overwhelmmg. My grandmother had died twenty-four years ago, but the sigh was the same and the rocking motion, the upper part of the body moving forward and back, was the same. The sigh was a lament passed on with generations like a cherished heirloom. Listening to the old woman sigh I remembered my grandmother. And strangely enough, the only audible sounds I remembered about my grandmother were her sighs. She had sighed more than she talked. She had sat in the marketplace in that small Ukrainian town, clad in coarse, patched clothes, huddling over a container of coal, her frozen red hands buried in the sleeves. She had sat there and rocked and sighed, and waited for someone to buy her clay pots. I had never seen her make a sale. Once, when I asked my grandmother why she sighed, she regarded me soberly and replied, "My child, a Jew who does not sigh is not a Jew." I was five or six at the time and the explanation puzzled me. "But I'm a Jew, and I don't sigh," I said. "One becomes a Jew slowly," she said in her kindly, patient voice. "One is not only born into it. One is beaten into it."

And now again I was tempted and I asked the question: "*Tante*, why are you sighing?"

The little old woman considered my question with that rocking motion and replied, "I do not need to sigh. After all these years of woe it sighs by itself."

A quarter of a century separated my grandmother from the little old woman who sat rocking despondently on an army cot in a Displaced Persons Camp somewhere in Italy; twenty-five years and another war and a continuous flood of tears. But little else differed between them. My grandmother had died in 1920, soon after her offspring fled from the Ukraine. Hers had been a life of woe, poverty of the cruelest kind, denial, and ghetto. In her declining years she had seen her people decimated by mercenary bands of Petlura, Denikin, and others. In one aspect my grandmother had been lucky. Her children had fled to America, to a haven. Later, death had come as a merciful gift from God. My grandmother had been more fortunate than the little woman in the DP camp. This one lived to see six million of her people exterminated; her own kin burned in *his* ovens while she and her husband had been spared. My grandmother had found her haven in merciful death. But this poor woman had no home. Her home was where she could sigh and rock, sigh and rock.

Had nothing changed? Across the space of twenty-five years the memory of the camps and depots and hiding places choked with refugees came back to me. The gaunt, terrified faces hurled me back to the days when we ourselves lived in fear and slept with our clothes on in attics and cellars ready to flee when the alarm sounded. From 1917 until 1920, when civil war raged in the Ukraine, it was a time of hiding in dark places and learning bewilderedly that for some reason a Jew must cower and hide and fear for his life. I had learned this before I learned my ABC's. And after that there were five long tortured years as a refugee. There was the crossing of forbidden borders from the Ukraine into Bessarabia, and the hunger for bread and home, of being separated from my parents, of being consumed by lice and vermin, of drinking water out of scummy puddles, of sleeping in gutters and haystacks and caves, of begging, of stealing food. And all along the route there were the gaunt, terrified faces in the refugee camps where old people sighed and rocked, sighed and rocked. And after that, how many years had it taken to shed the word "refugee"?

Twenty-five years! And nothing had changed. The victims were the same and so were the sighs. I recognized them and knew them and walked hand in hand with their sorrow. But beyond that, I was a man apart from their world; a "free" Jew, as one of them called me; a stranger from America, the fabulous, safe land where no bombs fell and Jews lived without fear of being massacred, and people ate white bread and meat and slept in peace at night. Were it not for the fact that I was a "bombardier" they would have resented my intrusion.

Mr. Weiss led me to the shoe-repair shop. "I want you to meet a survivor of the Warsaw Ghetto Uprising," he said. "One of the very few. You *do* know about the Uprising," he said, looking at me dubiously.

"Of course I do," I said.

"We Jews must be very proud of it!" the manager said hastily as if to appease any indignation that might have been aroused in me by his patronizing question. "It ranks with the feats of the Maccabees and Bar Kochba. It shattered once and for all the false legend about Jews not being fighters. This nonsense about the Jews being passive!" he said, stopping in the middle of the road. "We must tear that word *passive* out of our vocabulary. Enough! We've had enough of it! Our fathers raised us on it; we got it with the milk of our mothers, and it was all false. The meek shall *not* inherit the earth! Often our people were massacred while they were in their temples praying. Slaughtered like sheep. Our wise men taught us to respect the Word; to love the Word. But while we sat in our yeshivas and learned the Word, the enemies were building cannon." He broke off the tirade and ran ahead, as if he were done with the nonsense of emotion and was in a hurry to lead me to another of the many interesting points in the camp. "Come on, you will meet this man who fought in the Warsaw Ghetto Uprising. Let him tell you about it!"

I followed Mr. Weiss into the small alcove which had been turned into a shoe-repair shop. A young man in his late twenties sat on a low stool, driving nails into shoes. He looked up and stared at me; after we'd been introduced he went back to his nail-pounding. I sat down and reached for a cigarette and offered him one. He took it unsmilingly and his eyes rested on me again. His eyes were hard and they made him appear old. I started the conversation, about shoes, of all things, while, in fact, I wanted to hear about the Uprising. But I felt as soon as I'd sat down that he resented me and would not talk about that event. "I pound nails into shoes," he said to me harshly, "but it is a gun I want!"

"You were in the Warsaw ghetto," I said.

"That's a pile of rubble!"

"You were in the Uprising," I said, trying to bring him around.

"So were forty thousand others," he said. "Why are you interested in the past? Tell me better how I can throw away these nails and shoes and get a gun and fight those who murdered my wife and child. The past does not interest me. Why are you here?"

I told him about our crash landing, the hospital, and three-day rest.

He was silent for a while, ignoring me completely. Then he said, "You have excellent weapons! Imagine a Jew given an opportunity to fight from an airplane!" His blue eyes suddenly lost their hardness and the webs on his face melted and there was a suggestion of a smile. But it wasn't really a smile. Nobody in the DP camp smiled, not even once; perhaps their facial muscles were no longer capable of smiling; time and circumstance atrophied those muscles. "You have wonderful weapons!" he said, pounding the nails fiercely on the shoe leather. "What more could a man ask for?" He looked at me across the little wooden partition and I wondered whether this man from another world, this stranger and yet brother, suspected that I was unworthy of the wonderful weapons. Perhaps he was aware why I was there, seeking courage from him and the others, trying to rekindle my anger and sustain my passion.

"A man needs much more than weapons," I wanted to tell him. "Hatred, like love, is a delicate thing. It must be nourished and tended; it must be fanned and kept glowing. Strange, how very strange. You envy me my weapons and I envy you your hatred which is pure and fiery. The crematoria has robbed you of your loved ones, and the barbed-wire fences of the concentration camps and DP camps removed you from the world, but you took with you that pure anger and fanned it and made it into a glowing, searing flame. Your wives bore children in the shadow of the death ovens — in defiance — and suckled your young ones on the milk of anger. I envy you because for you there is no rationalizing, no choice, no retreat. For you the essence of living is resistance — and if I could achieve that state I might indeed consider myself fortunate."

The shoemaker hardly said another word. But when I got up to leave, he followed me outside the villa and ran down the road after me. "I didn't want to talk in the presence of the others," he said. "But you must do me a favor. There is a Jewish brigade fighting up north. I'd like to get in that brigade. Will you help me? Perhaps you can prevail upon the higher-ups to assign me. I'm an excellent shot, a sharpshooter, in fact. Please, I'll be forever grateful to you, I, I'll never forget you. If I remain here, pounding nails into shoes, I'll go insane." We stopped on the road. Around us were the soft, tender little noises of peace: the birds, the lazy palms, and the sparkling Adriatic. And we stood there momentarily, oblivious of the peace. "The fact is," my friend said, "we have enough young people right here in this camp to make up a squad. But the British will become suspicious if many of us run away. And I can't wait. If you could arrange to smuggle me up to Naples in one of your trucks, I'll get up to the brigade somehow."

"But how is it possible?" I said helplessly. "Naples is two hundred miles north of here. Besides, the brigade consists largely of Palestinian Jews, under British command. And they're up around the Po Valley —"

"You can't refuse me," he implored, "I'll die if I remain here."

I shrugged my shoulders impotently and lied, saying, "I'll speak to people. I'll try." And we shook hands, my friend and I, and suddenly we embraced. We walked up the alien road, arm in arm, and he told me about the Warsaw ghetto. . . .

· · · ·

In the evening there was a moving picture on the terrace of the officers' hotel. The dialogue and the music reached up to our room and mingled in my mind with thoughts of the Jewish DPs. It was a most fantastic setting: dialogue of a Western thriller, thoughts of refugees, Santa Casada. I lay in bed, my eyes shut, but I could not sleep. The only aspect in the whole mosaic that did not seem fantastic was the roll of the waves against the shore. This was the one reassuring aspect: waves rolling against the shore sounded alike everywhere. Closing your eyes you could well imagine yourself listening to the waves of Lake Michigan beating against the dunes, or the slightly more angry variety of waves at Miami Beach in late September. They were like the South Atlantic waves I heard in Belem and Natal in Brazil, or the Tyrrhenian Sea waves licking the shores not far from our base. Theirs was the kind of Esperanto you understood and did not need to translate. But everything else seemed out of joint, unreal, incongruous. In the movie the bad men were riding, and I could hear the gallop of the horses on the sound track, but before my eyes were the gaunt faces of the refugees and the survivor of the Warsaw Ghetto Uprising, savagely pounding nails into shoe leather. I pulled the pillow over my head and stuffed the ends of it in my ears to shut out the noises coming from the terrace. I wanted to dwell on the story my friend had told me before we parted late in the afternoon. Out of that story of the Uprising I was determined to carve out at least one clear image that might serve me in time of need, when my anger faltered again and the corrupt thoughts of survival came to plague me. But the picture was vague: for twenty-eight days several thousand Jews, the remains of three hundred thousand, rose against the might of *his* armies that were hemming in the ghetto. Only forty thousand were left by that time, too late, too late, but suddenly they rose in a final magnificent gesture and struck back. They were entombed behind the ghetto walls and underneath the rubble and corpses of their people. They fought, famished and skeletal, out of the holes in the ground, fought barehanded, but with a fury and a passion that came only from knowing there was no other choice. For a month the whole Nazi garrison of Warsaw blasted at the entombed Jews. But they burrowed in the ground, deep into the death caverns, emerging periodically to hurl their defiance. But soon their homemade grenades and rifle bullets gave out and soon their strength gave out and when the incredulous Nazis finally stormed the ghetto walls, after a month, they found smoldering rubble; not a Jew alive, not a Jew in sight, only a huge, slow pyre with the smoke curling toward heaven the last active token of resistance. "Too late," my friend had said, "we rose much too late. But at least we fought. And we stunned *them*. And we killed *them*."

Suddenly I heard Trent's voice, which came in a low conspiratorial whisper: "Sh, my *amico* is sleeping."

A girl's voice whispered: "He want signorina too?"

"No," Leo replied, tiptoeing into our room, dragging the girl by the hand so she would not stumble in the darkness. "No, he's too old."

"That is too bad," the signorina said, articulating her precise speech with an Italian accent.

"Take your things off."

Leo's bed being right next to mine, I could almost feel them fumbling with their clothes. The room remained dark. I peered from my refuge underneath the pillow, annoyed at the turn of events and terrified at the prospect of remaining still in my bed while they went through their act. I wanted to leap from my bed, naked though I was, and run away. But I remained in my rigid position, paralyzed and fascinated.

"I swear," Leo said, breathing heavily, "I can't get these damn Brazil boots off my feet." He giggled and I could tell he had had a lot of cognac. "Oh, wait," he said, "I knew I forgot something. I meant to ask you downstairs. How much do you charge? *Quanta costa?*"

The girl pondered his question as if it were out of place. She was a slightly-built girl with small breasts and a slim waist. Everything about her was frail and delicate. She looked like a schoolchild. "For a whole night it will be a thousand lire, ten dollars," she said softly in surprisingly good English.

"I don't want the whole night," Trent said, somewhat cross. "I want just one ride over the target. *Capito?*"

"Yes." She was pulling at his boots. "For one time it will be three dollars, three hundred lire."

"The hell you say!" Leo grumbled. "That's highway robbery. All the goddamn officers' fault," he murmured in feeble protest. "There was a time you could get a piece for a can of C rations, but the officers drove the price way up. Well, okay," he added, "hop in bed and get to work for your lire. Only whatever you do, don't wake my *amico* over there, 'cause he's an old bastard and needs all the sleep he can get."

"A signorina will do him much good," the girl said in a shy, unaffected tone.

"He's saving his for the wife back in the States," Trent informed her. "Meanwhile I think he beats his meat. Like everybody else."

"That is not healthy," the girl said.

They were both in bed and I could hear them moving around, seeking a comfortable position. "People who do like that," she said, "lose their hair."

"In that case all the guys in the United States Army will be bald headed," Leo observed with a chuckle.

They were silent for a moment. I moved my head slightly underneath the pillow to keep from suffocating. I cursed Leo silently, but instead of making an attempt at escape, I stayed on, pretending I was asleep. A morbid curiosity triumphed in me over the annoyance at Leo for bringing a signorina to our room. I did not question his right, only the propriety. He certainly had a right. According to the new Wing ruling, signorinas were allowed to circulate through the two hotels and offer their services, provided they had been cleared through the pro station downstairs. Wing had instituted this "service" only recently, after many protests from the enlisted personnel who had been forced to seek their signorinas in whorehouses and in Off Limits areas where VD was rampant, while the officers, particularly in Rome, were given room service.

The stories we heard about the goings-on in officers' hotels in Rome simply made our mouths water. We heard of beautiful signorinas parading through the rooms exhibiting themselves like models while the officers reclined on their beds, smoking their cigarettes in real hot-rock, bored fashion, eyeing the girls, snapping their fingers, calling for the next one, sweating it out until they found the one they liked and instructing her to take off her clothes and get in bed pronto. And the prices they paid outraged the enlisted men. Fifty dollars a night! A hundred dollars a night! (The British were furious, saying the Yanks were ruining the "natives.") The enlisted men complained. "You call this a democratic army? The officers get all the nookie and we get the s— — end of the stick."

An enlisted man, when he came to Rome on a three-day pass, would have to find himself a room if he wanted a signorina. The Roman landlady usually asked him: "Do you want a room with or without a signorina?"

A room with a signorina cost ten dollars per night, one without cost only one dollar fifty.

The damned officers!

If you offered a signorina less than what she asked for, she'd turn on you and cry indignantly: "Take it easy, greasy, you got a long way to slide."

Tough babies.

The best thing for a man who came breezing into Rome on a three-day pass, was to turn over to the signorina the one hundred dollars he'd saved up for the occasion. This flat arrangement entitled him to everything, and the girl took care of the details. If, during the three-day pass he had need of money, the signorina would give him some.

The damned officers! (The British said the Yanks would never make a good colonizing power because they were giving the "natives" all the money they asked for.) The men of the Fifth Army raised holy hell and complained: "You wild-blue-yonder boys with that fifty percent extra flying pay sure snafued the deal here! Used to get a gal for a bar of chocolate before you airplane drivers came. You sure f— — up the detail."

The damned officers!

The EM bitched so loudly their squawks must have reached headquarters in Bari and some of the big brass broke down and instituted a little democracy. Not too much. That's how it came to pass that they ordered a pro station set up at the Santa Casada Rest Camp.

This sort of thing embarrassed the hell out of the two Red Cross girls who worked in the hotels when it was under the aegis of Wing. Something had to be done about it because you simply couldn't have American girls living under a roof where there were such goings-on, so the two girls were moved out to a *casa* and they carried on their work of mercy between sunup and sundown, at which time they left the hotels. They acted like you'd expect American girls to act: by simply ignoring what was happening in the hotels at night. This was a war, and after all, one had to adapt oneself. And the girls did magnificently.

And that's how democracy came to flourish at Santa Casada, between sundown and sunup.

I expected Trent and his signorina to get to their business, but Leo was feeling maudlin and wanted to talk. "I was just wondering what you think of us *Americani*," he said. "You must think we're a bunch of suckers paying you all the lire for a quick ride. Well, maybe we *are* a bunch of suckers," he continued when she failed to reply. "But what the hell? What's the difference? Here today, gone tomorrow, as your dad always says. That's me. Once every twenty-four minutes a gunner gets killed some place; my time may come up soon. I had an *amico*, his name was Mel Ginn and he was a *molto buono* guy, and the *Tedeschi* killed him . . . *Capito?* . . . *Guerra non buono*," he mumbled, forgetting the signorina lying next to him spoke English well. "*Non buono*," he repeated, self-pity creeping into his voice. "So what does it matter if I shack up with a whore? Might as well get all the fun out of life —"

"Yes."

"There's a girl back home, a nice girl, mind you, but she's been fooling around with a *guaglio* who is not a *soldato* but a *civiliano*. What hurts most is that this guy was my best friend. Got a letter from her the other day and she writes she doesn't know if she loves this *civiliano* or me. How do you like that? Bust my eardrum and call me 4-F!"

"What does that mean?"

"The bastard is a 4-F. And she's *non buono*. I think I'll give her the air when I get back home. I'm getting my whoozis shot off here and she's carrying on with that jerk!" He seemed to be speaking to himself as well as the girl.

"She should not be doing a thing like that," the signorina said, "to one as fine as you."

"I'm no good," Leo declared. "I shouldn't be doing a thing like this with Mel dead only a few days —"

"You come to me," she said. There was a movement under the bedsheet.

"Get the hell away! I'm no fukken bono and you're nothing but a goddamn whore."

"You come to me —"

"Get the hell out of my bed!" She sat up in bed preparatory to obeying his wishes but he seized her by the shoulders and dragged her back. He resumed his semi-drunken monologue, insulting her in turn and whispering gentle words and calling her honey.

"Honey, I swear you're the nicest Eyetie whore I met in a long time. You don't even smell like an Eyetie. And I'm a crank on smells. With me its the first whiff that counts. That's the way I am. You know I'm from Hollywood."

"Cinema, huh?"

"*Si!*"

"Joan Crawford is very pretty."

"Used to be —"

"And she is a very good artist."

"I know them all, baby," Leo said expansively. "Why, I have close friends, *amicos*, in the cinema."

"Are you artist?"

"Naw. I like dogs. After the *guerra* I'm going to raise dogs. *Capito?*"

"That is very good," she said.

"What is very good?" he inquired suspiciously.

"What you said."

"Guess everything I say is very good until after you get your lire, eh? I swear, Nina, you're a devil, I think maybe I'll like doing it to you. Tell me," he said, wrestling with her briefly under the sheets, "do you know the difference between unconditional surrender and a negotiated piece?"

"No."

"Three dollars," Leo said, amused. He chuckled and asked chummily: "Tell me, honey, what made you go in this — I mean this *business?*"

"An Italian *colonnello*," she replied quickly, as if she'd memorized the answer and held it in readiness for the naive American twenty-three-year olds like Leo Trent. "He seduce me," she said with enough of a catch in her voice to make any man feel a rush of sympathy mingled with passion.

"Was he good?" Leo asked eagerly.

"He was brutal," she replied.

"No kidding!" Leo chuckled. "Gave you hell, huh?"

I thought the girl would recoil, but she continued with her story, feeding his curiosity, knowing too that she must be feeding his passion. "But he was divine in bed," she said without any conviction.

"After him, what happened?" Leo urged her on impatiently.

"He run away and left me," Nina recited. "Then came a *capitano tedesco*. Very handsome and dashing."

"Where did all this screwing go on?"

"I lived in Rome with my parents. I was an art student —"

"Oh, oh, you're giving me a line, baby. You're giving your old dad a line. I swear, you're a real devil. But let's forget this *art* business, just tell me about the nookie. This German captain, did he know how to do it?"

"He was very — what you call manly," Nina said.

"And you liked it," Leo insisted, playing his cruel streak to the end.

"I could not help it," she whispered.

"And after that, I suppose the *Americani* came, hundreds of them. Never mind, I don't want to hear any more. I —"

He grabbed her. There was a desperate scuffling under the sheet. The movie dialogue reached up to our window again: *Which way did they ride, pardner?* And the hoofs of the cowboy horses clattered on my brain. The waves rolled against the shore with their ageless, peaceful, measured strokes.

The sound track mingled with the roll of the waves, mingled with the image of an emaciated young Jew pounding nails savagely into shoe-leather, mingled with Leo's labored breathing. All this did not last more than a few brief moments, yet it was an eternity of torment.

If Leo had suspected that I was awake and heard him these few anguished moments, he would have killed me. But I was less concerned with Leo's anger than I was with his dejected state when they uncoupled. "I wasn't so good tonight," he said bitterly. "Maybe I was too eager. Well, I'll show you. Oh, I can do better than that. I think maybe it was the rubber. Screwing with a rubber is like taking a bath with your boots on. You come back tomorrow night and we'll do it without the rubber."

"Why not tonight?" she asked.

"Not tonight!" he retorted. "Now put your clothes on and wham it out of here. My *amicos* ought to be back soon."

"I'll come back tomorrow," she said, putting on her clothes. "I like the way you make love," she added kindly. "Much better than the *colonnello fascista* or the *capitano tedesco*. Much gentler —"

Leo knew she was lying, lying like a trooper, but there was nothing he was able to say, except, "*Grazie*, thanks."

When Dooley and Couch came back from the movie, Leo was lying on his back, smoking. "How was it?" Charley asked.

"*Molto buono*," Leo replied. "I was layed, relayed, parlayed."

"Didja give her hell?"

"Had her hanging on the ropes," Leo said. "She was moaning so loud I had to stop up her mouth 'cause I was scared she'd wake old Ben."

"With *your* little pecker?" Charley said dubiously. "What's more, whores don't moan."

"That girl was no ordinary whore," Leo said feebly. "You should hear the way she talked English! Better'n me. She used to be an art student in Rome."

"S — —!" Charley roared. "There's only one kind of art old Musso taught the Eyeties, and that's the art of nookie. Why, man, that Musso was the biggest pimp the world ever did see. And he made Italy the biggest whorehouse in the world. Why, even old Studs Lonigan himself couldn't —"

"I'm going to lay her again tomorrow night," Leo said, charting his own thoughts.

Dooley, who had sat by sullenly, said: "We're going back tomorrow morning."

"Yep," Charley said, "going back to fly the big-assed birds. Vacation's over. Lucky Strike Green's gone to war, who are we to shirk *our* duty?"

"My aching back," Leo whispered dejectedly as the others got in bed. "So soon —?"

After that it was quiet. Santa Casada bedded down for the night. I wondered how the refugees at the DP camp slept. I wondered whether Nina, the frail little prostitute, slept well. And I wondered too about the broken-down Italian generals and the blind accordionist who slept with his wife on a mattress on the floor, and the two Red Cross girls who had a guard stationed outside their *casa* at night. For the four of us who were going back to combat on the following morning, sleep was a problem. But one fixed image in my mind was a welcome substitute for sleep: the image of an angry refugee pounding nails into shoe leather, saying: "You have excellent weapons! What more could a man ask for?"

29

ONE DAY after his return from Rome Dick Martin flew as bombardier with a new crew. The plane was shot down over Bucharest. In the officers' tent we found the can of insect powder which Dick usually taped onto his chute harness. "If he'd had that can along," Dooley observed, "he wouldn't of went down."

"He was a queer duck," Trent said.

"He was a nice enough guy," Billy Poat said. "What tickled me was how he'd scream like a girl every time the bombs went away. Now what made him do that?"

"This world is made up of all kinds," Charley observed.

There had been other changes. Our copilot, Schiller, was put on a new crew. While we were away in rest camp, Trent's pup, Stowaway, was stolen. Leo was disconsolate. He ran to Group and the four squadrons, searching madly all over the field. Unable to find the pup, Leo broke down and wept, and in the evening he hung a star over his cot with the inscription: "STOWAWAY. MISSING IN ACTION." All the gunners in our barracks thought it was very touching, and Leo felt much better.

Andy Kyle started drinking. Our navigator, who had never touched liquor, not even the ounce of combat whiskey we'd get after coming down from a mission, started drinking. Billy Poat said Andy was drunk throughout their three-day stay in Rome.

Unlike most men, Andy cried when he was drunk. He slobbered and grinned, his big teeth protruding, his face giving the appearance of a boy who was aware of doing something wicked. After a few drinks, Andy came stumbling to our barracks, sat down on one of our cots and started mumbling the sheerest nonsense in our ears. "What's the shot?" he said. "The shot is," he replied, "I'm drunk and don't care." Andy didn't cuss. He just drank himself into a stupor in the evening, and when Squadron Operations sent Delmonico to wake him in the morning, Andy was out like a light and he'd he taken off the mission. After the planes went up, he sobered. But he was so ashamed, he would not come to our barracks when he was sober.

His face had suddenly grown older, grayer, and his eyes took on a furtive look. His step became jerkier and he walked on the alert, as if at any moment there might be a need to duck or sidestep. But the change was mostly in his eyes. Andy's eyes which had been smiling and friendly suddenly grew harder and bigger, the pupils distended. The softness in his eyes only came back when he wrote to his wife. And that he did religiously every day, although he had given up the correspondence course in merchandising.

There were instances when we succeeded in sobering him up sufficiently to fly a mission. He didn't beg to be excused. He did not protest about going up. But he was useless up in the air. Every time the ship lurched, hitting an air pocket or prop wash, Andy grabbed the nearest solid object and there was a terrified look in his eye. On the way back from a mission he'd be on the interphone constantly, pleading with the engineer, "How's the gas holding out?" It did not matter if he flew with Dooley or another engineer; he did not trust any of them, nor did he trust the pumps. "You'd better look again. I'm not sure we have enough gas. You can't trust those pumps. Just take another reading, will you?"

After the mission he felt ashamed of himself for having caused so much bother and fuss. "I know I acted like a kid," he said, "but believe me, men, I couldn't help it. Something's happened to my nerves. Suddenly they're gone. I don't understand. What's the shot?" He eyed us quizzically, but we all looked away because there was no answer. Yes, there was one answer. Andy was through. His usefulness as a combat flyer was finished. He was a liability up in the air, and after a pilot flew with him once, he refused to fly with Andy again. "He's a nice guy," the pilots in our squadron said of him. "Used to be one of the best navigators in Group; could split a field with his head in his ass, pretty near, but he's *finito*. Ought to be grounded."

We of his old crew flew with him out of loyalty and the past. But we knew this would not last long because we were no longer a crew, although we pretended we were.

Dooley said, "Why don't you get yourself grounded for a while?"

"Not while the rest of you fly," Andy said indignantly. "I'd rather get killed than do that!"

Drinking was a way of postponing. We wondered how long Squadron would countenance him.

It hurt when you looked at Andy and remembered the far-off days when he talked of a dream crew. It hurt, remembering that Lieutenant Kyle had been the mainstay of our crew. Truly the crew had revolved around him, although you'd hardly suspect it, considering his unobtrusive ways. He had been one of the minor suns, you might say, but he always had given off the most warmth so that we gravitated toward him without realizing it. Now, at twenty-three, he was a hysterical kid with the eyes of an old man. The only thing that reminded you of the old Andy was his flight cap with the inscription: "MO MULES THE SHOW-ME STATE."

30

EARLY IN August much of the air force concentrated on southern France. We hit Toulon and Marseilles regularly. The missions were long and weary, and Toulon, which had Jerry submarine pens, threw up a heavy barrage of flak.

Around our base there was an air of secretive expectation. Everyone had his own set of rumors and ideas as to what was in the offing. It was difficult to remain aloof and apart from the general excitement and anticipation. Dooley was constantly at Squadron Operations volunteering to fly. He didn't care whether they flew him with us or with another crew. He was afraid of staying idle. When forced to do nothing he drank himself into a stupor or ran off to Mandia where he invariably got into trouble. And every time he did something obnoxious in Mandia, Dooley gave a pack of cigarettes to Luigi, our barracks boy.

Our engineer had ceased talking about his experiences aloft. Unlike most gunners, who chattered a lot after a mission, Dooley said nothing. You'd think he was determined to drown his guilt by scorning the fear of death. Perhaps this was his way of purging himself of the guilt he felt for Mel's death. Perhaps he did not care if death struck him down. But the worst part of it was that he seldom said anything. For one who had been so garrulous Dooley gave the impression that he had lost his power of speech.

He flew more than the rest of us. When he flew with another crew, we waited for him to come down and brought along his cup so he might have his coffee from the Red Cross. This process of "sweating in" Dooley was done more out of a sense of custom than spirit. This was one way of showing that we were still together, pretending we were still a crew, still our brother's keeper, although, in reality, there was little that bound us. We were comrades only in the experiences and deeds of the past. In the present we were, each one of us, completely subjective and alone. The fact of the matter was that we were too frightened to fly with one another, and there was talk at Squadron of breaking up whatever remained of our crew and assigning us to other crews, or fly us as extras. I hoped that would happen soon. The waiting was worse than the flying. But while waiting, we clung to one another. We went to chow together and to the movies, and we played cards. We were like an exclusive fraternity, and yet the only thing we had in common was our wounds. We sat and gossiped: about Pennington who had a new crew and who had risen to be one of the best pilots in Wing; about Chet Kowalski who had dropped out of sight after hanging around the field for a while doing nothing. Chet had drifted out of our lives completely; disappeared, through channels, naturally, but gone as if he had never been one of us. He had left nothing behind except the ache that comes with knowing that a human being with whom you shared terrors and some joys had gone out of your life irrevocably.

Billy Poat became parachute conscious. Everytime something went wrong in flight, he strapped on his chute. "I warn you, men," he was forever saying, "if something goes haywire, I'm not staying around

to see what it is. Out the waist I go." And Leo started suffering from attacks of diarrhea. Usually he got the attacks in the briefing shed, and
only when the red ribbon pointed to a particularly rough target. But
Andy was in the worst shape of all. Dooley, Charley, Leo, Billy, and I
went to see Doc Brown and suggested he ground the navigator.

"Let him come and talk about this thing to me himself," the flight
surgeon said. "Why does he send you?"

We told Captain Brown that Andy had not sent us. We had come
on our own.

"This is most irregular," Doc said. "Besides, I can't be grounding
men all over the place. Hell, there's a war on. But one of these days
I'll have a talk with him."

Doc couldn't give us any more of his time. The medics' *casa* was
filling up with venereals who had come for their shots.

31

On MONDAY, August 14, 1944, all
combat troops were restricted to base. Squadron bars were declared
Off Limits. Pilots were briefed at 1800 hours, and the bomb racks
were loaded with one hundred pounders. At midnight we were ordered to go to "breakfast" and then catch a few winks of sleep. When
we returned to barracks, the lights remained on. The whole field was
lit up, as for some festive occasion.

This was to be our first night mass strike. There was no doubt in
anyone's mind that we were going to hit southern France. And
though we gave some thought to the opposition, men beleaguered
Squadron trying to volunteer for the mission. Gunners, as a rule,
seldom volunteered, but we suspected that this mission would be in
support of our infantry; perhaps we would get a chance to bomb
enemy troops, rather than cities. There could be nothing more direct

than bombing enemy troops. We were sick of bombing non-German cities, constantly saturating them with bombs, killing civilians week after week, month after month. Take Ploesti, for instance: thousands of men lost over the target — to hell with the money it cost — but consider the men and the effort. Yet Ploesti went right on producing oil. Or take Vienna. We saturated the city with bombs — although in the papers back home it said we bombed military targets — with the aid of our omniscient Norden bombsight. According to the papers the bombsight was one of the gadgets winning the war. Most bombardiers ignored the sight, and either toggled their bombs or pushed them off the racks with their feet. There was not one target we ever knocked out. We couldn't even put the Ferrara Bridge out of commission. No sooner did we bomb it than the Jerry engineers set about fixing it. We could almost glimpse them setting to work as our ships wheeled away from the target on the way home. Once a week we traveled north to take a poke at Ferrara. Each time we came back minus two or three ships. But one thing about bombing enemy troop concentrations: when you killed a Jerry soldier he stayed dead. And maybe that was the reason why the men were so eager to fly this one.

We returned from "breakfast" and Billy Poat sat down on his cot, straddling it cowboy fashion, and shuffled his cards for his never-ending game of solitaire. He had lost much weight since the crash and acquired a tic in his left eye. "I'm going on this mission," he said in his gruff voice to a gunner across the aisle, "and if I get shot down, you'll say, 'I sure miss the Shuffler.' And if you take my wallet with the hundred dollars in it, I'll haunt you."

"I guess I could use that hundred most bestest," the gunner said. "You ain't gonna do nothing with it nohow."

Billy rode along with the joke. "Got a letter from my ma," he said, "and she writes all the windows in our house are dirty. We got seventeen of 'em, you know."

"Seventeen windows? What you need so many of 'em for?"

"I don't know," Billy said with disgust, "all I know is it's my job to wash each one of 'em. My ma never lets anybody else do it."

"Well, now," Billy's new friend drawled, amused, "ya got yer work all cut out when ya get outa the army. Whar ya think we going tonight?"

"France," Billy replied, studying his cards.

"Think gonna be rough?"

"I don't give a s— —," Billy lied. "Don't matter to me where they send us. I seen 'em all. They're all the same to me."

The gunner, a new man, seemed very much impressed with Billy's indifferent attitude. "I bet you seen plenty, Sarge," he said with admiration. "Real rough ones, too."

"I seen 'em all," Billy said, looking up from his cards. "You name the place and I've been there." He spoke thickly but not loud enough for the others to hear him because he was a little bit ashamed of this hero role he always assumed with new gunners.

"Ploesti real rough, sarge?"

"Rough?" Billy said. "Roughest fukken target in the world. A couple of guys from the Eighth Air Force tried it once and haul-assed it back to England; they'd rather fly over Berlin than f— — with Ploesti, take my word for it. Why, Ploesti's got flak guns mounted on railroad cars that follow you around the target. They shoot at you for twenty minutes. That sonofabitch is rougher than a cob."

"Rougher than Vienna?"

"Nothing's rougher than Vienna. Vienna's the roughest target in the world. That's where we got it, and my buddy, Ginn, got his." Billy moved a few cards across the blanket and said thoughtfully, "Mel was a nice guy — from your part of the country. He was married. Me, I'm single so I don't care. I figure if they get me, okay. My ma'll find somebody else to wash the goddamn windows. That's no big job. Anybody can wash windows."

"What was your racket?"

"Bookkeeping, before I got tied up with this thing they call the army."

"How many missions ya got?"

"Thirty," Billy said with a mixture of pride and humbleness.

"I only got three," the new gunner said. "Wisht I was over the hump, like you."

"Oh, you'll get there," Billy said loftily but without any assurance.

"Thanks, Sarge, I shore hope so."

There was a flush on Billy's cheeks. He looked like a different man when people approved of him. But not many people bothered doing that. Everybody was too busy looking out for his own skin. He made friends with new gunners, but new gunners didn't stay new very long; they either grew old or went down.

"Let me give you a clue," the radio operator said, "your best pal is your parachute."

"I see what ya mean, Sarge."

"Tell you why I say that," Billy said, expanding on the subject, "in the infantry you buddy up with a pal or a foxhole or a plain, solid tree. You got something to depend on. But up in the air there's nothing, nothing but your chute. That's the only pal you got up there. Don't depend on nobody else. That's why I always take along an extra flak vest, so's to wrap my chute in it. I'd rather lose my right ball than get a hole in the chute."

"Not me," the new gunner said.

"You're like my old copilot," Billy said. "He used to wrap vests all around his *cojones*. But what good are your balls when there's a hole in your chute?"

The new gunner thought it over while Billy went back to his card shuffling. He held the cards in a firm grip and each card exploded in his fingers. He squeezed the cards with a passion and intensity as if all his anger and frustration were released through them. He started laying out the cards on the olive-drab blanket again. "You know, talking about those windows," he resumed, "I had a dream about 'em the other night. Dreamed I heaved a rock through a couple of 'em. You should of seen the look of surprise on my ma's face. And you should of heard me laugh!" He scratched the back of his head. "Now how do you dope that one out?"

"You got my hole card, Sarge. I don't know s— — from Shinola about dreams, excepting when they're wet dreams."

There was a familiar screech of brakes and Sergeant Delmonico's beaming pumpkin face was framed in the doorway. The Operations clerk stumped into the barracks and cried, "Awright, you hot rocks! Time to fly the big-assed birds! Earn your living! This is costing the taxpayers money. Let's get our asses off the fart sacks and into the briefing shed. Briefing in fifteen minutes. There's a war on, re-member?" And he grinned.

"How would you know?" he was joshed good naturedly.

"I seen it in the *Stars and Stripes*," Del replied, laughing.

"When did *you* learn how to read?"

"When I went to West Point. Me and the colonel."

"Where we going, Del?"

"Ploesti," the clerk replied.

"F— — you, mac. Where we going?"

"Vienna."

"You talk like a man with a paper asshole. Where we going?"

"France, you jerks, France," Delmonico exclaimed, shaking a few gunners who were burrowed underneath their blankets trying to get a few winks of sleep. "Big show tonight! History! You hot rocks'll be making history."

"I'd rather make love," Trent said.

"Need something bigger'n what you got for lovemaking," Del said.

"Why don't you take a flying f— — to the moon?" Trent retorted.

"'Cause I'm on ground status."

"What are we hitting this trip, Del?"

"Who says you'll hit anything? Didja ever?"

"Sure. According to photo-recon we destroyed all the whorehouses in Bucharest." ————

"The Jerries rebuilt 'em next day."

"How many ships going up?"

"Maximum effort," Del replied, wiping his brow as if he was weary of answering all the questions. "What the hell you asking me for? Am I G-2?" But he went right on giving information. "Each squadron is sending up eleven ships. Group oughta muster about forty-four."

"We carrying anything besides one hundred pounders? How about frags or antipersonnel?"

"What am I, the briefing officer? Just one hundred pounders."

"What do they expect us to do with 'em? Hit Jerry troop concentrations?"

"Dig latrines in France," Del said, escaping through the door on his way to awaken men in the other barracks.

We were all ready to start for the briefing shed when Andy Kyle came reeling into our barracks, grinning and drunk, waving a bottle. "Here I am, fellas." He put one arm around Dooley, the other around Trent. "Let's go fly."

Dooley freed himself from the navigator's embrace and took the half-filled bottle of liquor away from him. "You're alerted to go with us, lieutenant," the engineer said angrily, "what's the idea of drinking?"

"Ooooooh, I'm going," Andy said. "I'm all ready to go. Flying with my buddies. I wouldn't let 'em down for the world. I'll fly with you if you guys'll have me."

"You're too piss-eyed," Trent said. He liked Andy but he never passed up an opportunity to say something derogatory to an officer.

"You're just too full of firewater, Andy, old boy." He took the liberty of calling the navigator by his first name, knowing the man was drunk.

"True, true," Andy said dejectedly. "I'm just a no-good coward that's drunk while my buddies are getting ready to fly. I'm pretty chicken. I, I don't like myself, and I bet you guys don't like me either. And I don't blame you."

"We like you fine, Lieutenant," Charley Couch said politely. He never overstepped the bounds allowed by the army. "Now if you'll just sober up a little maybe we kin all fly this one together."

"Oh, I'm no good. No *buono*," Andy muttered, shaking his head, his eyes on the barracks floor. "But if you'll have me, I'll fly. Damn it, I'll take you right over that target like I used to. Remember how I split that field at Dakar? Made it right on the nose. Wasn't a drop of gas left when we came in from the ocean. That was some flying, eh? Some navigating, if I have to say so myself." He let himself be helped from the cot and led toward the door. "Oh, we had us a crew," Andy said, his arms around Dooley and Trent. "Best in the AAF. Just had a few tough breaks, that's all. Streak of bad luck. Got to expect that in war. Heck, men, if we stick together, Billy, Charley, Leo, Dooley, Ben, we still ought to come out on top." He vomited near the ship but we put him in the waist section and attached a portable oxygen bottle and mask to his face to sober him up.

The ships taxied off the aprons and onto the runway, their brakes moaning as they were maneuvered into position. Inside the waist section, where we took ditching positions for takeoff, it was pitch dark. It was only three in the morning and the whole world seemed asleep and only we were awake. The Libs' powerful landing lights stabbed at the new runway asphalt. We were still on the ground but already we were studying the new pilot, a Lieutenant Fitzimmons who was so small he had to sit on an extra cushion. He was using his brakes a lot, causing the ship to rear forward and settle toward the tail like a frightened bronco. Charley Couch, fearing takeoffs almost as much as flak itself, was wet with perspiration. The rest of us in the waist section held our breaths and said our own individual prayers and rubbed our good-luck charms — those who had them.

After we were airborne I got up and looked out the waist window. Below us, on our field, two ships were burning, one having exploded on takeoff. But other ships were taking off on the alternate runway, as if nothing had happened.

The world was wrapped up in stars. The sky was a sparkling, gleaming, twinkling lid, velvet soft, yet menacing. We flew in loose formation, spread out all over the sky to make sure the huge, delicate wings of our bombers would not tangle and break off. Charley stood glued to the window, as if he were on guard, trembling unashamed, showing his naked fear. "Look at that sonofabitch coming close," he cried. "My aching back! How do they expect Mama Couch's boy to ever get back to Arizona when they fly 'em that close? Get the hell outa there, you shave-tail bastard!" he screamed.

The rest of us lay around the waist section, clearing our ears by blowing our noses, or just staring into space. Each one of us retired into his own thoughts: thinking how alone man is on the way to a target, how terribly alone a human being is when he is facing death.

Andy woke up when dawn poked in the waist windows and through the camera hatch. "Where are we?" he asked, disturbed.

"Over Corsica," Charley said from his self-imposed guard at the right waist.

"What time are we supposed to hit the target?"

"Seven twenty-nine."

"How's the gas holding out?"

"Everything is holding out fine, Lieutenant," Charley said soothingly. "You got nothing to worry about. It's getting light outside. One thing I don't like and that's flying in the dark. 'Cause when you fly in the dark you never know where you're gonna land — if you jump. Ever think what would happen to ya if you jumped in the dark and landed on a church steeple? Some reaming you'd get!"

"Think I'll go up front and find out about the gas," Andy said in a worried tone of voice. "I don't like the way the engines sound. Sound to me like they're missing." He picked up his chute by the little cloth flap and started toward the catwalk leading to the flight deck. "I'll be back later," he said.

From fifteen thousand feet we saw the Mediterranean shed its deep green for a dull gray. Starting at the mountainous island of Corsica and stretching all the way to the French Riviera, where the invasion was to take place, troopships, naval vessels, barges, and all manner of watercraft looked frozen in the water like toys in a miniature pool.

Only the small PT boats and motorships were alive, scurrying about like water bugs, leaving little ribbed trails behind them.

Our effort exploded at exactly seven twenty-nine on Tuesday, August 15, 1944. Our heavy bombers came in at fifteen thousand feet, dropping the hundred pounders on the beaches. Troop-carrying barges followed us in and unloaded the infantrymen. The men were like tiny ants crawling up the sandbars. Low-flying medium bombers — B-26s, B-25s, A-20s — bombed enemy troop concentrations at low level. Our fighters — P-51s, P-38s, P-47s; navy fighters; British Spits, Hurricanes, Beaufighters, Mosquitos — came in at low level for strafing. Several battleships stood offshore and curtained the landings with a violent barrage. In the background two aircraft carriers sat broadly in the water with planes coming off them. And near them were the troopships, freighters, barges. It was a whole angry world afloat. The sky was filled with aircraft, thousands of planes at various levels, each bit of sky apportioned and staked out for this one blow.

We dropped our load and veered sharply back toward the sea, avoiding our own battleships, fearing their angry antiaircraft guns. Perhaps air force had been warned by navy: "If you boys drop some bombs on us, we'll shoot you down. Remember!" We moved out to sea and I sat in my turret watching the invasion. The enemy hardly responded. There was some desultory firing and antiaircraft from inland at the place where our gliders were coming in like papier-mâché toys buffeted and torn by the wind and tree branches.

If men down below were not dying, and you did not know how their hearts pounded fiercely, you might have called the spectacle majestic. Sitting back in the turret you might well have said to yourself: this is a ringside seat on history, and you're part of it, part of the effort, part of the kinship, one infinitesimal grain contributing to victory. You belong, yes, you belong in this bit of transplanted, angry America. You might even shout with joy into the interphone, and maybe you would be heard by the shoemaker, the survivor of the Warsaw Ghetto Uprising.

Our ground troops hit the beaches at Cannes and Nice and all along the Riviera, the playground of Europe.

"Those poor bastards!" Trent said, peering out the waist. "There's only one arm of the service I'll take my hat off to. That's the infantry! I wouldn't want to be in their shoes, believe me."

"Me neither," Charley said. "Just looking at 'em makes my head throb like a sick mockingbird's ass. I could never do it. Not me."

We waited for Billy to say something but he was strangely silent. He did not say one word about "transferring to the infantry."

Pointing toward home it almost felt like old times, and one could almost forget the old dream crew was only part of a crew, and one's mind flew ahead of the formations to a future, a dream of America. It was pleasant in the warm approving sun to speculate on how things would be in America after the war. The millennium? No. But a good life and a free life. Dooley would go back to Pittsburgh and Trent back to Hollywood and Andy to Kansas City and Billy to Rhode Island, and you would go back to Chicago, maybe to your old job, maybe not. But all the millions of men going back would henceforward judge their fellow men by their deeds, as they remembered them, and not by the sections they came from, the sound of their names, and the color of their skin. And there would be no more suspicion, like Charley saying the first time we had spoken: "So you're a Jew, huh? And from a big city. Funny! You look like ever'body else. Wonder what made me think you'd be diff'rent." People would no longer wonder because the ex-GIs would tell them that there were no differences between human beings, though their backgrounds may differ. And Europe would no longer be a place on the map or a target to destroy. We would remember, and tell about Anzio beachhead, Cassino, Foggia, Volturno, Regensburg, Bad Voslau, Steyr, Graz, Vienna, Bucharest, Genoa, Munich, Osijek, Brod, Ploesti, Bolzano, Budapest, Marseilles, Bratislava, Bologna, Miskolzc, Ora, Innsbruck, Salonika, Brenner Pass, Sofia, Po Valley, the Apennines. . . . We might even tell them about Lili Marlene. . . .

"We're losing gas out of the Number Four engine!" Andy cried on the interphone.

Andy's cry awakened me out of my pleasant dreams. We sat up and listened and those who could see, looked to starboard. Finally the pilot said calmly: "Nothing to get excited about." His voice carried the assurance that seemed to come automatically with pilots. "I saw the leak," Lieutenant Fitzimmons said. "It's not serious. We should get home without any trouble."

"You won't have enough gas," Andy argued. "We're a long distance from home."

Fitzimmons called Dooley. "Pilot to engineer, pilot to engineer, gimme a reading on the gas. Over."

Dooley got on the interphone after a moment: "We got enough gas. Got a thousand gallons left, more than enough for a three-hour trip."

"I don't trust the indicators," Andy disputed Dooley's words. "Maybe the indicators point to a thousand gallons, but I don't trust them. And *you* should know better, Dooley," he added as a significant afterthought. "I think what we ought to do," Andy continued excitedly when the engineer failed to take up his challenge, "is to drop out of formation and head toward Foggia where we can refuel."

"There's no need for it," the pilot said. "We're staying in formation."

Andy said no more. Several minutes later he came along through the bomb bays dragging his chute. When he came in the waist section we were lying about smoking, napping, or looking boredly at the green mountains of Corsica or the Mediterranean, which was blue from our height of eight thousand feet. Andy's face was ashen gray and his lips were trembling. His whole body was shaking uncontrollably as if he'd been seized by a malarial spasm. Andy put down his chute and came to the right waist window and peered out. "That engine's leaking badly!" he said. We got up to look. The gas that clung to the trailing edge of the wing showed a slight leak.

"It's nothing, Lieutenant," Charley said.

We sat down again, leaving Andy at the window. But we did not take our eyes off him. Finally Charley said calmly and deliberately, "Why don't you come and set down, Lieutenant?"

Andy paid no attention.

"Come on, Andy," Leo said. "Come sit here."

But the navigator seemed transfixed by that small glistening spot underneath the wing. He did not notice that we'd moved closer to him. Leo was lying down at his feet, dragging on a cigarette, keeping his eyes on him.

"Lieutenant, get away from the window," Charley said, after almost twenty minutes of this vigil. "I wanna close it."

"I'm staying right here, Sergeant," Andy said distantly and formally. He had never used the term "Sergeant."

The pilot, calling from the flight deck, said: "Close the goddamn window, Lieutenant Kyle. This is a direct order!"

Andy refused to obey.

"Close the fukken window!" Fitzimmons hollered.

Andy started saying something but instead he leaned his body into the wind, attempting to jump out. Leo tackled him by the legs and the rest of us seized hold of him and dragged him away from the window. He resisted violently, fought, bit, and screamed. There was foam at the corners of his mouth and his eyes had an insane fix in them. We held on to Andy for the rest of the trip.

32

PARIS FELL on August twentieth. The Queen of Cities was liberated by the *Maquis!*

Charley Couch won six hundred dollars in no-limit poker and sent the money to his father instead of his wife. He kept enough lire so that any of his victims might borrow some money for a poker game.

Lieutenant Andrew Kyle was grounded by a board that sat in Bari and adjudicated these matters. Andy had not wanted to go before them, but he was Finito Benito.

"I told them," said Andy, recounting his experience, "so long as my buddies are fighting a war I'll stay overseas, even if I don't fly. I asked for a job in Navigator Interrogation. But the brass said nothing doing. Have to get away from the sound of planes, they said. But I don't mind the goddamn planes!" he cried. "Why don't they let me stay around awhile? I'll get back in shape after a rest. And once I'm back flying I ask for nothing more than a gun. What kind of a war is it when a man that's fired on can't fire back? They can have their sextant and as-trodome. I said to them: give me a gun and I'll show you how to fight this goddamn war. So they looked at me and said: You're finished, Lieutenant. I begged them to let me stay around at least long enough to see you men finish your missions. I'd feel terrible if anything hap-pened to one of you while I was safe back in the States." He was lost in thought for a while. "Day and night I dreamed about the States. The States and Opal and a pair of slippers when you get home from work. Now that they give it to me, I don't want it." He looked at us pleadingly. "What'll I tell Opal when she asks how come I got home before the others? Tell her I cracked wide open while my buddies are still fighting? Look, men: what's the shot? All my life I considered myself a pretty rugged customer. Why should I fold up while the rest of you keep going?"

"What do you care, Lieutenant?" Billy Poat said. "They order you to go home, you go home. I wouldn't argue with 'em. We don't run this war. The politicians do. If they told me to go home, I'd go."

"But what about the rest of you?"

"At the rate we're going, it won't make no difference," Billy said. "If you want my opinion, the human is not fit by nature for air war. You just can't fight a war unless you got some place to duck once in awhile. That's why we got so much combat fatigue. No place to duck. And that's why we got a hundred percent turnover in combat personnel."

"I can't tell that to Opal," Andy said, staring dismally at the cracks on the floor. "I can't."

"How do you know your wife will ask?" Charley inquired.

"Even if she doesn't ask, I'll have to tell her. It's the right thing to do. The right thing to do," he repeated. "Funny —" A sickly smile played on his lips. "You can do the right thing all your life and everything turns out wrong. I was always fair with my buddies. I shared what I had. I gave away my liquor rations, my combat whiskey. I gave away my cigarettes. I never swore. I never abused the natives. In Rome, on our three-day pass, a signorina bust into my hotel room and I didn't chase her out because she might be hurt so I let her undress and stay in bed with me all night though I didn't touch her. I didn't even talk to her. In the morning I paid her as if I'd used her because I wanted to do the right thing. The right thing was to be faithful to my wife and to my buddies and the things I believed in. But in the end nothing turns out right."

"You gotta take these things as they come," Charley said softly. "When the fickle finger of fate gets after you, there's nothing you can do."

"But why does it have to happen to me?" Andy demanded.

"We bear you no grudge," Dooley said. "You done the best you could."

"But *you're* still flying. In fact, you volunteer to fly. All of you are in there pitching while I'm going home."

"If I had a wife like yours waiting for me," Charley said, "I wouldn't mind so much if they sent me home. Hell no! They could even send me 'fore I finished reading *Studs Lonigan*. Got a saying back home: it's better to go here than further up the creek. If my wife wasn't a bitch I wouldn't be here in the first place."

In the end Andy said: "Thanks a lot, guys." He tried to hold back his tears although at that moment it would have been right to cry.

33

ALL OVER the field men got drunk to celebrate the capitulation of Romania and the removal of Ploesti from the target list. In our barracks the celebration was more subdued. In our little corner there wasn't any celebration. Billy Poat was gone. In the morning, flying radio with a green crew, he threw himself out the waist window over the flak-ridden skies of Vienna. The crew came back and told the story how Billy had warned the pilot the Number Two engine was smoking, and the next instant he was out the window, his arms tugging frantically at a chute that failed to open. But even if the chute had opened, it would have made little difference, according to the men who had seen him go out, because Billy's dive was over the heart of the city where several hundred heavy cannon were tearing the sky to shreds.

In the afternoon we found out Billy had been to Flight Surgeon Brown pleading to be grounded. "He was here a couple of times," Doc Brown said. "He said to me now that he didn't have a crew it was easier for him to ask what he'd meant to do for a long time. He said he couldn't take the air war any longer. In the infantry he wouldn't have minded it. He said if we didn't ground him he would do something terrible. Really threatened me. But you can't ground every man who requests it," the captain said wearily. "What a hell of a job this is! Try and sort out malingerers from those who are on the verge of a breakdown! Nothing shows on the surface. Except the eyes, sometimes. Your navigator, Kyle, his eyes gave the clue. Looked like those of a frightened rabbit. So did Poat's. He showed me his hands were trembling, but anybody can make his hands tremble. He said he couldn't sleep nights and suffered from palpitations. I examined him and found nothing organically wrong. A lot of people have functional symptoms — it's fear. Attempt to escape from reality into pains. I advised him to fly a few more missions, then come back and see me." Doc field-stripped a cigarette, then threw the contents on the clay floor of the medics' *casa*. "What a hell of a goddamn job they gave me! I'm supposed to be a doctor. I'm supposed to make it easier for you men to fly those missions, but I feel more like an executioner. When I do take somebody off flying status for a while and put him on DNIF temporarily, Group tells me I coddle you men and deprive the air force of combat personnel. Is it any wonder I'd rather treat the mess personnel for venereal diseases?"

· · · ·

On that same day Lieutenant Andrew Kyle was placed on Orders to proceed to Naples by plane and from there sail to the Zone of the Interior "at the convenience of the army." But when Andy heard Billy Poat had thrown himself out the window over Vienna, he tore up the orders and ran away from the plane, screaming like a madman. The four of us, his former crew buddies, started chasing down the ramp, shouting after him, pleading with him: "Lieutenant, Lieutenant, wait a minute."

Andy ran among the planes and plunged down a company street. On both sides GIs and officers and Italian laborers who were working on *casas* stopped to look at the spectacle of a lieutenant, running and screaming like an insane man, being chased by four enlisted men. Near Group Operations a couple of ground men tackled Andy. The colonel ordered two guards to take him back to the plane which was scheduled to leave for Naples with a dozen men who had completed their missions.

Inside the ship Andy became violent again, screaming that he would not go home, he would come back, screaming until they gave him a needle and mounted guard over him.

Andy was asleep before the Liberator took off for Naples. He lay in
the waist section and we came in and took his hand and shook it
good-by. But Andy was already snoring. Next to Andy a gunner who
had finished his tour of missions was reclining easily, happy and grinning at the prospect of home and absorbed in a book: *How to Win
Friends and Influence People.*

We clambered out of the bomber and walked off to the side as the
ground crew removed the blocks from the two side wheels and the
ship moved off the apron. Charley Couch crossed his fingers watching the clumsy bomber lift slowly off the ground. It cleared the mess
hall, pulled in its flaps and folded in its wheels like a bird.

And then the four of us wandered off, lonely and empty.

34

Early in September they started
trickling back from the prisoner of war camps in Romania. Of the
four thousand men shot down over the Graveyard of the Air Force —
as Ploesti was known — one thousand came back. They came back
emaciated, bedraggled, legless, armless, weak, limping, hobbling,
hairy, ridden with lice. There was little difference in their appearance
from that of the refugees who clogged Europe's roads. The stamp of
war and defeat and humility was there. This was the way men with no
hope have always looked. But it was strange seeing Americans in this
guise, temporary though it was.

Dooley, Trent, and I circulated among the returnees, inquiring
about Dick Martin who had been shot down over Bucharest. Nobody
had heard about Dick or the crew with which he flew. Maybe they'd
been repatriated to another field. We inquired of each returnee, de-
scribing Dick's fat buttocks, his waddling gait, and his high-pitched
voice. These men who had come back from another world listened to

you distantly and shrugged their shoulders. All over the field these men had little clusters of listeners surrounding them, touching them, listening to tales of miracles and tales of prison camp horrors. And everywhere there were the exclamations:

"I sure thought you was a dead duck!"

"You'n me both."

"Howdya ever get outa that burning coffin?"

"Beats me."

"Well, now they're gonna delouse you, decontaminate you, desyph you, then they'll load you up with medals and send you back to the States to tell the civilians how rough it is and buy war bonds."

"How *about* that!"

You sensed a detachment about these men. They were removed from the rest of us by a set of experiences with which we were not familiar and a suffering which we had not endured. Many of us envied them because they were going home soon, going home heroes, and many of them no doubt resented us because we had not tasted their bitter life.

35

With the complete breakup of our crew I was relegated to the position of an extra gunner. They flew me only when one of the squadron tail gunners was on the sick list. Being cut adrift was a lonely and frightening business. One who had no crew had no buddies, although the four of us retained some bonds.

Around me there was the bustle of crews flying, of men going down, of flyers being reported KIA and MIA, of barracks emptying out and of new, bewildered faces appearing. Charley and Leo didn't seem to mind their new roles as extras. Charley said this leisure would give him an opportunity to finish reading *Studs Lonigan*, while Leo said he would catch up on his sack time. Dooley and I, however, were eager to fly the rest of our tour of missions, for our own reasons. Beyond a certain point, one felt useless hanging around the field while others were fighting the war. I was becoming a fixture around the base, and I didn't like that. Green gunners called me "pop" almost at first glance, and this made me feel terribly old. And it broke a pattern I had followed most of my life. Ever since I could remember I always associated with people older than I. Now the role was reversed. I was not accustomed to this father-image role, although it would be a lie to claim that I disliked it. But the change from being the youngest to the oldest was disconcerting. I felt ancient among the bright youngsters of nineteen and twenty.

As the record stood, I was stranded, without a crew. I was thirty-five years old and had thirty-four missions to my credit. At the rate I was flying I expected to have at least thirty-nine missions by the time I was forty. At which point life allegedly began. . . .

36

 THE LEAVES on the olive trees turned from green to a rich yellow and red. The sky was covered over by a dense mantle of angry gray clouds. With the clouds came the steady, pouring October rains of southern Italy. At night there were Alert Lists posted for the following morning's mission, but with the cloudy dawn came the order for a stand-down. What the Jerry could not accomplish, the weather had done. We were helpless against the weather, although we sent out radar ships at night to harass the enemy, and our formations, when they did defy the cloud front, were led by Mickey (radar) ships.

We wandered about the muddy field, seeking a break from the dullness and tenseness. In the library, operated by Information and Education, Captain Wilkinson and his enlisted men were dug in for the fall and winter — playing poker. A few small volumes of armed forces editions were strewn about the gaping shelves: Carl Sandburg, Bolitho, Zane Grey, Norman Corwin, and endless titles of books nobody was interested in. The books were there because they had been sent along from some USO in the States that no longer had any need for them. In the mess hall the rain came through the roof and into the mess kits on the tables. Outside the mess hall the army of dogs, which grew constantly, waited for your drippings. The dogs were mangy and wet. Everything was damp and wet.

In Mandia, where we ventured like tired sleepwalkers, the streets were almost deserted. The housewives, who had sat crushing beans for hours on end during the summer, were inside the dark hovels. The rain drenched the walls and the last signs of Mussolini's chipped image were obliterated. His admonition, CREDERE — OBBEDIRE — COMBATTERE, appeared like a pitiful joke out of the past. In the Laundry for American Solder, the four laundresses, Angelina, Maria, Lenora, and Gina, were working over GI and officers' shirts and there was hardly any light with which to see. The girls were wrapped in torn sweaters and their hands were red with dampness and cold. The Negro corporal sat in the gloom of the laundry, listening to the raindrops on the windows and the rapid chatter of the women. In the bar where Luisa worked, one lone New Zealander, his beret moved back on his blond head, sat glaring hungrily at the swarthy young barmaid who was behind the bar with her stump of a pencil. Just the blond Kiwi and the girl in the dark, damp, formless room; and the Kiwi telling the girl what a *dinkum* place was New Zealand, and Luisa saying, "No undershtanda." In the American Red Cross, Nellie Bullwinkle appeared even sallower with the change of the weather. Her complexion looked sickly and her face was lined with little folds of flesh. But she was as cheerful as ever, bustling about the place, giving off little sparks of benevolence.

37

THE OCTOBER rains grounded our ships and imprisoned us beneath a low canopy of black clouds. The rains put us out of the war and made us prisoners and shriveled us up with loneliness and boredom and uselessness. The Alert List was posted each evening, out of sheer habit, and my name began to appear on the list as flying with a new crew whose tail gunner was ill with yellow jaundice. Mornings we were briefed to hit Vienna. Some mornings we took off, but the formations turned back, usually after a fatal collision in the soup. We made attempts to break through the cloud front, but the clouds were packed in solid from the Alps at the Po Valley back to southern Italy. Coming down from a scrubbed mission our nerves were mutilated. We wandered over to the War Room to scan the large map and find out what was doing with the war among those who did not have to contend with cloud fronts. Every day at eleven A.M. Axis Sally came over the radio with her sugary, maudlin slop, and her dire warnings that the Germans were aware of our attempts to break through the cloud front to Vienna and were lying in wait for us. Sally pleaded with the flyers, telling them to throw away their guns and refuse to fight for the Jew-Bolsheviks who had imprisoned Roosevelt. This was no war for clean American boys, she said, telling them to go home. "Your wives and sweethearts need you," she cooed. "Don't drive them into the arms of the Jews and 4-Fs." Sally panicked the frazzled minds of many young flyers. Her predictions of doom spread terror among some, especially when she told them how many ships we had sent up on the previous day, what kind of bombs we carried and who led the formations. Where *did* that bitch get all the facts?

. . . .

Dooley lay on his bunk staring at the leaking, boarded ceiling. "This laying around is worse'n flak," he said bitterly. "It's enough to drive you nuts."

"You're forgetting," said Charley Couch, looking up from his volume of *Studs Lonigan*, "that you're living in the most int'resting period of history."

"I'm going batty," Dooley said.

"If you think you're bad off, you ought to hear how the boys on the Aleutians get along," Trent said. He was bent over his little table, composing a letter to his girl in Hollywood. "I knew of a guy in the Aleutians and he was so batty, he all of a sudden wanted to become an ocean wave. He said if they let him become a wave he'd take off and nobody'd be able to check up on him. 'One thing about a wave,' he said, 'nobody knows what becomes of it.' Ever hear such thing! I heard of another fellow stationed in the Aleutians. This guy, he went up to the CO and told him one way to keep the guys from going batty was to build 'em a roller-skating rink. 'Boost your morale one hundred percent,' he said. Imagine!" Leo made his point and returned to his letter.

"All this don't mean a damn to me," Dooley said. "Maybe you guys feel okay laying around, but I gotta fly. Got ten more to go and I wanna finish 'em."

"Just lissen to that rain," Charley Couch said reflectively. "Pissing a storm. Lake Frantic must be filling up outside. We'll need pontoons to get out for chow." He lay on his back, his corpulent little body covered with a blanket. He lit a cigarette and said: "I heard Axis Sally this morning. You know that gal's got something."

"What gal ain't?" Dooley said, maintaining his sullen tone.

"What I mean is," Charley said, his eyes on the ceiling, "she knows how to lay it on. Now you take the British Broadcasting Company, they don't know how to make you lissen. You tune in and what do they give ya? Mozart's Unfinished Fourteenth Symphony. The Jerries are smarter. They put on this bitch, Axis Sally, and she plays popular songs, then she says: 'You guys *getting* any lately? I'm getting plenty.' Now that's what I call art!"

"She's a whore," Trent said, turning away grudgingly from his letter writing. "I wouldn't lay her with Dooley's dong. Why, I hear she's been diving for every guy up in Florence. According to Intelligence she gave birth to a little bastard up there after screwing around with Axis George. I bet you she smells bad."

"But she sure makes you feel sad and lonely," Charley said. "Them records she plays!

> 'Oh, I'm sa-ad an' lonely, feelin' blu-ue,
> I can only think of you.'"

"If I got my hands on her," Dooley warned, "I'd shave every hair off her head like they do in France to them women that's traitors. She's no American girl, if you ask me. No American girl would sell out like that, broadcasting for the enemy. Now I got no use for this fukken war, but you don't catch me peddling my ass. I tell you I better not catch her walking around here!" he said, rising from his cot. "I'm going over to Operations and see if I can get myself a mission for tomorrow."

"And I'm staying right here in the sack," Charley said, sighing comfortably. "'Back the Attack in the Sack' I always say. Figger if it rains like this a coupla months the infantry'll win the war for me. I ain't particular who wins it for me just so long as I kin finish reading this here Studs book. At the rate I'm going I'll never finish it." He yawned and stretched. "Infantry! Them poor bastards! I kin just see 'em up there in the Apennines, soaking wet. My aching back. Kills me just thinking about it." He turned over on his side. "Think I'll put in some sacktime." He belched and said: "Excuse me, men, musta been something I ate. Burping ain't polite, I know, but it saves wear and tear on the asshole." He sniggered and added in a sleepy tone of voice: "Man, I'm a dirty sonofabitch! But I come from a good fam'ly."

38

THE RAIN BEAT on the leaking roof and came through the holes where the windows had been a long time ago. The men, having moved their cots from underneath the holes in the ceiling, were lying about sleeping, staring at the ceiling, or playing cards with pained boredom.

Two gunners stood several feet from one of the barracks doors, tossing daggers at it savagely, betting ten lire a throw. The daggers whammed at the thin door with explosive sounds and made my nerves curl. I was trying to write a letter to Ruth. I had received a letter from her in the morning and in it she wrote how she'd told a friend that I'd completed 35 missions. For some reason this information upset me. I felt Ruth should not have anticipated my missions. She knew full well I'd flown only 34. So why had she claimed the additional one? I resented the ease with which my wife (a civilian!) marked down missions which had not been flown. And I was annoyed with myself for resenting her. I wondered whether I should write and remind her again I had flown only 34 missions. Or should I forget the incident and write her the usual, cheerful, meaningless letter? Letters were so unsatisfying. You were always putting up a front. And so were the people in the States. The great American Indoor Sport! Everybody was lying like the very devil. Since the censors did not allow me to tell Ruth that some of my crewmates were dead, that one had been sent back to the States a broken man, that another had jumped out a waist window, I went to the other extreme and told her that all my buddies were in tiptop shape; we were literally burning up the skies over Europe. In return, Ruth wrote me that she was getting along splendidly, and she was lying too. I knew damned well she was consumed with ennui and pain. I knew that living with her parents in Michigan City was a living death — for her.

The two gunners were becoming more grim about their dagger game. Their daggers bit into the door with loud explosions, as if the men were taking out on the rotting wood the frustrations stored up in them. "You know what would be more fun than this," one of the gunners said. "Breaking a window. A great, big window. Smash it to a lot of fukken pieces!"

"You got something there, mate."

"You damn right!" Wham.

The daggers were hacking the door to pieces.

Across the aisle a gunner named Art was also poring over a letter. "I'm writing to my girl in Buffalo," he said, "and I'm having a tough time." He was speaking to no one in particular. "I don't know what to do," he continued somber faced. "I wanna break with her, but I don't know how to put it to her. I guess the best thing to do is tell her it's all over between us. *Finito*. Am I right?"

The two dagger-tossing gunners halted their savage game and said almost in unison: "That's a tough one, Art."

"But I don't care about her anymore," Art said.

"If you ask your old dad," Leo intervened, "I'd say don't break with her now. Keep writing till you're finished with your tour of missions. You can never tell what'll happen. You might go down or have your head blown off. It's always good to have someone mourn for you and say you were a hero. Get it? But if you break with her now, who'll cry after you?"

"I see what you mean," Art said solemnly. "You got something there. But still — it's not fair to —"

"Start giving her subtle hints," Leo counseled, "prepare her for the break. Get the point?"

"I'll try," Art said, "but it won't be easy."

At the far end of the barracks, near the door leading to the water-logged latrine, a gunner named Tex was picking on a guitar, humming mournfully to the accompaniment of the rain:

> *The Lib'rator's a very fine airplane,*
> *Constructed of rivets and tin,*
> *With a speed of over 200,*
> *The ship with a headwind built in.*

Oh, why did I join the air force?
Mother, dear Mother knows best.
Here I lie 'neath the wreckage,
Liberator all over my chest.

If you should go on a mission,
With plenty of money to burn,
Any old crewchief will tell you,
Two to one you'll never return.

And if you should run into trouble,
And don't know which way to turn,
Just reach up on the dashboard,
Push the button marked: Spin, Crash and Burn.

Dooley came back from Squadron. "Got some poop from Group," he said, throwing off his drenched helmet liner and raincoat. "The Alert List is up for tomorrow. I'm on it. And so're you, Ben. We ain't flying with the same crew. Charley's on, so's Leo. All flying with different crews."

"What about me, sarge?"

"Who's your pilot?"

"Pyniak."

"You're flying."

"Where we going?"

"Where you think?" Dooley replied. "Only one place, Vienna, that sonofabitch!"

"How are we going to break through the cloud front?" Leo asked bitterly. He was aware that nobody could answer his question, not even those who planned the missions in Bari. "After what happened last week when we lost a flock of ships, they ought not try it again. Clouds are a messy thing. I like to see where I'm flying. I don't like my eyes tied."

"They'll prob'ly put a Mickey ship at the head of each box," Dooley said, "fly by radar."

"We did that last week," Trent retorted, "but that didn't stop the collisions." He sat back on his cot and shook his head sadly. His face, which had grown thinner since the crash, had a drawn look about it, the worry and concern stamped on it like an indelible mark. He went over to sit on Art's cot. He put his arm around Art's shoulder and started whispering animatedly to him.

Art was a new buddy to Leo. Art was like Cosmo had been, someone to put one's arm around and whisper to and feel close to when danger was in sight. Art was a Polish boy from Buffalo and Trent was of Anglo-Saxon stock out of Hollywood. They sat for hours and whispered to one another and laughed and found strength in their companionship. They'd never flown together. Everything about them was dissimilar. Their cots were next to each other. But that's not why they were buddies. Trent had a penchant for picking buddies among those who were less articulate than he. And he usually chose them outside his own crew. Perhaps he had the notion that we, his old crewmates, were always sitting in judgment on him. He was deeply ashamed of the attacks of diarrhea which occurred whenever the red ribbon in the briefing shed pointed to Vienna. Leo had chosen Art deliberately — for his gentleness, his inarticulateness, and for his ignorance of Trent's flying habits. One had a feeling about Leo, whose mustache was no longer razor sharp and whose prancing had slowed down to a walk, that he was always thinking and worrying of what his kid-brother war hero might say about him.

●   ●   ●   ●

We were keyed up for the mission. You could feel a coiled tenseness in the barracks, going through like a spark among the thirty-odd men alerted. The talk was suddenly less boisterous and the two young gunners had ceased hacking the door to pieces with their daggers. Gunners sat on their cots talking in quiet tones. The boredom had vanished and instead there was a silence of retrospection and humility. The cussing and brawling had ceased as if the men were hurriedly trying to get on the good side of the Lord. Suddenly Delmonico barged in with the news that the mission had been called off. "Standdown for tomorrow," he said. "Order just come in from Bari."

"Well, what do you know!" someone shrieked happily. The tenseness snapped like a taut cable and the loud voices and curses rolled forth, drowning out the rain patter on the roof. Several gunners dug into their hoarded rations of combat whiskey and started passing the bottle around. Tex began picking on his guitar strings:

The Lib'rator's a very fine airplane,
Constructed of paper and wood,
It's okay for carrying whiskey,
But for combat it's no goddamn good.

Oh, why did I join the air force?
Mother, dear Mother knows best.
Here I lie 'neath the wreckage,
Liberator all over my chest. . . .

At our end of the barracks the four of us sat in semi-darkness, talking in the quiet tones of veterans whom life and time had subdued and made reflective. Charley was arguing mildly with Dooley, trying to convince him that the scrubbing of a mission was not a tragic thing at all. "I ain't gonna moan about it," Charley said. His words came out like a song with a nice lilt, as if he were cradling each word. "The way I figger it, every stand-down is a day longer to live, and one day longer away from my wife."

"I got too many missions to fly," Dooley said. Recently he had got the notion that along with his missions he must complete those of Mel and Petersen. We tried to argue him out of this quixotic scheme, but Dooley refused to listen to our reasoning. "I got ten more of my own to fly, and then the others," he said. "At the rate I'm going I won't ever be finished."

"Well, I ain't gonna hurry it," Charley said, leaning back on his cot and tucking his hands underneath his stubby neck. "I'm getting fond of this college life. Why, it's getting to be so you don't have to get outa your cot to get washed in the morning. All you hafta do is stick out your hand and the raindrops do it. Ever get that in the States?" He continued: "Nothing to hurry about. The way I look at it, life is ten miles of bad road. If you take it easy, it ain't so hard on your kidneys. I tried telling that to my wife. She's always in a hurry to get no place. Nervous in the Service. Now, supposing I was lucky enough to finish my fifty. What then? They'll ship me to the States for thirty days, then over to the Pacific I'll go, flying B-29s. Well, you know I ain't fit for no more flying. But if I hurry it and tear-ass back to the States, they'll sure as hell do it to me."

Tex's guitar and the loud voices of the gunners at the other end of the barracks floated in on our conversation. Leo said: "If God grant I finish my missions, I'll go back to the States and get lost."

"Get lost among civilians?" Charley said. "I don't know. I don't think I'd know how to act among civilians no more. I'd be scared."

"Not me," Leo said. "Soldier, you just let me among 'em."

"I'm scared o' the States," Charley said. "Don't ask me why. Was a time I wasn't scared o' nothing. Was a big shot; had all the dough in my pocket. Played a thousand smackers on a card. Was worth molto dough, and I ain't saying I'm pore now. But I'm scared. The air war done it to me. For a fella that's tunneled underground for gold like I done, was kinda strange working so high up in the air. Made me rabbit-jumpy so I got my ears cocked alla time for all kinds o' noises. Right now I don't feel like I'm fit to live among normal people no more."

"What are you gonna do after you're done with your tour?" Dooley inquired.

"Cross the bridge when I get there," Charley replied.

"What about you, pop?"

"I'll take my thirty days in the States," I said.

"Then you gonna fly some more?"

"That depends on air force. If they think I'm fit —"

"At your age?" Dooley snickered. "Throw in the sponge, pop. Why don't you do yourself a favor and get grounded? I'll finish the war for you."

"Thanks, pal."

"You proud?"

Dooley's spite did not have the old sting. His attempts at spite were desultory and weak, throwbacks to the past when he had attacked people savagely and without let-up. His voice was more subdued, and though he still walked with the springy crouch of a tamed panther, sometimes hours passed before a word crossed his lips. The scowl and frown were often gone from his face. And though he was wrapped up completely in his brooding, there was in him this new ability to reach out for people. He was able to talk of himself and listen to others. Only on occasion did the spite rise in him and then he sought me out to rid himself of it. This was a "Jewish war," and I was a Jew.

> Oh, if you should fly this old coffin,
> Or aircraft of similar ilk,
> Whenever you run into trouble,
> Remember — resort to the silk!

Tex's voice warmed up with the fiery combat whiskey. The two gunners who had tossed daggers at the mutilated door earlier in the evening resumed their game with renewed frenzy. They bet fifty lire a throw instead of ten, and the one who made the dagger stick was the winner. "Funny thing'd happen if somebody'd open the door while we're tossing 'em," one of them said. He was so amused with this he doubled up with laughter.

"I see what you mean, mate," his opponent said and he too roared with laughter.

Toward the center of the barracks the six enlisted men of Lieutenant Smiley's crew sat in a tight little knot, sipping their small savings of combat whiskey and pledging eternal friendships. They were pounding one another on the shoulder and embracing.

"You're my good buddy forever," Smiley's engineer said to the little tail gunner who evidently could not hold his liquor because he was swaying already. "We're all good buddies forever."

The tail gunner nodded and the radio operator said, "You goddamn right. This is the *best* crew ever. An' it's gonna stay that way if I got anything to say about it." All six nodded in unison on this, and the radio operator cried solemnly: "One for all and all for one! That's what I say!"

"Me too," the right waist gunner chimed in. His eyes were swimming but they encompassed lovingly the little world which consisted of his five buddies. "Best crew in the world! And when we get back to the States, we're all gonna be together."

"I'm married," said the ball gunner, "but I'll bring my wife along. All gonna stick together."

"'At's it. All together."

"We'll have reunions alla time," the engineer cried. "Get together in some big hotel in some big city, and brother! We'll pitch a bang till the bells ring. Just our crew."

"Damn right!" the tail gunner said jubilantly, waving his pistol. Suddenly he stopped, his face clouded with concern. "But what about the officers?" he demanded. "They gonna be our buddies too?" His lips were curled in utter distaste.

"At our reunions they'll be," the radio operator reassured him. "Just at the reunions — once a year. But the rest of the time it'll be just the six of us."

"Okay," the tail gunner said, appeased. "Jes wanna ta know. 'Cause I got no use for officers, even good 'uns. They're all chicken, f'ya ask me."

"I got a better idea," the right waist gunner said. "Why don't all of us move to Detroit after the war so we can see each other alla time, 'stead of waiting for reunions?"

"Hey, how *about* that!" the radio operator cried. "There's an idea. All of us moving to the same town."

"What about them that's married?" the ball gunner asked, distressed at having to place obstacles in the way of an otherwise excellent idea. "My wife likes to live near her old lady who wouldn't move from Harrisburg."

"It's okay," the engineer reassured him. "We'll think of something before we're finished with our missions."

"Roger-dodger!"

"Here's to the crew!"

"To the crew!"

"And to hell with civilians!"

"F— — the civilians!"

"Hurrah for us!"

"Yeah, hurrah for us!"

"'Cause nobody cares about us," the engineer continued the toast while the others chimed in, "and we don't care about nobody. Hurrah for gunners!"

"Down the fukken hatch!"

"San' Ant-onnnnne!"

The barracks was a bedlam of shouts and screams and blood-curdling cries. The lid had been pried loose.

Men were navigating among the tightly placed cots, swinging bottles. Men were embracing and calling each other "My good buddy!" Men were cursing civilians, the war, the rain, B-24s, Italy, the mess sergeant, Vienna, and the fickle finger of fate. "F— — everything!" they said.

The engineer from Smiley's crew came up to us and offered his bottle. "What's the matter you men ain't drinking? Ain't you gonna take just one swig with us to show we're all good buddies?" We took the bottle from him and drank. "Well, now I feel better," he said. "For a minute there I thought you guys was chicken — the four of you sitting off by yourselves while everybody in the barracks is getting pie-eyed."

"No, we're right with you," Dooley said without any enthusiasm. I noted what fatigue there was in him when he spoke. Dooley was only twenty-two but already gray hair showed on his temples. "Only thing," he added, not wanting to hurt the man's feelings, "the rain might let up and you can never tell what them eager beavers at Group are liable to cook up. Liable to call an alert again."

"Not now, they won't," Smiley's engineer said. "Stand-down tomorrow. Why don't ya take a real swig?"

Dooley seized the bottle as if it had been denied him all his life. He swallowed greedily and wiped his lips. Suddenly he was on his feet, shouting, "Now the rest of you are gonna drink too." He stood over Charley while he drank and then he pressed the bottle on Leo and me. "If I'm gonna get drunk," he cried, "so will the rest of you!" He lunged out of the barracks and several minutes later he returned with three bottles of American liquor which he had bought from some officers. Then he ran across the road and stole some C ration cans of sausages and bread. "We'll have a real party!" he cried. "Like we usta!"

The cots were moved away, turned over, folded, shoved out of the way. Dooley was in charge. Dooley roaring commands to open the bottles and fry the sausages; Dooley bellowing defiance at the rain and the boredom and Mel Ginn and Petersen; Dooley as I knew him, way, way back.

Charley put away his book and said: "Might just as well set up and pitch in and let the pieces fall where they may."

•   •   •   •

I drank until my body was too heavy to move. I heard daggers whamming against the door. I heard a pistol shot, and then they took the gun away from Smiley's tail gunner and he began to weep: "Gimme back my gun."

"You mighta killed Al," he was admonished, "playing with that gun."

I heard Art shout in disgust: "Oh, f— — that letter. I can't do it! Tomorra I'll write and break with her."

"I swear you're a devil, Art!" Leo said. "Why don't you take your old dad's advice and wait till you're finished flying?"

"I can't, I can't. It isn't fair."

"And supposing you get your head blown off?"

"I don't give a s— —."

I heard Dooley's voice. His voice was always louder than the others. "Lemme sing you, lemme sing you an Irish song!"

And I kept muttering to myself, "This has happened before. It has been going on all my life, this rain and scorching whiskey. The world has always been khaki and always will be. And before my eyes there have always been the faces of frightened men crying: We're too young to die."

Mist moved over my eyes and clouded my brain like the clouds that hung over the barracks. I felt Dooley tugging me, dragging me, shouting in my ear: "I'm gonna sing "Ave Maria" for the guys that's gone. And after I'm finished I wancha to sing "Eli, Eli" for the Jewish fellas. Now let's do it right, Ben, for all the men that's died." And we sat around the circle in the middle of the barracks, singing, weeping, and embracing. Dooley was hugging me and I felt his salty tears against my cheek and he was shouting: "You old Jew bastard, I love ya. You're my buddy till the day I die. You and me been through hell. We seen 'em come and go." He was on his feet and searching for Leo who was drunk and lying somewhere quietly underneath an overturned cot. He dragged Leo over to where I sat and started hugging him too. "Now we're all together. What's left of the old crew. We been together from the start. We brawled together and drank together and whored to-gether. I love youse both, you bastards, so let's get on with the singing."

At some point, as we moved drunkenly about among the broken cots and shattered glass and exhausted, liquor-sleeping men, I heard the screech of the brakes of Delmonico's weapons' carrier. He came into the barracks and cried: "Got new poop for you hot rocks! The mission's on for tomorrow. Everybody whose name was on the Alert List is flying."

Delmonico's announcement was received with snickers and laughter.

"Oh, yeah?"

"Go blow it out."

"That's a crock, too."

Someone who was sober enough and cared enough threw a bottle at the Operations clerk. The rest of us didn't care.

39

IN THE EARLY dawn we sloshed through the slippery mud to the mess hall. Inside the low *casa* the tables were still damp from the rain that had ceased eight hours ago. I sipped the acid coffee with distaste. Near me sat Charley, Leo, and Dooley. Their faces had a yellowish tint as if they were all suffering from jaundice.

We regarded one another with bloodshot eyes. We moved as if in a heavy, overpowering trance, with a terrible weight pressing down upon us. But underneath our fatigue the tense fear of a mission was working its way to the surface. "This is the craziest idea I ever heard in my life," Charley said wearily. "The clouds are all socked in, the front ain't moved a blonde cunt's hair since yesterday, but they're sending us up anyway." He took a slow sip from his metal cup. "I can't figger it. You think they've went nuts at Headquarters?"

"Looks that way to me," Leo said, staring at the cracks in the table. "Probably decided they weren't going to let a little cloud front of ten thousand feet put something over on the AAF. Not them! The bastards!" He sighed, concluding, "Trouble is I know where we're going, too. And I do hope I don't get the GIs when I see the ribbon in the briefing shed."

"Maybe it won't be Vienna," Dooley said. There were dark shadows underneath his eyes. The stubbly beard made him look like a derelict. "Maybe it'll be a milk run."

"Maybe they'll get some sense and call this thing off," Charley said. "That sky don't look fit for no man or dog."

We came out and looked worriedly at the sky. The black clouds of the previous day had given way to gigantic white masses with black bottoms on them. The masses moved slowly like huge icebergs, linked in a terrifying whiteness, as if the sky above five thousand feet consisted of nothing but roaming, impenetrable clouds. Our faces were turned toward the clouds, and then we looked at one another with incredulity and our glances said: they can't mean to send us up in this weather, it'll be murder. . . .

And yet we dragged our weary bodies toward the briefing shed, resigned; questioning but resigned. I saw Leo's face turn pale when he noticed the red ribbon. The yellow tint on his face changed to a sickly paleness. "Oh, my God!" he sobbed, looking down at his pants. "I — I can't help it, men."

The briefing officer, promoted to captain, was holding forth and his voice seemed far away as if it too was marching somewhere on the other side of the mountain masses. "There have been some breaks in the front," he said, "according to reconnaissance. The break, occurring up north, should hold for the rest of the day. At least, that's our hope," he said uncertainly. "Now, let me run over the plan quickly. You'll gain your altitude over the field. Should clear the weather at about twenty thousand feet. Then you set a course north three hundred miles where you'll rendezvous with the rest of the air force. From there, it is believed, you will be flying between two masses of clouds which will rise about five to ten thousand feet above your formations. Your escort is scheduled to pick you up over Lake Balaton and provide penetration. You will bomb the target through heavy overcast, naturally. And the target, as you see, is — uh — Vienna." The captain fidgeted on the rostrum and the stick with which he was pointing out our route slipped out of his hands. His uncertainty and misgivings about the mission came across to the gunners with his every halting word. Obviously he, too, was aware of the quixotic undertaking. He, too, had been briefed hurriedly and without conviction. He was not at all certain how far north we would fly before turning off into Yugoslavia. He spoke vaguely about a "corridor" and the "clear path" which awaited us when we joined the air force. His fidgety demeanor only confirmed our own fear that this would be a strike of desperation, an attempt to grapple with an enemy that had stopped us cold. The clouds were our enemy. The clouds were able to stop the army air force. (In basic training, in Gunnery School we had sung proudly: "Nothing can stop the army air force, not even Mabel.") The clouds stopped us and paralyzed our activities. The war was moving on all fronts: in France, the Pacific, Russia, moving in the air out of England. But stopped dead in its tracks in Italy.

After the briefing officer had finished, the Protestant chaplain said a quick prayer, blessing our endeavor. We stood with bowed heads, taking some comfort from the chaplain's words. But more than his prayer, we appreciated his rising at dawn to conduct these services.

After we were airborne I stood at the right waist window watching the planes poke through the clouds below us. We flew single file as a precaution against collision. The men in the ship were a crew of youngsters who had ten missions to their credit. Their eager chatter made me feel old. It pulled me back to the time late in spring when *our* crew had been together and whole, chattering over the interphone. There had been the feeling of belonging, although at the time none of us realized what comfort and warmth there was in belonging. The gunners in the waist section deferred to me as if I were a grisly old veteran who must be respected on account of his missions and experience in combat. On my part I felt terribly lonely and stared out the window searching for the ships in which Dooley, Leo, and Charley were flying. Each one of us was in a different plane; we were truly apart and severed. But the hope that they might be thinking of me or looking out their windows to catch a glimpse of my ship warmed and comforted me and made me feel less alone.

We were climbing slowly. Climbing through the labyrinths of clouds, through layers of white tablelands, through corridors, climbing, pointing upward. Ahead of us flew the colonel in the control ship, a two-engine plane, trying to whip Group into some semblance of formation. The colonel was pouring admonishing words over Command and his voice sounded thin and gurgling as if it had been processed and wrung out over the wires: "Awright, awright, let's get some kinda formation here. Come on, Number Four, get your ass in the slot . . ."

From the right waist window I saw the lead ship, flown by Captain Pennington. Big Wheel was leading the Group, and flying copilot with him was Major Schneider, our new squadron commander. Dooley was in the ship flying deputy lead, Number Two position, off Pennington's right wing. And we were off his left wing, flying Number Three. Behind us were an additional thirty ships, making up Group's strength for the day. I saw the ships come through the soup and then they disappeared again. They swam into view, little objects coming over clouds. They looked as if they were nestling on the clouds. There seemed no pattern to our flying, no purpose or rhythm. Only the knowledge — which was more of a hope — that at a certain altitude we would all be reunited and proceed on our course, gave this any semblance of reason. But as we continued climbing, gaining altitude over our own field, it became increasingly apparent that some ships had already lost their course in the mountains of clouds. These ships were probably poking blindly through the soup at one hundred and fifty miles an hour, and the men inside were praying, praying. . . . We were helpless in the cloud-fog, groping in the white, cottony substance which entombed us. Our instruments on the panel enabled us to tell altitude, but there was no way of determining how dangerously near was the wing of another ship lost in the soup.

The ragged formation was still over the home field when we went on oxygen. The temperature dipped down to twenty-five below, and a hundred-mile-an-hour wind lashed at our tail. I tuned in on Command, hoping to hear instructions from either the B-25 control ship or the tower that the mission was being scrubbed and the ships being called back. But Command was dead for long spaces of time as if both the colonel and the tower were unable to comprehend what was going on and feared to make a decision. Because someone lacked the courage to make a decision to call off the mission, we continued climbing, reaching hopefully toward those summits where there weren't any more clouds. Above these layers was the sun. The sun was separated from Mandia by twenty thousand feet of clouds, and somewhere in between were our men in the ships, sweating, praying, dying our own individual deaths, calling up our own dear images, mumbling in our own private ways the words that brought some succor and relief. Somewhere in that white, blinding universe were Dooley, Trent, and Couch.

We continued climbing in dead silence. The silence only made the folly of this mission seem more monstrous. It made it appear as if we had been stripped of any power to do the logical thing: which was to turn back. And in the absence of any such logic, we continued unresisting on this course of folly as if the ships had been set to fly by automatic pilot, thus eliminating such factors as human emotions and reason.

Command seemed to come to life only when the first box in our formation reached the summit of the cloud-mountains. We followed

Pennington out of the soup and came upon the flat white sea of clouds. The clouds were beneath us, stretching over the universe. Above the sun shone coldly. "Okay, move in," the thinned-out voice of the colonel came over. Only sixteen ships out of the thirty were visible. "Move in and get on your course," Command directed. "Fill up the lead box. Good luck to you. Over." The last word had been spoken. The control ship peeled off and went home while the decimated formation, half of what had been anticipated, continued on course. Leo's ship was missing and so was Charley's. I searched for them, I called the pilot, I could see very clearly from the tail-turret window that they were not there. Only Dooley's ship was still there, flying off Pennington's right wing.

The temperature dipped down to thirty-five below zero. I had plugged in my electric cord but I was shivering anyway and my teeth were chattering. The sun pointed thin daggers at my eyes, sharp, painful daggers with needlepoints that scratched the pupils. But there was no shielding the eyes because no matter where you turned there was the burning white splendor of sun, sky, and clouds. The clouds that stretched like a solid white floor beneath us cast a fierce glare about them, causing the eyes to tear and smart. I felt as if I were going blind and yet I did not dare close my eyes. There was something eerie about the vapor trails coming out like four parallel pencil marks from each ship. The vapor trails were the only manifestation of life in this white, glaring expanse. The shadows of the bombers mirrored on the cloud beds.

Pennington, flying a Mickey ship, was heading the formation in the northerly direction where we were supposed to rendezvous with the rest of the air force. But when we reached our point of rendezvous (which was nothing but clouds that looked like all the others), we saw only shreds of formations. We turned off toward the right and started across the Adriatic toward our destination. But even as we made this last turn there was a tentativeness, an indecision that seemed to permeate our small universe. At any moment I expected (and hoped) that someone sensible would assume command and instruct us to turn hack. But I hardly expected Pennington to do it. This sort of a challenge appeared to be made to order for Pennington. I felt that he would get through, or attempt to get through to the target even if the rest of the formation and air force turned back; he would make the bomb run himself, one bomber over Vienna, defying hundreds of cannon firing at him alone. Pennington's supreme moment had come. But even Big Wheel seemed uncertain today. Perhaps the clouds frightened even him. The clouds were like a sea beneath us, a deep, fathomless sea that removed the only thread of security a flyer has when he can look down on solid ground. The solid ground, even from a height of twenty thousand feet, made one feel more secure. Even only seeing the solidity made it easier. One wanted to see where he was going to fall. The clouds obliterated the world below. The world was space bounded by sky and clouds, with the hard, solid core removed. If you bailed out, you would never reach solidity.

In the distance I perceived the two huge masses of clouds which rose like white walls on both sides of our formations to what seemed like ten thousand feet. They were moving slowly, like two mountains shifting, heading inexorably toward the center which was our path. Between those two white moving mountains was our narrow corridor leading to the target. Along this shifting corridor our formation, separated from the rest of the air force, hurried toward Vienna. On occasion when the front broke, I noticed other Liberators bobbing in and out of the clouds like frightened rabbits fleeing in and out of bushes. But it did not appear strange that there should be no semblance of formation or plan. Nor did it appear strange when we did not find our escort over Lake Balaton.

The mountainous corridor came to an abrupt end and we were upon white ridges which were narrow and separated the boxes from each other. At times I lost sight of the ships in our own box. I knew we could not be far off the IP and the target, but a cold numbness took such full possession, my mind was incapable of grasping anything but the sound of my chattering teeth. I heard the last-minute feverish preparations, Pennington driving the formation into line, calling them to drop the bombs simultaneously with the radar ships. The radar ships, with the ponderous dreamlike kettles in which the detecting apparatus was lodged, were making corrections, lining up on the target, Vienna.

The bomb-bay doors ground open. The wind lashed and cut through to the flesh like a burning knife. The tinfoil streamed out the open waist windows and was lost in the clouds. Then I saw the black puffs. Black puffs coming through white clouds. Our ship began to rock from the near misses. Thundering hammer blows pounded my senses into a numb terror. I clambered out of the tail turret and strapped on my parachute and started moving toward the waist section and its open windows. As I moved up front, toward the windows, I noted that both waist gunners had been hit and were bleeding. Both of them had their oxygen masks on so I could not tell how deep was their pain. Our eyes staring above the masks were enlarged with horror, the pupils frozen. Near the right waist window I grabbed the gun mount to keep from being pitched by the tossing ship. I suddenly let out an anguished cry. My eyes were riveted on the lead ship; it seemed to stand still, nailed to the sky. Its two port engines had been sheared off by a direct hit. I saw a man come out the top hatch of the Lib and sway briefly above the plane's left wing. There was no mistaking the man. I wanted to scream: "Pennington, Pennington!" Ignoring the deadly wires on the ship, the rudder cables, the tall, lean figure moved cautiously toward the center of the ship, his arms extended as if he were balancing on a tightrope. Then he jumped. The bomber lost control and went into a death dive.

· · · ·

Dooley's ship took over the lead spot. One of its engines was feathered and its prop looked like a frozen cross. We moved into the Number Two spot and Lieutenant Heinkelman was flying Number Three. And that was all. There weren't any other ships. And if there were, we could not see them. Three lone ships with several wounded aboard, without any escort, flying back toward that shifting corridor of white mountains. We patched up the two waist gunners. Their wounds were on the surface, more frightening than damaging.

I was back in my turret, sucking greedily on a lemon that had been frozen into a solid rock. At twenty thousand feet it was almost impossible to light a match. Besides, every time I removed the oxygen mask in an attempt to take a few drags on a cigarette, a dizziness overwhelmed me.

The two mountains of clouds were closing in. It had been determined that we could not fly above them; the ships would not be able to climb to thirty thousand feet. And assuming we could gain that altitude, we would use up too much gas in the process and not have enough of it to get back to Italy. So the decision had been made by

the three pilots — all that remained of Group — to fly at the present
altitude, and if and when the two mountains of clouds closed the corridor, the three ships would fan out — in order to avoid collision —
and try and make Italy on their own.

Italy was far away, buried somewhere underneath white, impenetrable clouds, as was the rest of the world. It seemed incredible, and
you couldn't help thinking about it, that in these vast outer spaces
where oceanic clouds roamed at will, frightened men with pounding
hearts were asserting their own minor anger. But our anger was no
match for the wrathful elements; in addition to flying — which is
man's challenge to the law of gravity — and the brief encounter with
the enemy's batteries, we were taking on another adversary, the most
formidable of them all, clouds.

I longed to see the earth. Even the enemy earth. I would even welcome the sight of an enemy fighter-plane as proof that other human
beings inhabited these impenetrable white gorges. This whiteness
congealed into a solidity before the eyes. One could stretch out on it
and sleep on this vast, pristine, billowing sheet. And how I longed for
sleep. Fatigue moved crushingly on my body like the mountains that
were closing our path. I watched the ship in which Dooley flew
plunge into the soup. Our ship followed them in. And after that there
was nothing to see. Our sight was curtained with white. We plowed
through the whiteness, the ship groaning with the effort, the wings
flapping as if they were about to tear off.

"Well, it's all yours," the pilot said to the navigator who moved up
to the front end of the ship, near the nose gunner; where his instruments and charts were spread out on a table.

The navigator was silent awhile, as if weighing the responsibility
placed upon him suddenly. "Yeah, I guess so," he said timidly.

"I'll put her on A-5," the pilot said. "Let her fly by herself — for all
the good I can do her. Let me know when you want corrections."

"Okay, Al," the navigator replied uncertainly. I did not know the
navigator beyond having seen him walk jauntily down the base with
his broken garrison cap swept back on his blond head, smiling his
boyish, twenty-one-year-old smile. A college boy from Boston, made
warrior, like Andy Kyle. Now my life was completely in the hands of
this boy whom I'd never met. He was suddenly catapulted into a position where the lives of nine other men were dependent on his calcu-

lations. This awareness had a shattering effect on him. His voice which had been calm at first and replied evenly to the men's questions about our whereabouts, suddenly grew irritating. "I'm doing the best I can," he said, in response to our queries. "If you guys'll just leave me alone. . . ." We rode along in anxious silence, our ears attuned to the navigator. We accommodated ourselves to his moods and words and his well-being was our deepest concern. If we were silent, it was not because we were not eager to talk, it was because we feared to upset him. But our silence worried him even more than our words. "Why is everybody acting like this is a funeral?" he demanded.

"What's bothering you, Jimmy?" the pilot asked, worried.

"I feel a little dizzy, Al," the navigator replied weakly.

"You getting your oxygen?"

"Yeah, but I feel dizzy anyway."

"Now you just take it easy," the pilot said soothingly as if he'd sensed the navigator's malady and was trying to lead him along gently. "You just go on working and call me for corrections. You're doing fine."

"I'm not doing fine," the navigator replied. "We're lost. We're lost and I don't know how to get you out of it."

"You're kidding, Jimmy," the pilot said. "You're the best little navigator in the whole goddamn air force and don't let anybody tell you otherwise."

"Don't give me no snow job," Jimmy said, his voice choking with sobs he tried hard to stifle. "I know I'm lost. I, I can't get no bearing."

"Now listen to me, Jimmy. I'm not asking you to split the field, although I'll bet you're gonna do that today. All I want you to do is tell me where to turn off so we won't go over Zagreb and Belgrade and a couple more flak areas. I've been trying to contact Big Fence, but the signals I'm getting don't sound right to me. I have a suspicion Jerry's in on my line trying to steer us over flak areas. Get the point, Jimmy?"

"I'll try, Al." Five minutes passed and he spoke again. "Can't somebody spot a checkpoint for me? If I could only get a checkpoint to work from!"

"Maybe we'll hit a clear spot," the pilot said. But we continued riding in the bowels of the cloud mass. My mind returned to the target and the tall figure of Albert Pennington standing on top of the fuselage. No one else had ever bailed out of a bomber by going out of the top hatch. And yet it seemed the only thing he could have done, judging by the speed with which the ship had gone into its death dive soon after he had bailed over the side. I remembered Pennington's frequent warnings: "If something goes wrong, I'll tell you fellows, but don't expect me to hang around long after that." No doubt by this time Pennington had hit the ground. If his chute opened and the flak guns missed him and the enemy civilians didn't lynch him, perhaps he was still alive.

Then I heard the scream. "I can't, I can't. . . ."

The navigator's screams infected the crew. His hysteria spread through the fog-sealed ship. The ball gunner complained of the "bends." He was doubled up in the waist section, screaming from the pain in his joints. The right waist gunner started feeling faint. "I can't get enough oxygen," he complained.

Fear enveloped the men and brought on panic. I watched the puking, retching, hysterical boys, watched them thresh about on the floor like epileptics, but I no longer had the strength to get up from my spot near the camera hatch. I was stiff with fatigue and cold. I was beyond being afraid because I was beyond feeling any kind of emotion. I regarded the boys with a curious detachment. I wondered what I would do if one of them crawled over to the waist window and made a move to open it and fall out. Would I be able to stop him? It was absurd to think that I could stop any one of them, and yet I moved down off the camera hatch, closer to the windows. I moved in a horizontal position, a little at a time, as if I were unable to lift my body off the floor. My head was resting on my parachute. The chute harness cut into my thighs and the flesh was seared where the harness pinched against it. But the pain had become a part of me. I might have moved my hands to loosen the straps and free my thighs, but even that was too much of an effort because it required my sitting up. "Doesn't matter." This was the most inclusive of all thoughts. It best summed up the world. Beyond a certain point nothing mattered, and I had reached that point, and it was strange that it should be so unimportant and so undramatic and one should be so calm in the face of it. I didn't fear death any less; I simply attached less importance to remaining alive. Fear had been pressed out of me and instead there was the enveloping fatigue that held the promise of sleep and rest and peace. Perhaps life and death were not as far apart as people thought, and the change from one to the other not as painful as those who stood apart imagined. My eyes were heavy and my lids were beginning to close. Another comforting thought: it was not dying itself that was of any import, but how one died. Though we were lost in the clouds, the whole world knew of *us* and watched us and remained attuned to us — and approved of us. And that thought warmed me, and the thought of the angry refugee who pounded nails into shoes warmed me. And the anger which I had felt for those who had ordered this suicidal adventure was gone. Who was I to measure the cost as against the results? No matter how infinitesimal the damage we inflicted on the enemy, some progress had been made and the war shortened by a few ticks of the clock. It was absurd, I thought, patently absurd, to measure the individual against the gigantic effort. "You don't matter," I said to myself. "You, Ben Isaacs, are of no consequence." What sweet, calming, reconciled thoughts! How come the peace? I wondered. It didn't occur to me — and there was no way I had of knowing — that my heated-suit plug had worked loose from the socket and I was freezing to death.

Though my eyes were shut I saw the whiteness of the clouds. I thought I heard someone stirring and opened my eyes with the last measure of effort and curiosity. I saw the ball gunner move about. He sat up and reached down his left knee where his gun holster was strapped around the thigh. He pulled the pistol out of the holster and held it before his eyes as if examining it. I was propelled into a sitting position. I tried to get up and got to my feet. Suddenly the excruciating pain stabbed through my body as if my toes were on fire. I fell back with a cry, my mind awake with the realization that my toes were frozen and that my feet had turned into ice. At the same time I heard the shot. The man fell on his face. His left temple was bleeding. The oxygen mask was still on his face.

No one bothered removing the oxygen mask from the suicide's face. The sack of the mask had stopped inflating and we knew he was dead. And it didn't seem at all strange to me that I did not even remember this man's face. I had seen the face only when it wore an oxygen mask. There should have been a more formal introduction, I thought ironically. After all, he and I had practically gone through life together.

Two hours later we landed on a British fighter-strip north of Foggia.

40

ONE HUNDRED men were missing from Group. Six men were missing from our barracks. Lieutenant Smiley's ship had collided with another in the clouds and both of them exploded. Exploded, disappeared, wiped clean from the sky. No stench of dead, no guts spilling out, no blood, no dirt. Devoured by the voracious sky. Dissolved in the antiseptic air.

What other branch of service could boast of such clean working conditions? Compare your style of fighting with that of the infantry! Comparison proves!

Soldier, don't be bitter. What do you want? Egg in your beer?

Question: Was yesterday's trip really necessary? What did we gain out of the massacre?

Answer: You are here to fight, not to pass judgment.

Question: Granted. We're here to fight. But does yesterday's adventure come under the heading of fighting or suicide? What has been gained? Prestige for the air force? The fact was the Italy-based AF was suffering from an inferiority complex. And one of these cloudy days this inferiority complex would be the death of me.

The envy of our brass for the England-based air force was no secret. Whenever the boys in England achieved some striking success, our air force worked frenziedly to follow suit. Public relations officers at Group were constantly admonished about the fact that the other air force got more publicity in the States than ours. Press and radio were constantly featuring their achievements, relegating us to the Number Two spot. They made a movie called *Memphis Belle*. The movie was seen by sixty-five million, seventy-five million, one hundred million people. Our men saw it too and they laughed themselves sick. "You call that rough?" they asked. "Twenty-five milk runs, that's what them bums flew." Nevertheless it was good public relations. It made the England-based outfit the Glamour Air Force.

They were always ahead. They awarded more Silver Stars, Distinguished Flying Crosses, and air medals. In fact, the DFCs were being issued automatically in England upon completion of a tour of twenty-five missions, while in Italy a man had to fly fifty missions and even then he didn't get the Cross unless he was a pilot or performed some outstanding deed up in the air.

Group's public relations officer, after a dressing-down in Bari, ran around our base frantically, mumbling: "If we could only work up a congressional medal for somebody. That would show them!" Finally, you can imagine how overjoyed he was when he discovered an incident where a pilot had been killed after having given his parachute to a gunner who had forgotten to bring his own chute along. The dead pilot was written up good and proper. But the best they got — for his widow — was a Silver Star.

The public relations clerks in each of the four squadron PROs were on a twenty-four-hour alert — looking for heroes. They were driven to put out more copy for hometown consumption. Charts were hung on the office walls to indicate production of copy. There were pep talks all the time. Tonnage. Were we dropping as much tonnage as they? Hell, no. And there was talk among the men, and among the whores in Mandia who seemed always to know, that we were planning a "prestige" raid on Berlin. After all, hadn't they come over from England for a token raid on Ploesti?

Even among the enlisted men — they weren't medal-happy and publicity-hungry like the top brass, who simply looked upon the England-based air force as a rival business corporation with an enviable know-how — there were mutterings about the tough targets we hit, as compared with the glamour boys in England. "Just let 'em try Vienna once and they'd keep their big traps shut!" our men said. But the crowning humiliation was there for the whole world to behold: their commanding officer was a lieutenant-general, while our boss was only a major-general.

·   ·   ·   ·   ·

My frozen toes had turned purple. The flight surgeon told me I would be laid up for several weeks. Doc Brown came every day to change my bandages and apply salve. He did not linger in the barracks as he used to. He got over the habit of asking about the gunners' health. His eyes worked out a kind of evasive action, as if Doc were in mortal fear that if he looked about him, he might discover some problems crying for solution. He stayed in our barracks just long enough to check up on frozen toes. Then he escaped for fear there might be other complaints. Captain Brown walked with a constant shrug of his shoulders; that shrug appeared to be perched there in readiness for complaints about leaking roofs, sore throats, yellow jaundice, and combat fatigue. Group had forbidden the installation of stoves because one of the wooden barracks burned down. As a result everybody was coughing. But Doc didn't hear it. He couldn't afford to. The hospital was choked to overflowing. The medics' *casa* was always filled with sick. Many of the sick stayed in their barracks.

There had been a time during the summer when the men in our squadron were fond of Captain Brown. He had flown four milk runs "in order to get a taste of what the combat man faces." He had visited the barracks and talked and joked with the men. He had been like a father. Evidently he had been too solicitous because Group put the screws on him. In a few months you could see the change in Doc. He became an irritable, middle-aged man though he was only thirty-five. He turned on the flyers and accused them of malingering. "I won't coddle you fellows like I used to," he warned.

· · · ·

Doc Brown came to our barracks to look at my toes. Charley rolled over on his belly and became absorbed in *Studs Lonigan*. Trent started carving with his fierce knife, and Dooley walked away. Doc examined my toes, got up, tapped me on the shoulder, but instead of rushing out as usual, he hesitated. "Say, Ben," he said haltingly, "okay if I park on your cot a minute?"

"Sure."

"You flew with Lieutenant Mathias's crew this last time, didn't you?" He saw me nod and continued: "There was a suicide on the plane, right?"

"Yes."

"What happened?" Doc's tone of voice was that of a hurt and confused man.

"What's *your* theory?" I asked.

"His pilot told me today that this gunner suffered from the bends. He was in terrible pain. And then fear played an important part too, I suppose —" The latter part of the sentence trailed off as if he were afraid to voice his thoughts.

"Did that boy ever ask you to ground him?" I asked.

"No, not that I can remember," Doc replied quickly. "But even if he had, I can't ground everybody that comes to me. There must be reason and proof. You men have the peculiar notion that I can just go and ground people. My job is to keep the men in fighting shape, not on ground status."

"Well, that boy didn't appear to me to be in fighting shape," I said, "and incidentally, neither was the navigator. And the fact that we got back was more due to luck than what you call fighting shape."

"I'm not soliciting your opinions," the flight surgeon said abruptly. "I want the facts."

I was suddenly blinded with anger, and as is usual in such instances, I said a lot of stupid things about how a man could not be expected to risk his life for mom's apple pie or the corner drugstore or a jukebox. "Why the hell," I cried, "don't you tell the men why they're fighting? Guts alone is not enough." I heard my voice tremble and my palms were wet with perspiration, and even while I directed the words at the flight surgeon, the thought occurred to me that he was not the culprit; I was using him as a symbol of the army, taking out on him the hatred I felt for it. The obliqueness of this struck me, and yet I could not help myself. He was convenient, at hand, and my grievances had been choked inside me for many months.

"Shut up!" His voice startled me and I fell silent. His cheeks were crimson but he tried to control his voice. "Once and for all, cut out giving me your high-faluting opinions," he cried. "I don't want them, I don't hold with them, and I don't give a damn about them! I want the facts about the goddamn suicide. I want them direct, no trimmings. Tell me what you saw and not what you think. This is a direct order."

Charley was eyeing me owlishly and Trent looked up from his little table, pointing his huge nose at me. Dooley hung around, his face scowling, his shoulders hunched over as if anticipating trouble. The rest of the gunners, too, were regarding us with interest. Their conversation and buzzing had ceased and they were silent as if waiting for me

to fill up the vacuum of time. But I was choked up and the words refused to pass my lips. I was choked up with anger and impotence. I
had been challenged but I was shrinking from the challenge. What
harm could this man do me? I did not fear him, not nearly as much as
I had feared the drill sergeants during basic training.

I realized the gauntlet Doc threw down upset him as much as it
did me. He kept staring at me through his thick eyeglasses. His mouth
was set hard as if he were afraid to relax it and reveal his own fears.
There was something comic about him. So why did I fear him? Why
did I congeal? What had I to fear on my own accord? I was confined
to my cot with severe frostbite. All he could do was cite me for insub-
ordination, and in the face of my other problems, this was indeed a
minor matter. And even if they took away my sergeant's stripes, was
that so important in the face of combat?

"I'm waiting," the captain said. He, too, felt the silence. He was
aware also that the men hated him and hoped he would be van-
quished. "Look here, goddammit," he shouted, "I gave you a direct
order. I expect an answer!"

"What do you want me to tell you that I haven't already?" I asked.

"Address me as *sir*."

"Sir," I said. Inwardly I was saying to myself, "Look, the man is
afraid. He's trembling. Strike back at him." But I was paralyzed by the
silver bars on his shoulders. Those bars were his strength over me, but
that was enough.

"Okay, let's get on."

"I saw the ball gunner commit suicide," I said. "I tried to get up
and take the gun from him, but my feet would not support me. That
was the first inkling I had that my feet were frostbitten."

"Did the others in the waist section see him pull out his gun?"

"No, sir," I said, choking on my words.

"Then nobody else was involved," he said, a note of triumph
creeping into his voice.

"No, sir."

He got up. A little smiled played on his lips. "Why didn't you tell
me that in the first place, man," he said magnanimously. "That's all I
wanted to know." He stalked out of the barracks.

I heard myself saying what I'd heard many times before. "I'd like to
catch him after the war," I said. This had been said so many times by

those who had been humiliated and who had not fought back. I was ashamed to look into the faces of my comrades lest they judge me a coward. But instead Dooley came to sit on my cot and said, "You sure let that chancre mechanic have it with both barrels," he said.

"I'll say!" Charley agreed. "You had him sucking hind tit from the word go."

"Well, thanks a lot," I said gratefully. "Thanks a hell of a lot."

．　．　．　．

After the evening meal which Dooley brought for me from the mess hall in my kit, we sat on our cots covered by blankets. The clouds had turned angry gray again and it felt like rain. The barracks were cold and dreary and some of the men were acting up again, going stir-crazy. There were rumors there would be movies at the new indoor theater later in the evening. "They ain't sure yet," a gunner said sarcastically. "All depends on getting the projector fixed. Information and Education only got nine men working in their office. And that ain't enough to take care of a *whole* projector. You men know how it is being caught shorthanded!" he concluded sarcastically. The appreciative howls of the men pleased him. "I wouldn't be a bit surprised if they came down here and grounded a couple of you glamour boys so's you'd help out with the projector."

"Ain't that the goddamn truth!" another gunner said. "You went and hit the nail right on its fukken head."

The flurry of laughter spent itself. The boring silence set in again in our little world. It hung over our barracks like the homemade bulb shades which cast eerie shadows over us. It was as if everything that was to be said had been spoken, all the dreams laid bare, all the frustrations cursed, all opinions expressed, all the words used up. Beyond that each man was locked up in his own loneliness.

"I been thinking," Charley said reflectively, stretching out on his cot, resting his head on his arms. "For lack o' something to do I been adding up the cost of that mission to Vienna. Been exercising my mind, you might say. And you know something, if I was a taxpayer I'd he *molto* urinated off at what that fizzle of a raid cost. Lemme itemize it for ya, men. First take the bombs. Now each five hundred pounder costs one thousand dollars. Group sent up about thirty ships, and each ship carried ten bombs. That adds up to three hundred thousand smackeroos. Right? Now let's take the gas. Hundred-octane gas'll run you about one dollar a gallon and each ship carries two thousand, seven hundred gallons. That means purty near eighty thousand dollars in gas. You gotta figger Group maintenance and the salaries us suckers get for flying them ships. Then you gotta figger wear and tear on the ships. But let's leave that out. So far we spent purty near a half million dollars in the Group and we ain't off the ground yet. Now let's take off and see what happens. Only three ships get to the target, so we'll call the money spent on them well spent. But twenty-seven don't get there. Ten ships go down. Each B-Two-Dozen costs one hundred and seventy thousand, now that they got it down to mass production. So we lost purty near two million bucks on ships alone. Then you gotta add the insurance. Each of the hundred men that was lost was insured for ten thousand. That's another million. Include them dozen or so wops that got killed 'cause some o' the bombs was toggled over an Eyetie village; that'll cost dough. So we spent purty near four million dollars and what have we got? A lot of dead fish in the Adriatic from all the bombs that was toggled. Now you know how the pore taxpayer feels. It ain't easy for him, I'll tell ya that." He got up and looked with boredom at the dark barracks. "Think I'll mosey over to the dayroom and see if I can get somebody to gamble with me. Trouble is the guys ain't got the money to play no-limit but once a month. A fella can go crazy waiting for it to come around."

Tex started picking strings on his guitar, pitching his mournful voice on a high note:

> Oh, why did I join the air force?
> Mother, dear Mother knows best.
> Here I lie 'neath the wreckage,
> Liberator all over my chest.

> The Lib'rator's a very fine airplane,
> Constructed of paper and wood,
> It's okay for carrying whiskey,
> But for combat it's no damn good.

"You know, it just occurred to me," Leo said to Dooley, "it's about time I started thinking of the future. It suddenly hit me in the face and I said to myself: Trent, old boy, you're twenty-three years old and it's time you planned ahead."

"You picked a fine time," Dooley said, bored. "But I guess it's better than doing nothing."

"That's exactly what I said to myself," Leo said. "Why sit around all the time and go crazy waiting for the weather to lift so you could fly? Why not concentrate on something constructive? Think of your future. The yogis do that. They concentrate. On the West Coast some of the most important people in pictures practice yogi. That's why they're successful."

"I wisht you'd teach me how to do it," Dooley said.

"It's simple. I've been sitting here and concentrating on the future."

"And what do you see in the future, if I ain't gettin' too personal?"

"Well, I'm back in Hollywood and the sun is shining and the royal palms are swaying in front of our house, and my favorite pooch, Rex, is romping around among the hedges. I see Helen drive up in a roadster and she has on a low-cut unit and she smells of wonderful perfumes, the kind you don't notice, they blend in so well with her fragrant personality. And she says to me: 'Leo, old boy, forgive me! I have erred, spending time with George the 4-F, while you were fighting the good war. All them tough raids you went on, Leo, it must of been hard on you.' Then she touches my cheek gently and says: 'That scar, dear, it must be from one of your wounds. Let me kiss it. It makes you look so distinguished, like the Count of Monte Cristo with what's his name in the lead.' She kisses me and I can tell she's going loco, dying to have me put my arms around her. But your old dad plays a shrewd game. I lead her on. I say to her: 'Helen, how would you like me to show you my business establishment?' She smiles so beautifully, it just makes your heart melt. So I walk her around to the back of the house and show her my kennels. She looks at them, speechless. 'All them beautiful pooches,' she says, tears coming to her eyes. 'Leo, sweetheart, it's wonderful! Oh, I'm just crazy about them. However did you manage to get set up so swell, Leo?' And I said: 'I got a GI loan for a couple of thousand. Any ex-serviceman who has the ambition to go in business can get it.' Well, she can't get over it. Then she says: 'How about your kid brother? Did he get a loan too?' And I said: 'No, Phil doesn't care for business. He isn't ambitious like me. But as business keeps picking up I'll employ him.'"

"So that's what yogi done for you!" Dooley said. "What did you use for collateral?"

"What's that?" Leo asked.

"You don't think they'll give you a loan without collateral."

"I'm gonna be an ex-GI, aren't I?"

"Let's say you are," Dooley said, "just for the sake of argument. That don't make you automatically eligible for that dough. You'll have to prove ability to pay."

"My kennels are going to pay," Leo said heatedly. "I'm going to have the best pooches on the Coast. What's more, even if I can't show this collateral, don't you think I deserve some help from the government for spending five years in this army? Don't a guy deserve something for being shot at?" he cried, waving his arms about and pointing to the barracks.

"They ain't gonna hand it to you on a silver platter," Dooley said. "They ain't gonna say: 'Here's this hero, Leo Trent, and we gotta give him a loan.' Hell, no! You'll have to fight like a sonofabitch to get it. And you'll have to have collateral too."

"Well, I have no collateral," Leo said.

"Then it's just TS," Dooley said.

"But I have certain rights!" Leo cried.

"I been thinking about them rights," Dooley said reflectively. "There oughta be something coming outa this war where a man'd feel it wasn't for nothing. My old man was in the last one and all he got was the s— — end of the stick. Sat on his dead ass for a long time, then went to work in the steel mills. Me, I wanna go in the construction business. I wanna build. But I ain't got no collateral. I been walking around breaking my balls, thinking how I can get the collateral. Then I say to myself: f— — the collateral, after all you done for your country, they oughta take a chance on you. I think about it at night. I see myself fighting 'em, busting up the joint 'cause they won't gimme no loan. Then I say to myself: Dooley, you can't fight the fukken world all by yourself. You ain't as tough as you thought you was, and maybe you ain't as smart. Maybe the best way to get your rights is go into a huddle with other joes. After all, there's gonna be ten million of us ex-GIs. That's a lot of noise."

"Well, anyway," said Leo, "it doesn't hurt to think about it. I'm sick of carving my name on things and writings letters."

"Uh, s——!" Dooley cried, kicking the table viciously. "Let's do something before I blow my top. Let's all go to the movies."

"How about Ben?" Leo said. "Pop can't walk."

"We'll carry the bastard," Dooley said. "He don't weigh much. Come on, *paisan*."

"I don't feel like a movie," I said. "Those damned pictures are twenty-five years old. They drive me crazy. Then the projector keeps breaking down. Besides, it's cold in that barn."

"Take some blankets along," Dooley said.

I protested mildly but went along anyway. No matter how boring a picture, being with people and listening to chatter made it easier.

The men flocked to the large tin structure, wrapped up in their heavy clothing. They carried their jungle packs which were used as seat cushions on the bomb racks. The officers sat in the rear of the theater. The place was crowded and dark, most of the bulbs having been stolen. It seemed as if the whole field emptied into this barnlike structure. All the combat men were there and the maintenance men and ground grippers and orderly-room commandos and even some of the British antiaircraft gunners who seldom came to any of our functions because of our hostile attitude. They lived in a far end of the field and kept to themselves. The only time we saw them was when they were manning the antiaircraft guns on the field. Several of them sat unobtrusively in the front seats of the theater, strangers in this world of loud Yanks. Everybody off duty who could ride, walk, or crawl was there. The drone of engines came over loudly. But you no longer noticed the engines; they were part of your life.

I sat on the bomb rack huddled up in blankets, with Dooley on one side, Trent on the other. It was warmer and cozier in the theater than it had been in the barracks. Men sat closer together, and you expected something to happen, though nothing ever did. Nevertheless when the house grew pitch dark all eyes were on the high screen, and we were hoping for something wonderful and distracting; a miracle that would transport us to some enchanting isle of bliss and romance. We reached out for the celluloid American women, the most beautiful in the world. We devoured them with our eyes and remembered, possessively, that they were *American* women. And inevitably we compared these perfect specimens of womanhood with those of Mandia who had sores on their misshapen legs. "Look! Look at that babe!" one fellow in our aisle cried. "So firm, so round, so fully packed. So free and easy on the draw.'" There were sighs in the dark theater, sighs and exclamations. And how many of us, watching the American beauty, believed that our wives all looked like her! We had been away from home long enough to believe our wives were all Miss Americas.

The name of the movie was *A Bride by Mistake*. It was about a handsome air force captain, ribbons and all, and he was being pursued by a perfect pinup of an American girl. The epitome of feminine beauty. She'd offer her lips to him in passionate abandon but he kept retreating. "Kiss her!" the men in the dark theater roared. "Kiss her, you goddamn fool!"

"Look at the crazy bastard!" a corporal in our row cried impatiently. "Passing up a chance like that! If I was up there, I'd show him some pointers!" He fell into an uneasy silence and you sensed he was disgusted with the captain. "What's the use?" he cried anew when the officer staged one of his retreats after the temptress had cornered him in the sumptuous living room of her rich uncle's estate. The corporal let go a string of oaths but they were drowned out by ear-piercing jeers all directed at the reluctant captain.

"How can a guy be so stupid?" the corporal demanded of us in a whisper after somebody in the officer's section called for silence. "Didja ever see anybody so dopey, and him a captain too? If it was only me!" he said. "What's the matter with that sonofabitch? I'm fed up!" We lost the rest of the corporal's indignant words because the heckling rose to a high pitch. Then something wonderful happened on the screen. The timid pilot, as if responding to the catcalls and criticism of the men in the audience, abandoned his evasive tactics and went over to the offensive. "Now you're cooking with gas!" someone said jubilantly. "Let her have it!" someone else prompted. The heckling ceased, the theater was silent again. Trent, who never talked in a theater because "people work so hard to make pictures you gotta give 'em the respect and listen," broke the rule and whispered in my ear: "Now you watch that boy go to town!" Just then the projector broke down. Flashlights came on, stabbing the empty screen. Men started shouting, cursing, demanding more of the picture. Captain Wilkinson, in charge of Information and Education, called for order and said they were doing their best to repair the projector. But after half an hour the whole thing was called off. Dooley carried me out on his back, mumbling: "What do you expect of this fukken army?"

Trent, walking nearby, said: "That guy was a ham actor. Must be somebody new in Hollywood, a 4-F that got into pictures after I left."

Dooley was picking his way cautiously through the mud. I looked up at the sky. It was dark and it felt like rain. Nevertheless there were some bombers warming up in the dispersal area.

41

Six LETTERS arrived from Ruth and one from Chicago. It was obvious Ruth put in a great deal of effort to make her letters interesting with chit-chat about a small town. She must go insane digging for items. She said she was well; lying, of course.

. . . .

I started taking vitamin pills to combat low resistance. On the q-t, naturally. There would be the devil to pay if the men discovered me taking pills. Oh, the fun they'd have at my expense! Ruth must not know either.

. . . .

I received my four cans of beer from PX. There was no need to drink them all in one sitting because it was not likely there would be a mission on the following day and one was reasonably sure of being around to drink the stuff — unless the deluge drowned us all.

. . . .

My activities from October 15 to the middle of November consisted of: coughing.

Dooley's activities: coughing.

Trent's: coughing.

Charley's: coughing something terrible.

But according to the map in the War Room we were advancing on all fronts.

42

THE RAINS soaked the field for weeks and everywhere there were puddles. Boxes floated about and in some instances men used boats to get to the mess hall from their tents.

Everywhere there was mud, except on the runways which were kept open for the bombers to take off. The planes took off whenever the layers of clouds in the sky parted. There were days when the sun peeked out grudgingly. But it was a cold, friendless sun, bleak and temporary.

In the barracks it was freezing and damp and the men coughed and many were lying under blankets on the cots burning with fever. Charley's face turned yellow with hepatitis. He coughed with the dry heaves. He coughed and his face grew red with pain, but nothing came up. Trent's nose turned blue with the cold. He was dressed in his fur-collared winter flying clothes and wrote letters with his gloves on.

One day, when the skies parted briefly, we hit Munich. On the way from the target we were intercepted by Nazi jet fighters. They came in like greased lightning but did not stay long. They caused no damage, though plenty of anxiety. The flak over Munich, as over most targets, seemed heavier. Having failed to halt us with fighter interception Jerry was concentrating on his antiaircraft defenses.

·   ·   ·   ·

The Munich raid brought my missions up to forty. This entitled one, automatically, to membership in the Forty Club, to which Dooley,

Couch, and Trent already belonged. This Club was as exclusive as a centenarian fraternity because few gunners ever stayed around long enough. I remembered the flight surgeon telling us many months ago: "A man is no good after forty missions. Until then, he's fighting a war and taking his chances. But when he reaches the forty mark, with only ten more to go, he's too nervous to fight. He just concentrates on staying alive, at all costs."

The Forty Club men were young men, often boys, with shattered nerves and gaunt faces and always preoccupied expressions. They jumped at slight noises and often their hands trembled. Their talk revolved around the few remaining missions, and it was humble and restrained talk. Nothing else was of any importance, not even the war. With the goal almost within grasp, each one was taken up with survival. Life beckoned across the few remaining missions.

Dooley said: "Glad you made it, pop. Didn't think you could do it."

Charley stopped coughing long enough to make an observation: "Life has little meaning till you're on the verge of losing it, or finding it again. You take me, for instance. As you men well know, I'm a no-good, sinful ole bastard. I said to myself after they told me I was qualified for combat: Brother Couch, if you hafta go, might as well go here as further up the creek. You'll even get wrote up in the papers if they kill you. Back home folks meeting on the street or over a drink will say: 'How *about* that Couch fella! Wasn't he the hero, though!' And even them that thought you was a bastard, would call you a nice guy. What more can you ask for?" Charley demanded, coughing into his palm. "But no sooner did I get in combat than I become the scardiest *paisan* mortal woman ever bore. Men, I tell ya you never seen nothing like it. I'm scared of my shadow, but you oughta see my shadow: *it's* scared of itself. I ask myself: how come life is so precious all of a sudden? What's life anyway? Worry, work, gambling, liquor, hangovers, mean temper, and unhappiness. I was really never happy. And since I married, life's been downright hell! So why don't I relax and fly my missions? But try hard as you please, it don't work. You just hang on to this thing called life like it's the sweetest tit you ever sucked." He coughed and his face turned bloodred and his false teeth rattled and he shoved them back into place quickly. "Tell ya something else," he resumed. "I had a plan when I first started flying. Plan was to get even with my wife by getting myself killed off. That'd give her something to think about. Like to see the expression on her face when she saw the news. But I give up that plan too," he said in disgust. "Now that I got only seven more to fly I'm sweating them out something terrible."

Charley was seized by the cough again. The pain of it brought his attention around. "This sickness sure has knocked me on my ass," he said. "But I ain't going to no hospital. If it's gonna kill me, might as well do it in my own sack."

Charley was not the only one refusing to be moved to the hospital. There were at least six gunners in our barracks suffering from hepatitis, influenza, and sore throats. They wore all their clothes and over their shoulders were draped the olive-drab blankets.

Leo had the flu. He lay on his cot, surrounded by five cats. He had picked up the animals several days ago when they moved in underneath our barracks seeking shelter from the wind and rain. They had cried all that night and their plaintive feline voices woke us. Leo swore a blue streak at the "goddamn cats." Cats, Leo said, were less trustworthy than women. But the rest of the men felt sorry for the animals, and Leo was our only animal expert. The men appealed to him. So Leo, grumbling, got up from his cot and brought the mother cat and her four kittens inside the barracks. In the morning he sniffed the animals with his long nose, turned away in disgust, said he wanted nothing to do with them. "My business is dogs," he declared. "But since you jokers insist on having these animals in the barracks, why, I'll supervise their care — as a favor to you." He ordered the men to bring canned Vy-ennas from the mess hall and feed the cats. Then he built a little crib for them out of a box and placed it underneath his cot where Stowaway once lived. The cats started gaining weight and they were happy, and at night they romped among the cots chasing mice. We all grew very fond of the animals but Leo forbade any coddling. "The old lady won't stand for it," he said. "Wait till she gets used to you guy's first."

We suspected Leo was lying, putting us off, so he could have the uninterrupted pleasure of playing with the cats himself. But we were afraid to infringe upon the rules set down by our expert for fear of offending or alienating the cats. Supposing they *did* decide to move to another barracks!

In the meantime Leo was having all the fun. He crawled into his cot and the cats purred all around him, keeping him warm and smiling. "Come to think of it," he said, "these fukkers aren't so bad after all, if you bring 'em up right."

43

D OOLEY CAME IN dragging mud all over the barracks floor. He brought our mail from the orderly room and passed it around to the men who were confined to their cots. "We got a letter from Sharon Ginn," he said. He handed the letter to me grudgingly, suspiciously, saying: "I shoulda wrote to her." I realized he was jealous because it was addressed to me. I opened the letter and started reading aloud:

Dear Ben and buddies:
   I just been on the go. I left Ozone after I heard about Mel and went to Houston to visit my sister before I went home to Fresno, Calif. to moms & dad. & from there to Los Angeles to visit my other brother. So you see I been on the go. I sure don't like Fresno & miss Mel more than ever, it seems like he is just stationed some place where I can't go. Well Ben I guess it won't be long until you can come back to this side. Gosh! The rainy season has set in here in Calif. & it is so lonesome. Is it raining where you are? I am planning on going to work next week. How is the rest of the crew, fine I hope. Tell them all hello for me. Ben are you next to Mel in the crew picture toward the middle? Are you the Jewish gennilman Mel wrote me about from gunnery school? Well, I sure appreciated your letter. I will close for this time & God Bless you all & take care of yourself.
   Your friend,
   Sharon Ginn.

"You didn't know her, didja?" Dooley asked after I had read the letter.

"No, I never met Sharon," I said. "But after Mel died I sent her his farewell letter and added a few words."

"Oh —" Dooley crushed his cigarette on the floor. "I shoulda wrote but I never got around to it. You know I ain't much of a letter writer."

"It must be tough on her, the poor kid," Trent said, crawling out from underneath his cats.

"She'll marry again," Dooley said. "If I remember Sharon, she was pretty and young. She'll marry again." Then, with an abruptness which was obvious to all three of us, Dooley changed the subject with a stream of oaths. "Look at this sonofabitch," he cried, throwing down on the cot a new copy of *Yank* magazine. "A piece in there how the German prisoners of war in the States are being coddled. They live in comfort and eat steaks! An' if they don't get steaks every night for supper, the bastards go out on strike." He seized the magazine and thrust it at Leo and cried: "Look, you look at it!" Then he turned and addressed the other men. "Ever hear anything like it! We're getting our *cojones* shot off and them bastards are living the life of Riley. Why, the fukken USO even entertains 'em. We don't get entertained, but the Jerry PWs do! And lissen to the payoff," Dooley shouted, "American girls are provided for 'em at dances!"

For a moment the coughing subsided and a torrent of abuse descended on the barracks.

"The sons o' bitches!"

"I'll sure write home and let 'em know about it!"

"I'd like to take my forty-five an' line 'em all up against a wall!"

"What the hell do ya expect fum the army!"

Our anger was like a glowing fire that warmed our insides and sent the blood racing through our veins. But it did not last long enough and soon we were shivering again in our cold and in our helplessness. After that the outbursts against the army and the civilians, and especially the girls who entertained Nazi prisoners of war in the States, were sporadic and weak.

"If I caught *my* girl doing a thing like that," Tex said, "I'd break ever' bone in her body."

"I'd beat her into a pulp," another gunner said.

The threats were strung out along the barracks, each man devising ways to punish the erring girl. But none of them believed that *his* girl would ever betray him. At the same time the men agreed with Dooley that you couldn't trust women at all. They were two-faced creatures, Dooley argued, and even the best of them must be watched.

"You can deal me in on that one," Charley said.

"Me, too," Trent said. "Women are a very fickle lot. I wouldn't trust them further than I could throw a B-24."

"There was a time," Charley said wistfully, "when women knowed their place. There wasn't any of this running out to play bridge and fukkin around generally. They let a man take care of 'em. Ever'body was better off. One thing about women, most of 'em, even the purtiest ones ain't got a brain on 'em. You take my wife. I ain't ashamed to say she ain't got a thing 'xcepting that purty face of her'n an' more sass than she oughta have. When I finish my fifty and get home I aim to make some changes around there. Believe me."

"Atta boy, sarge."

Delmonico came in with the Alert List for the next day's mission. "Most of you guys that can hobble around on crutches are flying tomorrow," he said. "The rest of you are gonna stand inspection. Yes," he repeated, "Inspection!"

44

THE OFFICER from G-2 came into our barracks and stopped at the door. He shivered involuntarily at the sight of unshaven, unkempt men, wrapped in heavy clothing and blankets. "I'd like to speak to Sergeant Trent," he said, pitching his voice so that it would not sound too much like an order, yet making sure this was not to be taken as a social visit.

I watched the corners of Dooley's mouth tighten. He was about to say something, but clamped his jaws together. We both glanced at Leo's cot. It was disarranged, as usual, with the mattress cover and blankets and underwear all knotted, just like he had left it in the morning before going on the mission. His wallet was on the table, in its usual spot, thick with lire. We never found anything strange about the contrast between Leo's unmade cot and piled-up table and his always immaculate person, particularly the razor-sharp mustache. Perhaps Leo did not have enough energy for both. Perhaps this was Leo's way of defying the army.

"That's the cot over there," I said to the officer. I don't know what prompted me to say it. I could have come right out and said to this stranger, whom I had never seen and who was violating our sorrow, that Leo had not come back from today's raid. Instead I found myself taking a morbid pleasure in the thought that our buddy was finally beyond the reach of G-2 officers who had plagued him constantly over his fantastic letters home.

"Are you his buddies?" the officer asked. He was evidently new in his work and he hesitated.

"Yes," I answered. In his hand were a sheaf of letters. They were Leo's letters.

"Can you tell me where he is?" the officer asked, fidgeting uncomfortably as if he were aware of being in an enlisted men's barracks and did not know quite how to act. He saw us glancing at Leo's cot and the disheveled emptiness of it disturbed him.

"He went down this morning."

"Oh, I'm sorry," the officer said. "I —" He held up the sheaf of letters. "I guess it doesn't matter now. But — uh — I came to discuss these letters with him. He's sure been violating security regulations." He threw them on my cot and wheeled around to the door. "Well — you can have them now. You might as well tear them up." And he left quickly.

We looked at the letters. They had been written in the past two days. One was addressed to Helen in Hollywood and one to his kid brother, Phil, the marine fighter pilot in the Pacific. To Helen he wrote: "We are preparing for a suicide raid to Berlin. One cru is being selected for this purpose, all voloonteers. I'm on. From all I've been able to find out this is going to be a low-level raid. We'll come in over the rooftops, like that daring raid over Tokio. I do not try to minimize the danger of this mission. But if something happens and I don't 'make it' adios and may you be happy with whoever it is that comes in your life. . . ." And to his brother he wrote: "I hear you guys down in the Pa-

cific don't face much flak. Here it's flak all the way. Guns fire at you
soon as you cross into Yugo. And don't let anybody kid you that we
don't meet up with much Jerry fighter opposition. For some reason
they always pick on our Group. The other day the Jerries knocked
down 14 of our ships. I've got at least five Jerries to my credit, and now
I'm trying to confirm them. The chicken-shit officers at Interrogation
refuse to give me credit for 'em. My gunnery has been first rate, everybody here admits that, and I have been promised a chance at flying.
Probably go into jets after my tour is finished here. If you ask me the
conventional engine plane is too damned slow for my taste. I like
speed! How are the gook women down your way? They tell me after
awhile even the darkies get to look real white. Here we have some
beauts. Almost like being in Hollywood. Believe me, I get my 'share.'"

I folded the letters without any comment from either Dooley or
Charley Couch whose only reaction was a series of dry coughs. I tore up
the letters slowly, thinking back to the mission. It had been a milk run to
Novi Sad in Yugo where our Group busted several bridges to cut off the
Jerries' retreat from a Russian pincer. There had been no enemy opposition, no flak, no fighters. Coming off the target the ship in which Leo
rode went into a tailspin. It never came out. And no chutes came out.

Dooley and I started going through Leo's belongings, gathering
his personal effects to be sent home, distributing to the gunners his
razor blades and other knickknacks a man gathers through the years
in the army.

In the evening Supply took away Leo's blankets and we stood up
his cot in the corner of the barracks. And where Leo had been there
was a hole, a big, gaping hole, except for the cats' box. The cats continued scampering around the barracks as if nothing had happened.

Staring at the hole I thought it had been there from the beginning
of time, and nothing would ever erase it.

45

"I<small>F</small> I <small>AIN'T</small> mistaken this is Saturday night," Dooley observed. "But you wouldn't know it unless somebody told you. Back in the States you'd somehow know it was Saturday night without anybody telling you. The lights was brighter, like there was magic in the air. I remember when I worked in the mills, I'd come home with my pay and get all duked up and meet the gang and we'd go up to the City Market over in the Polack neighborhood, and beat the s— — out of the Polacks. Boy, we'd have fun! Then, after I started going steady, it was even more fun. Usta drive out and meet the dawn. You fellas don't know what the dawn looks like till you seen it come up over them mountains around Pittsburgh. Ain't nothing like it!" He lit a cigarette and looked at the bluish smoke curling up.

"Fun is right," Charley said softly, his gaze lost in the darkness of the ceiling. "We sure had it while I was courting my wife. On Sattidy nights we'd drive out to Lemmy's Place, a roadhouse clear out in the desert. I had me a roadster and plenty of lire in my jeans. Spending fifty didn't mean a damn to me, still don't. We'd dance and hang one on, and I'd do a little sociable gambling. Was a bad Sattidy night when I didn't clear five hundred. Then I'd order Lemmy ta close the doors, and buy ever'body in the house drinks and chow. Remember I usta make a lil speech, said: 'Folks, Sattidy night don't come but once a week so ya might as well raise hell and put wheels under it. Eat and drink and be merry. It's on me.' Then I'd walk around the tables watching folks having *more* fun with their clothes on. And sometimes I'd have a hangover so bad my head'd throb like a sick mockingbird's ass. But they was nothing like Arizona desert air to clear a hangover. I never seen nothing to compare with it. That was 'fore I got married." He cut off his story abruptly as if not wishing to spoil the mood by reminiscing about what happened after his marriage. He turned to me and asked: "What did you do on Sattidy nights?"

I tried to tell them about my Saturday nights, going back to the late twenties. Saturday nights for me were divided into distinct periods. The first was one of great hunger when I tried to assume the mannerisms of Americans and thought them best epitomized among the young men and women who frequented dances. I worked five and a half days a week as a shipping clerk in a box factory, but I lived all week long thinking of Saturday evening and a dance at Mirro Hall or Logan Square Auditorium. At one of these glittering affairs I met my first girl. She was a fine dancer and I fell in love with her. Once we won a prize for dancing. I got a cigarette case, which tarnished a week later, and Eleanor received a bouquet of flowers. I was a skinny customer at the time, weighing one hundred and five pounds; and because I worked days and went to night school, the Saturday night sleep was essential. But there was always this rebellion against going to bed on one's only free night. I'd wander up and down Division Street or visit a pool room in search of the elusive experience that wrought its magic on Saturday night. I would never allow myself to go home before three in the morning. The period I went with Eleanor was one of physical hunger. We spent our Saturday nights in the cold hallway of her father's house. We stood there for hours embracing and freezing, grasping frenziedly at the bits of happiness afforded us by the few fleeting hours. It was only after I started teaching and met Ruth that Saturday night lost its urgency. But I never got over the feeling that it was an important night, a special night, endowed with more potentiality and mystery than any other night in the week.

"I wonder what I'd do if I was home right now," Dooley said. His gaze wandered involuntarily to the emptiness where Leo had been. "I don't suppose Saturday night'll ever be the same again. I usta be able to have fun just being with people. Now I can't have fun unless I get pie-eyed. I feel like an old man. Think if I walked down the street in Pittsburgh tonight, I'd be touchy as all hell. Instead of having fun, I'd pick fights. I'd be browned off if I saw people laugh and enjoy themselves. My girl wouldn't like me. And maybe I wouldn't like her either," he added thoughtfully. "No, I guess I wouldn't be fit company for civilians tonight. Wouldn't be sociable. Not the old Dooley. They wouldn't recognize me."

"Nothing will ever be the same," Charley said. "If God grant I come out alive, Sattidy night won't mean a s— — to me. But the funniest part is — I don't know what *will*."

I said hopefully that time would heal the wounds and restore the inner peace and out of this crucible of suffering and violence something good must emerge. Dooley shrugged his shoulders, saying: "I don't believe nothing good will come of it. I feel something oughta, on account of what happened to Leo and Billy and Mel and Petersen and Big Wheel and Dick Martin. But something tells me the politicians will snafu the detail again. And I know what'll happen to me when that day comes around. I'll go off my nut and start swinging."

"Swinging at what?" I asked.

"At the whole fukken world," Dooley replied. "I ain't got no more faith."

We argued mildly and I reminded him what he had told Leo not very long ago about veterans getting together.

"You're dreaming, pop," he said wearily. "Trouble with you is you're a dreamer. *I'm* a realist. I don't trust anybody. Right now I don't even trust myself."

We were silent for a while, each listening to his own loneliness, each reaching for the warmth one human being affords another. In our uncomplicated little world of engine throb the only thing separating us was individual fear.

Dooley broke the silence. "Right now I'd like a little drink," he said. "Mission or no mission tomorrow. A little drink wouldn't hurt nobody. After all, it *is* Saturday night. Hey, Tex, play *The Lone Prairie*."

"Roger-dodger," Tex said.

The barracks door opened and we saw a drunken, wizened face peer cautiously in. The ground man was in his late thirties and wore PFC stripes. He was happily drunk. "I come to apologize," he said, gathering up courage and entering what was to most ground men forbidden territory. "I love you combat men and I come to apologize," the drunk said. "You stick you' necks out. You risk you' lives. You're fighting and winning this heah war. Wasn't fair what the brass done to ya, making you stand inspection! The colonel had no business making you men drill. Wasn't fair. I come to apologize for the colonel and myself. I love you. I love ever' one of you. 'Cause you're brave and you ain't afraid to die." He finished his piece and closed the door lovingly and was gone.

"Every little thing helps," Charley observed, amused.

"It's starting to rain again," Dooley said, listening to the drops of water striking the roof. "And it's only ten o'clock."

And I suddenly remembered the gunner who would bellow each night at ten: "Jeez, how I hate this fukken place!" And I wondered whether he had gone down or gone home.

I got up and put on my fleece-lined boots and heavy coat and helmet liner, and started for Squadron Operations to find out whether there was an alert for the next day and whether my name was on the list.

46

THE DAMPNESS and cold penetrated your very bones. The flesh was sick with pain. Men were coughing and spitting and their throats were husky and sore. Overhead the clouds marched across the sky, black clouds with the menace of a cold rain and white clouds like huge mountains traveling in the direction of the Po Valley where they would be stopped by the massive Alps.

Half the men from our barracks were at the Fifty-third Field Hospital suffering from pneumonia, influenza, hepatitis, and frostbite. There had been several deaths. Sergeant Sawyer had been ordered by the desperate Captain Brown to clean up the mess hall, especially the rinsing pots where men washed their mess kits after chow. Doc Brown, terrified of an epidemic, was the busiest man in our squadron. Group started building its own hospital on the field.

The cold rains beat down on the barracks and pyramidal tents and tufa *casas* where permanent party men lived. In the tufa *casas*, there was gambling and drinking, and occasionally each of the squadrons had a blowout and a naked signorina was paraded in front of the shouting men.

The missions were few on account of the clouds, and Group head-quarters was worried about the morale of the troops. Information and Education inaugurated a series of lectures on "The Meaning of the War," but most of the men in our barracks were too sick to go or care. They were even too sick to eat. There were Christmas packages strewn all over the barracks, but hardly anyone ate.

"If they don't fly me soon," said Dooley, "I'm gonna blow my top." He coughed like the rest of us, and his face was suffused with blood.

"I heard a rumor," Charley said, "we're getting ready to move to France. The whole air force. War going on *there*."

"I heard a million rumors!" Dooley said with disgust. "If we're moving to France, how come they're adding on to the runway? If you ask me, there'll be Superforts coming in here one of these days."

"Somebody told me," I said, "that we're going to move up north, past Foggia, so we would be nearer our targets."

"Well, I heard our Group is gonna disband and we'll all be sent back to the States and train for B-29s," Tex said.

Nobody took any stock in the rumors, but we repeated them anyway because they gave us a feeling of hope and change. Change from the cold, dampness, inactivity, and boredom that were driving men insane.

Besides Ruth's daily letter, one had little to look forward to. Except perhaps the daily cigar. That too had become something of a ritual. At any rate, it consumed time. It was too cold to read. There was no place to read. And there weren't any books.

Somehow, I had to fly those last five missions! The barracks and the puddles and the clouds pressed down on one like a heavy lid. And there wasn't any place one could escape. In Mandia the wet, cobblestone streets, the ill-clad children, the squalor, and the beggars made one sick. The Red Cross building was crowded with men who just stood around and stared at one another or past one another. They gathered at the club if only to keep warm and to keep from being alone. It distressed me to see Miss Bullwinkle and her two assistants trying so desperately to make the boys "happy." Everything about these three women was exaggerated: their smiles, their voices, their movements. They only made one more unhappy. I felt less constrained among the laundresses on Via Cavour. They were blue with the cold and did not pretend to be happy. They had seen the misery and loneliness of Mandia in previous winters. They were first cousins to misery. Their men had been away since the start of the war. But despite it, they laughed when they said: "*In America lavorano poco, molto mangiano; in Italia, poco mangiano, lavorano molto.*"

I sat with the laundresses for hours, and often little or nothing was said. Their patience always amazed me; it was a monumental patience and as old as the so-called Arch of Triumph that stood at the gates of Mandia for almost two thousand years. If there were only some way of learning from them this patience and calmness and good humor! I felt keenly that the time was short and soon many of us would be leaving Italy, and there must be some way we could atone for the indignities we heaped upon them and the humiliation we caused them. We fouled their beds and bought their sisters. They had greeted us with kisses and roses when we first came. But by our deeds they learned to hate us. We became the loathsome *Americani.* They had hoped we would clear out the *fascisti.* They had hoped for understanding and bread.

I tried to alibi, but my words were wooden, apologetic. "This is a war after all," I said to the girls. "But after the war it will be better for all of us."

"If you do not clear out the *fascisti* now," Gina asked delicately, as if fearing to hurt my feelings, "who will do it after you leave?"

"You will," I said.

"Not if your American money supports them," Gina said. "On the one hand you accuse all Italians of having been *fascisti*, but on the other you put the *fascisti* right back into power. In Mandia the mayor was a *fascisti* party member and your people knew it. And in Rome your important officers spend much time with friends of Achille Starace and Edda Ciano. I do not understand this." She went back to ironing a GI shirt. Her thin face was somber and grave.

Gina was seventeen but she looked like a child. Her child's face was stamped with suffering and resignation. Only her eyes looked old. Gina's eyes, like the eyes of all the children one saw on the streets and refugee camps, were disturbing and filled one with guilt. What shame could be greater than for a grown-up to stare into the face of a child whose eyes had grown evil and corrupt and all-knowing? Our guilt was so enormous, we would never expiate it,

"You know Luisa who tends bar at Tony's?" Gina asked.

I said yes, certainly.

"Well, do you know she is with child, having been raped by your *fratello* with the Oriental face?"

"No," I said, stunned. "I did not know." I tried hard to recall any mention Dooley might have made concerning Luisa. He had said nothing about her for months.

"The whole of Mandia knows about it," Gina said, "She was ill many days after your *fratello* attacked her. Only a week ago, Tony drove down with her in his wagon to the gates of your airfield. He tried to see the *commandante* and show him that Luisa is pregnant and your *fratello* must marry her. But the guard at the gate refused them entry. He would not even take a message to the *commandante*. He drove them away from the gate. Tony shouted and wept and said Luisa has been ruined by an Americano and he would appeal to the bishop of Lecce for justice. She paused and regarded me with her twinkling eyes. "What does your *fratello* say about all this?"

"I have not heard," I said.

"If Luisa had been *bad*," Angelina said, "it would have been different. We have many *bad* ones, and with them it makes no difference. But Luisa remained good. She avoided the *fascisti* and the Germans. Your *fratello*, he did a terrible thing."

. . . .

The rain washed the cobblestones and the clouds turned day into sorrowing twilight. The lights were on when I came back to our barracks. The smell of damp wood and unwashed bodies and medicaments hit my nostrils. Dooley sat on Charley's cot, talking to him. When he saw me come in, the engineer said, "Here's another letter for you from Sharon Ginn." He handed me the letter. "Say, how come she don't write to me?" he demanded. "Me and Mel was close buddies."

I opened the letter and stared at it absently, thinking of what I should say to Dooley.

"Read it out loud," Dooley said.

Dear Ben:

Well, its only me again. I just got to thinking about you & thought I would drop you another letter. How are you makeing out over there, I bet you are homesick. Well, soon it will be X-mas, it sure did come around fast this year, matter of fact every thing seems like it has been on a 90 mile-a-minute run. But I guess time passes pretty slow to you over there.

Lt. Andrew Kyle wrote me from Kansas City and said he would like to visit me.

Ben, I don't guess you like to talk or think about my Mel much because of the feeling it gives you. Can you tell me if he ever shot down enemy plane? If you can get it pass the 'bogie man.'

I have try almost every way I know how to get the address of Lt. Petersen that was hurt so bad, can you send it to me?

I know every one at one time or other has a craveing for something or other to eat. Or if you need anything at any time, I would sure like to be the one to get it for you. And that goes for the whole crew.

Well, Ben its awful lonely here, except for Halween. Did we have the kids at our door, after trick or treat so we treated them so they wouldn't hand us a trick. I help mom & busy cutting cake for them. But it makes you feel good to know the kids here can still have fun without being scared to move, its that way in so many countries now. I would like to know, is there a cross on Mel's grave?

Your friend,
Sharon.

"I sure wish I could do something for that girl," Dooley said, trying to hold back his tears. "Like to buy her a present for Christmas. But what can you buy in this stinking Mandia? They ain't even got cameos for sale, like in Naples." He lit a cigarette and dragged on it. Charley made an observation about Sharon and how she ought to forget about Mel and think of marrying again. And my mind was crowded with a deep resentment toward Dooley. One couldn't help juxtaposing Luisa and Sharon. He was at the point of tears where it concerned Sharon. But Luisa . . .

"Dooley, I found out about Luisa today," I said.

"What about her?" he said belligerently.

"She's pregnant."

"What's that to me?"

"Did you know Tony brought her to the field a few days ago to complain you raped her?"

"I didn't rape her," Dooley retorted. "She done it on her own."

"Gina told me the girl was sick for several days after it happened. Did you know that?"

"Say, what the hell business is it of yours?" Dooley cried, rising from the cot and thrusting his excited face at me. "Who the hell asked you to judge what I do? Why, you bastard, who set *you* up as my conscience? You mind your own fukken business or I'll smack you one in the jaw." He seized hold of my jacket and started shaking me. I tried to free myself but he shoved me and I fell back on my cot. "You mind your own business, you Jew bastard!" he cried. "Don't go taking the wops' side against your buddies or I'll toss you out on your ear. We don't want no wop lovers in this barracks. You — you" he began stammering. "How do you know it was me that done it? Luisa been laid before me and after me. I — I didn't do nothing to her she didn't want done. These Eyetie gals, they're all on the make. They suck you in and lead you on so you'd marry 'em and take 'em back to the States. How do you know Luisa didn't do that to me?"

"The story I heard was that she almost died after you raped her. Everybody in Mandia knows about it. And now there's just a little more hatred against me because of you."

He flopped down on his cot heavily. "I offered her money," he said wearily. "What do you want me to do? I'll give her all the money I got. But I can't marry her. You guys don't expect me to marry a wop, do you?" He looked at Charley pleadingly. "She won't take any of my money. What can I do? Jump outa B-24?" He clamped his jaws together and ground out the cigarette on the floorboards. "I been to Group," he resumed in a low voice. "Group surgeon gimme a physical to see if I'm fit to fly after my fifty. They said okay. It's never happened before, and I'll be the first one. So I'll keep flying, see! I'll fly till it kills me!"

47

THE MASSACRE of American soldiers in the Malmedy Sector in the Battle of the Bulge came over the radio. For a while we listened shocked and speechless. Then it dawned on us that an important battle had been lost, and to our shock was added astonishment and anger. It had taken some time for our men to realize that Americans, too, were capable of losing a battle. In G-2 I heard some officers blame the terrible Bulge calamity on "faulty intelligence." But among the men in the barracks a pure hatred was kindled against the Nazis, and there were dark mutterings of revenge. I had never seen such anger before. (We fought our air war relying too much on the Geneva Convention even when we knew the enemy violated that convention.)

"Oh, those sonsabitches!" Dooley cried. "Killing innocent Americans! Killing prisoners of war! I'd like to load up the whole air force with frag-bombs and drop 'em on every fukken city in Germany."

The skies opened briefly as if responding to our pleas, and every ship, airworthy or not, was sent aloft. For three consecutive days we saturated Axis Europe from Bolzano in northern Italy, to Brennero, Vienna, Brux, then over the Alps to Munich. There weren't any gripes among the men, and even those who had complained of ill health were suddenly recovered and eager to fly.

On the fourth day the clouds closed in again. My mission credits added up to forty-eight. I had two more to fly.

48

DOOLEY, CHARLEY, and I ushered in Christmas at our squadron bar, No Brass Inn. We sat at a table, sipped vermouth and talked about the morning's mission. All three of us had flown to Bratislava. The raid gave Dooley fifty missions; Charley forty-four; it gave me forty-nine. Dooley had suggested a little celebration on account of the completion of his "first tour," and in honor of Christmas Eve.

I sipped the tasteless vermouth and abandoned myself to the warm talk and chatter. The Inn was crowded with gunners, ground-crew men, and orderly-room commandos. There was festive bunting on the windows and Christmas tinsel hung around the electric bulbs. One gunner, already drunk, was buying drinks for the house. He had completed his tour of missions, and was boisterously happy. "I'm *finito!*" he cried. "Going back to the States and screw this war! Tonight I'm buying the drinks! Everybody in the house have a drink on me and Merry Christmas to you all!"

The bartender, a corporal with cross-eyes, set up the drinks and the men around the bar grabbed them and drank. The gunner shoved past the men at the bar. He stumbled among the tables as if he were searching for someone. When he saw us, his face lit up and he came over to our table and asked if he might sit with us. "I wrote a little poem," he said tenderly. "And nobody'll understand the meaning of it that ain't a gunner himself. I ain't gonna read this to no ground grippers," he whispered secretively, gathering the three of us in with his large arms. "You men will understand it! Mind if I read this poem to ya? I call it my Fifty Mission Poem, and I'm sending it to my sister in Travers City."

"Wish you *would* read it," Charley Couch said with a mixture of curiosity and hospitality. "Go right ahead."

But our guest was not quite ready to read. "You fellas are my buddies," he said, "even though I ain't flown with any of you even once. But that don't matter. Even if you never flown with a man, he's a gunner like you and he knows what the score is, and he's your buddy. So you fellas are my buddies." We raised our glasses and drank and the gunner wiped his lips and resumed eagerly and grimly. "I lost my crew awhile back when Major Wilson went down. Won a raffle that day that entitled me to see a USO show in Bari. So I went and seen *This Is the Army*, and when I got back to the base, no crew. Went down! There I was alone in a tent, my five crew-buddies gone. I went plum' outa my head. You fellas must remember how I carried on. They took me down to the Fifty-third and put me in a straitjacket. I wanted to kill myself. I wasn't gonna live — not while my buddies was down. You won't believe it, men, but I had a feeling God was punishing me for winning that raffle and seeing the show while my crew was flying. Well, they kep' me in the hospital coupla months. Kep' me in the Violent Ward, and the *head* doctor come around every day to have a talk with me and explain to me it wasn't my fault I didn't go on that mission. Wasn't me that fukked up. I couldn't help it winning that squadron raffle. And when you come right down to it, I *couldn't* help it. I come back to this base and they started flying me extra, like you fellas." He took a sip of vermouth and looked pointedly at Dooley. "You finished up today, didn't you, Sarge?"

"Guess so," Dooley said.

"But you're flying some more, ain't you?"

"Yeah."

"Well, I take my hat off to a guy that flies after he's *finitoed* his fifty. I'd like to do it myself. I honest to God would — for my buddies' sake. But I'm all shot to hell inside. Got stomach ulcers and they get so bad sometimes I feel like creeping up a tent pole." His big face was perspiring but he paid no attention to it. His eyes were fixed on Dooley in supplication. His palm was around Dooley's biceps. "I sure wanna take my hat off to you, Sarge. You and all gunners," he added, taking us in with his glance. "I don't know yar names, but you'll be my buddies the rest of my life. And if you ever come to Travers City, Michigan, look me up. I wish you would. I mean it."

"How about that poem you was gonna read us?" Charley asked.

"Oh, yeah," the gunner said, unfolding a sheet of white paper with a picture of a Liberator at the top of it. "It's to my sister. She's all I got back home." He looked at the paper tenderly and cleared his throat and read:

> The thing has came true what I've been wishin',
> No more combat for me, I've flew my last mission.
> Within a short while now I'll be sailing west,
> Toward the "land of enchantment," and a long-needed rest.
>
> How long it will take me I really don't know,
> But I hope to be home in six weeks or so,
> So pay up the butcher and grocerman too,
> 'Cause I'm plenty damn tired of c ration stew.
>
> Shine up the Ford and save up your gas,
> I sure will appreciate riding in class.
> Don't get impatient, it may be quite a wait,
> So don't be expecting me till I reach your front gate.

He wiped the perspiration off his face with the crook of his arm and folded the poem lovingly. There were tears in his eyes when he got up. His lips were trembling. "I'm obliged to you fellas for listening," he said. "Merry Christmas to you and God bless you!" He returned to the bar and resumed buying drinks in a loud tone of voice.

No Brass Inn slowly filled up with ground-crew men whose faces and hands, though scrubbed, retained the indelible marks of oil and grease. Their faces looked wind pinched and raw, while the faces of the orderly-room men and medics and mess personnel were sallow. The chairs and tables were all occupied. There was hardly any room to stand, but the men continued piling in as if the Inn were the only place in the squadron area where one could usher in Christmas.

The talk around me was like a loud buzzing. I found no need to look up. The faces around me were not new. I had seen them all before; all of my life, as a matter of fact, though I knew few of them by name. There had been no need to learn a name. "How ya, Sarge?" seemed enough. "Fine. How are you?" "Still kicking." And that was all. And yet the feeling was there that I had known these people since the day of my birth. Somewhere in back of my mind, and against my better judgment, they had been arranged in categories according to their occupations: ground engineers, armorers, radio repairmen, ground-crew chiefs. With them the exchange of greetings had always been warm because they serviced our ships and worked out in the open through rain and mud, and during the summer, through the fierce heat. And then there were the men who worked in the orderly room: desk sergeants, typists, clerks; one hardly paid any attention to them because they sat underneath a roof that did not leak, and they were kept warm by a stove. And into that same category went the men from Supply who lived in *casas* that often had showers, and their clothing was always the best. Then there were transportation, the medics, Information and Education, and a host of others. For each gunner there were six or seven ground men. And it seemed as it they were all at the squadron Inn, all trying desperately to gain a foothold on a bit of pleasure. I closed my eyes and thought: if only something soft would brush against me; if only I heard a female voice. Could it be, I wondered, that there weren't any females left in the world? What would happen if a woman, an American woman, walked into our midst? Would the hard, tense faces relax? Each one of us in that crowded room was charged, like a stick of dynamite, hidden behind a thin facade of amiability. We were all sincere in our greetings and shoulder thumpings, but each one of us moved cautiously, afraid that if he let go something terrible might happen. I thought back to a picnic our squadron had had during the summer. There bad been a lot of beer and chicken. After we had eaten and drunk, we wandered about the beach like madmen searching for release. The picnic finally broke up into a free-for-all and several men had to be treated for wounds.

"How ya, Sarge?" Sergeant Sawyer said, pushing his way through the crowd. "Merry Christmas to you all."

Several ground-crew men came up and patted Dooley on the shoulder and congratulated him on finishing his tour. "I hear you're gonna fly some more," one crew chief said. "Well, you must have a good reason, Sarge, but darned if I know what it is. Why, you wouldn't get me inside a B-Two-Dozen with a team of horses! Tell you," he cried, grinning, "anything that's off the ground more'n ten feet is *altitude* to me! No, sir. Gimme the good old terra firma." He offered to buy us all a drink, but the offer was purely academic. One could hardly get within shouting distance of the crowded bar. By this time one could hardly breathe, but the men continued piling in.

A PFC with a flat nose started singing Christmas carols and that made Dooley sit up and take notice. He sang a few bars and gave up. "I been thinking about our crew," he said, directing his words to me. "Remember all the good times wc had! Every place we went, we had a good time. Remember up in Massachusetts around Springfield and Chicopee Falls? The babes was terrific! All you had to do was take a bus in town, walk in a bar and there they were! You could scoop 'em up with a shovel. I never seen anything like it," he said wistfully. "Why, old Chet Kowalski, he was so busy loving up the women he didn't have time to brush the dandruff off his blouse. Nice fella, Chet was," Dooley said reflectively, "even though he was always scared to death of having his *cojones* shot off. I never seen a guy so hepped up about his balls. Wonder what happened to Chet. . . ." He lit a cigarette and resumed quickly, as if the train of thought animated his speech. "And then, remember we was shipped down to Savannah to train for overseas, and I picked up this chick that worked at the crummy PX. Kind of on the husky side, but I like 'em well stacked. I don't go for this 'the closer to the bone the sweeter the meat stuff.' There wasn't many nights I missed with her. Something about the southern gals, once they get revved up, brother, they keep going at 2400 rpms. Must be the climate. Then Andy Kyle got married. Boy, we had fun that night walking up Bull Street and little Cosmo raising particular hell. He was a swell kid, Cosmo. Woulda been a monk — if he lived."

"When your number is up," Charley observed leisurely, it don't matter if you was going to be a monk or a gold prospector. When it's up, it's up."

"That kid didn't even shave once," Dooley sighed. "If he'd of shaved once, at least. There's lots of things he never done, but this being a holy night I won't go into that." He shook his head slowly and looked absently at his thin vermouth glass. "When you think back, we had a damn nice crew. Swell buncha guys. It's just that we run into a streak of hard luck. That can happen to any crew."

"It happened to my old crew," Charley interrupted. "If you told me a year ago I'd be all by myself drinking vermouth this Christmas with the rest of my crew strung out all over Germany, Austria, and Romania, I'd of spit in your eye. 'Cause really, we had us a crew! Out in

Charleston, where we did our overseas training, we was top crew in Bombing and Transition. But I guess their numbers was up. And me, sinful ole bastard that I am, nothing'll kill me."

"Fate's a funny thing," Dooley said, "fight it all you want, but in the end it'll come out on top. Now, you'd figger a guy like Cosmo who was right next to God alla time, you'd figger him a good bet to come through. Hell, the way that kid usta pray! And then you take some other guy, I mean one that's whored and drank — me, for instance — and he goes ahead and finishes his fifty."

"It's how you're dealt the cards when you're born," Charley said weightily. "Either you got 'em or you ain't."

"Old Andy," Dooley said, listening to his own thoughts and paying little attention to Charley's words, "he always talked about a dream crew. I guess that wasn't in the cards either. Outa the whole crew just Ben and me left. And soon Ben'll finish his fifty and go back home and I'll be all by myself."

"*I'll* be around," Charley said comfortingly. "Don't guess they'll finish me 'fore I get th'ough reading *Studs Lonigan*. Wouldn't be fair."

"But I mean my old crew," Dooley said soberly. "Be kinda funny when you leave," he said to me.

"I'm not going yet," I said. "That one mission has to be flown. And I'm thinking about it right now."

"Oh, you'll make it," Dooley assured me. "I'll sweat you in."

Around us there was the buzzing of voices and the forced laughter and the frenzied movements of men who were drinking themselves into a stupor, determined to have the good time that always eluded them.

Talk and chatter and always the underlying hunger and yearning.

A voice: "Wrote a letter to my wife and told her to keep looking at the floor when she's in bed, 'cause, brother, when I get home she'll be seeing the ceiling, that's all!"

A voice: "Got a letter from my wife and she writes: 'When you get home you won't be able to pinch me like you usta 'cause the kids are grown up now.' How do you like that!"

A voice: "I wonder what my wife is doing this very minute. She wrote she was going to her old lady in Milwaukee for the holidays. Jeez, what I wouldn't give —"

A voice: "Let's have another drink!"

A voice: "Yeah, let's."

And many voices: "Merry Christmas to you!"

At midnight we started back for the barracks. The sky was dark, black, and little lights shone out of the barracks and pyramidal tents where men stayed up to usher in Christmas. We sloshed through the mud with the aid of flashlights, and every few steps we halted to look at the slits of lights spilling out of the makeshift dwellings.

"Night before Christmas," Dooley remarked sadly, "and there ain't no singing."

The tents were quiet and inside men sat around little box tables on bomb racks and in the center were the fruitcakes which had been sliced tenderly with daggers. And there were cans of Spam and cold turkey, and there was salami and Christmas candy. In some tents a little tinsel was hung around the tent pole, the same tinsel that we used going over a target to distract the enemy's radar. And in some tents GI socks were hung up and they were filled with hard candy. And in the distance, on the ramp, a bomber was having its engines revved up.

"It just ain't no Christmas 'less you sing 'Silent Night,'" Dooley observed. "Why don't the three of us do it?"

"I couldn't carry a tune in a suitcase," Charley said, "but you can deal me in."

All three of us sloshed through the mud, our hands entwined around the shoulders, singing "Silent Night." Dooley's baritone soared over the tents and pygmy olive trees. His words came out with an ache and nostalgia: "Sle-eep in heavenly peace . . ."

Suddenly we heard a carbine shot. Charley screamed, "Duck!" We fell flat on our faces into the deep mud.

There were several more carbine pings, and somebody answered the fire with a forty-five pistol. And we stayed in the deep mud, listening to the shots and the exchange of angry words. The men who were firing the shots were obviously drunk. They were firing into the black Italian night: the brutal, alien night that sat over their yearnings like a heavy, suffocating blanket.

The bullets zing-pinged, and we hugged the muddy ground, and Dooley murmured: "My aching back, a fella can get killed around here."

49

Six p.m. Eighteen hundred hours. The Alert List was up at Squadron Operations. My name was on the list, flying tail with Lieutenant Short.

I wondered, I wondered where we'd go for my last ride.

· · · ·

At dawn Dooley and Charley accompanied me to the briefing shed. They were not alerted to fly, but out of the goodness of their hearts got out of their sacks in the raw morning and came along to give me support. All three of us looked quickly at the ribbon as soon as we entered the shed. It was not Vienna!

"Innsbruck oughta be a milk run," Dooley observed with the weight of a man who has been around a great deal. "They prob'ly got about twenty guns shooting at you. But I never seen 'em do much damage. What's more," he added slyly, "don't forget you was born in a caul!"

Charley said: "I wisht I was flying *my* last one."

They drove out to the bomber with me. Dooley held on to my gear and carried it off the truck to the plane. "Don't knock yourself out now," he said, half in jest, "lemme carry this stuff. You just take it nice and easy." At the ship, Dooley went up to Lieutenant Short, the pilot, and said: "Lieutenant, my buddy is flying tail with you today. Wancha to take good care of him. He's all I got."

As I was getting inside the ship through the camera hatch, Dooley said: "Don't forget, pop, we'll be waiting for you right here. We'll eat lunch together."

"Okay," I said gratefully, waving to them from the waist window.

Then I heard the disembodied words over interphone: the words, the world of air war.

"Start the putt-putt."

"Clear the props —"

"Starting Number Three engine."

Then the control tower clocking the squadrons, coaxing the ponderous, bomb-laden ships onto the runway. And the whole world trembling from the engine roar.

The wooden blocks were removed from underneath the wheels of the plane and we taxied off the apron, the brakes screeching in anguish as the pilot maneuvered into position.

We shot down the runway and the wheels bounced off the asphalt and we cleared the olive trees and the squadron mess hall where a nice, peaceful smoke was curling up to the sky through the chimney. As all these actions and sounds and landmarks registered in my mind, I thought: the last time . . . All these things I'd seen and done before. I had known the roar of engines since the day of my birth. The churning emptiness in the stomach had been with me all my life. All my life I'd been airborne and tasting the clammy, rubbery surge of oxygen hissing out of a tube, and seeing formations of bombers and hearing the tinny, inhuman voices over Command: "A-Able calling B-Baker. Over." The last time. In the past I doubted that there would ever be an end. But this *was* the end. No matter what happened to me on this mission — this *would* be the end. And just the thought that an end does come suddenly made me feel jubilant and unafraid. A terrible weight was removed from my shoulders and I thought: "You made it, you made it, you made it." What I wanted to shout was: "You did not quit, you did not quit, you did not quit." And now it was too late to quit! We were airborne; the verdict was sealed. The battle with self had been won, and in the face of this, I was too happy to dwell on what might happen in the battle with the enemy.

I was intoxicated by the thought of self-conquest. The will had triumphed over emotion, which was represented by vacillation and cowardice. I was suddenly unafraid of death. For the first time in my life I was not afraid. "It does not matter," I said to myself, sitting firmly in the tail turret. "It does not matter. They can't kill me now." Even death was no longer a terrifying thing.

I was aware that all these thoughts of self-intoxication were detached from the war itself. I was reveling in personal triumph, indulging myself immodestly, admitting I had been a poor risk all along.

Inevitably my mind veered to the youngsters in our barracks, in this very bomber, who were truly the heroes of this war. Most of them fought on sheer guts, with hardly any knowledge of the causes for the war. I wondered what made them persevere. An innate courage. But courage was a flower that blossomed slowly. One could learn and gather courage. What was it, then? Approval? Was it possible for men to go out and die because others died and because their environment approved of and demanded such acts?

We flew up north along the Adriatic. At the Po Valley, which had been flooded by the Germans in their retreat, we came upon our first range of the Alps. The mountains stood at the end of the flatlands, rising sheer and black, like massive walls defying penetration. Their jagged peaks scratched the sky, rending into shreds the clouds that tried to enter the forbidden land beneath us. We flew two thousand feet above the highest of the peaks, keeping a respectful distance. The vastness of the mountains made one freeze with the cold terror of their beauty. They were beautiful, despite the gorges which meant certain death if one attempted to land among them or even parachute down. They were majestic despite the sharp peaks that rose like nails, a forest of nails and steeples and cones and sawtoothed crests. From the air, the Alps were an enchanting death trap. And it was among these gorges, hidden in a large valley, that we came upon our target, Innsbruck. We made a sharp turn in order to line up the formations for our bomb run. We turned without warning, as if we'd come upon our prey suddenly and had not allowed sufficient time for the ponderous echelons to maneuver. Our ship banked and I seized the turret and suddenly, looking down toward the earth there was empty space where the Alps had been. We swung crazily and I had lost the earth and the mountains, and where both should have been there was empty, white space. I sat up and then I caught a rim of the mountains and they were falling away from me like a huge black wave to be replaced by nothingness. I searched desperately for a horizon, trying to reestablish my contact with the planet. For a moment I had the sinking feeling that we were detaching ourselves from the earth and its law of gravity, and being sucked into space. And in my mind there was the crazy refrain: this is the last time, no matter what happens. Shout your defiance; you're not afraid. It is too late to be afraid. But I seized the turret doorjamb and held on for dear life until the Alps hurtled into view again.

And then everything went wrong. As if the gods were mocking me, testing my resolution, throwing obstacles in my path to see if I were truly my own master. It suddenly occurred to me a diabolic game was being played. One of the bombs hung up, and our Number Two engine quit. We were maneuvering in the saucer of a valley, trying to escape the batteries that fired at us from all the rims of the saucer. To the left of me I glimpsed one ship peel off. Her two starboard engines were both dead. And then it suddenly penetrated to me that the ship hurtling toward the jagged peaks was *Flying Foxhole*. It turned crazily as it fell, sucked down by some powerful magnet in the bowels of the gorge.

The formations fled across the Alps and we fell behind, trying to unfreeze the prop of our dead engine. We were losing altitude, flying barely above the mountain peaks. The winds lashed at the tail turret and my eyes were turning into icicles. I felt how tensely the pilot handled the ship among the downdrafts. "What a majestic graveyard!" I thought. But in the next instant I rejected such a fate.

We were alone in the Alps, one solitary ship, and I hugged my guns. The escort of Mustangs had gone ahead with the formations and we were a perfect target for the Nazi jets and ME-109s that prowled in the area from Munich to the Po. Though the temperature dipped to 50 below, I was perspiring. Sweat was coursing down my neck. I experienced a stinging sensation along the small of my back and a moment later I knew my electric suit had shorted and I was being set afire. The fire was concentrated along my back where the short had occurred. The delicate wires of the electric suit were burning through the lining and the flame was singeing my skin. I felt is if a nail were stuck into my flesh, and then I smelled the burning cloth. I tore the suit plug out of the socket and the burning gave over to a slow smoldering. Then I felt cold. It was a matter of time, and I knew it, that I would be seized by the subtle clutches of frostbite that always came on without warning, but rather with a lulling whisper of sleep. And yet I continued perspiring and ignoring what might happen to my extremities if I did not exercise them vigorously to keep the blood circulating. Instead I was peering at the sky, searching the mountain crags for enemy pursuit ships. Somewhere in my mind I decided that freezing to death was for some reason less horrible than being shot down on one's final mission. And with my eyes, my whole being stared out past the iced windows of the turret, while my gloved fingers which were quickly going numb, stayed glued to the guns. My hands trembled, but I did not attribute this to fear alone. A gunner's hands trembled after a while, perhaps all his life. And my heart beat furiously, and that too may have been more a result of the war than the momentary fear. I felt suddenly as if my whole body was arrayed against me, hurling its war legacy of pains at me, demanding submission. And I retorted with numb lips: "It is too late. There comes an end. This is the end. And I'm not afraid."

50

I REMEMBER that morning. I remember how out of the blackness of the receding Alps three aircraft rose in our direction. And suddenly I awakened from my numbness and my lips whispered over the interphone: "Three unidentified aircraft at six o'-clock high!" I raised my guns and suddenly I dropped them and a cry of joy burst forth from me. "They're ours! P-38s!" I cried.

I remember that morning and the three pursuit ships which were the loveliest of all sights. I lowered my guns and we lost some altitude and I felt warmer. And the sun came streaming in through the Plexiglas and I began to cry. How splendid were the mountains receding along the Po! And how beautiful the earth! I cried for the deep serenity inside me, a serenity which made me forget, momentarily that the war was not over and tomorrow men would be dying.

Yes, I remember that morning and the tears and the sorrow, and finally the calmness.

A NOTE ON THE AUTHOR

LOUIS FALSTEIN, an aerial gunner in World War II,
was awarded the Purple Heart and the Air Medal four
times. He was educated at Chicago and New York Uni-
versities and wrote two other novels and a biography of
Sholom Aleichem. He died in 1995.

A NOTE ON THE BOOK

The text for this book was composed by Steerforth Press
using a digital version of Electra, a typeface designed in
1935 by William Addison Dwiggins, Electra has been a
standard book typeface since its release because of its even-
ness of design and high legibility. All Steerforth books are
printed on acid free papers and this book was bound by
BookPress of Brattleboro, Vermont.